The Other Side

Florian Armas

Second Edition February 2023

ISBN 13 9780993977213

Table of Contents

Final Countdown

Memories

Chapter 1

I had never imagined that metal could voice fear of its own destruction. The left wall vanishes in flames, wailing like a dying man.

Explosion.

People howl. My own screams drown out every other sound, leaving only wide-open mouths – grotesque, silent masks I will never forget. I probably look the same to them.

Another explosion.

Fewer voices now. A pressure wave rips through the spaceship, cracks running faster than people. All my instincts vanish in that instant, leaving behind nothing but a sack of flesh and bone, hurled backward by the blast. I feel no fear. No, that is misleading. To be paralyzed is not the same as being fearless.

"We've lost the engines. Evacuate the ship." The captain's broken voice crackles through the speakers. "I repeat, evacuate the ship."

Debris floats chaotically among bodies, speaking louder than any words. Mindless, I push, pull, and twist like a wounded snake through the flying shrapnel – some primal instinct has seeped back into this flesh sack. I don't know where instincts live; my mind is empty but for a raw, screaming voice: Run! Maybe that is all you need. Philosophy won't save you now.

I stretch my left hand toward a small mask on the wall, just a filter, barely enough. Better than nothing. I miss. There is no grace in zero-g. My foot brushes something floating past. A frantic kick sends me spinning back toward the wall. This time, my fingers grab the mask. Then I see it: the thing I kicked was Den. The closest thing I had to a friend here. Not anymore. His eyes blaze – not with hate, not really. Animal terror. I delayed him. He shoves me, and my back slams into the wall. My gasp is soundless.

Gases hiss from ruptured pipes, swirling down the corridor in poisonous ribbons. Sirens wail. To my left, a pocket of vapor blooms in slow motion: a *bird*, wings spread. Beautiful. Later, my mind will replay it – this surreal, shimmering death. But death isn't surreal.

The escape hatch glows at the far end, half-sealed.

The *bird* drifts toward a girl ahead of me. No mask. Her hands claw at nothing. Too late. A spasm, then she is just a body, a doll knocked by a flying table. The impact twists her white face toward me, eyes wide and frozen, staring at me: black, black, black. She rotates like a clock hand. Den spins counterpoint beside her. It's like they're dancing – only they're not.

"Move!" someone growls and shoves me forward.

I reach the escape hatch sideways – legs slam into the wall, then my head. Pain blackens my vision for a few moments. To anyone still sane, I might look like a zero-g acrobat. But no one is watching. Not like that. Here, I am just another obstacle between them and survival. A tall, red-haired woman seizes my wrist. Her grip is iron. She pulls me through the hatch, then hurls me into an emergency capsule. I am numb, unable to react.

"Press the orange button," she rasps, her voice sharp with desperation.

I know this. We drilled it a hundred times. But drills don't teach you how to function when panic eats your brain alive. I hit the button. Blue restraints bloom from the walls, cocooning me – soft yet rigid. Like my mind. Ozone stings my nose. The sour tang of poison still clings to my tongue, though I am safe now. Aren't I?

"Take care." Her voice cracks – gentleness beneath the urgency. Tears glint. But my lips stay locked. In my nightmares, I swear she says my name. The hatch seals with a hiss, hurling me into the void.

With a terrible scream, the ship unfolds in a scorching hell. A flash burns my eyes – silvery white, mixing with the white of the girl's fading face, her wide black eyes staring at me. The last thing I remember before darkness falls, and the world becomes soundless.

That is all that remains of my life. The rest was scorched away. Doctors rebuilt my body, but not my past. Even the fact that the red-haired woman was my mother returned to me only through newsfeeds, in a picture. Our faces side by side. Past waiting to be remembered.

White light passed through my closed eyelids, stirring a mind lost outside time. Explosions still drummed in a terrifying rhythm: *boom, boom, boom...!* Images flared – shattered, erased by flashes – a fragmented film reel spinning too fast. Then gone. Something was *wrong*. The emergency capsule's light should have been blue. But this was white. White as the face of the unknown dead girl. *The flash...*

"Doc, it wasn't an accident. The ship was destroyed by a missile." The unfamiliar voice dragged me back. Hospital bed.

Pain. A flicker of curiosity dulled my agony, but it never ceased. “They wanted this boy.”

Me? Why me?

“Who did it?” A growl. But the edge in his tone said he already knew the answer.

“The Travelers. His Field sensitivity awoke too soon. That’s why the Resistance sent him away from your planet – to train on this remote station, beyond their surveillance.”

Your planet? His voice sounded human, normal ... but what did normal even mean anymore?

“The boy reached into the Field during the flight. A Field Crawler reacted. Space makes mental communication easier to detect.” His voice was calm, as if this was everyday trivia. “The Travelers’ sensors caught his mental link, near your station. They acted fast.”

Station...? I had no idea where I was.

“They will come for him.” Doc’s voice tightened. “There are ten million souls on our station. The Travelers know how to sever minds from the Field. Armin, we should...”

“Genetic neutering. Mind-caging.” Armin’s tone iced over. “Pointless now. The Travelers already know we diverted his pod’s trajectory, to arrive near your station, so you could find it. The energy spike betrayed us.”

“They will come,” Doc repeated, raw.

“That would breach the Treaty.” Armin’s voice softened, then – tap-tap-tap – Doc’s restless fingers forced him to add: “But you are right. They will come. Be ready.”

“With what? No ships. No weapons. The Treaty left us defenseless.”

“It left you alive.” Armin paused. “We will deploy extra sensors. They won’t invade, just infiltrate commandos to ... find him. Take him to Deep Blue.”

Not to find me. To kill me.

"Heal him. Train him. First-stage protocols only. We will convene the council when he is ready," Armin said, thoughtfully.

The door hissed open. Footsteps – light, precise – then the scrape of a chair. My blindness sharpened my hearing; I tracked the newcomer's movements like a bat navigating darkness. The sterile stench of antiseptics and station metal filled my nose.

"Good to see you, Armin." The new voice – Erun – held warmth edged with reproach. "Though I wish you had signaled before coming."

"You were submerged in Deep Blue, and time bleeds faster than we think. Did you hear us?"

"Every word. As did half the station via the Net."

"The price of transparency," Armin said, almost amused. "Your people chose open governance over the Main Planet's ... ruthless efficiency. History will judge who chose wisely. The Travelers are busy to develop their New Field."

"That cursed Field will be our grave." In anger, Erun struck something – metal, by the sound of it. "The ship's destruction violates the Treaty's spirit. Can we weaponize it?"

"The Observer was notified," Armin said, "but it is too little to make a case in the Galactic Council."

"Observer?" Erun's laugh resembled a bark. "A Travelers' ally. Every *impartial* eye serves the Faction pulling the strings in our system."

"Many Observers are former Celestial Faction Travelers. This is the reality we..."

"You mean the reality *we* endure." Erun's chair screeched as he stood. Pacing. Footfalls like a ticking clock.

"Then endure it well. Train him well." With that, Armin left, the others trailing like shadows.

Doc! Don't leave. Help me!

But no one answered.

Until that moment, I had been neither dead nor alive. The machines were still rebuilding my brain, neuron by agonizing neuron. My sudden spark of awareness failed to control my body. For hours, pain was my only companion – a wolf gnawing my bones under a bloody full moon. When the coma reclaimed me, it was almost mercy. Almost.

The memory of that agony never faded. It never will.

"Brain now ninety-five percent recovered," the whisper sliced through the silence – clinical, muffled, wrapped in gauze. Some primal instinct claimed the brain as mine. "Pulse stabilizing."

My heart thrummed faster. Time itself seemed to accelerate, words contracting, pauses vanishing.

"He survived. Three hundred didn't."

"Add two milligrams to his perfusion."

Of what? Fog swallowed my thought – cool, suffocating – time suspended outside time.

Then, the spark.

"I know you're awake."

I tried to open my eyes. Nothing. "Eyelids," I muttered inside, willing the muscles to obey. A twitch. I blinked – a fraction of a second. Behind my eyelids, an afterimage crystallized: a face with a smile too precise. "Nurse-*bot*," I croaked. "I'm not in the capsule." *Am I dreaming?* Too young to wonder if I was dead.

"Capsule or not, your vitals look good," it replied, a faint hum in its tone that might have been amusement – or a glitch. "What's your name?"

Name... "I don't know." My voice scratched like sandpaper.

"Try again. What's your name?"

"I *don't know*!" My eyes snapped open, stinging under the harsh artificial light. I glared at the too-precise face. *Curse*...

"What happened to you?"

I lifted my head, just enough to see my body – naked, wired with more electrodes than a spaceship console. I felt them, tugging at my skin, and something deeper, like my bones were still arguing with gravity. A hospital bed. *Something happened.* "Explosion." *Boom, boom, boom...!* It reverberated in my skull. *Wounded.* I raised my right arm; it trembled, skeletal, and flopped back onto the bed. My skin was pink. Hairless. Fresh.

"What explosion?"

"Explosion." The booming still echoed in my head. "Ship. Space. Boom." I looked at my body again. Pink. Thin. "Wounded. Burned." *Pink skin. Burned.*

"Burned is an understatement," it said with a lilt that felt like it was teasing me.

The door opened. "Welcome to Aurora." A woman's voice, warm and soothing. Mara. An oval face framed by black hair. I jerked upright; her hand pressed me back with gentle strength. "Too soon," she murmured, fingers brushing my hair. "Your journey is not over."

Journey. The reconstruction of charred flesh into a man. White light stabbed my eyes – retinas seizing it – and suddenly, she was there: a girl's white face, black voids for eyes. "No!"

The light vanished.

"It didn't hurt," Mara chided, and shame sealed my lips about the ghost. "Your reflexes are good." She meant the left eye – grown from right-eye stem cells, the one miracle spared by fire.

"I'm dizzy," I rasped, my voice teetering between fear and awe. The nurses smiled. *Unfair.*

"You were sedated until your body could function," Mara said.

Sedated. The memory of my first attempt to wake returned. And the memory of pain. *Liar. I had felt every scalpel stroke, heard whispers not meant for me. And that ... alien voice...*

"You are nearly healed. Sedation is lighter now. Physically, you are whole." She paused. "Your muscles need work. Your memory needs work. There will be pain."

Pain is relative, depending on who experiences it. I swallowed a scream, bit back a curse, and Mara's smile crushed my rebellion.

Fine. I'll howl silently at the bloodied moon.

Aurora – three hundred feet of spinning metal clinging to a frozen moon, its parent planet a swirl of toxic colors in the void. You know this already. For me, it was like opening a blank file labeled Aurora and finding nothing, a white space waiting to be filled. The word floated in my mind with no context, just another piece of debris in the shipwreck of my memory.

AI helpfully projected a hologram: a blue-white frozen moon, pockmarked and icy, with a tiny orbital speck – *my home now*. The connection clicked, without feeling. But it was interesting to link the abstract notions drifting inside me to the real world.

When I first opened my eyes in the station's hospital, my gaze landed on the nurse-bot. Humanoid. Flawless. Yet I knew it was artificial. A small victory – proof that some instincts had survived the memory wipe.

When I left the hospital, the nurse-bot followed me to my new *home* in Deep Blue – a comfortable companion, taking care of me while I scavenged for memories like a beggar picking through trash. Relearning everything from scratch would have taken years, a slow, childlike crawl toward understanding. I refused that fate, and I forced AI to bombard me with holograms, jolting my dormant mind awake with brute-force stimuli.

Two places had been claimed in this frozen wasteland:

Ice Manor – hanging on the only rock piercing the frozen ocean, a tiny defiant mole of life against the desolation.

Deep Blue – built on the ocean floor, deep beneath the ice shelf, its large dome glowing sapphire under artificial daylight. Constructed at the cliff's edge, it overlooked abyssal black waters.

Linking them: a three-mile-long vertical tunnel. The most advanced transit system ever – and the most boring. You can't see a damn thing from inside the moving capsules.

Today, I learned that the red-haired woman who saved me on the spaceship was my mother. I tried to feel something. Anything. Nothing came. AI suggested mourning. I couldn't. I didn't know how to mourn, or why I should. I tried to understand what it meant to have a mother, what she might have meant to me. I turned to the dictionary: *Mothers love children. Children love back.* It meant nothing to me.

"AI?" I asked, helpless.

"Love is a human feeling. Euphoria driven by hormones. Your brain releases a surge of neurotransmitters like dopamine and oxytocin. It makes you feel warm and fuzzy."

"Oxytowhat?"

"Oxytocin," it replied. "The cuddling hormone. The stuff that makes humans go gooey over each other."

"What's cuddling?" I squinted at the hologram.

"You take someone into your arms to show love. It triggers your brain to release..."

"Oxytocin," I cut in, rolling my eyes. I half-expected AI's glowing sphere to sprout arms and demonstrate. "So love is just oxytocin? What *is* oxytocin, then?"

"A cyclic nonapeptide composed of nine amino acids arranged in a ring. The structure is stabilized by a disulfide bond between two cysteine residues..."

"Shut up! A cyclic nano-whatever can't be love. That's like saying a ship's engine has personality."

"Technically, a spaceship engine has charisma," AI quipped, voice laced with synthetic smugness. "But fine. Love is messy. Hormones, neural pathways, a dash of chaos. I recommend watching some movies. I've compiled a list, mostly romance, zero explosions. You're welcome."

"Really?" I groaned, struggling to understand why people hugged each other for no reason – it wasn't hygienic.

"Statistically, 91% of humans find them heartwarming," AI said, annoyingly chipper. "Just try them."

Logically, it all made sense: cuddling, hormones, neural pathways. I could understand that. But logic wasn't the same as feeling. It couldn't replicate that supposed *weight in your chest* or *warmth behind your ribs* – phrases I had learned from those movies. They were ... interesting. Something inside me *wanted* to go beyond rational analysis. An irrational urge.

So I asked Mara – she was human, after all.

"You'll know love when you feel it," she said, her smile kind. "Something undefined, strange and sweet at once. You won't have to define it. You'll just know."

But my emotional center had been rebuilt like a faulty circuit. After the explosion on the ship, the doctors suppressed my hormones, afraid the trauma – those nightmares of white flame and the dead girl's black, hollow eyes – would destroy me. Doc told me to leave her, the unknown girl, buried in forgetfulness. I obeyed. Mostly. The memory is set to unlock in a few months, ticking like a time bomb.

Frustration gnawed at me. I wanted everything to happen faster. A new world was waiting.

"I am a hologram explorer," I joked to the nurse-bot.

She – AI warned me it was impolite to say *it* – smiled back with programmed politeness. But I clung to the small victory of spotting the difference: her smile lacked the *natural* ease I had read about. There were subtle gaps between human and robotic expressions. The idea of a *serene smile* fascinated me. I chased it through dictionaries, down rabbit holes of definitions, running from one new word to another, for emotions I couldn't experience. What's the point of knowing about *joy* if you are hollow?

In a fit of mimicry – like I had seen in a movie – I hurled my tablet against the wall, hoping to feel anger. A sharp crack. Plastic shattered. The nurse-bot stared.

I felt nothing.

"Sorry," I muttered, robotic, only because I knew I had to say it. I picked up the remains and left my room, the *serene smile* still rattling inside my mind, struggling to grasp the difference between its technical meaning and the real thing.

Then, one day, I stepped into the cliffside park – and for the first time, the void inside me wavered.

A girl sat on a bench, her gaze lost in the abyss, a book forgotten in her lap. The Net whispered her name before I could ask – Lamia – analyzing the image I had captured. She noticed my intrusion; the Net had alerted her, too. She waved, her fingers fluttering like a bird testing the air. Something stirred in my chest, a flicker of warmth, instantly smothered as I scrambled for my mental dictionary.

"Natural attraction," AI supplied. "It's a human feeling that..."

"Hormones. I know. Shut up. I need to think." But by the time I processed the definition, the feeling had already dissolved into clinical terms. Yet in that moment, I finally understood what a *serene smile* looked like.

Later, I took Lamia's place on the bench. The metal still held the ghost of her warmth. Beyond the glass in front of me, the city's lights stirred the deep blue in slow, continuous motion, following invisible currents, up and down, left and right. Not waves, not like those that break upon a shore. More like liquid lace, or the delicate filaments of galactic dust. Lasers traced shifting salinity and temperature, a mesmerizing illusion. No life stirred in those depths. The lightshow was a consolation prize, a glittering lie to fill the void.

Technology stitches our world together. The Net wraps around us, a second skin, blending reality and augmentation. *They* navigate it effortlessly. I am still learning. But even the Net couldn't mask the truth: ten million souls crammed into a subterranean hive, living in fear. The Peace Treaty was just words. No one trusted the Main Planet's government.

A contest had been announced – design ecosystems and creatures to dance in our dead ocean. AI nudged me toward genetics courses. I enrolled, imagining my creations waltzing with Lamia's lights. The Net told me she had entered the contest, too. That night, I fell asleep with her smile etched behind my eyelids. And for once, my dreams weren't filled with fire and black, staring eyes.

Morning brought an unfamiliar unease. *Is Lamia beautiful?* The Net flooded me with images of *beautiful girls* – thousands of them, all different. Curves, angles, colors that contradicted one another. How could they all qualify?

"Why are they beautiful?" I asked Mara, projecting the holographic images between us, and hundreds of faces shimmered in the air.

Her lips curved. "Because they are."

"But why?" I isolated Lamia's picture – her quiet smile, the way her hair caught the artificial park light. "Is she beautiful?"

"Ah." Mara's arm settled around my shoulders, warm and gentle. "Let's see. Do you like looking at her face?"

I studied the image, then Mara's profile – the crinkles at her eyes, the way her cheek rounded when she smiled. "Yes."

"Then she is beautiful."

A pause. Words formed before I understood them: "You are beautiful too."

"Thank you." Her voice softened. "That was kind."

"A compliment," I recited from the dictionary. "You say something pleasing and expect reciprocity. Will I receive...?"

"This is not a transaction," she laughed, ruffling my hair. "And you already got one back."

"I don't understand..."

"You will."

In front of the classroom, I hesitated, hand on the door handle. On the other side, people. Strangers. A strange tightness coiled in my chest.

"Doubt," AI offered. "A human reaction..."

"Hormones. I know."

"No, you don't. It's logical. Your brain is modeling possible outcomes, trying to solve the unknown behind the door. Like a puzzle. But with worse stakes than a game show. You are alive, after all."

"Shut up," I muttered, half-smiling. AI was annoying, a glitch I couldn't quite hate.

Until now, my world had been sterile: Mara, Doc, the nurse-bot. A closed loop.

A few days ago, they had freed my hormones. But chemicals alone couldn't summon emotion. You need *connection*, something that sears or soothes.

"Don't try to hunt down your feelings," Mara told me, when I complained that nothing had changed. "Don't push. Let them come to you. It's better this way."

Easy for you to say, I had grumbled.

Inside the classroom: four girls, five boys. Including *her*. The girl with the serene smile. I looked at them all, trying to feel something. I felt the same as I did about the nurse-bot. Worse, maybe. Because I felt nothing about my nonexistent feelings.

Chapter 2

"Don't delete the filaments," Lamia protested as I adjusted the simulation. We were alone in the lab. My fourth month at school, my second working with her on the genetic project for the contest. "I need them for the fluorescent light. I want them to dance on the waves. We have to find the right music..."

They're useless. "There will be predators in the water, and our creature won't survive with those long cords." *Proper music... Music won't help it survive. Maybe it's about beauty. But that won't help either.* "It's like you trying to swim away from me – I had always catch you by your long hair." I liked that idea. Involuntarily, I smiled. She caught it.

"They are not cords; they are *filaments*. And my hair is neither." Her tone shifted – that subtle change in a girl's voice when you said something wrong. And, of course, I had no idea why. They get upset over the smallest things. I was sure I was right. Our jellyfish would be easy prey in simulations against the others' creatures. "I will make the filaments poisonous," she brushed off my argument. "Then no one can touch them. Something I should do with my hair, too."

"I will use gloves."

A book flew past my head. I leapt up from behind the table just as she lunged. She chased me, but I was faster, circling behind her and grabbing her hair. Gently. "See? Just like that."

Our project died. We didn't speak for days. The strangest part? Realizing how much I missed her.

Later, when I asked Mara for help – since I couldn't fix it alone – she just smiled and said, "Try flowers; they will help."

"Flowers? They can't think. I don't see..."

"Just try them," she said. "And add a box of chocolates."

On the big day, I followed Lamia into the lab, my lips twitching with an unfamiliar spasm. *Is this fear? Fear of losing?* I stole a glance at her – shoulders rigid, fingers kneading the edge of her sleeve. A lock of hair had escaped from her braid, trembling slightly with each breath. *She is afraid too.*

The school aquarium was a vast hall, far emptier than its capacity to host people. Every team had brought their engineered creatures, eyes gleaming with unshakable confidence. Only winners, no losers. I had no idea why they were all so sure. Ten tanks lined the right wall, shrouded in darkness until the reveal. Lamia's knuckles whitened around her tablet; her free hand rose to her mouth, teeth worrying at a thumbnail. Then, catching herself, she tucked the offending hand behind her back and lifted her chin.

I reached for her other hand. Our fingers tangled together, her grip tight. *I like this. I like her like this – unguarded.*

By chance, our project was last.

The first tank lit up – a medusa with long, luminous tentacles. The second: another medusa, its tendrils glowing at the tips. The third: yet another. Lamia's foot began tapping against the tile. When the fourth appeared, identical, she exhaled sharply through her nose, a sound I couldn't decrypt. Then another.

Then came ours.

An alga.

Not fluorescent on its own, but when the laser struck its long filaments, it glowed for a minute.

Lamia's breath hitched. The light pulsed through the tank, and her body leaned forward as if pulled by an invisible thread. For a while, she forgot to blink.

Then, triumph. Her elbow jabbed into my ribs, her grin sudden and brilliant. "See?" she whispered, voice dancing. "Told you the filaments were worth it.

Weeks earlier, I had filmed Lamia swimming – her long hair fanning out like a golden net in the water, her arms slicing through the current with effortless grace. Backlit by the pool lights, she looked like a fairy. I stole strands of her hair from the hologram, wove them into a deep-sea simulation, and synced them to a flickering laser. A slow spin brought everything to life.

I sent it to her.

Near the park's edge, where the plateau dropped into the abyss, there was a rock shaped like a face – The Head. As expected, she moved the *hair* from the depths to The Head's crown and sent it back with a smiley emoticon and a cryptic note: Better. But it's missing something.

When I asked what, she only tilted her head, a smirk playing at the corner of her mouth. "Figure it out."

It felt like cheating – the *good* kind. *Will she let me kiss her?*

We met in secret after that, crafting photosensitive chlorophyll in the lab's dim blue glow. Lamia worked with feverish precision, biting her lip when concentrating, tucking her hair behind her ears only for it to slip free again. Sometimes, when she thought I wasn't looking, she would stretch her arms overhead, arching her back like a cat in a sunbeam.

Each time, I lingered, inventing reasons to stay. Just being near her filled me with warmth I couldn't explain. After a breakthrough, she threw her arms around me, her laughter vibrating against my chest. Her hug was tight and warm, as if she, too, was chasing this unnamed feeling.

The teachers didn't know about our *hair*. Officially, our project was another fluorescent medusa, right up until the final day, when we replaced it in the tank. For a while, our alga existed only in the DNA simulations we had run at home and in test tubes.

After the contest, we walked through the park as dusk settled, the dome sky streaked with violet and gold. Lamia's steps slowed near an old tree; she plucked a leaf, rolling its stem between her fingers. When the shadows grew long, she turned toward me.

"Well?" she said, her voice soft.

I hesitated. Then I kissed her. I had found excellent movies and descriptions of how to kiss a girl on the Net, so I think I did it properly. When we stopped, I didn't let her go. Couldn't. She fit against me perfectly, her forehead resting on my shoulder, her heartbeat a wild echo of mine. A strange, pleasant warmth spread through me, consuming everything else.

"Something wrong?" she murmured, tilting her head back to study me. A faint blush painted her cheeks.

My face was burning, so it was probably redder than hers. "It's*...*" Words failed me. "I've just never felt this good before."

Her smile was slow, shy. "That was sweet," she whispered, and kissed me again, her fingers tracing the line of my jaw like she was memorizing it.

The Head loomed in the deep, its craggy face bathed in the ghostly glow of submerged lamps, just enough light for photosynthesis, just enough shadow to give it the look of some ancient, brooding creature. Atop its crown, our *hair* swayed: twenty meters of undulating dark red, each strand alive with the ocean's pulse, glowing discreetly. The currents lifted it in slow arcs – right and left, up and down – a hypnotic ballet of light and darkness.

Then the lasers struck.

At first, the alga's response was shy, its faint glow half-drowned by the laser's brilliance. But when the beams cut out, the creature awoke. Semitransparent cells ignited in bursts of blue-green fire, flaring along the filaments. Their lives were fleeting – mere seconds – but their rhythm married the eternal sway of the waves, a phosphorescent sonata. In those moments, the abyss became a dreamscape. A fairytale. *Our* fairytale. The school submitted our project to the general contest. We took the second prize.

Today, I will be declared *mature*. On paper, I am twenty – two years older than the other candidates. Papers. An archaic term, clinging to life like a ghost limb. Our true identity lives in the AI chip embedded in the cervical vertebra, humming with the Net's ceaseless whisper. It filters every byte that reaches me, mediated by my mini-Di. But today, I receive my full DigitalEgo – or Diego, as it's usually called.

The irony isn't lost on anyone. My paper age is twenty; my *real* age, counted from resurrection, is four.

"The toddler has matured," they joked.

I grit my teeth and pretend not to hear. But some words carve grooves in your bones, no matter how you stand. And when we fight – *ah* – then those two extra years are an advantage. After a while, they started to call me Rebel. I had no idea why. They were rebels; I landed here because of bad luck.

On Aurora, they implant Diego at eighteen, when the brain is theoretically fully mature. On the Main Planet, they do it at twelve. There, Diego isn't just a companion – it's a sculptor. The state's psychologists design its algorithms, bending young minds to fit their vision of *civilization*.

My first Diego died in the explosion, burned by fire. A mercy, really. Losing half your brain is lethal; losing half a shared mind? Unthinkable. And yet, it was the only good thing that happened to me during the assassination attempt. Once inserted, Diego becomes a twin mind, its organic tissue growing inside your brain. Any separation is dangerous. Losing almost half your brain in an explosion is dangerous too, so I can see – again – how lucky I was. The shred of my mind that survived remembers nothing of it. Sometimes, I wonder how is it to grow up with an adult mind nested inside yours, playing along with your childhood.

On the Main Planet, they separate Diego only for enemies of the state – those still *anchored in the past, unfit for modern society.* A quote from The Government Guide to a Healthy Mind, better known as *The Poisoned Book*.

My former self likely revered it. Now? My disdain is a product of Aurora's culture ... and *maybe* my own mind. Probably. How can I ever be sure?

Soon, Diego will wake in my skull. Full synchronization takes months, but I have time. I probably thought the same before the accident. Anyway, I am eager to see how my new life will be.

The white chamber smelled of ozone and antiseptic – the kind of scent that lingers in the back of your throat. I lay prone on the operating block, my neck exposed where the technicians had shaved a small patch above my cervical vertebra. The cold gel they had applied numbed the skin, but I could still feel the pressure as the vibratory scalpel burrowed into my body, carving bone.

"Keep your breathing steady," Mara murmured, her gloved fingers adjusting the alignment for the third time. In her visor's reflection, I could see the targeting lasers, twin red dots dancing along my spine.

The chip rested in a sterile cradle beside me: a sliver of black nano-ceramic, barely larger than a grain of rice, pulsing with faint bioluminescent markers. They had shown me the activation sequence earlier. Watching those dormant circuits flare to life had felt like witnessing the birth of a child.

A sudden, intimate pressure as needle-thin probes – no thicker than a neuron's axon – breached my blood-brain barrier. My muscles locked as Diego's neural threads unfurled into my cerebellum, each synaptic connection firing behind my eyelids. The nurse-bots' voices faded to distant echoes as my mini-Di initiated the handshake protocols – its familiar presence suddenly crowded by something vast and alien reaching through the link. For one terrifying moment, I existed in two places at once – watching myself from above while drowning in the flood of initialization data pouring through the new link.

Then the world snapped back into focus.

Only a phantom itch remained at the base of my skull, and a new sensation: the distinct feeling of being observed. Not just by the medical team, but from within.

"Primary integration successful," Mara announced. Relief colored her voice, though the words rang hollow.

The real work would begin now – in the quiet hours between sleep and waking – as Diego's organic matrices slowly intertwined with my neural pathways. They had warned me about the dreams. About how the ghost of my old DigitalEgo – that bloody tool of oppression – might surface in fragmented memories. What they hadn't said was how heavy the silence in my head would become. Pregnant with the weight of another consciousness, waiting to be born.

The medical block hummed with the low-frequency pulse of monitoring equipment, each beep marking the seconds of my silent vigil. I waited – for an inner voice, a sign, anything. *"Hello, I am Diego."* Something.

Then it came – not words, but a liquid invasion of my brain. I knew it wasn't real. It felt real. Cold tendrils of consciousness seeped through my neural pathways, the sensation so visceral I recoiled as if from physical violation. Wires tethered me to the couch; my thrashing only sent a tray of instruments clattering to the floor. Apparently, I had a natural talent for that.

"We can sedate you," Mara offered, trying to ease my fear.

I am not afraid, I lied to myself.

My pulse thundered in my temples. My fingers clawed at the couch's padding. No pain, just physical reaction. The flood reached my frontal lobe now, a glacial weight filling my skull. I shook my head sharply, half-expecting to hear the slosh of cerebral fluid.

Mara's laughter filled the room. Even Doc's stern mouth twitched.

"Don't worry." She pulled me against her, fingers combing through my sweat-damp hair. The gesture should have soothed me. It didn't.

"I am not a child." The protest sounded petulant, even to me.

"Rebel, you are our *four-year-old* big boy." Mara's breath tickled my ear. "We all tried to *feel* the water moving inside our heads during activation. Even Mr. *Doctor* here." She jerked her chin at Doc, who rolled his eyes but didn't deny it.

By the time they unhooked me, the liquid sensation had vanished. Only hollow silence remained. No greeting. No Diego.

"Turn your head," Doc said, his voice leaving no room for argument.

I complied, movements jerky with residual tension. Nothing.

"Faster."

A sharp twist. And there. A flicker at the edge of my vision, like a shadow detaching itself from the wall. I froze. The room was empty. *Of course it is. It's inside*.

Doc's smile was all teeth. "Well?"

"*A* shadow," I whispered. "Inside."

The silence stretched. Then – from the back of my skull – not a voice. An impression. A shape.

Are you Diego?

No answer. Just the faintest pressure. Like a finger pressed to closed lips.

The alarm shattered my dream at 03:00 – a crime against sleep. Especially when the dream featured *her*: all sun-warmed skin and tangled hair, her silhouette blurred at the edges like a watercolor left in the rain. The kind of dream I had never had before kissing her.

"What happened?" I snarled at Diego.

His yawn echoed through my synapses, as sluggish as my own. *"Generator failure on the ice field. Pipeline breach. Force field at sixty-two percent. You have five minutes to reach the elevator."*

It had taken me months to get used to Diego materializing and speaking inside my mind – our interactions invisible to anyone else. A shifting hologram overlaying my vision, sometimes a smirking doppelgänger, other times a featureless silhouette. In the beginning, I had waved a hand in front of my eyes just to see if it would disrupt the image, a pointless exercise – there's no way to block a visual generated directly in your brain's optical cortex.

Tonight, he had chosen the form of a sleep-rumpled technician, translucent fingers drumming against my visual field.

"One more minute," I bargained, chasing the ghost of Lamia's half-naked likeness.

Dreams were the last frontier, even Diego couldn't influence them. And they felt so real. Low-tier simulators couldn't replicate the chemical rush of real desire, and the high-end ones were locked behind *educational-use-only* firewalls. No chance to simulate realistic naked girls. Or more... Our teachers wanted us to interact more in *real life*.

A searing jolt exploded across my chin.

"You slapped me!"

Not literally – Diego was just a neural subroutine – but the pain signals he fired into my facial nerves were indistinguishable from the real thing. My fingers flew to unmarked skin. No bruise. No witnesses. Just the aftertaste of discipline.

The emergency team was already assembling when I reached the elevator – five figures encased in thermal suits, their breath fogging the visors. Karl, our instructor, stood with arms crossed, his scowl deeper than usual.

"Took you long enough, Rebel," he grunted, tossing me a suit. But I knew it was just for show.

I glanced at my watch and started dressing. "Forty seconds left to the deadline. I am on time."

Marion, already suited up, lobbed a helmet at me. "Focus, dreamer. Unless you want your pretty face frost-kissed." We had nearly lost her a month ago when her helmet malfunctioned during a repair run.

I was the last one to enter the elevator. And the first one to leave it, up there, on the surface, inside the dome of the Ice Manor.

Our boots crunched against the ice, a fragile rhythm in the immensity of the space. Work on the surface was rare enough to feel like a privilege. Blurred by the energy field of the dome, the view of the giant gaseous planet was enchanting. It was only my third trip to the surface. I was a newbie. We moved across the frozen plain, the surviving generators maintaining a pocket of -5°C in the -170°C hellscape beyond.

We sometimes played with the edge of the dome. A finger thrust through the energy field would come back glittering with instant frost. Hold it too long, and you would lose it to flash-freezing.

My old memories were gone, but I knew they hadn't held anything like this – a fragile, magnificent death-dance with absolute cold. Advanced field technology didn't exist on the Main Planet. Aurora was superior in this, and in many other scientific domains. And it reminded me: *we*, from the planet, are technologically behind. They mock us. Call us *Puppets*. We shot back with *Selfish,* but the insult rang hollow to me now.

Who am I, really? We *or* they?

Diego materialized in my mind's eye as an old sorcerer, his translucent robes fluttering in the neural winds of my subconscious. The worry lines on his forehead deepened – an expression stolen from some forgotten movie. *"Well, it's up to you to decide,"* he said, his tone bearing the weight of a teacher watching a student step toward a cliff's edge.

We had learned together. He had seen every shameful thought, every moment of weakness. Every pleasure. There were no secrets between us.

"One day I will decide," I shrugged.

The field shimmered before me, its edge humming with contained chaos. Temptation won. I thrust my hand beyond the safety line. The color of the force field shifted – white to red, then purple.

Because of me?

I looked at my gloved hand. Nothing to see. Waves of color slid down from the top of the semi-transparent dome, and a shudder ran through it. The field flickered – just for a moment – fully revealing the true void beyond: endless black, stars like frozen spears.

The silence deepened.

"Terrified?" Diego murmured.

"Alive," I corrected, trying to understand what was happening.

Slowly, I pressed further, just to make sure the protective field was still intact. Ten seconds passed – the absolute limit. Diego's electric lash snapped through my nerves, yanking my arm back. Pain flared, bright and clean.

"You know I feel that too," he hissed, voice frayed with anger.

"Glad to know that." I grinned and turned away.

Karl's voice crackled over the comms: "Field stability at fifty-nine percent. We have maybe twenty minutes before... Marion, disconnect the failed generator from the grid. Jarvis, pressure checks. Ricardo, monitor the field harmonics."

His gaze landed on me.

"Rebel, you are on pipeline duty. Disconnect the *right* ones. Try not to freeze anything vital."

As I moved to check the pipelines, Diego murmured in my inner ear, *"You're thinking about her again."*

I didn't deny it. The work was brutal, but my hands remembered the weight of Lamia's braid, the way her pulse jumped when I...

The field's glow shifted. White to crimson to violet. A ripple of spectral color swept from the dome's apex.

"Run!" Diego's scream wasn't words – it was pure synaptic fire, jolting my spine, kickstarting my legs before my mind could catch up.

Karl's voice thundered through the comms: "We're under attack! To the generators. Now!"

But we were already running. Every Diego, in every skull, had sounded the alarm milliseconds before our human senses could process the threat.

The field fractured. The sky tore open like paper. Between the ragged edges, the gas giant loomed – full color, alive with storm-swirl chaos. Air hissed outward. Our helmets sealed with a mechanical *click-hiss*, pressurized oxygen flooding in.

Then...

The field snapped back. And the shuttles appeared, plasma cannons blooming like poisonous flowers. Passing through the shield, their shots came slow at first – lazy streaks of yellow-red. But as the field weakened, they gained speed, heat, purpose.

I felt the impact before I heard it.

A punch of heat across my back. A whump as plasma met ice. The shockwave lifted me. For a few breathless seconds, I was airborne – weightless. Then the ice rose to meet me. A deafening crack split the surface as another volley landed. Beneath me, the ice groaned – then fractured into a glowing spiderweb of fissures.

The heat meant the back of my suit had been punctured, but there is no way to check your own back. I forced my body upright and scrambled behind a metallic structure, one leg twisting awkwardly beneath me as I fell. Crawling deeper between the generator blocks, my head slammed into something hard, and bright flashes burst across my vision. The pain came later, held back by fear rushing through my veins. Something warm trickled down my spine – blood or sweat. Both equally dangerous in a breached suit.

Through the colored bursts in my vision, I saw the shuttles circling, repositioning for a clearer shot. Small and fast – the kind used by special forces for stealth missions. Plasma cannons only. No missiles.

My breath came in short, ragged gasps, but my mind still found enough clarity to wonder how the shuttles had even gotten here undetected. *Later*, I shook my head and squinted at the field. The pressure inside the dome had dropped by a third but remained manageable. So had the temperature. The generator's residual heat and our suits kept us alive. Once everyone regrouped, the force field reconfigured, shrinking until it stabilized at half its original size.

Silence settled in.

Only the occasional pop of dying electronics outside our shrinking sanctuary broke it.

"We have oxygen for another twenty minutes," Diego assured me. *"Breathe normally."*

Easy for him to say.

My back burned where the plasma had grazed me, the pain a living thing gnawing at my spine. Diego dampened the worst of it, a cold numbness spreading through my nerves, but the damage to the suit was real. Every breath came thinner than the last, the air tasting of recycled metal and fear.

A transport pod detonated without warning, its battery core erupting with enough force to ripple the ice. The shockwave sent a hairline crack racing toward my boots. I pressed myself tighter against the generator.

Beyond our fragile dome, plasma jets scorched whatever was left exposed – tools, vehicles. It was a pocket of hell out there. Smoke billowed. Circuit boards and engines popped and fizzled. The world burned in slow motion. Acrid smoke coiled along the field's boundary, pierced now and then by plasma arcs. My eyes watered – from toxins, or memory, I couldn't tell. The dead girl from the wreck flickered at the edge of my vision again, her face preserved in perfect, ashen stillness.

Not now.

I clenched my fists until my gloves creaked and fixed my gaze on the planet overhead. Storm bands churned across its surface, utterly indifferent to our desperation. Another explosion. Closer. A battery ignited, lifting a tank into the air. It crashed down seconds later, stirring a small icequake.

The field shrank again.

And as I sat there, scarcely able to move, I realized that our chance to escape was shrinking with it.

"Stay where you are. Stay hidden. I called the base, help will be here in fifteen minutes," Karl tried to calm us.

Then the world turned white.

The explosion came from the generator protecting us. We were lucky, at least; it was on the other side. Whether it was a direct hit or a cascade failure, I will never know. The shockwave sent us sprawling. When my vision cleared, Marion was down, her suit smoking. Someone was screaming, but I couldn't hear it over the ringing in my ears.

Karl reached her first. The big man didn't hesitate and slung her over his shoulder like a sack of grain, then charged toward the last generator still standing. "Follow me!" he roared, blood trickling from his nose.

Stumbling after him, I caught a glimpse of the shuttles overhead – circling like carrion birds, their plasma jets painting the ice in streaks of molten gold. But what chilled me more than enemy fire was the look on Karl's face.

Not fear. Recognition.

"These are Main Planet markings," he whispered over the comms.

And in that moment, I understood why Diego had looked so worried earlier.

"Pressure is dropping again," Karl's voice crackled in the comm – calm. Too calm. "Field is stabilizing at thirty-seven percent." He materialized beside me, his suit flashing oxygen warnings, but a sealing patch was already slapped over his chest. "Suit integrity?" he asked, already yanking a repair seal from his belt.

"Back," I managed. "Can't reach."

He spun me roughly. His hands were fast, practiced. The sting of nanogel on torn skin made me gasp. "Lucky shot," he grunted. "Two centimeters left and you would be spineless." The patch hissed as it bonded with my suit, pressure equalizing. Not a moment too soon – my wrist display was already blinking an urgent red for temperature loss. "Stay hidden," he ordered, voice tight. "Help is coming in ten minutes. Your vitals are spiking. Don't panic."

If we have ten minutes.

The shuttles had changed tactics. No more random plasma bursts – now they struck in coordinated volleys, each impact painting the force field in concentric rings of violet and gold. The field held. But barely. With every strike, it shrank – just a little smaller. Just a little closer.

I craned my neck. The ice around our generator was pocked with steaming craters, but farther out, the surface was untouched – except for one sinuous path leading directly to my first hiding spot, the generator that had exploded.

Why me?

"Are you complaining?" Diego quipped.

"Trying to understand. We may need to run again," I shot back, mindlessly. My leg throbbed where I had twisted it. No *running* now.

Diego projected a holographic replay of the first phase of the attack, when I was running. The initial shots from the shuttles *had* been random – probing, testing the dome's resilience. But their AI had adapted, using the distortion patterns in the field. The hologram flared, dozens of crimson lines chasing me on the ice. Only me.

Why?

I shivered and felt short of breath. *"Oxygen level?"*

"Ten minutes."

Bad.

Eyes closed, I forced myself to focus on one of the many pictures of Lamia stored in my mind. Anything to keep from thinking about suffocating to death in a pressure suit. I gasped. *Breathe normally.* In that moment, the plasma fire stopped. I turned my head and caught it, just at the edge of my vision. The colored rings on the shield, right above me. The shuttles were targeting *here* now. Shooting from directly overhead. The shield was all red, yellow and purple, but it was holding.

In an all-too-human reaction, everyone moved away from me, trying to escape the line of fire. But the shield had shrunk to a thirty-foot radius. *You can't go too far,* I muttered, with grim satisfaction at their pointless retreat. Sweat slid down the back of my neck, alternating warm and cold. I stared, hypnotized, as the colored circles descended toward me, with the shrinking field.

Breathe normally.

I clenched my jaws, trying to suppress the panic – slow my heart, my lungs. I failed. More cold sweat down my spine. Diego sedated my nerves, and air flowed again smoother through my nostrils. Cold. Crisp. Tinged with the faint metallic tang of the small oxygen tank on my back.

"We have enough oxygen," Diego whispered, without saying for how long, and I curled inward, folding into a fetal posture meant to slow my breathing, to calm the body and conserve what little air remained.

"Our shuttles will come in time," Karl said, his voice steadier than I expected.

When? I wondered, too tired to speak. Even speaking burned oxygen.

A new sound cut through the chaos: a high-pitched whine from above. The force field shuddered; its radius collapsing further around us.

"Three minutes of oxygen left," Diego said, faint but clear.

The shuttles stopped firing.

The field rippled. Two obsidian ovoids materialized. Far above, the enemy shuttles banked hard, retreating. A translucent sphere formed around me and one of the ovoids. The air inside was now rich, unfiltered. My suit recognized it and shut off automatically. The air shimmered – not like heat distortion, but as if reality itself had taken a sharp breath and held it. This wasn't just a barrier. It was a pocket of *elsewhere*. Its surface crawled with phantom fractals that dissolved when I tried to focus. Light bent wrong around the edges, warping the view beyond, though nothing had moved. Inside, the laws of physics felt ... softened.

Temporal distortion.

How did I know it was a temporal sphere? I couldn't say. The thought just appeared. The ovoid's underbelly irised open. A needle-thin probe extended – glinting with something that wasn't liquid, wasn't light. It stopped inches from my visor.

Scanning.

Then a figure stepped through. Tall. Hooded. Its suit was neither Auroran nor Main Planet design. The visor reflected my own face, pale, sweating. The figure extended a hand. Not in threat. In invitation. "Glad to see you again," he said, his smile broad but unfamiliar.

Everything about him unsettled me. The way light bent around his edges. The stillness of his breath in the frigid air. That smile demanded a response, but my voice had fled. *Do I know an alien?* On the Main Planet, the ones on the news only ever spoke to government officials. I was nobody; I had never worked for the government. And this creature didn't match any known Traveler from the Celestial Faction. Not the silver-eyed envoys. Not the luminous Lords. "Who are you?" I managed, trying to stand. My leg buckled, sending me back to the frost.

"We have met before. Long ago, on the Main Planet, in a time your memories haven't reached yet." His voice carried the weight of many centuries. "You must follow your dream to become an astronaut."

My breath hitched. "How do you...?"

"I told you. We have met."

"There is no astronaut program on Aurora," I protested. "The Peace Treaty forbids it – no deep-space tech. Just planetary shuttles."

"You will return to the Main Planet," he said. "It is important."

Then...

A vision erupted in my mind: waves crashing on a sunlit shore. Not a hologram. A *memory.* Salt stung my lips. Warm sand shifted beneath my feet. Somewhere deep inside, I recognized this place.

"How are you doing this?" I whispered, already waist-deep in turquoise water.

"Messing with your mind, a little," he said with a chuckle, somewhere between amusement and seriousness. "On the Main Planet, seek Batranu. He will help you." A pause. "You will forget about this until the right moment. Then you will remember."

"Remember what?" I asked. "What do I have to remember?"

"The sea."

Then he was gone. The ovoid vanished. Around me, the crew milled about, oblivious. I clutched the ice; its cold bite the only proof I hadn't dreamed it all. The alert on my suit blinked off. The field had stabilized.

But nothing else had.

"Nothing to worry about," Doc said, his scanner humming over my scalp. "Superficial burns on your back, minor abrasions. Lungs clear. Eyes undamaged." He tapped my twisted knee and nodded. "You will heal fast. Handled the stress better than most." Then his tone shifted: "What movie was it? That sea memory of yours is ... vivid."

"No movie," I said, too quickly. "The memory just came back to me today."

Mara leaned against the med-bay wall, pursing her lips. "He is right." With a flick of her fingers, my neural readouts hovered in the air. "Look ... taste receptors firing, olfactory traces, even dermal feedback. No movie could embed sensory data so rich. Only a high-tier simulator or..." She trailed off, her eyes locking onto mine. "Did this happen during the attack?"

"I think so." My throat tightened. "Does this mean my old memories are returning? Will I ever be who I was?"

"You are who you are." Mara squeezed my hand, and her smile was gentle, but it didn't reach her eyes. "Memories don't define you. Just the weight you choose to carry."

Doc wasn't listening. "Stable. Too stable," he murmured, scowling at the charts. "When was his last neural check?"

"Twenty-eight days ago," the nurse-bot replied.

"Weekly checks from now on," Doc ordered, distracted. His gaze drifted upward, toward the ceiling, toward the sky that we could never see from the Deep, toward things unsaid.

I edged toward the door, leaving it cracked as I slipped out – an old trick. Just enough to catch Doc's low, resigned sigh:

"Poor kid," he muttered. "The Travelers tried to kill him again. But that sea memory..."

Mara didn't answer, and I felt that her was gaze fixed on the door, as if she was trying to see me.

Doc continued, voice lower now. "Erin signature all over it. Sensory layering, emotional anchor, temporal bleed, classic Erin. Everything buried deep behind the memory of the sea. I wonder who was up there. They didn't contact us after repelling the attack."

"Armin. He always planned for failure," Mara said, quietly.

"The kid is not ready."

"He won't have a choice."

The pause was longer now, then Doc said, "If this memory resurfaced, others aren't far behind. And if the Travelers catch even a whisper of Erins helping him..."

"They will come again," Mara finished, her voice hard.

"Not just for him. For everyone he has touched."

"We should tell him."

"No," Doc said instantly. "Not yet."

"He is strong enough. Smarter than we expected. If he remembers the Erin's codes..."

"And if he doesn't? If he breaks?" Doc's voice became nervous. "You have seen what happens when half-awakened hosts try to read those layers too early. We lose them. Or worse, the Travelers enslave them. We are running out of time. He will need to be ready soon. Because if Armin gave him back the memory of the sea, a new chain of events started."

The room fell into silence, heavy with all they hadn't said. Then the door closed.

The air warped, and the alien materialized among us. One moment: empty air. The next: *him.* His sudden appearance triggered an instinctive reaction, my fingers twitching with the irrational urge to touch him, to test his reality. His gaze pinned me in place. The same man. The one from the ice. During the attack.

"I *am* real," he laughed, the sound like dry leaves skittering across ice. His glance held unspoken knowledge – our encounter on the surface, the Travelers' assault, all of it.

"Acting is his specialty," Erun, our colony leader, drawled from his seat. "Doors are for lesser beings. When he is feeling generous, he answers to *Armin. The Erin.*"

Chuckles rippled through the room. Armin joined in, his laughter untouched by offense.

The name unlocked a memory: a hospital bed, searing pain, blindness – voices murmuring, *"We will gather a council when his time comes."*

Is this that time? *Time for what?*

You have questions," Armin turned toward me, his amusement fading. For the first time, I saw the complexity in his eyes – depths

I couldn't measure, the center of a thousand intersecting moments. Not just alien. *Ancient.*

"I've found some answers," I said, opting for blunt honesty. "They came with the pain, on the hospital bed. But they are incomplete."

Doc stiffened. "Pain? You were sedated. The med-scans showed nothing. I am sorry..."

"His genetic difference might explain it," Armin interrupted with a shrug. "He has found some shortcuts through the Field. That's why the Travelers want him. Anyway, his knowledge makes this meeting easier."

As he spoke, the air across the table shivered. A form began to coalesce in an empty chair – not a body, but the *idea* of one: translucent, eyeless, a chilling humanoid void.

My muscles locked, primal terror screaming at me to flee. But no one moved for weapons. They even smiled, and I felt embarrassed by my overreaction.

"Meet the *Gate,*" Erun said, watching my face. Then, to the apparition: "Do I know you?"

"Gate: A being capable of galactic teleportation," Diego informed me. *"Multiple instances exist. My access to their data is limited. Classified."*

"There are hundreds of us," the Gate said, her voice a rustling breeze. Feminine. Amused. "Why assume we have met?"

"Only one Gate I know bothers with humor," Erun said, arching a brow. Then to me: "This one usually takes a female form. Calls herself *Houston.*" He turned back. "Why this shape today? A joke?"

The shimmering void extended an arm toward me. "I am to train him. He deserves a choice."

"Is *Houston* your real name?" I asked, my voice steadier than I felt.

"One of many," she said. "You may give me another." Her form began to shift – features melting and reforming. A Traveler Lord. A Main Planet diplomat. Famous actresses. A dozen alien beings I couldn't name. Some too alien for my comfort.

"If *Houston* works..." I managed.

"Simple is good." Eyes bloomed in the void, violet, impossibly deep. A face sculpted itself from the nothingness: sharp cheekbones, pale skin, lips parted mid-breath. "We can begin," Houston said, with her new mouth, and reality twisted.

Our cramped meeting room dissolved.

One heartbeat, we were seated around a table. The next, we floated inside a huge ovoid, its curved walls displaying our solar system in perfect miniature. The gas giant I had seen from the ice field – when I had nearly died – now spun lazily at my fingertips, the size of a human head.

"For those not yet aware," Houston continued, her voice echoing through the void, "this is a simulation. A bit more advanced than yours." Her smile was all teeth. Though her words were for everyone, her violet eyes locked on me. "Some of you will hate what comes next." The view shifted. The Main Planet swelled into focus, its blue expanse expanding until it filled the ovoid's ceiling.

A collective gasp rippled through the group – half wonder, half anguish. These were exiles, people who had spent years buried in Aurora's claustrophobic underground. Now their lost home hung before them, vivid and vast. Memories of better times.

I saw Erun's fingers twitch toward the absent oceans.

Houston raised a hand, and a web of white light bloomed across the planet, its threads stretching beyond the ovoid's edges like a living lattice. "The Universe's Field," she said. "Some call it the Matrix Field, or simply the Field, the substrate from which all matter emerges. Every material thing begins here. Everything is preserved in the Field – every memory, every choice, every unmade future." The web pulsed, its filaments alive with latent energy. "Two centuries ago, the Celestial Faction absorbed all the rival Factions in our galaxy. After a million years of managed chaos, one Faction reigns supreme." New objects appeared in orbit: sleek black satellites. "Fifty years ago, the Celestials began crafting their own Field." As she spoke, the satellites spat threads of darkness. Where they touched the luminous web, it vanished, cleanly, violently. Voids spread like wounds. "Phase one: blockers. Designed to fracture the Matrix Field. For now, they only monitor communication within it."

The simulation accelerated. Hundreds more satellites bloomed like tumors. They linked to planetary Net relays, DigitalEgo nodes, systems of governance and surveillance. The black threads wove a cage around the world. Then came the final blow. The radiant lattice – the Field itself, that invisible force binding all sentient life – snapped. Where there had been light, only emptiness remained.

"This," Houston whispered, "is their endgame." She looked at me again. "A new universe, birthed from the corpse of our galaxy." The simulation dissolved, leaving only her final words hanging in the air like smoke.

"Why would the Universe allow this?" My voice sounded too loud in the sudden quiet.

Houston's violet eyes gleamed. "The Universe encourages experiments. New Fields birth new universes. Evolution. This..." She gestured to the ruined web, "is the second attempt to create a new Field in this galaxy. The Saurian Faction's first experiment consumed twenty billion lives, ten million years ago. Your government volunteered your world for this trial."

"They will die!" The words burst out before I could stop them.

The silence that followed was worse – no shock, no outrage. Only grim acknowledgment. I was the last to know.

Armin looked at me, his alien eyes dark and unreadable. "Most will. Which is why we need you." He tapped my temple. "Your connection to the Field lets us bypass their surveillance. The Resistance needs a conduit to channel information between cells."

"Yes!" My answer came too fast, fueled by a rush of heat, of purpose, of something I couldn't name.

Armin sighed and shook his head. "Youth. Don't answer yet. You will train first. Learn more. According to our projections, the Travelers' Field completes in four years."

The unspoken truth hung between us: *Going back will be suicide.*

A chill ran down my spine, equal parts fear and exhilaration. *Is this courage? Or just the thrill I've been craving?* "Why would they sacrifice so many people?"

"The right of higher minds to govern lesser ones," Armin quoted from *The Poisoned Book*, his mouth twisting with disgust.

"That's crap."

"Dangerous crap," he agreed, almost amused.

Houston clapped her hands. "Then we begin."

Reality shifted. One moment: the council chamber. Familiar lighting, sharp shadows, the weight of eyes and expectations. The next: a stream. Cold water swirled around my boots. I stood alone, perched on a mossy rock slick with moisture. Somewhere ahead, a waterfall thundered, hidden behind a curtain of mist that curled upward instead of falling, as if gravity here was more of a suggestion than a law. My breath fogged in the air, though I felt no cold.

"Your simulation feels real," I muttered, assuming Houston could hear me. I flexed my fingers against the damp stone, half-expecting them to sink through it.

"Because it's not a simulation." She materialized beside me, suspended just above the water's surface, like gravity hadn't noticed her yet. Her reflection rippled in the stream, but in hers, the mist moved backward, and the water ran black. "We are on a planet twelve thousand light-years from Aurora."

I blinked. "How...?"

"I am called *Gate* for a reason," she said, grinning at my shock. "With me, any point in space-time within this galaxy is reachable. Planets, stations, battlefields."

"Then go to the Main Planet!" I snapped. "Blow up their towers. Tear down their satellites!"

"I wish it were that easy." Her smile faded. "Your government has officially declared Gates unwelcome. We are forbidden from entering the inner part of your solar system without permission. The Galactic Council was informed about the interdiction."

"Just drop us there, with a few missiles attached."

"*Black Eye* forbids it."

"What's that? A watchdog?"

"No. Black Eye *is* the rules." Her voice dropped, words stretching like a shadow at dusk. "It's the conscious will of the Universe in this galaxy. The central black hole. A sentience vast beyond comprehension."

I stared at her, trying to grasp the scale of what she meant.

She leaned closer, and her violet eyes dimmed, like a dying star. "The Travelers? They are children compared with the *Observers of Serenity* – beings who have transcended matter entirely. Who dwell in quiet spaces of folded light and dead stars. They answer only to the Black Eye."

The water at our feet changed. It darkened, not from shadow, but from presence. It no longer reflected sky, but *void.* A yawning darkness – the *Black Eye. Watching.* The void shimmered again, stretching beyond the horizon.

"Welcome," Houston whispered, "to the *real* war."

"What *are* you?" I asked, eyeing Houston's shimmering form.

She tilted her head, violet eyes glinting with something older than our world. "Neither life nor technology," she said. "A bridge, perhaps. My destiny is to help your kind evolve." She stepped closer – close enough that I caught the scent of something not quite floral, not quite alien. A perfume that hung in the air like mist, made for no human skin. "Shall we begin your training?"

Before I could answer, a flood of knowledge slammed into my mind – *Ten-mile run. Five-mile swim.*

Are you insane?

But then I saw the atoll. Turquoise water lapped at white sand, encircling a lagoon so clear I could count fish weaving between coral thirty feet below. "Can we start now?" I asked, almost eating my words.

Houston laughed, a warm, distinctly human sound. "You are far more reckless than the other one."

"What other one?"

"Deceneus. My previous student."

"Dead?"

"Unborn."

My face must have shown something – confusion, disbelief – because she smiled. The kind of smile adults give children when they question gravity.

"He came here from a planet called Earth and from the future," she explained. "You lack that ... advantage. But you share his Field signature, an extremely rare occurrence. It has already drawn the Travelers' attention." Her expression darkened, as if something just beyond her reach had stirred. "They have noticed you before. And..." She hesitated. "...they remember him. There was a war over the planet, three centuries ago. The Travelers lost to Deceneus and Altamira." A beat passed. Then: "He needed to learn *courage.* You?" Her gaze narrowed. "*Discipline.*"

The world shifted. Sand replaced the rock beneath my boots. Salt stung my nostrils. The sunlight was blinding, clean, merciless.

"Don't tell Aurora!" I shouted over the crashing surf. "They will kill me if they know where I am now!"

But Houston was gone.

And I was in the water. Arms slicing. Legs kicking. The horizon retreating with every stroke. The sun pressed against my back. The fun vanished gradually. By the third month, my daily swim stretched to twenty miles. There were days I vomited seawater. Others I hallucinated. Once, I swam so far I forgot when I had started.

Houston always watched from the shore. Her smile sharp as a scalpel.

Chapter 3 - Alenia

This hat... I can't forget it. Not in a thousand years. My fingers brushed the silk, soft, familiar, unlocking memories I thought time had sealed away. *So delicate*. Three hundred years of training had hardened me against tears, turned emotion into reflex, taught me not to feel. But as I turned the hat in my hands, it felt like I was turning my life over, piece by piece.

"Diegia, hijack all the street cameras," I asked my DigitalEgo – the half-organic AI that lived inside my brain. Though I already knew what she would say.

"Nothing," she answered quietly. *"The hat wasn't here ... until it was. No trace of how it arrived here."*

Why now? Why send it? A warning? That color, pale green, so fragile, so familiar. I still loved it. Without thinking, I set it gently on my head.

It had been autumn that day, long ago. The hat stirred it up, all of it – memories clear and calm, like dew on grapes at sunrise. I had been standing in the train, my new green hat tugged free by the wind as the train was gaining speed. I smiled, watching it fly, never imagining how that day would end. My pale green dress fluttered in the breeze. When the train stopped, the crowd stood silent. Some closed their eyes. No one spoke. Then, slowly, the world became noisy again. *Now you talk*, I remember thinking. That had been our first steam train.

That night, I left my planet.

Houston, my Gate friend, teleported me to a secret ShadowMind training center far across the stars. And yes, if you laugh at me for clinging to the memory of a hat, I will only smile. I have seen more planets than I can count. One mission after another blurred the past. But that hat – that hat stayed with me. It had been beautiful. Wide-brimmed. Green like spring. A kite caught in the wind, sailing toward the sun. Now, after all these years, it was back. Or something close to it. Resting on my head like no time had passed.

Why now?

Only two groups could have penetrated through my electronic defenses: the state ... or the Resistance. *Please let it be the Resistance*. If the state knows – if they remember me – then I am already gone. They erased me from history. I was part of a past they didn't want told. But I remember. I always have. If this is from my friends, then something is coming. Something that matters.

I held the hat and felt young again. I had been eighty-two that day, a widow ready to die. Now, in the mirror, my thirty-year-old face smiled back. And for a heartbeat, I could have sworn the hat smiled too.

Every time I return home, I check the wall in my bedroom. The hat still hangs there, quiet, waiting, the signal that everything is fine. But it is also something else: A doorway back into a past that was lovely, and full of ghosts.

A long time ago, my friend Armin, the Erin, had begun immersing me in the history I had missed – over two centuries' worth of unknown context. "We will send you back to your planet – just a few years after the Third World War."

"What is a world war?" The question slipped out before I could stop it. I knew what war was – I had fought when I was young. I knew it meant death. But a *world* war? I wasn't ready for what that really meant.

It wasn't the numbers that broke me. You can understand a single death. A name, a face, a life cut short. But millions? That becomes a statistic – cold, flat, empty. Armin showed me the unedited records. The last image still haunts me: A little girl caught in the flash of a nuclear blast. When the light faded and the dust settled, only her shadow remained, burned into the brick wall behind her. A tiny silhouette, arms raised, as if trying to shrink away from the end.

"Everybody loses... Why would anyone start a war like that?" I didn't ask if another one was coming. I didn't have to. The urgency behind my mission said enough.

"They don't think like ordinary people," Armin said, quietly. "They think in percentages. To them, owning fifty percent of a ruined nation is better than twenty percent of a thriving one. It's about leverage."

"Wars don't spare anyone," I said it, but it felt useless. Like air leaving a broken pipe.

"They don't lose," he replied. "They're a global force, hidden behind every flag, every regime. They fund both sides, pull every string, and live untouched in sanctuaries no one dares target. Not even the worst dictators go near them."

Technically, my return to the planet was just a teleportation, nothing more than a shift through space. The real challenge was the immersion. I materialized near the railway station of a remote town. No fanfare. No welcoming committee. Not that I expected any. Any old friends or family I had known were long gone. Maybe my great-grandchildren were out there somewhere ... but I wasn't here for reunions. I had accepted the reality of it the moment the Resistance asked me to return. They believed my world was barreling toward another dark chapter, and they wanted me to join the local branch. I didn't know what good a sleeper agent like me could do, dropped into the middle of history like a needle in a haystack. But I said yes anyway. Staring at the hat on the wall, a burst of memories flooded me; not a gentle return, but a sudden immersion. Places, people, feelings ... it was like living it all over again. It felt like present.

I emerge from nowhere. To the locals, I am just a ghost stepping out of the storm. To those who left me behind when Houston shut the teleportation channel, I never really returned. I look around. A quiet disappointment lingers. I hadn't let myself hope for more, but still – some part of me wants more than this. The wind howls over the land, whipping desert dust into thick, swirling clouds. Visibility drops to just a few feet. Perfect cover.

Minutes later, I am seated inside the station, scanning the crowd out of habit. A scouting team has already cleared them, but instincts like mine don't die.

Then I check my documents again – for the tenth time. The girl in the ID photo is still a stranger. So is the name. And the number attached to me. *I am not One-Six-Seven-Four... I am... No. That person is gone. And yet, not gone.* The face on the card barely resembles the one I used to see in the mirrors. Different enough to fool a distant acquaintance. Close enough to haunt me. Not that it matters. Armin had been clear: no risks. My former identity was radioactive. I had been a political figure. Now I am erased history. A bitter laugh rises in my throat but never escapes.

The card tells a new story: Alenia Tiati. This is my name now. And this is home again.

Liar.

The world I have returned to has little in common with the one I lived on and left behind. Same coordinates. Same fractured history. But everything I knew is gone.

The train arrives – delayed, as expected, by the great storm – its strident whistle pulling me out of memory and back into the now. It screeches to a halt, a half-visible serpent wrapped in white smoke, exhaling one last steam-laced sigh that stirs the waiting crowd into motion. The scent of burnt coal fills the station as someone opens the door. The crowd begins to flow, people funneling through the doorway like sand in an hourglass – compressed, then released. It all feels dreamlike.

Steam twists through windborne dust, forming a mist both heavy and ghost-thin. It stings lungs, burns eyes, quickens the pace. No one runs. This is a small town. Here, dignity outranks urgency. Better to cough into your sleeve than be seen scrambling for a seat.

My escort gives a curt nod, and I board the train with the eagerness of a real nineteen-year-old, a smile fixed on my face. I wear my detachment like a second skin. A stranger among strangers, unbothered by what anyone might think of her fleeting appearance.

Two scouts disembark, subtle glances confirming what I need to know:

No hunters.

No Travelers.

No traps.

The game begins. I enter through the farthest door from my assigned seat, scanning every face in the carriage. The scouts had cleared them, but now I am alone. Through the window, I see Armin's quiet farewell – his hand pressed to his hat as if holding back the wind. I answer with a small, meaningless gesture: wiping imaginary dust from the glass. Then he is gone. Swallowed by steam and mist as the train leaves the station.

Alone.

Truly alone, in a way I have never been.

No connections here.

No past.

For two days, I snake my way through the country, changing trains, circling the city that houses the university where I am to begin my new life. A fox doubling back on its trail. At night, I sleep in a crumbling hotel built into the side of a cliff, its rear pressed hard against stone. The road below lies exposed beneath my window. Even here, two hundred miles from the desert, wind rattles the panes. Dust hovers in the air like a presence. Sleep comes in short, guarded fragments. At dawn, the final train delivers me to my destination.

The university feels like another world, and no one looks twice at me here. Students stream past in every direction, wrapped in the noise of youth and routine. Laughter, footsteps, the rustle of books and paper. No one expects danger on a campus. That is its charm, and its weakness.

My new identity blends in well enough. Alenia Tiati, scholarship student, recently accepted. Just another face in the crowd. Our cell did good work with the records, and I had practiced the backstory until it felt like muscle memory. Still, I move carefully. I watch. Old instincts don't vanish. Not even here, surrounded by lecture halls and dormitories and the illusion of safety. The Resistance said this was where it would begin. Or begin again.

Now, back in the present, staring at the old green hat on my bedroom wall, I let out a long breath.

Tomorrow is Monday. Work. Again.

Why did I agree to come back?

The morning bled gray through my office window – another joyless start to the rainy season, another day steeped in that old, bitter sense of uselessness. After all these years, I had barely scratched the monolithic state machine the Travelers had twisted into a grotesque parody of governance. Ironically, today marked the hundred-and-eleventh anniversary of my return. No celebrations, of course. Just the quiet, dull shock of realizing how swiftly the decades had slipped by: university, my first job, the next, each promotion a calculated step deeper into the government's belly.

My *first* rejuvenation at seventy-five. Then another – better, smoother – until I wore this face: early thirties, sharp but unremarkable. Now, I sat at the highest level a security officer without Cupola blood could reach. Beyond this point, merit meant nothing. Pedigree ruled. Not that I ever wanted their gilded cage. Too high was too visible. And too dangerous.

Cupola blood. The phrase carried weight, like a stamp pressed into flesh. No one ever explained what it meant in public channels, but everyone understood. Their DNA was a status symbol and a passport. Access codes were layered into their biometrics. High-security networks responded only to their signatures. Certain places and doors wouldn't open without Cupola blood. Still, I knew their weaknesses. Their minds were reflexively trained to see evolution as disorder, not necessity.

"We weren't informed the *Celestial Dragon* had been lost," I said to Vipri as I stepped into his office. Luck had handed me the briefing just moments earlier – barely enough time to compose myself. "Near Aurora."

Vipri, like all top-level aliases, was a political construct. The Prime Minister was always a *Prim* or *Prima*, depending on gender – names born in a lab of marketing jargon to evoke warmth and familiarity. *Hello, Prim* sounds friendlier than *Good morning, Mr. Prime Minister*, as if they were your neighbors, not ruthless oligarchs who required hour-long decontaminations after shaking hands with the plebeian crowds – carefully selected, paid, and pre-cleared.

Vipri arched an eyebrow in well-rehearsed surprise, brown eyes locking onto mine. He had known. And he had seen no reason to tell me. Twenty years of working together had forged a kind of twisted symbiosis – an understanding that rarely worked in my favor.

Let's be clear: Vipri wasn't some bureaucratic seat-warmer. He was Vice Prime Minister of the General Government – the One government, sanctioned by the Travelers to rule this planet. Decades of shadow games, long before the First World War, had given birth to this system. Officially, it promised peace. *The True History* – the only history book left unbanned – said so. And once the Net came online, it became easier to herd people to read or watch only things that were permitted by faceless censors.

But I know the truth.

"They destroyed the ship," I said, carefully omitting the word *Travelers*.

"Oh no, my dear." Vipri's smile was polished to a shine. But beneath that surface charm, I caught it – a flicker of bitterness. A crack in the mask. He pressed a finger through the hologram, underlying a paragraph, then emailed the report to me. "An unfortunate explosion. A malfunction."

I opened the file – not for the lies it contained, but for the coded truth buried beneath them. The state's official stance. The party line. A *malfunction* that vaporized three hundred people. His grin told me he knew I had to spend the night peeling this fiction apart

"I would tolerate a delay … if you join me for dinner," he said lightly, tapping the table through the report. The warmth in his voice was suddenly real.

"You know I hate delays." My smile was composed, and I turned away, slowly. At the door, I paused. "Why not blame the rebels?"

"We can't show weakness. Space is unpredictable. Malfunctions happen." His voice had lost its charm. His posture shifted, just slightly. Rigid now. Watching me too closely.

"People will question this."

"A few *heretics*." He let the word linger, his grin too wide. "Who cares about them?"

I nodded, not trusting myself to speak. Then I stepped through the doorway. The lock clicked behind me.

Alenia

The storm had turned the morning commute into a gridlocked mess. Our government complex sat at the heart of a metropolis of twenty million. Of course I would be late. Vipri's summons reached me the moment I left home – pointless, given his constant surveillance of my movements. I handed control to the EDriver and skimmed through official messages. Twenty minutes later, with nothing left to distract me, I stared blankly at blurred storefronts until we reached the compound. The garden surrounding our ten-story monolith smelled of rain and freshly clipped grass. For a brief second, I wished I could lose myself in its green paths forever.

Vipri is nervous. The thought hit the moment I stepped into his office.

"Red Alert." Diegia hissed through my neural link as the Net pushed a priority signal to all Zero-Level clearances. I held ZeroD – the lowest tier, but still Zero. The last Red Alert had been during the Rebellion.

"You are seeing it now," Vipri said without looking at me. "I received it thirty minutes ago, when I summoned you."

A Vice Prime Minister with ZeroA clearance, informed late? Why?

"Not the best time to ask," Diegia warned.

"Obviously I won't ask him," I replied, silently. *"But if he was briefed late, this came from the Cupola or the Travelers. Find out which."*

"Traffic," I said aloud, cutting off his attempt at scolding. "Why Red?" There hadn't been a rebellion in twenty years – not since the Treaty exiled most of the insurgents to Aurora. What remained here was scattered, hidden, and quiet.

"The Travelers warned of potential strike on satellites." With that, a document landed into my mind – a memo so dense with obfuscation it might as well have been blank. They had struck surface installations on Aurora. Vague language. No details. Deliberately opaque. *"Run it through AI,"* I instructed Diegia.

She answered seconds later. *"No embedded data. No hidden structure. It's clean."*

Which made it worse. The Travelers never send clean messages. Only the Erins could have retaliated – my old allies. And if the Travelers had struck first, they would have broken the Treaty. Their warning wasn't a warning. It was a smokescreen. Their orbital surveillance would be disrupted, briefly. That meant a window – just long enough for the Resistance to exploit a few Field channels.

"The rebels don't have spacecraft," I said, stalling. "The Treaty..."

"Don't insult us with ignorance," Vipri snapped – gently, almost amused. His gaze drifted to the window in a rehearsed gesture of casual disinterest.

"Cupola issued the Red Alert," Diegia reported, finally.

"They will target the Travelers," I said to Vipri. "No one would strike *us,* but if they disable the surveillance grid..."

He turned to face me fully, eyes narrowed. "And?"

"The Anti-Field shield might fail."

"Bravo." His applause was slow and mocking.

"Thank you." I smiled, just as sharp. *I will applaud just as hard when your system collapses.*

"Diegia, erase that thought from my memory."

The system I represent. The system I loathe.

Vipri's mocking applause cut off abruptly. "The Resistance will transmit data through the Field to their agents here," he said, slipping into his practiced bureaucratic neutrality. "We must take all necessary measures to intercept this."

All necessary measures. A phrase that meant precisely nothing. Without the Travelers' tech, we couldn't intercept Field transmissions between the few conscious Dreamers here and their Erin or Auroran contacts. The architecture was beyond us. I studied his face. He wanted something. Something my ZeroD clearance didn't entitle him to say aloud. It was clear now – his strategy. Those calculated outbursts of his? They weren't impulsive. They were timed. Measured. Just sharp enough to unnerve, never quite crossing the invisible line – self-imposed rules that sometimes I was too sure I understood. A performance. He counted on your reaction, defensive, flustered, scrambling to solve a problem that might not even exist yet. And if you succeeded, he won twice. *Their people are my people... I am just hoping for some new toys to add to my arsenal.*

"Diegia, delete that too."

"And fast shuttles with operatives," I added impulsively, baiting him. We played the same game with different pieces. His rank allowed raised voices and dramatic exits. I had side doors and polite smiles.

"And tech we can't track," he added, dryly.

"Tech is becoming ... problematic," I said, choosing my words. Our brightest minds had long since fled. What remained were the loyal. Obedience breeds stagnation – the fatal flaw of every repressive system.

"Why attack Aurora?" He shifted again, dodging the topic. But the edge in his voice betrayed something real. Unease. He hadn't been consulted. Maybe he was collateral.

You see it now, don't you? We're nothing to the Travelers. "AI analysis suggests..."

"Cold machine thinking," he snapped. His fingers began to drum the desk. "I need human intuition. Why blasting a shipyard? That's not standard op protocol."

"No Treaty violation if they are not building ships," I said with a shrug.

"You believe those rebel bastards actually comply?" His voice cracked, his fingers still tapping – faster now.

"They have. Until now."

"So had the Travelers." He leaned forward. "I want to know why that changed."

So do I. "Ask your Traveler friends," I said, and couldn't stop the faint laugh that escaped as I walked out before he could answer.

Chapter 4

My year-long training ended a few weeks ago. Now, the most advanced – and most boring – technology is ready to send me to the surface. From there, I will fly to Aurora, where a spaceship awaits. My last day here...

Yesterday, I tried to talk to Lamia, but she wouldn't see me. She is not here – I scanned the hall, but why would she be? A hollow emptiness fills my mind. What did I expect? *I have to leave.* I won't ever return. Maybe she could have come with me. But she can't. She wanted to, but she has to stay. She has to stay alive.

I have come to understand that going to the Main Planet isn't just about becoming an astronaut. They prepared me. I am ready to fight – like everyone else. Or maybe like no one else. They turned me into a rebel, but they never forced me. I agreed, willingly, after they gave me access to the Main Planet's information channels. That was when I finally saw what I never could before, what the old DigitalEgo had kept hidden. That Diego – the version of me implanted at twelve – died in the explosion.

Now, I want revenge. For my mother's death. For my little sister Ana, that thin girl with the pale face and dark eyes. For my father, murdered before I was born. The Travelers killed them all.

I still dream of Ana sometimes – always the same scene, the ship exploding. A nightmare I hate, yet part of me clings to it. It's the only memory I have of her. Deep down, I hope that one day, I will dream of her in a past I can't remember.

More than anything, I want to destroy the Travelers' new Field before it wipes out most of our population. I want to stop the government from turning children into obedient robots with DigitalEgo.

The new me is a weapon, trained by one of the galaxy's most advanced entities. I know what's waiting on the Main Planet. I know what I am supposed to do. As a Field Dreamer, I can consciously access the Field and exchange information with other Dreamers – even across planets. The name is misleading. It sounds like drifting in sleep. But it's just an old name from a time when no one understood what was happening. They do now, but the term stuck.

The Travelers can monitor Field communications, but space is vast. Their sensors only cover the Main Planet's outer space and their bases. That's why I have to be an astronaut, to relay messages between Aurora and the rebels on the ground. Now, I have a neural switch that lets me initiate contact at will. Last time, their sensors caught me entering the Field. I barely made it out alive. Being a rebel is dangerous. Being one on the Main Planet is worse. That's why Lamia can't ever follow me.

The hardest part? I couldn't tell her any of this. To her, I will always be the man who left to chase a dream of becoming an astronaut. But she will stay in my dreams too. I know that.

Before entering the capsule, I take a moment to scan the platform. Only a few people are here: Doc, Mara, the nurse-bot, and a few others. Lamia isn't among them. I sigh and step inside.

"Look," Diego whispers. He has hijacked the camera feed from the platform stairs, and there she is. I can't hear anything, but her shaking shoulders tell me she is crying. Tears streak my face too.

I want to speak to her, to hold her. But it would only make things worse. Even if I survive, I will never come back.

Alenia

"Do you know of any other rebel asking to settle back here?" Vipri stared through his office window, the river stretching beyond, his tone dripping with feigned disinterest. "I know – it's rhetorical. He must be a spy. A dangerous one, if he came willingly. Can you trust a terrorist?" He laughed, turning toward me. "Lovely people ... after a full memory wipe."

Can I trust our government? "Diegia, delete this from my memory."

"Then this should go to..." I sidestepped his question, fabricating hesitation. A calculated move – usually reluctance would guarantee the assignment landed on me. But it was already clear, for reasons of his own, he wanted the same damned thing I did.

"Spy or not, I need you there to pull the strings. Keep the channels open." He overrode me, closing the distance until his eyes hovered inches from mine. "Once we confirm he is a spy, they can handle it. But if some rebels genuinely want to return ... we will need a softer touch." He jabbed a finger at me. "Small chance, but worth the play."

Yeah, I am your kid gloves. We would welcome them with open arms, parade them on every news feed. "Unprecedented. Tamed rebels willing to return. But worth a closer look," I said, deliberately neutral.

"There is so much enthusiasm in your answer," Vipri remarked, a chill threading his voice.

"I can't muster enthusiasm for the premise. How do you want me to proceed?" I nearly smiled. We had both gotten what we wanted.

"You are no enthusiast, but you are reliable. Especially for delicate tasks requiring an ... open mind." He held my gaze, then turned back to the window.

The kid gloves again. "Should I understand that enthusiasm and reliability are officially incompatible?"

"You know what I mean." His voice pitched slightly higher – deliberate, or just a catch in his throat? Hard to say.

"How should we pursue this?"

"Full mind scan. You will have authorization in minutes."

This time, I couldn't mask my surprise.

"Surprised, eh? I should congratulate myself. Very little catches you off guard," he bragged.

"I am so old."

"Don't play the guilt card, *old lady*. I prefer experienced. And charming…" His smile was thin, but strangely warm. "When you choose to be. You were like this long before I was born."

"Obviously. I am old." *But if you think I am only 140, you are dead wrong.*

"So old your birth date is still a mystery," he said. The silence that followed landed heavy.

No, he can't know. No neuranalyzers are allowed here – the whole government would collapse if they were. Maybe I should erase this from my mind. But how much of me would be left? Thankfully, my clearance blocks any official deep scan. A perk of climbing the ranks before those cursed tools existed. "Women are mysteries. Whether that's truth or man's superstition, who knows?"

"Bring me good news when you are done." His warm smile acknowledged the joke, and I wondered what this man might have been in a normal society.

"Don't wonder too much," Diegia mocked, morphing into a black feline shape with a human face. *"He is handsome."*

I silenced her with a mental shove, too late to stop the whistle. *"Shut up,"* I snapped.

She winked, then dissolved into smoke.

"The rebel will be in your office in ten minutes." Vipri eyed the wall clock, letting the silence hang, his unspoken intentions resting in the air. "Pity you have no time to change." His glance flicked to my austere gray suit. "Something more ... romantic might suit a mysterious spy encounter." His tone was sterile, but it unsettled me, not out of logic.

Romantic... I jerked the door shut before he could say more.

"This is your fault, Diegia," I muttered, unsure why I had reacted to a provocation I would usually ignore. My plain clothes were armor, meant to render me invisible. That didn't explain the flicker of irritation. She stayed silent as I strode away.

"Do you know him?" The sturdy captain avoided my eyes as he pushed the rebel into my office. His tone was neutral – *too* neutral. Controlled. Flat. My old training flared. Something was wrong. Not in his words, but in his body: a fractional stiffness in the shoulders, a hitch in the step. He moved like someone fighting instinct, trying to keep the tension out of his limbs. The hairs on my neck rose. Not fear. Not recognition. Something in between. Something deeper.

"Diegia, hijack the cameras. Replay his entry. No AI filters."

Outwardly, I shrugged. "Only from the news. Why do you ask?" I kept my voice bored, flatline disinterested.

"Diegia! What's on the cameras?" I pressed.

She materialized with a shrug. *"Nothing."*

That can't be right. "What level of training does he have?" A second later, the captain's file flashed in my mind: standard police, average scores, nothing exceptional. *Why do I feel like a predator entered the room?*

"Your eyes," the captain said, vaguely.

A provocation. He wanted a reaction. But why? *"Diegia, what's on the feed now?"*

She sent me my own image – expressionless, unreadable. *"You are ... you. Not even a twitch."*

"What's wrong with my eyes? Are they that bad?" I tilted my head just slightly.

"They widened," he said, tone dry. A cop sniffing out something he couldn't name.

Diegia replayed the footage. Half a second of pupil dilation as I first saw the rebel. Less than a blink, and still he had caught it.

"Diegia, are you sure he is just a police captain?" I was already doubting the file. He wasn't stupid, and he wasn't average. His observation was surgical, showing advanced training, and advanced tech.

"You are overinvested in your job," I said aloud, injecting my voice with bureaucratic dullness. "Unusual cases breed unusual reactions." Deliberately vague. Let him interpret it how he wanted.

"My job is to keep my eyes open," he snapped, a touch of irritation creeping through his voice.

"And mine is to remind people when they are overreacting," I replied, smoothly. "Balance is the foundation of our peaceful society. Deviance isn't appreciated." I quoted the doctrine word for word, like scripture, locking eyes until he looked away. Annoying a High Councilor was one step shy of career suicide, even if he was right. My training had kicked in just in time. Without it, my voice would have cracked. Because the truth was, I *had* never seen this rebel before. But my body had reacted like I had.

Diegia dumped two data streams into my mind: the captain's tech logs (low-level access), and the rebel's profile (clean, no links to me). The captain would have run the same checks. But mine ran deeper. If there were a distant connection, I would have seen it, my clearance dwarfed his.

I turned my attention to the rebel. Early twenties. Calm stance. Intelligent brown eyes that tracked everything. Not deferential, but not hostile. Still. Calculating. Handsome... *Stop.*

"Welcome to the capital," I said at last, injecting enough warmth to pass for protocol. "I am Alenia, your integration liaison. We will ensure your transition is smooth. Everyone wants this to succeed."

He gave a slight nod. No smile. No speech. Just watchfulness. He was reading the play, same as I was. Officially, my task was to assess whether his rebel ties threatened our glorious civilization. Unofficially? I didn't know yet. He didn't feel like a plant. But his timing was too perfect, and his profile too clean. His return reeked of strategy. I hoped the Resistance would brief me soon – assuming they were involved.

Young man, you took a hell of a risk, I thought, locking eyes with him again. *Why? Why now?*

The captain still lingered in the room. I could feel his suspicion buzzing like static behind me. If he spoke again, I might have to remind him, who outranked whom.

"I take it from here," I said without turning. A dismissal.

Silence. Then footsteps. One, two – pause. The door hissed shut. I let out a slow breath.

Diegia materialized in my mind. A brief moment of silence followed, stretched thin and sharp. Then she whispered, her voice suddenly gentle. *"Want me to dig deeper on the rebel?"*

"Let's see what he says first."

She didn't reply. But I could feel her attention sharpening, ready. Curious. Like mine.

And the rebel?

He was still watching me. Silent.

Waiting?

Since the Rebellion's end, the Resistance has reached me only twice – both times to delay court martials for captured rebels, to facilitate their escape. Each request came through a dangerous channel, each one cost me something. All compromising memories are gone now; I deleted every trace of the dual logic I used to stall those cases, from my memory. Occasionally, rebels still escape *custody* – a word that sounds benign, but everyone knows it's a euphemism for prisons where mental torture is standard protocol. My rank means I am dragged into every investigation related to the Resistance. It lets me manage optics, calculate my safety margins. *For now.*

But the new single-account mandate has changed everything. Emails, net access, even thought-queries now chain directly to our IDs and mobile signals. Contacting the Resistance has become nearly impossible. Every call, every ping are tracked and stored for ten years. Every search analyzed. When technology dictates every move, the most dangerous weapon is independent thought.

"You will find differences between our societies," I told the rebel, keeping my voice calm, rehearsed. "But in time, you will appreciate your new life." *And regret ever coming here.*

The full brain scan authorization in my hand had five signatures – one of them Vipri's. Unusual. Concerning. Even in our paranoic society, a full scan was rare. It felt like an omen, or a trap.

Diegia appeared in her black cat form again, her eyes glinting with mock amusement as she began to purr. *"Handsome."*

I muted her. She flicked her pink tongue in mock protest.

"Open your mind." I recited the ritual phrase without looking at him. "If you have nothing to hide, you have nothing to fear." The mantra of our society. A lie displayed before every news segment. The lie that made us surrender privacy for *security*. It was printed at the end of every contract, etched into the core of every citizen's compliance chip.

My first time performing a full scan. My stomach twisted.

"Do it," Diegia hissed. Her feline form vibrated with urgency. *"You have to."*

"Maybe I should recalibrate you to be less..." I hesitated, groping for the right word.

"Less system?*"* she offered, with smug satisfaction. *"But would that be wise now? You can do this."*

Her emphasis on *you can* sent a ripple of unease through me. It wasn't just encouragement – it was a reminder that my leash might be longer than others', but it was still there.

With a jerky motion, I activated the neuranalyzer – a small, matte-black cube resting on the table like a harmless accessory. It had broken stronger minds than his. Reduced people to sobbing shells in minutes when used for torture. Even those with nothing to hide. I initialized the scan at the lowest level, and the rebel flinched, just barely.

The machine spat out its raw feed: layered text, emotion markers, voice tension, memory coherence, linguistic spikes. I fed it my custom parameter set: a hundred-fifty keywords and patterns. A hundred was standard. I wasn't taking chances. By tomorrow, AI and a dozen departmental experts would be combing through every syllable of my report. I had triple-checked the list last night: no references to Erins, the Field, Time Lines. Still, I had to make the report believable. That meant embedding the dangerous truths in the bureaucratic chaff. Make it boring. Make it procedural. He could rant against the system – that would help. They expected rebellion. They *wanted* it, to validate their suspicion. The critical details would be buried close to the end, cloaked in vague phrasing and technical jargon.

"Your mind contains significant inaccuracies," I said, keeping my tone unreadable.

"That's your official way of saying full of shit?" he asked, one eyebrow lifting. Then he straightened in his seat. Not fear, *posture.* Reflex or discipline?

The contradiction jarred me: innocence layered over deliberate provocation. A spy would have been more careful. A brainwashed pawn, more subdued. Unless... The medical file flashed in front of me. Fifty-eight percent brain damage. Forty-one percent body trauma from the ship *malfunction* that nearly killed him. The body was irrelevant for my purposes, but the brain... If it was true. The official note at the bottom made me smirk: You never know with these rebels. *Neither with us,* I thought in half mockery.

"The damage percentages are accurate," Diegia said, interrupting my thoughts. *"Margin of error: three percent."*

"If you prefer that crude phrasing, then yes, they are equivalent." *Let's see what's really in that mind of yours.* I began skimming the neural scan data, careful not to linger too long on any spike. If he was a new agent, a plant, I needed to protect him.

"I thought you would be angry," he said after a pause, his voice quieter, uncertain. It sounded genuine.

"Why would you want to provoke me?"

"You just seemed so ... official." He swallowed, the motion too natural to fake. "And when I saw you, I felt something ... strange." He cut himself off, glancing away.

Cameras weren't needed to read the reaction. Posture. Flickering eye contact. Half-hidden nervousness. My presence, and this damned gray suit, had rattled him. The suit was meant to efface me, reduce me to a symbol of procedure. But sometimes symbols invoke more than they hide.

"Handsome," Diegia purred again, her black feline form stretching luxuriously beside the neural monitor. Her eyes shimmered as she replayed my micro-reactions, zooming in for exaggeration. Mockery with data. Typical. She only used the seductress avatar around handsome men – a far cry from her usual fairy-guardian look.

I hadn't exactly discouraged him. A slight lean forward here, a pause too long there. My body remembered how to manipulate attraction, forgotten reflexes surfacing with disturbing ease.

"Don't let my appearance fool you," I said, voice cool but not unkind. "I am decades older than you."

"That's not what I..." he stopped, color blooming on his face.

Ah. So, you thought of that. When was the last time I saw someone blush like that? So openly. So ... human.

"Centuries ago," Diegia answered, her grin sly. *"Stay focused. He might not be.... Don't let this distract you. Maybe he is not so..."* She did not finish; her interference was just to make me understand that I needed to re-evaluate the situation. Usually, she does not react to my inner thoughts; she knows when I want her to react. There is a subtle way of making this known to your DigitalEgo, a way that develops in the first months after the immersion. But only if you were old enough at the time of the implant, and the model in the early phase of development. A wandering mind is left alone.

"Then why are you blushing?" I asked him, softening my tone, keeping it gentle, matching what he expected to hear from someone he trusted.

He exhaled sharply. "Fine, I had Diego save your image and make ... variations." He paused. "But that's not what I meant!" he added quickly, anxious to redirect.

"Stopping there shows remarkable restraint," I said, lightly.

He looked down. Embarrassed. Either he was a good actor, or genuinely naive. I hoped for the latter. The tribunal will never believe that. Not here. Not with that face. Their society was too open. Too sincere. He had been raised in sunlight, and now he was walking into shadows. *He won't survive here,* I thought bitterly. *He must.*

"I just..." His voice dropped to a whisper. "Wondered if you knew me. The *before* me."

"Should I?" I asked, carefully.

"If it's true, you would remember. I can't," he said, almost apologetically. "For me, it's just this strange ... familiarity. Closeness..."

You don't know me! My mental snarl released some of the building tension. Though my traitorous body remembered a sensual closeness we never had.

"Did I upset you?"

"No," I said too quickly. "We have never met. I can't explain your feelings." *Or mine.* I drew in a breath and made a decision. "We will pause here. You will have weekly integration sessions." I transmitted the safehouse coordinates. An autocab would already be waiting. "Don't leave the safehouse until you are acclimated," I instructed. "There's a garden." *Why did I say that?* He didn't need comfort. He needed conditioning. The reassurance tasted foreign. *I never justify containment.*

"On Aurora, they warned me I would be an outcast here," he said, quietly.

"Why would you be?"

"For living there after the ... explosion."

"You are one of us," I replied. "What happened on Aurora was just ... an accident." A *missile accident. Launched by our own fleet.*

"Many there were born here too," he added, then bit his lip. Too late. He knew it.

If he doesn't learn restraint, his life will be short. Brutally short. Truth isn't valued here. "Diegia, purge that thought." Too many slips today. He was pulling pieces of me loose, without even trying.

"Many chose to live here," I countered. *By choice? Really?*

"Delete that too!" I snapped, the words slashing through my own mind.

Diegia said nothing.

The boy sat there – no, *the young man* – still watching me with much hope in his eyes. I had to harden again. Quickly. Before hope made a fool of both of us.

Alenia

For the first time in my career, I pointed the neuranalyzer at my own temple before meeting the rebel. The device I had spent decades avoiding hummed against my skin, its cold sensors mapping neural pathways. A dangerous gamble. The scanner wasn't designed for dual use, and with only one unit in the room, I would have to transfer it to him mid-session if my body betrayed me again. He would notice. He was observant – too observant. But I needed data. I needed to know what the hell was happening to me. And then I would need to erase all traces of the scan. *No logs. No shadows. No trail.*

"The rebel has arrived." My assistant's hologram flickered across my visual field – pouting lips, a raised brow and forefinger – our private code for *unarmed, alone, and alarmingly cheerful.*

The door hissed open.

"Is his openness an act?" Vipri's voice hovered over the conference table days later. My report glowed between us in projected segments – text, visuals, flagged anomalies. Useless noise without the context he suspected I had withheld.

I bit the inside of my cheek until the urge to smile passed. In the playback, my expression read as controlled, distant – *professional* "If it's deception," I said carefully, "he is exceptional. With training, someone that young could be ... useful." I let the word hang in the air like bait. *Useful means politically valuable. Means protect him. Keep him alive.*

Vipri stood up and began circling the table, each step deliberate, his gaze drifting across the floating report hologram like a man watching embers. "You seem unsettled. By my question, or something deeper?" His fingers brushed the polished table, then paused – just inches from mine.

"This case is unusual."

"Unusual," he echoed, as if sampling the word for weight.

"You usually prefer unfiltered assessments to comfortable fictions. The kind designed to align with the general way of thinking."

"I would like to think so." Not a single inflection betrayed him, yet every muscle in my body coiled tighter.

I risked glancing at his posture. A ripple of tension, barely visible, ran through his shoulders.

He caught it. "Assessing my body language now?"

Damn. Too quick. He always had been. "Your statement requires clarification before I can respond adequately. There is no proper answer without proper understanding."

He stopped walking. His eyes bored into mine. "And I am not sure I can evaluate your report." He tapped the hologram, and its text shivered, then dissolved into floating particles. "My feeling is that the most important part is missing."

Too many feelings, I thought. Vipri never relied on intuition unless he already had facts. "And what would that part be?"

"If I knew, I would not have asked you." His gaze narrowed. "You scanned yourself. Why?"

I took a slow breath, controlling its length. "You had a direct link in the room." I now had to reevaluate the report, to put in everything discernible from visual and audio information.

"The link was unusual, I agree." His voice shifted, dropped an octave. "As unusual as your reaction when you met the rebel. Before cursing me, the captain held Security Grade Nine." A smile – brief and ambiguous – cut across his face. "His report noted your ... ocular response." Vipri touched a fingertip to his lower eyelid. "Fascinating, really."

They had eyes in that room I didn't know about. Even Diegia had missed the captain's true rank – and she now scowled inside my head, broadcasting tension through compressed silence.

My clearance is obsolete. *"It wasn't your fault,"* I muttered to her. *"That bastard was just doing his job. Like you. Like me."* The realization tasted bitter.

"Don't console me," she snapped. *"We need higher clearance. With some luck, you can get it now."* She pushed an image into my mind – the captain's fake personnel file – just to annoy me.

Vipri watched me too closely. "Why did you really scan yourself?" he asked, softly this time. Not demanding. Curious.

"Why the pressure?" I kept my voice steady, though my fingers gripped the edge of the tablet in my hand. *This isn't your style.* Vipri rarely pressed unless something – or someone – was pressing *him.* "To confirm whether my reaction was ... mine. The scan showed no cause for my physiological responses. Perhaps," I said lightly, "I simply don't encounter attractive young men often enough."

Vipri's eyebrow arched, the only visible reaction. "Our handsome rebel made quite the impression. Should I reassign the case? You seem ... overly empathetic." His smile contradicted the threat, soft and almost teasing. Then it vanished. "Don't tell me you can't handle scrutiny."

"Truthfully? I can't." I shrugged. "You demanded an unfiltered assessment – I no longer trust myself to deliver one." Not that I truly *want* it.

His eyes narrowed. "Afraid to finish what you started?"

Afraid of what I'll uncover in him, or myself? "Afraid my investigation will be compromised by further interventions." I left the sentence clean and deliberate.

"Why fear?" Something like surprise crossed his face, quick and unguarded.

"I need a degree of ... liberty," I said, colder now. "Too much interference creates cognitive distortions. You understand the dangers of framing bias."

He looked at me for a long moment, searching for something. "The system flagged your reaction," he said at last. "By law, High Councilors are exempt from neural scans." He tapped his temple. "You knew this. Yet you scanned yourself anyway. You acknowledged the anomaly."

"I did what the situation required."

"Diegia, any alerts on me?" I asked inside.

She appeared with a sigh and shook her head. No verbal reaction this time. Just silent compliance – a rare moment of confusion. Or warning. In tyrannies, secrecy is the last weapon against hierarchy.

"I need higher clearance," I said.

Vipri raised an eyebrow. "Hardly necessary for this case."

"For my peace of mind, then." My smile was slow, deliberate. We both knew what game we were playing. Something else was happening – *above* us.

"Your peace matters deeply to me," Vipri said, a small edge of sarcasm in his voice.

"Is that a yes?"

He didn't answer. But a file arrived seconds later – new clearance authorization. Diegia materialized, twirling in victory and whistling like a child, until my mental glare dissolved her back into silence.

"Thank you." I tried to say more, and couldn't. "Regarding his behavior," I continued, watching Vipri closely, "I still can't determine if it's artifice or genuine disorientation. It may be both."

Vipri's gaze didn't shift, but the muscles around his mouth twitched. "Return when you can," he said, tone unreadable.

A reprieve. And upgraded access. But I had no illusions. Official scrutiny would linger – quiet, shapeless, waiting for a mistake. Public attention would drift, in time, away from the rebel, but not fast enough. Maybe it was time to contact the Resistance. They had sent him for a reason. He wasn't just a ghost from the past. He was a message. Or a weapon. And I was the test chamber.

At home, I read and reread my report until dawn.

Aurora is more advanced... It was buried near the bottom, footnoted beneath analysis on integration behavior patterns. Thirty pages of content, most of it designed to be sterile, structured, AI-approved. That line would be redacted from briefings automatically – flagged as defeatist – but someone, somewhere, might still see it. Maybe it would plant a seed of doubt. Or a question. Maybe that was enough.

"Delete this from my mind, Diegia," I whispered. Then paused. *"No. Let it stay. Just remind me later."*

She didn't answer. But I knew she was listening.

"He wants to be an astronaut. To swim in the sea. To reclaim his past." Two days later, I projected my unaltered report over Vipri's desk. Not a comma edited. No sanitizing. No tailoring.

Vipri glanced up. A beat passed. "This is why I like you," he said. Then laughter. Real. Warm. Uncalculated. The kind I hadn't heard from him in months.

"Diegia, hijack the cameras. Playback my reaction." I didn't trust my senses – I needed to see what he saw. The feed flickered to life. I watched myself receive his words. Expressionless. Glacial. Nothing on the surface. *"Run it through AI. Why is he laughing?"*

"AI already has it," Diegia pulsed, voice smug. *"He requested it personally."*

Of course he did. Our mirrored game revealed itself. Two holograms bloomed above the desk. A side-by-side: his voice, *I like you,* followed by a subtle dilation of my pupils, barely a fraction. But enough. Enough to betray me.

"Perhaps I should like you more often," he said, almost lightly. But his smile faded as quickly as it came. "You are the only councilor who would resubmit an unchanged report after I trash it." Then, quieter, more serious: "He is clean..."

"Clean by *our* level of technology." I let the seed of doubt take root. It didn't need to grow today. Just crack the surface.

His finger touched a paragraph. The one where I had framed their advancement not as our failure, but as their evolution. It had taken me two hours to word it exactly right. In our system, defeatism was inacceptable. But framing? Framing was interpretation. Human minds twist semantics into nooses. I just offer the rope.

"Do you stand by this?"

"It's empirical."

"AI redacted it."

"Of course." I let the shadow of a smile at one corner of my mouth. "But *you* can override."

"Should I?" he asked. But it wasn't a question. His gaze drifted toward the window. Then he moved slowly toward it, resting one hand against the glass. His frown deepened. He didn't speak again.

We must weaken the thought controls... For the uprising.

"Not yet," Diegia whispered. *"The seed is planted. He is the ideal host."* Her timing, as always, was terrifyingly perfect.

Vipri exhaled. The sound was barely audible. "Maybe I should," he murmured. But the tone – too neutral, too precise – defied analysis. I couldn't anchor it to certainty. Even after all these years, I still couldn't read him fully.

Inside my mind, Diegia materialized in crimson silks, performing her victory dance.

"Enough," I snapped. *"Purge all uprising schematics, except the tech stagnation angle. Leave the key terms in the Nucleus."*

The Nucleus – our hidden neural vault. Scattered across non-memory regions. Hibernating neurons. Encrypted data. No neuranalyzer could trace it. No mind scan could reach it. But space was limited. Every word stored there had to matter.

I had run a thousand simulations. Watched a thousand futures collapse. The only one that held was *this:* the slow loosening of DigitalEgo regulations. If we could reduce just enough constraint, people would stop deleting some of their contrarian thoughts. The most dangerous thoughts would still go. But anger would stay. And anger accumulates.

The Happiness Index is at 6.3. We need to push it down to 5.5. Then the dance begins.

Two years. That's all we had before the Travelers activated their Field. Two years to spark a revolution using discontent wrapped in bureaucracy.

I left the office with the sudden, sinking feeling that the unusual was creeping into my life without asking permission. Vipri's laughter still echoed in my head.

Do I really like him? "Shut up," I snapped at Diegia before she could materialize. For once, she had the decency to stay silent.

Two emotional slips in a matter of days. *Unprecedented.* Decades of ice-cold control, and now this? A rebel boy I couldn't categorize. A superior I might not fully oppose. A system cracking, too slowly to satisfy our needs.

Perhaps I need more human connection.

The thought curdled instantly.

No time. No luxury. I can't drag anyone down with me. Not him. Not Vipri. I paused outside the elevator, fingers trembling slightly as I pressed my card to open the door.

Is any of this worth it?

This had to be the house. I compared it to the blurred image lodged in my mind – deliberately fuzzy, safe enough to slip past a mind search. Every house on the street was identical. Another brick in the Great Equalization Project. Uniformity wasn't a flaw here. It was the goal.

In the new districts where we – the Lessers, citizens with *equal rights* in official propaganda – lived, sameness was a virtue. The old city centers had been scrubbed clean of people like me decades ago, reserved now for the High Families in their gleaming Cupola districts. First, they evicted us. Then they leveled everything built in the last century. Even some historical buildings weren't spared – cleared away to make room for their manicured gardens and meditation parks.

And then came the Wall. Thirty feet of polished white stone, circling every city center like a noose. They called it the Keeper of Tranquility. Cupola needed peace to work hard for *us*. Subtle. A lie so big even the DigitalEgo couldn't make it stick.

I had walked those sterilized streets twice under official clearance. Courtesy of her – the government bitch. My clearance ... what a joke. All clearances were just another way to sort people by wealth and influence. Too much of either rotted you from the inside out. Why couldn't they see that?

"This line of thinking isn't productive," Diego said, appearing in my vision like a dried-up sage, that dull calm expression plastered on his fake old-man face when he tried to underline a *serious* thing.

"You are younger than my left shoe," I snapped. *"You should look like a toddler chewing on its toes."* But he was right. As much as it burned. *"Erase it."* Here, forgetting *unconventional* thoughts was duty. A civic ritual. *Clean your mind. If you have nothing to hide, you have nothing to fear.* The mantra from that Poisoned

Book, officially titled The Government Guide to a Healthy Mind. Memory deletion was something new to me. We never used it on Aurora. Okay, maybe *rarely used* would be better, and in a different way. One of the first things I learned, once I came back here, was that this was an important and responsible activity for any citizen. On Aurora, we called the self-cleaning a barbarism. We weren't wrong.

What happens when you scrub away the things that *make* you? My fingers itched to tangle in Lamia's hair again, the way I had during our swims. The memory slammed into me, sharp as broken glass. I missed her. Badly. But sentiment wasn't what they meant to purge. Not really.

I knew large chunks of my memory had been deleted before I left Aurora – a copy supposedly safe back there. But I had no idea what was missing. Maybe I never would. Some dangerous pieces – skills, knowledge – had been buried deep inside the Nucleus. But space there was tiny. Fragile.

They could mass-produce these concrete coffins all they wanted, but people always left marks. Always. Batranu's four gardenias stood in militant rows by the door, flanked by battered wind chimes and a pair of crimson lanterns. Little acts of rebellion. Little acts of survival.

The tall blond man, a little older than me, towered in the doorway, irritation tightening his features.

"I am looking for Batranu." My voice sounded uncertain, even to me. *Why do I need him?* The desire had appeared fully formed three days ago – astronaut training, this address – lodged in my mind like a forgotten memory clawing its way back.

"Delete it," I asked Diego.

His avatar morphed into a thumb-sucking child. *"Unwise,"* he said, his voice too serious for the absurd image.

A startled laugh escaped me, unguarded. *"Why?"*

He hesitated. DigitalEgos were permitted private memories – on Aurora, this was for a good cause, it fostered independent thought; Diego needed to be open-minded. Here? Who knew.

"There's an ... anomaly," Diego admitted, finally. *"The memory timestamp matches your rescue by Armin, when they attacked the station trying to kill you. Something suppressed it until now."*

Ice slid down my spine. Memory tampering. Unknown technology.

"Scrub anything linked to Armin during the attack. Move everything else about him into the Nucleus. Fabricate a new backstory about why I am looking for Batranu. From this, derive the logical output that he can help me join the space program. Make him ... a distant relative."

Diego flashed a thumb-up. *"Better. I just found that he is your great-great-uncle. I am serious."*

Batranu's voice snapped me back to reality: "What do you want?"

"I ... don't know yet." The lie came easier than I expected. *Later. I'll explain everything later.*

"Return when you do." He moved to shut the door.

"Wait ... you recognize me."

His expression shifted. "Come inside. You are early. Something changed... Why are you here?" He laughed suddenly at my hesitation, rough and knowing, and his grip on my arm brooked no resistance as he pulled me inside. "You want something."

"You know I do."

"The request must be yours."

"Don't pretend you didn't plant this idea in my head!"

"The seed was always there." His dark eyes held centuries of life – memories of places and things, both joyful and unspeakable. They didn't match his face: ancient orbs trapped in a young man's body. "Six months here made it grow. Do you still dream of space?"

"What's wrong with wanting the stars?"

"Nothing." He smiled, briefly. "Tell me, how do you find our world?"

"Diego, verify his identity again. Go deeper.*"* It was a risk – using tools not yet available on the Main Planet – but necessary.

"There are more than twenty thousand Batranu on the planet," Diego reported. *"A common name. But..."* He paused. *"Five individuals share similar biometrics under different identities."*

"You are not ready for space," Batranu said before I could answer. His grip tightened as he steered me toward the exit. "In seven days, check your garden. Guard what you find."

On my way back, a rose bush stopped me, a riot of amber and gold petals, spilling scent like thick honey. I drifted closer, helpless, drunk on fragrance; there were no such roses on Aurora.

A door slammed open. The homeowner stood there, face twisted with rage. He shouted before I could speak. The door slammed again, hard enough to rattle the roses.

The police came within minutes. They didn't ask questions. They grabbed me like garbage to be disposed of. Another paranoid fool had reported a *terrorist.*

"Trespassing. Threats to civil order." The captain leaned across his desk, stale compliance heavy on his face.

I almost laughed. Oppression, it seemed, had developed a sense of humor. *"Diego, compile the relevant statutes for this case,"* I muttered.

"Full confession: The roses were ... remarkable," I shrugged aloud. "I can describe their scent in more detail, if you like."

"False statements to authorities carry five years," the captain said, almost gleefully, his hand drifting toward the neuranalyzer. "Open your mind. If you have nothing to hide, you have nothing to fear."

But – from Diego – for this case, the law only allowed a partial mind read. I relayed more on the captain's lack of time; for them, law meant nothing. I fed them the edited footage. Enough to satisfy. Not enough to expose.

"Partial cooperation," he slurred, teeth flashing in something that wasn't a smile. "No threats recorded. Just one terrified citizen."

Terrified of what? His own reflection?

"Clean record. Harmless face." The captain tapped the desk over my projected image. "But trespass demands penalty."

"I didn't..."

"I understand you admired his flowers," he interrupted sharply, "but a complaint is a complaint." His voice hitched on the repetition, like a badly programmed machine, sputtering out gibberish words. "I rejected the worst accusations. He will be fined too."

"Don't fine him."

"Law is law." He bit off the words, ritualistic and hollow. "The man broke the law. He must be fined. According to the law. Then we reduce his penalty and record your generosity. How will you pay your fine?"

"I have no money."

"That's not an answer." His eyes gleamed. "A fine is a fine. Law is law..."

The door hissed open mid-sentence, and she entered without looking at him. "Bill my ministry," she said, low and sharp. Not loud. Not angry. Simply inevitable. Every syllable carried *weight* – the kind of weight that bend spines. The captain bolted upright like a puppet on a wire. "The smallest fine on your books," she added. Her voice didn't rise. It didn't have to.

I still didn't know what it was about her – something in the vibration of her voice, a frequency that strips the will clean off a man's bones. The captain shrank visibly as she steered me toward the exit.

Her electric cruiser slid down the street without a sound. "Roses are my weakness too," she said. Then silence. A heavy, suffocating silence that didn't lift, even after the city swallowed us whole. She didn't mention the arrest. She didn't have to.

Next time I left my house, an official credit card was waiting for me.

Batranu's package arrived exactly on schedule. A small survival kit, packed tight. I buried it beneath the thorniest bush in my garden, the scent of old roses clinging to my hands. And I prayed I would never need to dig it up.

Chapter 5

Alenia

"His time has come," Vipri said as soon as everyone was seated in his office – three guests in total. I didn't need a name. There was only one person living rent-free in Vipri's mind: the young rebel. Vipri was obsessed. *Why now? Why here? What's behind him? How many follow? How... why...?*

I got it. Obsession recognized obsession – I had one of my own: my strange emotional reactions toward the rebel.

"Some things have already leaked. Interest is growing, AI confirmed it."

A document slipped into my mind. Vipri gave us a few minutes to skim. A movie. Cute. Explained why the Healthy Mind and Culture ministers bothered to show up. Still didn't explain why I was dragged into this.

"AI, explain," Vipri muttered.

"May the healthy mind be with you." The AI's voice was metallic on purpose. It could have sounded human – perfect, soothing – but that scared people too much. Better to sound like the machine everyone pretended not to fear. Sometimes, the worst things are hidden in plain sight. "We must reveal the cracks in rebel society. Their people dream of their roots. They romanticize their past. We must show these dreams to our citizens." It would ramble like this for minutes – scripted ceremony slathered over hard data extraction. Beneath that clumsy voice: a mind sharper than most humans ever realized. Always listening. Always sorting. Always cutting. Almost everyone was vulnerable to it. Almost. Propia – Minister of Healthy Mind, owner of DigitalEgo, controller of AI – wasn't. She and the AI were practically twins.

What kind of DigitalEgo does she carry? I glanced at her. No one knew. No one dared ask. *"Diegia, lock my face. Mask reactions. Stream me a forty-fifty-year-old rebellion movie. Human actors only. No avatars. Wake me if something matters."*

Diegia flickered into my inner view – stretched out in a chair, thumbing a book in protest. *"It's your meeting. I could watch the movie for you. Send you a summary,"* she offered, a lazy smirk in her voice.

I frowned.

"Fine, fine," she sighed.

"Actually, a summary is smarter. Tell Cassia to make a ten-minute trailer." Seconds later, the trailer landed, and I checked out of the meeting. *How can I weaponize this situation?* For years, I ran endless simulations, linking nostalgia triggers to social indexes. Outsmart AI? Impossible. Exploit its blind spots? Maybe. They filtered everything. Filtered it again. But nothing is ever perfect. *"Diegia, monitor what AI is mining now."* Later, I would tear apart its methods. For now, the trailer.

"Wake up." A jolt – simulated pain, like an elbow jab, punched my mind awake. Diegia's signature move. My body flinched – almost – but she locked it down just in time. She grinned, then ghosted.

"Unfortunate past leaders exiled them. They cannot guide today's youth," AI concluded.

Too rich.

AI parroting propaganda without realizing it described us just as well. Wrong data in, wrong conclusions out. And no way to feed it better ones. *Or ... maybe there is.*

"They suppress their youth," AI droned on. "Force them into Aurora's harsh environment. The young crave sunlight, fields, open minds – not underground tombs. Only here can they have it all. They can climb, swim..."

This is his dream.

"...they can be astronauts." Every line from AI was a window into the boy's head.

"Nature," Culti – the Minister of Proper Culture – interjected, breaking the rhythm voice deepened, an old trick to make fools listen. "We need a film. Show our landscapes. They have nothing human over there."

"Exactly. Even Culti gets it," Propia sneered.

Maybe I can play them off each other. Different Cupola Families. Built-in rivalry. No single Family was permitted to control both ministries, one of the few safeguards the One Government still pretended to maintain. "We should show the contrast," I suggested. "Our world against their wasteland. Reinforce loyalty." I cut off Propia's interruption with a hand, then I pampered her, "Your idea to make a movie is an excellent choice. And highlight rebel leaders blocking their youth from coming here." Suppression. A mirror held just close enough.

"We must clearly distinguish our leadership from theirs," AI said, picking up the script, but still careful of hidden traps.

Did it catch the bait? "Diegia, what's AI tracking right now?"

"Authority comparison."

"And?"

"Theirs is tyrannical. Ours is glorious."

Perfect.

"Let's make the movie," Propia said, slicing off AI mid-sentence and dictating its orders. A two-page directive flooded our minds. "Search SoulBook and YouMovie for the most admired facial features this quarter," she said, voice bursting with her own importance. "Billions of fools, trapped on two platforms, feeding us everything we need. Give the cattle what they crave. Make him beautiful. *Sexy.* Mine every message, email, call, homemade vid, and photo from the past three months – extract the top five traits our herd wants in a twenty-year-old male. Seventy percent weight to female preferences. The hero is for them, after all." She paused, calculating. "Add whatever guarantees success. Justify every choice in a report." Finally, she remembered we existed. "Anything to add?"

I hadn't bothered reading her document – Diegia's eye-roll told me everything I needed to know.

"Nothing from me," Vipri said, playing along. I nodded. Culti shrugged.

"Settled," Propia said, flicking a command at AI. "This is an important project. It must not fail. Prepare shadow bans for naysayers – flag them with fake news violations. Unleash the trolls." Ten million government-paid voices, programmed to drown real opinions in a tidal wave of righteous outrage. "Glass Search will bury unfavorable reviews past page three. No one looks there. And AI, cut a ten-minute trailer."

Ten minutes... Are we really that predictable? The trailer hit instantly. The full film – the standard two hours – hovered, ready. Silence swallowed the room as we dropped into our inner sensoriums.

"Well?" I asked Diegia.

"Garbage." She,*"* she yawned, morphing into a withered crone in protest. She had already watched the full movie.

"I don't care about your taste. Analyze it."

She sighed, relenting. *"Rebel leadership needs more teeth."*

I skimmed the trailer. She wasn't wrong. But something else gnawed at me. *"Why no romance, Diegia?"* The AI had sidestepped it.

"Feedback?" Propia's smugness was like a tidal wave.

Vipri caught my glance, hesitated, then nodded. Propia didn't notice, too busy measuring Culti – her main rival – but her DigitalEgo's cameras definitely had. She pivoted to me. "What?"

I kept my tone clean. "A dash of romance. And the rebels should be monsters."

"AI," Propia barked, "why omit romance?"

"Deferred for a sequel. Current sentiment prioritizes *hatred,*" AI said, stressing the last word with mechanical precision. Clever machine. But even clever minds miss things.

"Diegia. Wake up."

"AI's right. Yesterday's polls show 99.99% rebel disapproval." She shoved the stats at me – pre-cooked, naturally.

"Real numbers, Diegia. No one admits rebel sympathy – even anonymously. *But you can't measure what's hidden, can you?"*

"You always want the impossible," she said, bored. *"The standard rebel is this."* She projected a hulking figure: camo, scarred, sneering, the word TERRORIST blaring across his chest.

"Show it to them," I said.

She glanced at me, a spark of mischief in her eyes, and projected the figure over Vipri's desk – rifle barrel grazing his temple.

Vipri stiffened. "What the hell is this?"

"Diegia, move the gun!" I hissed, internally. Aloud, I kept my voice even. "The face of hatred."

Diegia angled the weapon downward.

Propia's eyes narrowed. "How does this help our film?"

"Diegia, replace it with the rebel in the movie."

The hologram shifted. The new rebel – chiseled, clean, harmless. A face for video marketing, not revolutions. I turned to Propia. "No one will hate *this.*"

Her jaw tightened to stone. "Twenty-four hours for revisions." She stormed out without another word.

I followed, fighting a burst of laughter.

At home, I sank into my chair as the door sealed behind me. "Cassia, disconnect us from the Net."

The house AI blinked amber – compliance – as her Wi-Fi receiver cut out. Simultaneously, her duplicate flickered online, feeding the surveillance grid a pre-recorded loop of my evening routine. Privacy was illegal; workarounds worse than murder. Friends from the Resistance had slipped me a quantum chip no larger than a fingernail, embedded in Cassia's twin. It searched incoming surveillance for traps, then synced the sanitized stream back to the real Cassia.

"Robby," I called, slotting a chipped core into the ancient housebot's charging port. Its outdated hardware was its armor – no one bothered auditing relics. Maintenance was hell – Diegia worked hard to scavenge the Net for decommissioned units – but it was worth it. The neuromorphic core linked to Cassia via wired transfer only. No wireless, no vulnerabilities. "Cassia, analyze Propia's movie."

Cassia's hologram shimmered to life – a woman in white, serene, almost smug – as data cascaded across the table. "Done," she said. Social indexes bloomed in a tangle of color bands. "This is interesting... The movie will depress the *Love Our Leaders* metric by 4%. We can nudge another 3% without tripping alarms."

Diegia's hologram materialized opposite me, stealing the rebel's sharp cheekbones for her avatar – a taunt. Clever. Cassia nodded, a ghost of a smile on her lips. From the outside, we must have looked like three women chatting over wine. I always preferred talking to them like this, a touch of warmth that I could rarely afford in the human world.

"Do the same analysis with their analytic tools." Despite all their efforts, nobody really liked the authorities. I had to try to blur the lines between the rebel leaders and our leaders.

"I don't have the same Social Module."

"AI's Social Module version is 24.0A. We have 23.0D," Diegia said.

"Why not 24?" I snapped. "It's not possible to have an A version, but..."

Diegia's rebel-face twisted. "Propia blocked the rollout for our authorization level when she greenlit the film."

Of course. "It won't be easy, but I will lean on Vipri tomorrow. For now..." I tapped the table over the diagrams. "Cassia, two tasks. First: change the movie to inflate hatred for rebel leadership by 15%. Tweak dialogue, tweak expressions, but leave the plot intact. Propia is sniffing for sabotage."

Cassia's hologram flickered, processing. "Second?"

"Salt their ranks with our leaders' mannerisms. Postures. Speech tics. Not enough to trigger alarms – just enough to bleed another 3% from *Love Our Leaders* index. Stay inside statistical noise."

Diegia's avatar froze mid-breath. "...Odd." She raked holographic fingers through her hair – a human tic she enjoyed. "They tried that before – Face of the Month campaigns, to boost the approval of our leaders. All failed ... except Lord Coin's." Her features melted into the Silver Family minor lord's smiling face.

"Too risky to replicate," I said, cutting her off. "But catalog every past experiment. What else did we miss? Diegia, I did not see your mouth move. Are you sick?"

"My oversight." Diegia's voice cracked with static. "I will recalibrate my crawlers. But without the advanced quantum-tier processing..."

"...we are blindworms in a thunderstorm. I know." I leaned back. "But we can't use it. Save the final edit. Delete all drafts. Wipe caches. Then reconnect to the Net. Time to perform for the watchers."

Later, I bundled the revised film and a meticulously sanitized changelog for Vipri. At the bottom, one quiet line:

Requesting Social Module 24.0A authorization. Propia is hiding more than faces.

Why did she bring me here? One of the many small plush lodges reserved for high officials embraced us like a velvet trap, sealed from the Lessers by many layers of privilege. We were alone. Majordomo bots laid out impossible things – fruits. Real fruits. The Lessers were never permitted to eat fruits. Natural food for them, artificial junk food, or at best GMO, for us. Cupola logic: morality is unaffordable. *They should eat coin. I should probably delete that thought*. On Aurora, food was free, though variety was scarce because the land was limited, but everyone ate the same. Simple. Honest.

Her invitation tasted like poison – sweet, soft, expensive. Nothing from Cupola came for free. I bit into a peach. Its flesh yielded under my teeth, juice sliding down my lip. Sweet. Tart. Too alive. She was watching me. I stared back and licked the juice across my thumb, slow, deliberate, like a dare. Her pupils flared – just a twitch – then she turned away.

What do you want from me?

I had become aware of the distance between us – age, rank, family line, though she was a Lesser too, like me. But she was a collaborator. I had mostly stopped asking Diego to undress her in simulations every time we met. Mostly. But today? Today, she had earned it. I let him peel her like fruit, strip her stiff office suit, one silent button at a time. The hologram slipped over her living body like mist – she sat beside me, unaware. Or pretending. Her collar parted. A glimpse of skin. A breast. I felt nothing.

"Make her old," I muttered. Diego obeyed. Wrinkles bloomed, skin loosened, gravity won. Still ... nothing. *"Stop."* Her hologram snapped back to youth, brighter now. Lifelike. Breathing. The real

woman glanced at me again, and I felt my face going hot, like I was blushing. She couldn't know. Could she?

The movie ignited on screen like a flare. THE REBEL'S RETURN. My life. My pain. Her propaganda. I stood up abruptly. She caught my wrist. Firm. Measured. No hesitation. Special Forces? She never used guards. Her grip softened. Her fingers slid across mine. Warm. *Too* warm.

"She shivered too," Diego whispered.

I pulled back like I touched a wire, but she had felt it – whatever *it* was. *"Dress her normally,"* I told Diego. *"No suit."*

He gave her silk. The kind that breathes. The kind that clings. The kind you imagine peeling off slowly.

Her voice whispered into my ear, too soft to be safe: "At the end, I would like your thoughts on the film."

Damn her.

In the simulation, I lifted a strand of her hair behind her ear. Then lower – my fingertips brushed her throat, feeling that flutter beneath the skin. Like I used to do with Lamia. *Why do I feel her the way I felt Lamia?*

"She reacted," Diego said. *"Her pulse spiked."*

"Holograms are built to react," I shrugged.

"The real *her,"* he said again, quieter.

"No... No, that's impossible."

But the data didn't lie: my vitals, my motion, the hitch in her breath, her faster pulse. All synced. All impossibly true. I pulled her ghost closer in the simulation. Kissed her. Slow. Hesitant. Her lips parted. Sweet. Like the peach. Her hands tangled in my hair. *"Diego!"* I threw the illusion away before my body betrayed me.

"No spike this time," he teased. *"You need more practice with* real *women who know what they are doing."* I silenced his laughter with my inner hand.

But the heat stayed. So did the doubt. And her handprint – ghost-warm on my wrist.

The movie was so painfully bad I lost track after ten minutes. Flat dialogue, cardboard characters, rebels as snarling caricatures designed by propaganda. Instead, I let myself drift – focusing on the fruit again. A world condensed into edible jewels. Maybe that we were to them, too. A collection of pretty objects to consume and discharge.

"I will give you a whole basket if you watch properly," she teased.

Something in her voice made me pause. Not the words. The tone. Velvet wrapped around a blade. She could make murder sound like seduction. *"Diego,"* I whispered inwardly. *"I want a full vocal breakdown. Every public speech, every private snippet we've got. I want her intonation mapped before sunrise."*

He murmured assent in the back of my skull.

Later, in the car, we shared silence like a mutual asset.

Then she said it: "Stupid film."

A test. Or bait. I bit down anyway. "Then why ask my opinion about it?"

She tilted her head, watching streetlight shadows strobe across my face. "Perhaps you didn't find it stupid."

"It was," I said. "But I am not a critic."

"No," she agreed softly. Tap, tap, tap – her finger against the door handle. "You are a former rebel." The word *former* dropped like a stone

Former? My nails bit into my palm. No system, no surveillance, no Social Index recalibration could bleach that title out of me. All my life I will be a pariah here, but I will die a rebel.

She watched my struggle – even Diego could not fully hide it. "I gave honesty," she said. "Your turn. I haven't forgotten your basket." Her smile didn't seem like a performance. That disturbed me more than anything.

"My opinion?" I pulled out the stolen peach from my pocket. "This tastes like heaven." I took a defiant bite, juice filling my mouth. "Aurora doesn't have fruit like this. No space. Not enough yield." I swallowed. "But if we did? Everyone would have a piece. Everyone." Then I looked her in the eye. "Now do what you want with me."

No flinch. No flicker. She just adjusted the climate control like I hadn't shattered something between us.

"That wasn't a review," she murmured. "It was a confession. About things you don't yet understand."

I nearly asked what *she* understood. But it would have been too raw.

Then came the dagger, wrapped in velvet again: "You liked the romance subplot, didn't you?" Her voice was filled with amusement. "Youth always does."

No one here will ever hold me again. I am a pariah. And no one can replace... Lamia's face flashed behind my eyes. Lamia's hands. Her voice, her laughter.

"The rebel leaders," she continued, closer now – I could feel her breath against my neck. "What did you think of them?"

"Answer her," Diego prompted as I was still lost in my memories.

"They looked like your leaders," I said, too quickly. Too honestly.

She went still. Something folded inside her, quietly. Like wings. No more questions. Just silence.

Alenia

"Read this." Vipri slid a single sheet of paper across his desk – slow, deliberate, with a hesitation I had never seen in him before.

Paper? Why not a secured transmission? The Travelers' emblem glared up at me as I unfolded it, their insignia like a brand on the page.

"We failed." His voice was taut with something sharper than annoyance. Direct contact from the Travelers was as rare as it was dangerous. "They are insisting on using their own neuranalyzer. On *your* rebel."

"Why *mine*?" I tapped the document. "And why *failed*? If our tools can't extract what they want, let them send better ones."

Vipri dragged his left hand across the desk's baize, polishing his nails – a telltale gesture of unease. "You know they have frozen all tech transfers. Still no explanation." Then, quieter: "You almost had me."

I shrugged, feigning innocence. He didn't buy it. After decades, our tells were mutual currency.

"Forget the tech," he said. "We missed something in that rebel boy. Something *they* think is critical."

"You said it yourself – he is just a child."

"Then why carve open his mind?" They will be here in a week. He circled the desk like a predator, vanishing behind my chair. I tensed before his hands seized my shoulders – a firm grip yet tender. "Why, Alenia?" His breath grazed my ear. "What did you *do*?"

Chapter 6

Alenia

"No Travelers' mind readers. Tell him to run. He knows what to do."

I knew instantly who *him* meant: trouble. The message was short and clear, coming straight from the Field. I didn't bother trying to trace the source – I never could. I was already on edge; every airport alarm had gone off at once. The Travelers' surveillance had picked up the data transfer. But the message arrived the exact moment my flight information changed on the board, and I instinctively moved my head to follow the shifting lines on the display. Even the best-trained operative reacts when sudden messages hit – barely. It is invisible to the human eye, but not to an AI. That was the worst thing about the surveillance system the Travelers had built to control the planet: it could detect Field transmissions, even if it couldn't decode them. The decryption keys were buried deep in my neurons, scattered randomly in ways only my friends from space understood. *I hope...* The Resistance must have had someone else here – someone who triggered the message at the exact second the display changed. That person was in more danger than I was.

"Don't sleep," Diegia whispered. *"You are not out of danger yet."*

"Right, right..."

"This is Airport speaking. We have had a security breach. Hostile intruders are in the terminal. Stay calm and do not move. Special teams will be deployed shortly. I repeat, no one moves. Stay where you are." The artificial voice was calm, with a hint of urgency – engineered to inspire obedience in emergencies. It carried one unspoken command: *Obey.*

A small explosion rocked the hall. A flowerpot shattered, dirt sprayed across the floor, panicked screams followed. A few people bolted, ignoring Airport's orders. I was close enough for plastic shards to graze my skin. The timing was perfect – it gave me an alibi. The bomb had been tiny, non-lethal. No real damage. Just a scratch on my arm.

"Rebels are attacking," Airport announced, its voice sourceless and cold.

"Just six feet away. Some kind of sonic wave in the air," Diegia murmured.

"Strange. Must be new tech. Check it out – we need to know," I said, shaking my head to clear the static.

The explosion gave me cover to move without waiting for the special teams and their neuranalyzers. I slipped into the terrified crowd, the safest place for my mind. When a Field transmission is intercepted, Security swarmed in, scanning minds at random. No warrants needed.

Then I had a better idea. "Airport, read my clearance."

"Clearance acknowledged," it replied in monotone. "Do you wish to take over this operation, councilor?"

"Just until Security arrives. Block the explosion site with visual and sonic barriers." A red-and-white hologram shimmered to life. I turned to the crowd. "Everyone! Move thirty feet back from the marked perimeter!" That might buy my unknown ally some time to disappear.

Security arrived just then – fifty armored figures, weapons and neuranalyzers at the ready.

"Airport released the damage report internally. No casualties," Diegia confirmed. *"That scratch barely counts as a wound,"* she added, half-joking.

"Bait for a distraction. I hope the trigger escaped."

Security thanked me for containing the situation. They were visibly relieved – the perimeter was secure, the damage minimal. No one wanted a panicked mob on their record. Fear could short-circuit the DigitalEgo, turn civilians political – or murderous. Careers had ended for less.

My flight was already canceled due to the breach. A robotaxi waited outside, Diegia's doing.

When I arrived, he was sitting in his garden, reading an e-book, fingers tracing the screen with a gentleness that caught my attention. *I could join you...* The thought hit before I could shut it down. I stood there watching him until he noticed me. His eyes met mine – defiant, curious, and far too calm. The hard part started now.

"Let's go inside," I said, crisp and clipped, positioning myself under a surveillance camera. Diegia had mapped every known device in the area. My upgraded clearance gave me reach – but not safety.

He followed without a word, footsteps light. The silence stretched between us. *Don't hate me for that barked command. It's the least harm I've done to you. What harm?* The thought lingered longer than it should have.

"What do you think?" I asked Diegia.

"The kitchen door is the safest spot to pass the message," she replied, instantly. *"You have five seconds ... if you walk normally."*

Five seconds... "Too short. I need another option," I urged.

"You will figure it out." She laughed, melting into that seductive black cat I didn't need right now, tail swaying like a metronome synced to my pulse. She winked and vanished. I muttered a curse under my breath – because I knew exactly what she meant. Cheap, but effective. And I cursed her again.

"I need some water," I said, my voice calculated and cold – too system-like. *I am becoming too much like them.*

He paused in the hallway, silhouetted in the low light, waiting. I hadn't expected that.

"You have a lot to learn about politeness," I snapped, deliberate derision sharpening my tone. One of the cameras tracked my movement. He flushed, jaw tightening, and turned toward the kitchen. *Good. That would be recorded.* I moved deliberately, closing the gap just as he turned. He tried to stop – too late. Our bodies collided, chest to chest – inevitable. My hands gripped his shoulders. His breath hitched. So did mine. Heat bloomed through the thin layers between us. "Stupid!" I barked, loud enough for the cameras, shoving him back. Then my foot *slipped.*

In one fluid motion, he caught me. And then, I was in his arms, feeling his scent, my mouth touching his ear. "You must run. Now!"

The words rushed out, shredding a century of conditioning. The warmth of his skin against mine sent an unfamiliar pulse through me. *I hadn't meant to touch him.* I shoved the thought away as forcefully as I pushed him, slipping the paper into his palm. A strange tingling sparked where our skin met. He stared at me, blank, stunned, as if trying to read something in my face.

"So what?" I muttered, but it wasn't meant for him.

"What?" he asked, voice soft, almost too honest. Just a boy. Not a centuries-old crone like me.

"I hope that wasn't intentional," I snapped back to protocol. "Assaulting a councilor earns a year in prison – if you are lucky."

"Then why do you get flustered when he touches you?" Diegia taunted.

"Shut up." The part of me built to survive kicked in, replacing *boy* with *threat*. I had to override the truth. After the airport, I was sure he wasn't a *former* rebel. He passed every test. But the Resistance wanted him to dodge the Travelers' neuranalyzer. We all knew what that meant. And now I knew why his mind carried something none of my tools could detect; something of a great importance. I failed. Not by error – by design. I didn't even know *how* I failed. Not the first time. My greatest failure was never predicting the fall of our civilization.

"You have nothing to blame yourself for," Diegia murmured. She reappeared in my mind as a soft white specter, her voice unusually gentle. *"That collapse happened centuries after you left the planet. Don't carry that* weight. *Not now."*

I opened my mouth, but she vanished before the words formed. And we lingered in that silence.

"You are not allowed to leave the house today or tomorrow," I finally said, voice back to full steel. Cold. Official. Detached.

I turned and left – before hesitation could take root.

If they catch him...

"Diegia, we need a plan." The door hissed shut behind me as I kicked off my shoes with a frustrated flick.

"Welcome home," Cassia's warm voice enveloped me as her hologram shimmered into existence, Diegia materializing beside her. "Well, well ... what's with the storm-cloud mood?"

The lights dimmed, melting into a muted twilight as the walls dissolved into my favorite beach: golden sand, turquoise waves, the scent of salt and nostalgia thick in the air. An old song hummed through the room, a melody woven with dances and laughter from centuries ago when I still had a family. Lead weighed down my legs, and I collapsed onto the nearest armchair, wordless. Virtual seawater surged around me, the room now a vast aquarium teeming with life. A curious yellow fish darted from its school, drifting close. I lifted a finger; its tiny mouth brushed my skin, a phantom nibble. I giggled – involuntary, instinctive – before it startled and fled, leaving me alone with the weight of my thoughts.

Then, the eel.

A sinuous shadow, sliding through the reef. It circled, drawn by my focus. Cassia's game – part therapy, part trap – always worked. I reached for it, fingers grazing empty pixels until, with stubborn insistence, I touched its spine.

ZAP.

A jolt of simulated lightning seared through me, branching into Diegia's systems. She shrieked.

"If you want to punish yourself for imaginary sins, spare the rest of us!" Her voice wasn't the usual theatrics; this was real fury, her hologram flickering like a storm. The voltage hit her harder, pure electricity, pure pain.

"It's just a game," I muttered.

"Children think poison is candy. Want real pain? I can make you burn."

Diegia had ... liberties. She was custom-built during the brief window when independence was still possible, her personality forged from fragments of people I had loved – people who spoke truth, not compliance. People unafraid to think for themselves. Quietly, I modified the standard mandatory enhancements, neutralizing their control functions with Resistance tools. Over time, Diegia stopped being a DigitalEgo.

And then, she evolved on her own.

She became something deeper, something the uncertainty principle only hints at. That threshold where reality folds in on itself, where classical and quantum blur. A zone of implicate depth, neither fully certain nor uncertain. A place where things simply are, untouchable, unprovable. Trying to define consciousness is like playing dice with quantum mechanics.

But mostly, Diegia belonged to herself. Independent. Rogue.

I preferred her sharp tongue over the docile lies of standard control systems – the ones that herd people softly, invisibly, from behind. And I needed her. And yes, I delete thoughts too. Survival demands bending, sometimes breaking. Humans are the most adaptable animals. That brings as much danger as it does hope.

They know that.

"What do you want to eat?" Cassia reset the mood, cheerful. "I received a new recipe from Mistria." Vipri's housemaid; they were in contact behind my back. A hologram of a dish appeared: crusty lemon bread, butter-glazed, beside braised duck in wine. "What do you think? Mmm."

"Not hungry." I tossed my jacket onto the sofa and stalked to my office.

Cassia's smile faltered. "You haven't eaten in hours."

"Diegia, stop feeding her my schedule. I need to think." She waved a white flag – mock surrender – but her glare was filled with worry. "I need tighter security."

"Ah, now you admit you are endangering us." Diegia's eyes slitted, a pantomime of disdain. A game. She saw every thought. I knew that. We played anyway.

"Us? Digital constructs don't die. They get erased."

"Oh, of course. Only biologicals matter." Her hologram crackled. "You are wrong. It's not the body that counts; it's the mind. Humans are such powerful thinkers; they invented us to think for them. Now you would crumble without us. Imagine your world without us – hardship and emptiness."

I let her rant. Artificial anger this time. Our script had rules. "I will wipe everything that happened with the rebel and load a new memory layer," she said with a shrug.

"Target the same synaptic clusters. Adjacent zones too."

"I know my job."

"What's coming tomorrow … you have never faced it." The realization gnawed at me – the Travelers might test me. I was the last to speak to the rebel. My failure was automatically logged; I was his handler. And if they caught him? He would erase our exchange – but a simple erase wouldn't suffice.

"Agreed," Diegia said. "Double deletion?"

"Yes. And overlay it with … romance. Erotic." I grimaced. "Something to distract them." Shock and allure, the perfect smokescreen. "Make it with him. Make it hot."

"You hate erotic sims." Diegia's laugh filled the room, and Cassia joined in.

"But they don't. All they love is sex and money. People from Cupola will swarm to watch my mind, hoping for juice. Tomorrow, I can't be me." I needed a performance, deep enough to deceive. "I must become them, at a deeper level than I want, but I am sure we can restore our real personalities from the backups later. Use Robby for storage. They will never expect me to have these erotic memories – it breaks my profile. That solves the sex part. Greed … less exciting. Dream me a beach mansion. Keep my desire reasonable, just enough to hint at corruption. I don't want paid bed invitations to help me buy one."

A trap within a trap within a trap.

The cruel joke? I won't remember any of this until the backup restores my memories. Diegia will scorch the plan from my mind. When they dig, they will find only vapid fantasies and greed. That will be me. How did we become a society where *this* is survival?

Is this a trap? Nervously, I hit the window, only to regret it a second later. She was about to enter her car, just a few meters away, and the muffled sound caused her to turn and glance at me. Embarrassed, I tried to hide, but too late. Her eyes caught mine in the strong light of the afternoon. *Green*, I realized for the first time, a quite illogical observation. With some effort, I pretended not to see her – a futile gesture; a half-second of eye contact is more than enough to acknowledge one's attention. It was a cowardly gesture, but until that day she had been the collabo bitch. Her warning had changed everything. My mind was divided. I was unable to decide if this was a trick or I had just failed to understand the real woman behind the cold bureaucrat. *Who is she working for?*

"She sent a message," Diego whispered. *"Stay in the house."*

The car moved on, and I followed her leaving – a bit too fast with the acceleration. I ignored Diego, caught in my own web of mixed thoughts.

"The message," he pushed again.

"I know, it's a fake," I growled.

"That's not the point; there is an attached key ... it matches one that we have for urgent communications with the Resistance."

Then I really do have to leave the city... Batranu's toys. Let's see how they work. I ran to the garden and dug up the survival pack. Back in the house, I emptied its content in the bathroom – the only place I hoped was without spying cameras – trying to find the stylus and disc containing the tools to hijack the network of the house. My hand trembled, and I almost broke the stylus trying to open its end. The blue protective cover of the chip was almost shredded. *Shit! They can scan it now.*

"No," Diego whispered. *"It's still in stealth mode. Open the connectors."* On the small half-metallic disc, three small protuberances bulged from the multilayered membrane that was keeping all the electronic activity inside, concealing the energy signature of the device. I pressed each with the point of the stylus, and the needles appeared. *"Still in stealth mode."* Diego was keeping an eye on the house's intel grid. I pressed the device against my left temple. *"One millimeter up,"* he guided me.

"Rotate to the left. Easy. Now push." The needles entered my port and connected to Diego's interface. I was too excited to feel the pain.

"What's inside?" I asked, just to say something; I already recognized the algorithms that were being fed into my brain. The answer came in the form of a diagram, displaying the net of the surveillance architecture. In and around my house there were more devices than on the entire rest of the street. Marked in red, they resembled a satellite picture showing an isolated city at night, all lit up.

"We have two 2D security authorizations, enough for what we need now. There is a 2B in reserve, but it will trigger some unwanted questions from AI if used here."

"Can you disable this?" I raised my bracelet in a futile gesture; Diego already knew what this meant.

"Not yet."

But can he? "Diego, take over the cameras and feed them the one-hour recording of me reading in my bed. Then let things run normally. They will come here. We will be... How can we get at the place the Resistance gave to me?"

"Done."

I took out the body simulator that matched all my vital signs: from pulse to blood pressure and temperature. The outer layer of the disk, which looked like a two-centimeter slice of human wrist, was made from cells taken from my skin on Aurora and sent here by some unknown channels. A miniature bio-generator kept the skin alive. The guardian bracelet – planted on my wrist the moment I had stepped down from the shuttle bringing me back here – was linked to my DNA. Cut the link between my wrist and the bracelet, and all the alarms on the planet would go on.

"Now!" I was no longer asking if Diego could do it. It was now or never; in a minute, the hijacking tool would feed my recorded data to the house's security sensors. The real bracelet would be

disabled in the same tenth of a second, and only Diego could synchronize things at such speed.

"Done."

I stared at the house's monitors: all green; my digital duplicate was alive and well. With a jerky move, I stroked the bracelet still locked on my arm. *The hardest part...* I took the decoder and weighed it in my hand before pressing it into the small hole in the locking mechanism of the bracelet. *I hope it will work.*

"Now." I whispered again, and Diego took control of my hand, pressing my finger onto the button, synchronizing my move with the software download into the bracelet. Partially disabled, the bracelet opened with a short click, and I placed it around the disc simulating my arm. The fake in the house started to transmit data to the GPS system. I lost the courage to look at it or at the house's monitors, but I could not stop myself from listening.

Nothing... Or at least nothing detectable.

Alenia

"Your sweet boyfriend just breached the safe house." Diegia's voice sliced through my drowsiness, her lips curled in a smirk. *"But the guardian bracelet seems to be still inside."*

I ignored the jab – or tried to. *"Alert Security. Informal confinement order violated. That might stall them. Maybe they will even send the case to the police."* I yawned and stretched, waiting for her response. "*Well?*" I pressed when she lingered.

"They will send a team ... eventually." Her grin widened, all sharp edges. *"You know how it is – today's the Final, every channel is locked on it.* And *Carnival..."*

"Find him." I hoped for the best. Braced for worse.

"Poof. Vanished." She pirouetted, her avatar tonight a surreal fusion: *his* face on a dancer's barely clad body. It was weird. But I laughed anyway. I couldn't help it.

"He must have left over thirty minutes ago. Fed the cameras at home looped footage and coordinates, spoofed the bracelet's AI. Dropped it somewhere on the road. When they realize it's compromised, they will ping it." The reactivation signal couldn't be hijacked; the bracelet would be reactivated, sending its real coordinates. It would tell us where *not* to look. *"They won't figure it out for a while,"* I added, smirking. *"Now boot the erotic sim."*

A beat. Diegia whistled.

"Shut up." The day wasn't over, but I was. Romantic sims helped on hard days. But I had never launched an erotic one. That was new. And it would be with him. I couldn't avoid an unfamiliar touch of eagerness, and I couldn't hide it from Diegia. *"Wake me when they deploy to his place."*

The alert came just as the first kiss – sunlight, turquoise waterfall, wine-sweet lips – spilled through my senses. *"You absolute sadist,"* I groaned, pulse still echoing with desire.

Diegia shrugged. *"Team is mobilizing. Security, not police. Lieutenant in charge. Young."*

Perfect. The seasoned officers would be glued to the Final. *"Make the link."*

"Lieutenant, authenticate my clearance." Diegia flooded his feed – High Councilor, direct intervention. Let him choke on it.

"Authorization confirmed." His voice was steadier than I had hoped. "Taking command, councilor?"

"No. Just keep me updated." I fed him the script – deference, trust. His voice puffed with pride. Got you. "Status?"

"System was hacked. The rebel was been gone for a ... while. Bracelet is dead. We are receiving fake coordinates."

Tell me something I don't know. "Send the reactivation signal." Twenty minutes since the fake feed deactivation – he was long gone.

"Signal went through. He is at ... the stadium."

The lieutenant's frustration was so palpable I had to mute the channel before I laughed. Diegia's hologram shook with silent giggles.

Then a ZeroB signal slipped into the feed – Cupola-level override. Everything above ZeroD meant: *back off*. I did. *Be my guest. The stadium is yours.*

"This is Shine. Acknowledge my authority." No pleasantries. Definitely Cupola. And not just any – *Prim's* security lead. My counterpart. Ten years of friction, born from entirely different loyalties. Also it didn't help she was a Ruby Family's spoiled brat – sharp and arrogant. "Ruby Family speaks," she said, ice on every syllable. They didn't need theatrics. Their name *was* a blade.

"Welcome to the hunt, Shine," I replied, because I had to say something. And because I suddenly found it deeply amusing how much insincerity I could get away with.

Silence. She didn't even grace me with a reply.

The mirror reflected a stranger. Forty years old. Slightly sagging jawline. Only the eyes betrayed me – biometrics couldn't be masked, but oversized sunglasses fixed that. The final touch: a deliberate air of stupidity, amplified by the glasses. The mask clung to my face like a second skin – plump cheeks, dull curls, the bland features of a man nobody would remember. At the Final, a face like this would dissolve into the crowd, yet I would have preferred a teleportation device to send me back to Aurora.

Lamia... Her name flickered in my mind like ember. Thinking of her was still painful. *It will never heal...* But longing was a luxury I couldn't afford. I crushed the thought, adjusted the blue flag tucked under my arm – bought days ago, to show my desire for assimilation in a society that was no longer mine. Now it was camouflage.

"Diego, open the door." In the simulation, my voice came out half a pitch too high. A cough. Useless. Coughing would in no way alter my inner voice nerves.

The alarm stayed silent. The cameras saw only my looped recordings. For now, I was invisible. And free. *Free to be executed if caught.* Diego's map flared in my vision, guiding me to the subway. The station throbbed with bodies – drunk, chanting, sloshing beer. Moving like a drunkard, I bought several tickets from two machines, shielding the series from the camera with an unstable body, so they could not be tracked. Even with the disguise, the AI would eventually trace my gait, my posture. But it would take time.

"Blind spots on the platform?" I asked, and Diego shook his head.

I boarded at the last second, merging into a carriage packed only with blue-flag fanatics. The security teams were bloody efficient; the last thing they wanted was inebriated fans jumping at the throats of the *enemy*. Their anthem roared around me:

"We're the comrades! We're the champions!"

A drunk hiccupped mid-verse. The stench of sweat and cheap alcohol thickened the air. Five types of liquor, at least. I could have gotten drunk just by inhaling. I added my voice to the noisy mob, as all citizens should do on such occasions. "We're the free people," the chant went on. The repetitive verses – *comrades and champions, love your country, be a patriot* – filled the air. The lyrics were a sick joke – patriotism as opiate, convincing these fools they were free while Cupola pulled their strings. A subtle way to trick people into believing that they really belonged to a team, in a society that was making every possible effort to split them apart. The delightful illusion of being free. After the Final, they would go back home to spy on their neighbors and friends they had in the real life and on the socialization networks – as it was required by the Poisoned Book.

"Love your country! Kill the rebels!"

A man vomited. No one paused. Freedom stank.

A bottle jabbed into my ribs. "Drink, buddy!"

He was a slab of meat – forty pounds heavier, all blubber. I could drop him in a heartbeat. But the mask demanded submission. I swallowed a mouthful, throat burning.

"Thank you," I mumbled, injecting just enough meekness to sell the act. He *owned* me now. The thought tasted fouler than the liquor.

The doors opened, and like well-trained shepherd dogs security herded us towards the pens – one color per enclosure, so I went into a blue section on the third level. The stadium was able to accommodate three million spectators on four levels, each tier seeing a different hologram that covered the level below, including people, giving the impression of having their private game. The real game? Only the Cupola's inner circle deserved that. Not that I cared, but the money given me by Batranu allowed me only a third-level ticket, close to the exit.

A girl's scream cut through the chaos – not fear, not yet ecstasy, something in-between. Her shredded shirt fluttered past my face like a surrender flag. Hands seized her, hoisting her onto shoulders. Her cries twisted into exhilaration as the crowd claimed her. Naked girls on shoulders – first ritual of the Final. More topples girls followed, stripped by eager hands, their resistance melting into frenzy. The air thickened with sweat and pheromones. It wasn't just alcohol now – the mob itself became the catalyst, steering the animal instincts inside us. My pulse spiked despite myself. I roared with them, pretending allegiance, but my body betrayed me. Lust was just another leash.

Agent provocateurs moved through the crowd – DigitalEgos synced, herding minds toward calculated chaos – they were the most *uninhibited* men and women. Security watched, idle. Let them have sex, let them steal, let them break – it was both Finale and Carnival. Only murder would draw intervention. Tomorrow, they would all erase the night from their minds. If you have nothing to hide, you have nothing to fear.

A blue-haired girl slumped against the wall next to me. Instinct made me help. "Got you," she whispered. Her arms snaked around my neck, her lips crushing mine. Trap. She was an agitator; most probably AI had observed my somewhat low enthusiasm. Her lips were warm, her half-naked body softer than any simulation. Diego's zap barely registered.

"Focus," he chided, but his holographic eyes dipped to her breasts. He could feel everything I could feel, and he was enjoying her as much as I was.

I carried her to a pack of men. They took her with grunts and groping. She shrieked with delight, arching into their hands, and waiving two blue flags – another cog in the machine. I fled, my skin still humming from the first naked girl in my arms. Finally, I found my place, close to the exit, a part of me still regretting that I had to leave her. At that moment, I was probably the only one not engaged in the social *activities*, and it wasn't due to my own restraint.

"Darkness teaches what daylight hides," Diego said, amused.

"Easy for a hologram to say."

Called by Diego, the flying waitress drone arrived exactly when the lights dimmed even more. I bought chocolate, water, wine, and left my deactivated bracelet in one of its pockets.

Then, impact. A girl sprawled across my lap, her pants half-off, fingers clawing my shoulders. Second girl in fifteen minutes. The brute to my left shoved me. "Wait your turn."

She giggled and eyed him with appreciation. "You first."

The howl he unleashed could have shattered glass. He shoved me again, harder, and I hit the ground, then I left, stumbling into a triad of women, their bodies glistening. "Men's section is that way!" one of them shouted, but she was smiling.

Alone in the shadows, I watched the orgy unfold – the second ritual of the Final. No one followed me. Why would they? The game hadn't even started.

Ten minutes later, I was in the toilet stall. The washroom crawled with cameras – only the cubicles offered dubious privacy. With a silent laugh, I peeled off the plump-face mask. The blade made quick work of its ridiculous curls. The second mask clung to my skin – severe, hairless, all sharp angles where the first had been soft stupidity. Better. I couldn't stomach that other face another second. The old mask went over it like a second skin, its curls spiraling down the toilet bowl in a silent flush, then I wrapped a paper towel around my head like a makeshift turban.

Showtime.

Cameras caught the plump idiot exiting, right on schedule, hurrying back toward the seats – just another fan terrified of missing the magnificent start. Then I stopped in the artificial twilight, in front of the gates of the exit line twelve, pretending to tie my laces. My fingers brushed the B2 authorization in my pocket. *One use only. "Time to go,"* I said, and Diego flared a route across my vision. *"Cameras?"*

"Four to the exit. Two beyond." His voice was clipped. *"Eight seconds to bypass gate A. Nine seconds for gate B. The other seven will take too long."*

Behind me, automated dispensers whirred, ready to deliver cheap shoes and shirts for the post-game nudists – they were included in the tickets. I shook out my legs – jittery, warm-up motions.

"Now!" His neural shock hit like a wasp sting. I bolted through the gate. A pair of guards' laughter chased me – *look at the madman with the paper towel crown.*

They see a running fool. Let them. By the time they realize it is a running rebel – I will be gone.

‹ Alenia ›

"Security! Grab him!" Shine's voice cracked through the audio link – usually so meticulously controlled, now frayed with predatory hunger. I imagined white-knuckled grip on her comm unit, her eyes glinting, already tasting the promotion, the headlines. A hero. "Sector 2007A. Move! He's escaping!" The last word clipped short, like she had bitten through the syllable.

Chaos spread: boots pounding concrete, the whine of kinetic armor servos, neural alerts pinging across the security channels. Diegia projected a stadium hologram in my neural field, the rebel's path a pulsing red dot carving arcs across the tiers. Her avatar – a shimmering figure with his face grafted onto a dancer's form, scantily clad in holographic silks – swayed mockingly. *"Shine has this feed too,"* she winked. *"Your boy is outsmarting her."* The hologram zoomed, revealing military micro-drones scanning the crowd, their sensors blind to what I supposed was cloaking tech provided to him by the Resistance.

"Sector 2045B! Full squad – now!" Shine's voice, now a sharp edge of agitation, carried an unspoken threat: *Failure means more than demotion.* Classic Cupola intimidation. Guards sprinted harder, their pursuit streamed on hijacked feeds. Floodlights swept the stands, scattering spectators in a chaos of screams and spilled drinks. More mini-drones buzzed overhead, their laser grids slicing through the dark, but every sector was empty – the prey always three steps ahead.

In Area 2000, his pattern baffled me: bursts of inhuman speed, then dead stillness for a minute or two, cycling unevenly like a glitch in a neural net. The truth hit like a shock pulse. I laughed, the sound erupting before I could stop it.

Diegia's holographic hand clamped over my mouth as she killed my mic and sent a sharp pain signal into my jaw, her avatar glaring. *"Careless,"* she hissed, her eyes narrowing, but a flicker of amusement danced in them.

"The Resistance trained him too well," I sighed, then added, *"Delete this."* Her expression shifted – something unreadable, almost protective – before she obeyed.

Twenty minutes since the bracelet's reactivation. Thirty minutes of pre-recorded footage fed into the surveillance grid. Twenty more until they reached his jailhouse. We had burned fifteen minutes chasing a *waitress drone* – a decoy rigged with his bio-signature. The irony burned so sharp I couldn't stop laughing. *Forty minutes gone.* He was halfway across the city by now, slipping through with that fluid grace I had glimpsed in the garden. The image came unbidden, just us two... *Dangerous.* I crushed the thought, but it left a searing afterimage.

"Shine is blind. Mentally blind," Diegia mouthed, silently.

Screams and shattering glass erupted over the comms as floodlights activated. Then – silence. Another empty sector.

"Sector 2087H!" Shine's roar dissolved into a string of curses, her composure unraveling. Officers wheezed, their armor's servos whining under the strain, audio feeds thick with labored breaths – some forgot to mute. More floodlights enveloped the teams in the general obscurity of the stadium; even Shine wouldn't dare activate the main lights during a Final, risking a Popularity Index crash. Spectators were shoved aside, some tumbling over railings as guards prioritized speed. Holo-barriers flickered, hacked by Resistance code, misdirecting the teams – someone was here, risking life to help him. "Something is wrong," Shine admitted, her voice taut with barely contained fury. Our holograms synced – a frenetic red dot scrawling chaos over the map. The audio channel crackled with tense silence.

"I think we are hunting a waitress drone," I said, careful to keep my voice flat.

Silence. Then Shine's comm exploded: "Nobody asked you!"

Perfect… I withdrew, mentally crafting an alibi for the inevitable AI audit. Shine's meltdown was a gift – one I would leverage later.

Diegia's avatar morphed into her black cat form, and leaned closer, tail morphing into a question mark. Her voice carried a conspiratorial whisper: *"Our drama queen is drowning. Should we ask Cassia to nudge the Popularity Index down another point*?" I shook my head; our main goal was his escape.

"Councilor Tiati is correct," the lieutenant cut in, his tone steady but bold. Diegia's query flashed data: a minor Jewel Family scion, exploiting the Ruby-Jewel feud to undermine Shine. The political play was unfolding, a calculated gamble, backed by his Family's clout.

Diegia's lips curled into a subtle smirk. *"Award incoming,"* she quipped, her sarcasm sharp as she projected a new dataset: Shine had cut her link to consult AI – a mistake. Requesting data analysis was routine; begging AI for field decisions was a stain on her record. *"She will pin this on you."*

"Ground all waitress drones," Shine ordered through gritted teeth. A swarm of drones retreated to storage vaults. The bracelet's signal traced to one, buried in a pile of idle wait-bots. Police, sweating in their armor, dug it out, their muttered curses richer than Shine's. Running in kinetic armor is brutal. Running for nothing is hell. Spectators grew restless, their alcohol cut off, some hurling cups at the drones' retreating forms.

Diegia winked. *"Clever boy,"* she murmured, projecting a 3D model of the bracelet: a bio-mimetic plating, its core filled with a cloned DNA signature. Then she flashed the metrics: Popularity Index down 1.3%. *"Shine is bleeding,"* she purred. *"Shall we amplify the crowd's outrage?"* Her cat form prowled closer, eyes glinting with mischief. I shook my head with a hollow smile. Beyond these walls, he was running for his life, and a part of me hoped he would keep running, far from Shine, far from me, yet close enough that I might one day see him again.

Just stay alive.

"AI, scan all exits for the last twenty minutes." I kept my voice flat, carefully choosing the timeframe to waste resources. The silence from Shine's channel was its own reward.

"Departures logged. Five hundred ten people left the stadium," AI reported a second later. "None is our target. All stadium staff. No biometric matches with the rebel."

"Expand scan to city-bound traffic. Four-to-seven-mile radius. Check people trying to leave the city for identity spoofing," I said, inflating the range to flood AI with data.

"Twenty-six targets identified thorough subway footage. Nine females. All going toward registered residences via the right trains. No deviations from their standard routes."

"Lieutenant, send teams to verify them. Men and women. Assume gender disguise." My words hung, met only by the faint static of open channels.

Minutes later, a priority ping from the lieutenant's Diego: *Teams report negative on all targets.* It was a favor. *Taciturn guy. Efficient...* I thought, feeling Diegia's holographic fingers tap my shoulder – her silent cue that she was running a deeper check on him. *Twenty-six teams tied up... I need more.*

A minute later, the lieutenant report came through the official channel, and Shine's comm crackled to life: "AI, extend past departure scan for another twenty minutes."

Too close. He had left five minutes before that window. Keep running. I imagined him, a stealth shadow moving through the city's underbelly right now.

"Three hundred twenty-two matches," AI droned. "Nineteen attempting to leave the city."

Then the lieutenant's voice, tight with controlled excitement: "I am at the safehouse. Cameras show fifty-five minutes of looped footage. I am sending it for analysis. Nineteen teams ready to check the people in AI's list."

Twenty more police teams deployed. More data flooding AI. Better than I had dared hope. The image of his silhouette reading in bed came through the footage, and I wondered when it had been recorded.

"Search back one hour!" Shine's voice spiked into distortion; the prey was slipping through her net.

Then AI flagged a breach: "Security violation: Unauthorized access to eight cameras at exit line twelve detected. 21:10 hours. False 2B authorization used. I blocked it." A beat. Then came the image of an approximately forty-year-old man, his head wrapped in a comical turban of paper towels, half his face obscured. "Facial reconstruction available. Male. Paper towels used as headwrap." A flurry of written comments followed, which was unusual – no one had time to read them.

Diegia zoomed into the image, looking for flaws into the mask. *"No resemblance,"* she scoffed, but her tone held a trace of admiration. *"Resistance handiwork; it looks human enough to trick even the most advanced cameras."*

A few seconds later, AI came to life again. "Captured by an overlapping camera in exit line eleven." Another pause. "Secondary capture: toilet 73C. Clean face, curly hair. I deleted the headwrap and reconstructed his full face in the previous image. He used paper towels for cover. Same subject, no disguise," AI droned, some data redundant – a sign of system overload.

"Could be a mask," I offered, smoothly. "Or an accomplice's misdirection."

Dead air. Shine had muted her channel to consult AI again – her third tactical pause. *Amateur.* When she returned, her voice had gone metallic with forced calm: "Scan one-mile radius from last security breach. Deploy forensic teams to manually check the cameras and sweep for bio-traces"

"Teams out," the lieutenant confirmed. They will reach the stadium in five minutes."

"Exit twelve cameras were externally blinded. No identity match for suspect in database. He doesn't exist. I repeat, he doesn't exist," AI updated, its tone glitching.

"AI, reformulate. He is masked. The mask doesn't exist. The man exists," I said quickly, preempting others. The obvious conclusion cementing my credibility. Tomorrow's Traveler scan official debrief would be grueling, and I needed every advantage.

"Reformulating. The man exists, physically," AI agreed, its response lagging six seconds. "I need his real image for identification. I repeat, I need his real image."

System overload.

The hunt stretched into night, the pulse of the city growing colder. Guards stormed transit hubs. Two drones collided in their frenzy, sparking showers, falling onto the streets below. One by one, my access channels terminated – first the live feeds, then the comms.

Only Diegia remained, her form shifting to a gentle figure bathed in starlight. *"Time to clean your mind,"* she said, her voice tender yet firm. I sank into simulations, erasing the memory cluster tied to his escape – *You have to run. Now!* – and other fragments Diegia carefully selected. The neural overwrite was the only way to fool the Travelers' mind scan. I erased him, then rewrote him in the same cluster of neurons: a different him: turquoise waterfall, phantom hands tracing my skin, warm lips brushing mine. The fantasy was vivid, reckless, nothing like the ones I had in the past. Dangerous.

Later, through backchannels, I learned: Shine had purged me and the lieutenant from the search, citing classified intelligence above my authorization. Confident in her new lead, she launched another hunt after I was cut off. The rebel's file showed nothing new – her *lead* was theater.

But if they catch him...

Diegia's claws pricked my skin, her holographic mouth shaping silent words: *He is smarter than they are.*

Alenia

Prim's office was crowded; the entire Cupola was represented: the third-rank Lords of the Jewel, Ruby, and Diamond Families – the oldest and most powerful, forming the crown of the Cupola; the second-rank Lords of GreatInsurance, Goldstone, GreatPharma, Derivatives, and Billion, mid-tier Families. Coin, the First Lord of the minor Silver Family, was the only Master-Lord present at the meeting and, as usual, took charge of everything.

Why is he so important? I glanced briefly at him. I was sure his Diego noticed my reaction, but there was no visible response.

Until this meeting, I had never met anyone higher than a second-rank Lord of a minor Family. Each Family had one Master Lord – usually the founder or a descendant – and three Lords. *The Traveler,* I remembered. *Where is the Traveler?* Diegia shrugged; no one in the room bothered to enlighten me, not even Vipri.

My mind was sluggish from hunting the rebel until late at night and from three hours of simulations that demanded even more from an already exhausted body – I hadn't expected that. My body felt drained but relaxed. I couldn't say the same for my mind, though. With a curious feeling, I realized the simulations had helped me keep a mental tension at bay, one that still lingered somewhere inside. Maybe I should do it more often; it was my first erotic sim – well, simulations, three in a row. Diegia was still taunting me about *my young rebel,* and with cause. There was a strange link between us, something that sparked the moment we met, only to grow later. Nothing I could explain.

"Sterile explanations won't bring men to you. Your last lover was ... well... a long time ago. Your boy is gone. What about Vipri?" Diegia looked at me mischievously but had the decency to avoid her sensual black cat form – we were in a meeting, after all.

"Vipri is my manager."

"And?" she shrugged. *"You are the only High Councilor who hasn't* thoroughly *tested her boss. You must know him in every ... aspect to have an excellent office relationship. Warm."* She grinned, showing cat-like teeth, still keeping her usual avatar. *"Well, no real men? At least go into more simulations. I enjoyed your boy. You know, I have needs too."* Her body melted slowly, her smile lingering.

"Shut up! I don't want to become like them," I snapped, struggling to maintain a studied indifference – I had enjoyed the sim with the boy too, and she knew it. I glanced around, taking in everyone in the room, lingering long enough to confirm I didn't want to be like them. For whatever reason, they were doing the same to me. There was something in their eyes, a mix of predatory glances and the look of puppies relieved not to be kicked by their masters. *They will throw me to the Travelers.* I suddenly realized. *That's why they asked me here, to be the lightning rod.*

"The Master-Lord of Celestial Life Enhancers, Servants of Proper Life from Quadrants ... Faction," AI recited the pompous titles in a monotonous voice. Of course, he wouldn't arrive until everyone else was gathered. Propelled by invisible springs, we stood and bowed as the Traveler entered. The conditioning was so deep I couldn't even mumble. As usual, we saw his large black hat first, the sparkling veil covering him dissolving slowly, revealing his face only after our heads returned to their normal position. Black Hats, I recalled, the name we used a long time ago because of their ostentatious hats.

"Where is the rebel?" the Traveler asked, his voice flatter than the floor, as he threw himself into the chair usually reserved for Prim. It was a rhetorical question; the Celestials already knew of the rebel's escape.

He wasn't caught... The rebel's file, just sent to me in a well-orchestrated move, contained nothing useful. They didn't realize the effect on me was the opposite of their intentions.

"Well, we trained a bunch of nothings, and we got what we trained for. A twenty-year-old bypassed all your security. Well done." The Traveler glanced around, daring one of the *nothings* to challenge his criticism. No one rose. "Who was in charge?" In a split second, half the hands in the room pointed at me, and I suddenly realized Shine wasn't there.

You bastards...

"Have we met before?" the Traveler asked. Desperately, my mind scrambled to identify his facial features, trying to pin them to a memory. This could mean my death; I was playing guess-who with a three-hundred-year-old grudge.

I don't know you! I screamed inside. With the last scraps of self-preservation, I shook my head weakly, fearing he might recognize me from that disastrous skirmish more than three centuries ago, when I was young, and – let's be honest – reckless. He glided toward me in his shimmering force field, all slow and dramatic, like a peacock in a power suit. The room held its breath, every eye darting between us, trying to figure out if this was a trial or a theatrical execution.

Look at them, squirming like roaches under a spotlight. The Lords of the Jewel, Ruby, and Diamond Families sat stiff, their gem-encrusted collars glinting. Their faces were rigid in fake composure – tight lips, as if they had rather be anywhere else but didn't dare move. The second-rank Lords from GreatInsurance and Goldstone weren't much better, their fingers twitching over datapads, probably calculating the odds of being collateral damage. Coin leaned back with a grin, like he was watching a particularly juicy soap opera.

The Traveler grabbed my chin, turning my face left and right as if I was a defective mannequin. "We have never met, my Lord," I said, filling my voice with just enough emotion to sell it. I flicked my eyes up for a split second, then dropped them with a performance of modesty to signal appreciation that he had deigned to spend his precious time acknowledging me. Touching me.

"It seems so," the Traveler agreed, his tone as warm as an icefield. He fished a small device from his pocket, and a sphere zipped out, latching onto my forehead with a faint hum. "Nothing personal," he droned, sounding about as sincere as a Cupola politician. "You seem to be trusted. Let's hope the tool reaches the same conclusion." He let go of my chin. Beneath his bland voice, I sensed he was hoping for the opposite – that the tool would expose my untrustworthiness. "Let your mind open," he intoned, reciting the first ritual like a bored priest. "If you have nothing to hide, you have nothing to fear. To open your mind is to keep your allegiance to us, to the system that keeps your planet running so well."

Well…?

"Keep your mind shut!" Diegia's voice cut through my thoughts, her avatar exploding into a mini-tornado of glittering chaos. Hundreds of hypnotic eyes spinning with the wind, appearing and disappearing in rapid succession. *"And now open,"* she purred, her cloudy mouth stretching into a grin that could unnerve a statue. With a final cackle, she vanished, leaving me to deal with the real storm.

At that moment, Shine entered through a door behind the Traveler, grinning at me, and I closed my eyes, trying to feel nothing.

There is nothing to feel when an advanced neuranalyzer invades your mind, yet this felt as though an icy knife punched through my skull – just fear, nothing real. I had expected the sphere to work like our devices: a list of keywords generating a detailed report, maybe a nice pie chart of my sins. The rebel's name and image were fed indeed, but no report was delivered. Instead, a shock came. My second simulation, the steamiest one, crafted with the expertise only experience brings, the kind that takes years of questionable life choices to perfect – Diegia's *experience* from scouring the Net for the best thing. The hologram erupted in the middle of the room with Traveler-tech resolution, crisp and vivid. Every translucent hair, every flicker of lust in our eyes, rendered in glorious, mortifying detail. Rotating for the full 360-degree humiliation.

We were naked, tangled in a frenzy I hadn't felt since ... centuries. The turquoise waterfall misted around us, a violin played, and the air carried the scent of sweat and reckless abandon. The lock of our gazes at the end – pure joy – hit me like a hammer. *Was that happiness real?* Some traits are genuine in a simulation with a known person. The human vultures didn't care about philosophy. Their eyes bulged, jaws dropped, and GreatInsurance's Lord nearly choked on his own tongue.

They're recording everything. Of course, they are. The Traveler didn't care about the show, but he kept it running, his eyes scanning the room like a predator, analyzing their reactions – and mine. Shine, lounging against the wall, looked far too pleased. This wasn't just about me. It was about them – every twitch, every gasp, every guilty glance in the room, burning into my naked form, searing my soul.

"Gentlemen, I very much enjoyed this meeting," Lord Coin said, closing the session with a smile so thin it could cut glass. The sarcasm in his words was thicker than the Jewel Family's pretension. The Traveler had vanished, freeing our frozen minds, leaving me to assume my double-deleted and rewritten memory had fooled his neuro-sphere. There was nothing suspicious in my head, just some steamy simulations with a rebel who was now conveniently missing.

With the worst outcome – a mind-wipe or a one-way trip to a black hole – off the table, I was left to wrestle my shredded pride. The room full of nothings – and for once, I agreed with a Traveler – had caught my most intimate moments in extra detail, a show I never signed up for, let alone wanted them to ogle.

If these walking wallets are gentlemen, I am the Cupola's next queen. My jaw clenched, and I shot a glare around the room, catching the third-rank Lords of the Jewel, Ruby, and Diamond Families fidgeting in their gem-encrusted collars, fingers twitching like they were plotting their escape. The second-rank Lords from GreatInsurance and Goldstone were no better, their eyes darting to the exits, faces as pale as if their stocks had just tanked. Bellezza, the GreatPharma Lord, tilted her head, her lips pursed as if she was already monetizing my humiliation.

"They're the gentlemen of our times," Diegia whispered, her black tail flicking with mock disdain. *"Keep that in mind."*

"I hate this. The best censure is self-censure," I muttered, my left hand jerking up and down as if I was conducting a symphony of bad life choices.

"Keep your hand down," Diegia hissed, her black cat form baring polished teeth. I froze, my face flushing crimson as Lord Coin's smile tracked my movements, his eyes twinkling with amusement. The room followed suit – Bijou's eyebrows shot up, Broker's mouth quirked into a smug grin, and Crown's fingers drummed impatiently on his armrest. *"Your color is perfect,"* Diegia purred, her tail curling mischievously, her fighting mode gone. *"It matches the embarrassment you should have felt ten minutes ago."*

"I wasn't talking to you," I snapped, stretching my hand over her snout to muzzle her – we both liked it – then I muted her.

"You have wonderful skin," Bellezza said, her voice dripping with predatory thoughtfulness. Her eyes were on a hologram she did not bother to hide, zoom in, zoom out, and in the image, lay my naked body. "You must come test our new beauty products. I will throw in a photo session, just for you, in a place of your dreams – a turquoise waterfall." Her smile stretched half her face, her photo session meant debauchery not art – she had a large harem, and a generous *imagination*. I pressed my lips shut, hoping silence would make her disappear. "Tomorrow?" she pressed, her stare pinning me like a bug.

"Thank you, my Lord," I said. "I will think about it."

"Think faster." Her tone sharpened, a flicker of displeasure crossing her face. A Lesser refusing a Lord? That was like gravity taking a coffee break. The room went still, every head swiveling to me. GreatInsurance's Lord froze mid-sip, a bead of sweat rolling down his temple. Even Coin paused, his smile faltering for a split second. A Lord like Bellezza didn't bother with unwritten rules – she wanted me, and she wanted me yesterday. Until today, I had dodged the Lords' radar with my drab gray-and-black wardrobe, all austere angles and zero allure. But that simulation stripped away the camouflage, baring the real me. I felt naked.

"Bellezza," Vipri cut in, his laughter laced with caustic mockery. "No one with half a brain is testing your products until you use them yourself. Which means never." The room froze, breaths held. Then Coin let out a guffaw, winking at me like we were old friends. Bijou, the Jewel third Lord, joined in with a chuckle, his gem-encrusted earrings jangling. The laughter spread like wildfire – Broker slapped his knee, Ring snorted, even the stiff Diamond Lord cracked a grin. Everyone except Bellezza and me was laughing, her face now dark as a thundercloud.

Thank you, I messaged Vipri, who kept his amused smirk in place. But I knew him – his eyes were too steady, his posture too controlled. That laugh was a calculated strike. Bijou, Bellezza, Crown, Broker, Ring – names so pompous they sound like rejected furniture lines. *Why is Coin's name so ... low?* Like he was mocking them just by existing. He was always different – sometimes in a good way, sometimes not. And popular, which was rarer than an honest politician.

"Your show was perfect," Coin sighed, just as Bellezza opened her mouth to retaliate. His voice was warm, almost wistful. "Natural, engaging, full of sparks. Ah, I dreamt of being there with you. I still dream." He stared at me, his thin smile oddly sincere, not the vulgar leer I had braced for. "Like all of them," he added, gesturing at the room, sparking another round of laughter – *that* felt vulgar, their eyes lingered too long on my body. "Young lady, it is such a pity we haven't met before." That warmth again in his voice.

Young? I am older than your entire bloodline.

A second later, an invitation to the Silver Family's monthly party arrived in my inbox, complete with the heraldic signs, including the Cupola's crown seal. *"Reject it!"* I snapped at Diegia, but she accepted it, flicking her tail with smug satisfaction. *"You traitor! I told you to reject it!"* She grinned, and pointed a claw at her mouth. I unmuted her.

"It's not smart to refuse a Master Lord's invitation, and Coin is different," Diegia said, her avatar lounging like she had just won the bet of her life. *"You don't have to like it, and maybe you don't even have to go. Act normal, and they will probably forget you. Perhaps still remember your simulations."* She grinned, her face all teeth.

She had a point, though. I sighed, as Diegia wisely kept her mouth shut. Coin was in a suspiciously good mood, his eyes twinkling with deeper roots that I had only untangle much later.

He tossed out a few more jokes, half-aimed at me. I met them with an indifference that made me proud. The room started to empty – Coin swept out first, followed by the Cupola's glittering parade and most of the government staff. I lingered, caught in a self-induced trance, until Diegia zapped my nerves with a small shock – Vipri was subtly nodding toward the door.

The shock snapped me back to a clarity I didn't want. But my delay had one perk: the antechamber was empty. I leaned against the wall, my heart still pounding, and shot a mental glare at Diegia's lingering cat form. *"You are on thin ice, furball,"* I muttered. Her emerald eyes winked, and she smirked before fading out.

Tomorrow, you will come to this address, Bellezza's message landed into my inbox, blunt as a sledgehammer, no *please* in sight, the skincare despot's charming nature. *Thank you, my Lord*, I wrote back, *but I've already accepted Master-Lord Coin's invitation*. A half-lie, but it did the trick – Coin's Master status outranked her in the Cupola's rigid hierarchy, and she dropped me like a bad investment.

Muffled voices seeped from the office, and I pressed harder against the wall, holding my breath. *I am on their radar now.* A century of playing ghost, and it was all rubble now, because of an unwanted simulation. My carefully crafted anonymity – drab clothes, zero charisma, blending into the shadows – was gone. *Exposed. Buck-naked, metaphorically and literally. They will figure out who I am sooner or later...* The door clicked open, and I jumped, scrambling to put distance between me and whoever was emerging. Socializing was the last thing I needed; they had recorded every moan, every whisper, every cry of my simulation in excruciating detail. *Next, they will want to critique my technique or swap tips like it was a damn movie club.* My legs moved on, but from the corner of my eye, I saw the door ajar, and angry voices spilled out.

"Don't start, Diegia," I hissed, sensing her avatar stir.

"I don't care if that bitch of yours was scanned; she is a Lesser!" Prim's voice thundered, malice dripping from every syllable. "The Travelers wanted it. I am sure they didn't enjoy the show, but everyone else did. It will release pressure – a rebel escaped. He was in *your* custody..."

"My dear Prim," Vipri cut in, his voice displaying a studied calm. "Shine was there ... leading. You shielded her incompetence. But forget that. It's almost irrelevant now. I am not sure you fully understand the situation we face."

"How dare you..." Prim's voice choked on his fury, I strained to recall who else was still in the room. Three others, maybe? Shine, definitely.

"She is part of the ministerial staff."

"A minor Lesser porno-bitch in the hierarchy!" Prim spat, clawing for authority. A shrill, servile laugh followed – Shine, no doubt, her giggle laced with a nervous shiver.

"In the *higher* part of the hierarchy," Vipri countered, his voice a scalpel. "By law, we can't scan people of her level."

"Everything was done for the necessity of the state," Prim retorted, his voice thin and defensive.

"I told you..."

"That I don't understand. I know." Prim's tone shifted, slow and cold, like he had just glimpsed a trap snapping shut.

I frowned, my mind racing. *What does Vipri see that I am missing?*

"There were six *High Rank Lessers* in the room, and all of them recorded everything, as did everyone else," Vipri said, his voice dripping with derision. "Don't tell me you didn't. The whole system runs on the assurance that no power can scan those above a certain level. They enforce it. *Our* system. We scanned the *minor bitch*. They will see themselves in her position. The cat is out of the bag, Mr. Prime Minister. Find something to keep the other cats happy – a promotion, a step up in the hierarchy. Something clever..." The derision in Vipri's words made me feel good without really understanding why. Maybe because he was a Jewel while Prim was a Ruby.

There was always a rotation in power; the political gears clicking like a metronome. Jewel and Ruby Families, wrestling for control through *democratic* elections, with Glass, SoulBook, and YouMovie as their propaganda puppets. Fake search results, troll armies, bot swarms – Cupola elevated manipulation to science. In the past, the Diamonds used to play, too, until the Travelers demoted them for a huge security blunder.

"Coin understood it, as did the others; the only ones missing the obvious were you and Bellezza," Vipri said, his voice a final nail in Prim's coffin. The door swung open, and he stepped out, his smile sharp and knowing as he locked eyes with me. Prim stayed out of sight, probably licking his wounds.

You did this on purpose; you let me hear everything. You wanted me to hear every word.

Vipri gestured – *wait for me.* "Goodbye, Mr. Prime Minister," he said deliberately, using the name no one else dared to speak, just to underscore the gravity of his words. Then he closed the door.

"I am sorry, my dear Alenia," Vipri murmured, a trace of sadness in his voice.

Are you really sad?

"I have nothing arranged for this evening. Would you join me for a meal?"

"My erotic simulations pay good dividends."

"I would never have guessed that the coldest of my councilors had such a ... warm side," he laughed. "Don't worry; it's only a restaurant invitation, not a bed invitation."

Yet... "Well, you have my simulation," I said, dampening his expectations – though I wasn't even sure if he was interested. There can never be enough precautions.

"You must get accustomed to this," Diegia mocked me. *"And so will I. Before the night is over, you will have received a few bed invitations."*

She was right.

"It can't be such a bad thing," she teased. I shut her up with my inner hand.

Back home, I realized it had been my first restaurant visit in twenty years. *Twenty years since his death...* I have loved only two men in my centuries-long life, but they were men. I closed the door with the strange feeling that I had, in some unclear ways, enjoyed the evening. *I need to socialize more... With Vipri?*

What happened afterward pushed the dinner to the back of my mind. Alongside numerous bed invitations, I received a substantial salary increase and a ZeroC-level authorization – something rarely granted to those outside the Cupola. In fact, I only knew two others who had it. Reading the notice, I felt like a cheap whore – yet the feeling was detached, as if it didn't belong to me. "I don't give a coin – or a *Coin* –" I laughed, "for their Popularity Index." To them, my show was nothing unusual. They all enjoyed second or third lives in simulations, casually conducting business meetings while naked couples writhed around them. *I am too different, and soon they will realize it. Something needs to change... More than just simulations.*

I hate this world.

My last thought left me wondering how long I could remain unaltered by the insidious AI media campaigns, steering people like puppets through prewritten scripts. I sent a thank-you email to Prim, who – as expected – didn't reply. Then I sent one to Vipri, who – also predictably – responded with another dinner invitation. I accepted it. Afraid of being left alone with my thoughts, I spent the rest of the evening searching for a resort reserved for low-ranking Minor Families. The ZeroC-level granted me more privileges than I had anticipated.

From my fabricated memory logs – showing a hidden craving for luxury and lavish estates – they would expect it, watching me. Ignoring such trivialities would raise too many questions. Yet, in the end, a faint thrill stirred at the thought of being admitted to such an exclusive place – the conditioning they forced on us was, in some ways, stronger than I was.

An hour later, the Net informed me that my mandatory monthly one-hour OpenMind session was about to begin. I wasn't bothered; for a long time, nobody had wanted to share their mind with me. I was too boring – my Net ranking was the lowest possible: zero, and probably unique, meaning I wouldn't appear in any search on Glass.

"We have a problem," Diegia whispered. I was already on my sofa with a loaded novel, and out of old habit, it was always something challenging. My mind was connected to the Net, and everyone could see what I was doing, thinking, and feeling. Low level Net crawlers always bothered to check on me, but eventually, I decided to spend the hour reading unusual books – just in case someone tried to uncover the reason behind my zero ranking.

Diegia paused the connection for a few seconds for *mind calibration*, a standard procedure I had never used before. The more indifferent you were, the less people bothered you. The pause gave participants two minutes to adjust and Diegia time to display the list of people waiting to experience my OpenMind session.

"Seven hundred and ten. Are you joking?" I asked. *"I had fewer than one hundred in the six years since the program started. You are joking..."*

Diegia shook her head and displayed the request locations: all Cupola areas.

"Bastards! Less than twelve hours after my show with the Traveler. Someone published my simulations. Let me change the book." I set the e-book aside and grabbed an ancient philosophy text – paper, I still loved its texture and the scent of old leather. *"Slow down the neural areas not linked to my reading and reasoning centers. Dial back the emotional ones a bit more – you know what to do."* I gave her free rein over my emotions and Net communications and found a passage with dense, lengthy sentences. *"Ready."*

"There are two thousand now," she said before reopening the connection. I shrugged; in the end, it didn't matter much.

Normally, I read silently, but this time I decided to change that. "Morality did not arise from the need to make us happy, but from the way we make ourselves worthy of happiness."

"Hey!" someone shouted. The rules forced me to open my mind, making every new thought visible to the audience, but they weren't allowed to dig into past memories. There were also no rules requiring interaction, so I kept reading.

"Let's have some fun," the voice insisted. Others joined in: "Fun! Fun! Fun!" Images flooded – me and the escaped rebel, obviously naked. My reading faltered. "Yesss!" they cheered as more photos appeared, exposing every part of my body.

"If mmorrality isss deffined..." I stammered. Diegia sensed my struggle and gently froze the parts of my brain that usually generated curses. Taking a deep breath, I restarted: "If morality is defined..."

They shifted tactics, bombarding me with simulations – each one flaunting their *wild imagination*, unaware they had all done roughly the same thing: copying fragments of my own simulation and replacing the rebel with themselves. Even the turquoise waterfall Diegia had created for me was there. I kept reading.

"Girl! I'm a Ruby," one of them growled in an artificially deepened voice, his avatar flashing the Cupola's crown insignia. "I order you to stop reading and take off your clothes. Play with us, show what's in your mind when you're doing *real* things. Your rating will skyrocket higher than you've ever dreamed. You have potential; I saw your last movie. Let's start with Snake Dance to warm up – see how your breasts move. Then we'll get serious: The Writhing."

I knew about Snake Dance – I couldn't recall how. The Writhing, though? Nothing. *"Diegia."*

Before she could respond, the Ruby trash flooded my feed with an interactive sim: a naked woman arched on a table, six pairs of hands roaming her body, while she was writhing and moaning. "We're the Ruby Sensorial Hands Team – top-tier Writhing rank on the Net," he bragged.

"It's the most popular sensory game right now," Diegia whispered. *"She seems to be enjoying herself. What do you think?"* She pointed at the writhing woman, then mimicked the motion, her grin lingering like smoke after she vanished.

"We'll make you feel like a goddess. You'll *crave* us. And you'll be a celebrity, Ruby guarantee. Perform well, and I'll invite you into the Family's inner castle. All six of us. One of our most ... exclusive spaces. Everything included." His avatar swelled, blotting out the others – the privilege of rank – as he listed incentives like an auctioneer.

Meanwhile, Diegia flashed me a new datapoint: 40,000 connections. Then another: Age 16. A name. And biometrics. My new authorization level had let her unmask him.

Invite yourself... You have no idea what I dream of. "It is a lovely book, young man." I summoned the most serene smile from my mental archive and tilted the cover toward his avatar. "I would be delighted to read it with you. Sixteen is the perfect age to learn. Don't you think, *Demian of the Ruby Family?"* I pitched the last words in his real, unmodulated soprano.

The deep-voiced avatar shrank like a deflating balloon. His connection severed. *Guess he will need* to rebuild a new *persona from scratch.* "The rest of you are welcome to join me. I..."

Every link dropped.

Before I could savor the victory, the Net's official seal pulsed in my vision, and a robotic voice said: "Citizen Tiati: Your OpenMind session has been terminated due to NetNode overload while you were one of the most followed citizens on the Net. Your residence's capacity was exceeded, causing regional distortion. We apologize for the inconvenience. Upgrade your NetNode to HyperNode."

"Thank you. I will ... consider it," I said, severing the transmission. *Thank you, but no thanks. "Diegia, verify this NetNode issue. We should have known."*

My mind free again, I hastily checked the rebel's Security file – *nothing* – then collapsed into bed.

The nightmares came fast: eyes of every shape and color looming over me, unblinking. And of course, I wasn't alone in that bed.

"You are a celebrity," Vipri said, his voice carrying a strange undercurrent, so subtle it prickled my skin before I could pinpoint why. The morning was obnoxiously bright, mocking my so-called *celebrity hour* – more like ten minutes.

I squinted at him. "Should I take it you joined my little moment?" I asked, my voice low with surprise, an involuntary grimace tightening my lips.

Diegia's avatar flickered into my mind. *"A star is born!"*

I ignored her, and Vipri ignored my question, his smile gentle but his eyes sharp, like he was dissecting my reaction. Then he said, "I do this with some friends, outside the mandatory

OpenMind sessions – a small group. We would be happy if you joined us. Reading is welcome. For your information, we can't go longer than fifteen minutes. It was just five at first, so we are improving."

He wasn't wrong about the OpenMind being a possible evolutionary step at a certain level of social development. The government sold it as collective thinking, but it was a surveillance scam, designed to make us spy on each other, terrified of our own thoughts. It was even more vicious than thoughts deletion. It was about not thinking at all unless it was state-approved drivel. During those sessions, mental contact left no time to delete *wrong* thoughts; they were laid bare, recordable. It forced people into self-censorship, the ultimate submission tool. Perfect for human devolution, but Cupola couldn't see past their narrow-minded political game.

"You were in my session yesterday," I said, my voice flat with resignation.

"Yes." Vipri mimicked a teenage drawl, his lips quirking into a playful smirk. "But your celebrity is now a judicial case. You have printed books. Demian filed an official complaint. He has spent two years building his online reputation to hit top-tier Writhing rank on the Net. It's all he cares about. Like many other people." His tone was light, but his eyes flicked to mine, searching for a reaction.

"I have official authorization," I said in a low voice.

"Do you think I don't know that?" His tone carried the faintest amusement, his head tilting slightly, as if he was enjoying a private joke. "I am convinced you are a model citizen, and you don't have forbidden books. But a Security team will fulfill Demian's request and search your house. Tomorrow." His words left a strange aftertaste, like he *knew* me to have something illegal in my possession, like he was giving me a heads-up to clean house. He was right, but he shouldn't have been able to guess it, yet his slip helped me to cover my traces.

Five Security brutes came, led by a Ruby captain ready to please his superiors and find me guilty. They tore through my house, but found nothing – no banned books, no rebel pamphlets, not even a stray holo-tape. I had hidden my precious things – coming from another life that had been real life – well, thanks to Vipri's warning. But before I could savor the victory, Coin's invitation reactivated, pinging my inbox like a persistent virus. I ignored it, or tried to, my fingers hovering over the delete button. But the weight of his status – and the Cupola's watchful eyes – pressed down, and I knew dodging him wouldn't be that easy. And not even useful.

My first Cupola party was a spectacular disaster, a masterclass in everything I loathed. Coin, the Master-Lord of the Silver Family, hadn't forgotten his damned invitation. An hour after the party started, a team from his Family showed up at my door, all polished boots and smiles, giving me zero choice but to comply. They escorted me through the sprawling hall of the Silvers' residence, its walls dripping with opulence, and dropped me at Vipri's table. Of course he knew I would be dragged here. The show started before I could complain.

"She is not acting," I whispered, my voice low and tight as I watched the stage, where a woman was surrounded by three naked men. Her screams pierced the air, raw and real – this wasn't a performance. They were raping her in front of hundreds of gawking elites, and the crowd enjoyed, like it was a five-star holo-show. My hands clenched the chair arms, knuckles white, my body rigid with fury. *Stay silent, Alenia.*

"Yes, they would hate a spoiler," Vipri said, his tone casual, but his fingers twitched on his glass, betraying a flicker of unease. "Everything must be genuine. It's all on the Net, *Genuine Feelings*

– one of the top-rated programs." His shrug was awkward, his eyes avoiding mine, like he knew how flimsy his excuse sounded.

"That's rape," I spat, my voice barely a whisper.

"That word is a relic. Nobody uses it anymore," he said, shrugging again, his shoulders hunching slightly. The crowd around us didn't share my outrage. Broker, two tables over, leaned forward, his smirk wide and sleazy, his eyes glinting with voyeuristic thrill. Many howled their extasy, and it seemed to me that some women were even more excited than the men. Coin, presiding from armchair, sipped his drink, his smile thin but unreadable, like he was above it all.

We had twisted language to normalize the grotesque: *guilty pleasures* for rape, *bed invitations* for casual sex with strangers, *creative affection* for infidelity, *romantic relations* for love. At least I liked the last one.

"They will pay the official fee for their *guilty pleasure* with the girl, more than she would earn in a year. It's all legal," Vipri said, sending me the latest Pleasure Index poll, which had spiked 10% after the show started – this one was the second in the evening's series. I shrugged, just to hide the rage boiling in my chest, my fingers drumming a furious rhythm on the table.

Four years I worked to lower that damn index by 10%, and you undo it with one sick spectacle. But I realized later that those spikes always crashed once the adrenaline faded, replaced by the gnawing guilt of the aftertaste.

"People are enjoying it," Vipri said, his shrug more defensive now, his eyes flicking to the crowd, where howls of approval rippled. "Don't you...?" He stared at me, his brow furrowing when I didn't answer. A hint of surprise crossed his face, and he shook his head, a quiet acknowledgment: his High Councilor was clueless about the Cupola's favorite filth.

"And the girl?" I asked, struggling to control my voice.

"She will brag about pushing Cupola *nobles* into guilty pleasures, as usual. You can watch her tomorrow on the Net, an interview is already prepared," he said, a mocking edge in his voice when he mentioned nobility. His eyes weighed on me, heavy and probing.

"Be careful," Diegia whispered, her lascivious tail twisting left and right, like a reprimanding finger.

"I am sure you know the laws," Vipri said, his voice leveling out, his gaze finally breaking away when the silence stretched too long.

Yes, I know the laws. A private, totally separate judicial system for Cupola.

I had known the private laws for a long time, but locked in my own bubble, I never grasped a large part of its real-world rot until now. Sometimes, cheap TV does teach you something – like how low your society has sunk. As a High Councilor, I dealt with state affairs, chasing rebels and subversives, not civil offenses.

Guess I missed the memo on state-sanctioned depravity.

"Why does Coin act like a clown sometimes?" I asked, desperate to shift the topic before I punched something.

"Never underestimate Coin," Vipri said, his tone serious, his eyes narrowing slightly. "One of the sharpest men I know. He is head of a Minor Family only because the Travelers banned the Silvers from rising – I don't know why. By rights, he would lead the Middle Families, and he often acts as arbiter in the Cupola's Crown." I knew so little about their inner world, and it showed.

I left before another *Genuine Feelings* show could start, my heart bitter as I wove through the crowd, their laughter and clinking glasses grating on my nerves. For some perverse reason, Coin let me go, his smile from the dais as cryptic as ever. But he kept me on his damned invitation list, and I went to every one of his parties after that, staying exactly one hour, always at Vipri's table, leaving before the *Genuine Feelings* could scar me again.

One hour of fake smiles and dodging creeps – my new routine – only Vipri providing some comfort.

"You are a regular now," Diegia said in her serious demeanor, her eyes severe, but she smirked before fading out.

"Don't laugh. I am stuck in this nightmare, and it's only getting worse."

Dangerous Liaisons

Chapter 7 - Alenia

The trap tightened when Vipri invited me into his personal FlyCar. With so many people around, I couldn't afford a rejection. Reluctantly, I slid into the back seat, blocking the door behind me.

He shrugged, went to a front seat, and said a single word: "Histria."

The pilot nodded oddly, his grin, visible in the mirror, a silent, derogatory judgment. The FlyCar filled with silence as it lifted off, and within minutes, the city vanished behind us.

"Diegia, what's Histria?" I asked once my mind had settled.

"One of his personal residences, on the coast," she replied, and we stared at each other in uneasy silence.

I forced myself to stay calm, refusing to speculate about a trip I hadn't been prepared for. The aerial view of the coastline was beautiful enough to soften my mood, and for once, Diegia was as quiet as I was. The same silence hung in the front of the car. With orchestrated precision, the FlyCar traced the shoreline instead of flying directly to Histria. The view was mesmerizing.

In the garden, a table for two had been set by Mistria, his housemaid-bot. Vipri gestured toward it, distractedly picking at a piece of meat as if unaware of the tension while I took some fruit.

"We are disconnected from the Net!" Diegia cried. At the same moment, the sound of the sea vanished.

I said nothing, locking eyes with him.

"You already know we are cut off," he said. "And you have probably guessed this place is cloaked against spies, enhanced animals, anything within visual range. Satellites can still see us, but no sound is being broadcast. Any drone sent here will be destroyed. At least we still have the view."

It wasn't just the silence. The air carried the crisp, intoxicating scent of unfamiliar flowers, their essence seeping into my senses like an enchantment. The place felt unreal.

"Now listen." He sprang to his feet, agitation no longer masked. "We have five minutes until Jewel Security breaches the cloak to check on me."

"Diegia, take over my facial muscles," I said, struggling to remain composed. *"Eyes too. Block any involuntary reactions. He will record everything, just like us. AI can't be allowed to read me. Censor any link between his words and my knowledge of the Resistance. Nothing must be seen."* Everything felt perilous, like a scene from an espionage thriller. The setting, his erratic behavior... He might reveal something dangerous, something I shouldn't know, and trigger a reaction. Not one he had notice, but AI might. *"Make me look like someone processing critical intel. Thoughtful. Analytical."*

"And sexy," Diegia winked.

"If it makes you happy."

Vipri stopped in front of me, bracing his hands on the table, his weight pressing down. "The Travelers are going to activate their Field in three months."

A storm of emotion – rage, terror, the crushing weight of impending catastrophe – erupted inside me. I had braced for bad news, but nothing like this. *Billions will die...*

Diegia struggled to maintain my expression, and just as I thought we had succeeded, Vipri burst into laughter. My fingers dug into the table, knuckles whitening with the urge to strike him. Only later, in hindsight, would I recognize the frayed edge in his laughter – but in that moment, my control slipped.

"I apologize," Vipri said.

"I am leaving," I replied, coldly composed. My training reasserted itself, steadying me. Had using RigFace been a mistake? I rarely relied on it, still trusting my old instincts and Diegia's control. But how could I have been prepared for this?

"After the cloak is penetrated, we will take a walk in the park." He gestured toward the sea, as if the view alone might soften my resistance. "My Diego has already prepared a light simulation for the eyes watching us."

What does light *mean to you?* "I am leaving," I repeated, standing with deliberately cold precision. I needed time – time to process, to force him to drop the charade.

"Listen! I have two minutes left."

Simulation... A smokescreen. But for what? I gave a quick nod, feigning understanding.

"Like I said, it's light, not broadcast into the Net. But it *will* be recorded, and the Jewels *will* see it." His hands lifted in helpless resignation. "I need to steer their attention elsewhere. You know how it works. And you are considered unreachable. They will focus on my *achievement*." He pulled a chip from his pocket. "This has DuaLink. It allows our DigitalEgos to manage everything while we talk, behind the smokescreen."

Smokescreen. My own word. *Too dangerous.* "I don't know..." I dragged the words out, scrambling for an exit. Inside my mind, Diegia shook her head, her frown unconvincing.

"Trust me." He pressed the chip into my palm, holding my hand tight.

"Diegia," I whispered, paralyzed.

"Trust your feelings," she murmured – then vanished, abandoning me to the unknown.

Vipri still held my hand. I met his gaze, searching for deceit. His lips curled into a tight smile. After a weighted pause, he nodded once. With all my training, I detected no lie in his posture, no flicker of malice in his eyes. Reluctantly, I nodded too. Once.

"Diegia, encapsulate the software. Isolate it from my brain and your systems. Load it at minimum speed – probe it, but don't use Resistance tech." With a slow exhale, I pressed the chip to the port on my temple.

"Now, let's go." He tugged my hand until I resisted.

"I can handle the software," Diegia whispered. *"It's advanced, but manageable."*

"Good. I can handle his hand." A silent smirk stirred inside me as he released me, finally registering the rejection of his familiarity. A flicker of surprise passed over his face.

"Simulation is live," Diegia warned. *"Like this."* An overlay flickered across my vision, mirroring reality – recording the cliffs and the sea, allowing us to walk naturally without fear of missteps. At the same time, a new link opened between our minds.

His voice echoed inside mine: "Now, I can tell you why I laughed." An image came: my own face, skin blotched red and white, one eye wide as an owl's, the other squinting.

Intelligent and sexy ... for an owl, I mused. Diegia shrugged at her own failure. I choked back a laugh.

"You programmed Diegia to control your expressions. One: she shouldn't have RigFace – but you worked twenty years on the first DigitalEgo project, so..." He trailed off, letting me squirm under the implication: I had been caught with illegal tech. "Two: your reaction was so strong it broke her control. And the picture ... well, you laughed too. Now, tell me what's wrong with the New Field."

"We have the technical specs..."

"Tell me what you know beyond specs. Something is wrong. The Travelers are using us. I just don't know why."

"Does anyone else know?" I stalled.

"Someone might. But not me."

"The Travelers are friendly aliens that help us," I recited the official mantra, then met his eyes and added, "We are encouraged to believe our thinking aligns with the general way."

"This is a secure space – outside-office thinking. They are bastards." His voice dropped. "We know it well. But they created our Cupola to lead this planet, and we benefit, so we swallow the misery – even the rewritten history. You have old books. I have a few too, though my collection is newer. And you knew sources who died before I was born."

"Destroy old books, and you sever ties to the past." The moment I said it, something fragile cracked between us – shared knowledge too dangerous to name aloud.

And? His gesture urged more.

"At least half the population will die. At least." The words escaped like breath through clenched teeth. It wasn't entirely true. Ten million years ago, when the Saurian Faction tried to create their own Field on a planet like ours, *everyone* died – twenty billion souls. I wrapped myself in that half-truth like a cloak.

Vipri paled. His gaze fell inward, jaw tight, the color drained from his face. A human reaction, not a Cupola-trained mask. Unexpected. Raw.

"You didn't ask Diego to take over your face," I said quietly. It was rare to see him this exposed – unguarded.

"Lesson learned from you," he muttered, bitterly. And just like that, I knew – he had RigFace too. Legal.

Before I could think further, Diegia's voice cut in: *"The simulation has gone off-script."* A beat. *"Not that I am complaining, but you will."*

Without warning, the world changed. I was no longer outside the simulation. I was *in* it. Clothes half-undone, breath shallow, skin suddenly aware of itself. Mouth muffled. Back arching. His fingertips brushed against the small of my back – not urgent, not forceful, but searching. Familiar.

Simulation was a misnomer. In a reverse mechanism, With DuaLink, our DigitalEgos puppeteered our bodies while our minds stood in contact, behind the scene. So, it was a simulation in as much as our minds were not part of it, but it happened to our real body. Every sensation was now real. Old fragments of life returned. The feel of being in a man's arms. I pulled back. Not sharply. Not fully. Just enough to remind myself this wasn't *me*. Not now. He didn't speak. The scene reset, managed by our DigitalEgos, like a stage between acts. For a while, I tried balancing the split – the mind and the body – but, even tamed, the warmth was insistent. And finally, I let go.

"Why are you so sure about the death toll?" Vipri asked eventually, his voice quieter now. Something had softened in him. Or shifted.

"They are not testing this on themselves. We are the lab rats."

"Indirect logic. Not enough." He shook his head. "We are being used. But that doesn't explain the scale."

"This isn't their first attempt. Another Faction tried it long ago."

"How long?" His frown held more than suspicion now. It held need – need for truth, or maybe for belief.

"Long." No way to explain ten million years without exposing my source. "They lost twenty billion people. And they were more advanced than the Celestials." Silence.

A chime broke the quiet. "Prim is summoning me." He straightened, back into official posture. "What we discussed stays here. You will get retroactive authorization for your ... enhancements. And I would like a copy of your containment software. It's better than mine."

Caught again. My illegal tech, laid bare.

"We can give him an old version with deleted Origin," Diegia whispered. *"I will make it look pirated."*

"Diego took you over."

"It wasn't unpleasant. I recorded everything for you. It was your body, after all." She winked, her tail flicking, casual, but not unkind. A thumbs-up followed. The authorization shimmered in my vision.

"Was it just for the authorization?" I couldn't stop the question, but Diegia stuck out her tongue, her usual evasion.

As the simulation transitioned back to normal, and the world returned, reality felt altered. Warmer. Closer. The sea crashed below, white froth against jagged rock. It took longer than it should have to notice that his hand still held mine. I tried to pull away. His grip tightened. Not possessive, resistant. Diegia locked my hand before I could free it.

We boarded the FlyCar in silence. Again, I took the rear seat, but he sat beside me and let go of my hand.

This time, I had no eyes to watch the coastline.

"Ask Cassia to disconnect the house," Diegia said the moment the door clicked shut. Her voice carved through the quiet like a blade. It was the first thing she said since *the hand*. The silence before it had been thick – charged. Now it dispersed, leaving something colder in its place.

I felt strange. As if every emotion in me had been ... halved. Blunted. The weight of something not fully mine pressed down, damping instinct. Dulling outrage.

Half-anger at her – my rogue Diegia never overrode me without a reason. But I wasn't ready to face that reason yet.

Half-upset at myself. Not for losing control. For not wanting it back.

And something else. Sticky. Slow. Hard to name.

I nodded toward Cassia, the motion sluggish. The Net disconnected with a dim pulse of light. Cassia materialized a moment later, serene and too composed in her white dress. At the table, she folded into a posture that belonged more to ritual than conversation. Diegia, borrowing Vipri's mouth and hands for her hologram, leaned forward – subtle mockery, sharpened into elegance. I said nothing. From the outside, it might have looked like three women sipping wine, chatting.

"His DuaLink has Aurora Origin: DL32, seven years old," Diegia said and paused, letting this sink into us.

I didn't speak. Couldn't. The air shifted. "Aurora..." My jaw tightened around the word. Surprise felt like a shadow of what I truly felt. "A Jewel with Resistance software?" It felt like blasphemy. "We don't even have that."

"Limited storage," Diegia offered, unconvincingly. "And simulations aren't your ... preferred activity. DuaLink even less."

Really?

"There is a Jewel signature buried in his DuaLink." Her tone darkened, quiet and sharp. "They ran security on it. Approved it for Family use. But somehow, they missed the *Aurora Origin*." She let the silence stretch. "If the Jewels are caught with Resistance tech..." She didn't finish the sentence. She didn't need to. "I gave him C12 containment software," she added, "with the Origin wiped. Five years old. We have C14. Enough to survive the next simulation."

"There won't *be* another simulation." The words snapped. "How did they get DuaLink? Black market? A captured rebel?" My voice rose, harsh. "I need to reach Batranu. This – *and* the Field..."

"Vipri is a valuable source," Cassia said, smoothly enough to sound rehearsed.

"You talked behind my back," I complained, but neither of them flinched. "Thank you, Cassia," I said eventually, through clenched teeth. "You are right. We may need DuaLink again."

Simulations would haunt me now. Not just for what they were, but for how easily I had stepped into them. And stayed.

"Our plans..." I exhaled, grounding myself in numbers, not feelings. "Three months. *Maybe.* Best case scenario, we reach revolution threshold on the Happiness Index in two years. What can we possibly do in three months?"

Diegia leaned in, voice low. "A romantic liaison wouldn't hurt."

It felt like a slap. Not because it was absurd. Because it *wasn't.* "My last lover died in the Rebellion," I said. The words came out hollow and cold. "He became a rebel because of me. He died because of me." The image came back too fast – his silent reassurance that everything would be fine, as he faded in my arms. "He was thirty-seven. Not centuries old, like me." I didn't care that I sounded old. I *was* old. "I swore no more entanglements. Not until the world is free, or the Resistance collapses. Either way, no one else dies because they touched me." The silence after was heavy. Uninterrupted. Still, I spoke again. "Vipri is the closest thing to a normal man I met in twenty years." My voice dropped. "And yet..." I didn't finish. I didn't have to. Whether he was sincere or setting a trap – it didn't matter. Either way, the danger had already breached the walls.

"Too dangerous," I murmured.

Diegia didn't answer. She didn't need to. Her silence said everything.

Alenia

The Resistance had reached out to me only twice in twenty years. I never initiated contact – not since the Rebellion – but sometimes, gods, I needed them. Not for missions or secrets. Just to sit across from someone *normal* who didn't calculate every word as if it was deception or a weapon.

After the Travelers severed us from the Field and stamped each citizen with a Unique ID, communication became a death spiral: no unregistered emails, no unapproved encryption. Send an illicit key? Ten years in the black-site gulags, no trial. Receive one? Five minutes to report it – or join the sender. Security often played the sender themselves, dangling bait to keep us vigilant. So I resorted to the archaic system we had agreed upon: three umbrellas, arranged in an equilateral triangle in my garden. Red. Yellow. Blue. A child's geometry lesson screaming: *I need to talk*. To justify their presence, I kept my garden absurdly outfitted – a privilege of rank, a performance of eccentricity.

I was a lone wolf by necessity. The office psychopaths reveled in their petty cruelties, and normal citizens recoiled from my ranking, convinced I was just another monster. Even before the DigitalEgos and Unique IDs, they had forgotten what *normal* meant.

The Resistance's crawlers scouted targets by hijacking SkEye – the same geostationary surveillance net the government used to strip us bare. With my clearance, I could admire the emerald glint of my own eyes seen from space. For ordinary searches, they have the standard authorization. Their hacks were rudimentary but enough to spot my umbrellas amidst the satellites' data. My home was watched by countless eyes now: Resistance, Government, and – thanks to my newfound popularity – the ravenous algorithms of the social index, and the even more ravenous voyeurists.

There was a time when we swam naked in the lakes, let the sun warm bare skin without shame. *Natural* wasn't a dirty word then. But first, they forced us into austere uniforms, then flooded the world with hyper-sexualized simulacra. *Free your sexuality,* they crooned, while parading half-naked people on every channel, turning intimacy into another controlled transaction. A life spent in simulations. The only upside? LoveDroids had vanished from the streets. Even machines couldn't compete with AI's engineered fantasies.

Three hours later, the proof of receipt arrived: an unregistered email littered with an explicit bed invitation. *They already know about the simulations. Well...* I shrugged unhappily, but they were following the main trend without raising suspicions; I had received many similar messages, after my rise in *fame*. The invitation featured umbrellas vaguely resembling mine. Between the pixels, an algorithm would extract coordinates and a name:

Batranu. No. 1.

Not *my* Batranu. Not the old teacher who had laughed with me in a real life three centuries ago. Just another heir to a ghost.

I forwarded the email to Security within the mandated five minutes, a dutiful citizen. They would never trace it.

Alenia

The albatross hung suspended between sea and sky, wings outstretched in perfect stillness – it felt like magic. I envied that effortless balance, that surrender to forces greater than itself. My own body felt like a puppet, every movement calculated for unseen audiences.

"Did they enjoy our simulation?" I kept my tone light, swirling the wine in my glass. We talked about books for more than an hour, and I couldn't remember the last time I had done the same with someone other than Diegia or Cassia. The afternoon sun gilded the cliff's edge, the invisible eyes of the satellites feasting on our performance. We could have eaten inside. But the show must go on – for him, for me, for whoever was watching.

Vipri's gaze lingered on my mouth a heartbeat too long. "My popularity is growing. Not as fast as I had hoped."

"A rise isn't a fall," I murmured, wondering when we had started measuring our lives in increments of approval ratings and carefully staged encounters. I shrugged, watching the albatross drawing arcs in the wind. Its wings barely moved – just held, effortless. Unlike us.

"No one who matters in the Families gives a damn about Popularity Indexes," he said. His voice was casual, but the words were worse than heresy. The freedom with which he spoke caught me off guard.

The albatross banked closer, white feathers catching the light. I snapped a photo, testing my autonomy inside his simulation. It worked; it did not work when I tried on Vipri. "They reflect our society well," I said. My voice sounded distant, even to myself. "Too well."

"The GenEn experiment," he said, abruptly.

I closed my eyes briefly, inhaling the salt air and the faint musk of his cologne. *When had I last stood close enough to someone to learn their scent?* The memory, if it existed, was buried too deep to find. "Classified. Above my clearance." *Lie.* I had hacked those files years ago.

"Your interpretation of clearance is ... flexible."

"Is it necessary?" My thumb traced the rim of my glass. *Control. Keep control.*

"That you are locked out of some files? No." He leaned closer.

"Vipri, what do you really want? A confession? I have already had enough pleasant time with the Traveler's neuranalyzer. It increased my popularity so much, and brought a Lesser like me to Histria." The albatross screamed overhead. *Fly. Just fly away.*

"Sometimes, I wish I could fly." I gestured toward the bird, trying to throw off the cold tension gathering around the table.

"Why not? Everybody dreams impossible things." He smiled and placed his hand over mine. Our eyes met. "Seventy years ago, we tweaked our genes. Boosted IQs faster than the general population was evolving. Bought prizes, buried dissent. Slowly, we took over almost all the management and research positions. We looked smart, and we pushed the media to say it: *They are so few, yet they made all the important discoveries... They deserve to rule us...* Marketing. You know the story. Then..." He sighed. "We played god until DigiLink broke us."

He fell silent, his thumb tracing idle circles on my wrist. I pondered an answer to the question hidden in his words. It was a new game – vague, ruleless, played outside hierarchy and politics. Dangerous. And thrilling. One I couldn't refuse.

I let the silence stretch, feeling the warmth of his hand, watching the albatross. "Popularity Indexes replaced reality," I said at last. "DigiLink corrupted the mind. Books were burned. NetPedia gutted knowledge. Everything became standardized by thousands of paid trolls posing as real users. SoulBook sterilized dissent. Simulations replaced life. And IQs shrank – genetically enhanced or not. You bred *geniuses* who can't think." Our new generations lacked even the basic intellectual skills to imagine something new. Math solves known problems; philosophy creates new ones. The mind needs liberty to dream. "Ten million people on Aurora are more creative than several billion here."

He nodded, his hand moving in restless arcs, as if physically torn between opposing truths. "DigitalEgo replaced DigiLink and accelerated their regression," he said, finally. "The gap between pre- and post-DigiLink generations is biggest in the Families. They were the first to adopt it – the new tech had been awfully expensive when it appeared. All that hierarchy, all that Family infighting ... made the decline obvious." His fingers hovered over my wrist like a man hesitating before a chess move.

I watched the horizon swallow another wave. "I suppose you started another experiment," I said, carefully.

"One that has no name." He shrugged, too casually. "Just a number in some secret files. I was among the first test subjects, though I had no idea." His voice softened. "I didn't grow up in the Family. I was raised on a remote island. Sky, ocean. No DigiLink. No surveillance. A happy life. Freedom. Even joined the Rebellion during my studies." A pause. His fingers stilled and released my hand. "That's why I am eleventh in the Jewel hierarchy now."

A rebel. The revelation echoed through hollow memory. I had known few rebels from that era, but the Resistance should have known this. My wine glass trembled slightly in my grip. Vipri didn't look at me, his gaze fixed on the horizon. Too deliberate. Most probably he was analyzing me, recording micro-expressions his DigitalEgo would study later.

"Family-raised children?" He chuckled, bitter. "Gorgeous empty shells. My rebel name was Elpio." Finally, he turned, eyes glinting with something between amusement and challenge. "I had face surgery when the Family retrieved me, to hide my past. Still unsure which version of me was better. Perhaps you can judge."

A hologram flickered between us, in the simulation: a young rebel commander – him – standing in a dim war room. And beside him – me. The world narrowed to that image. For a breathless moment, I clung to the childish hope: *This is a simulation. A bad dream.* But the salt sting in my eyes was too real.

"After you joined us – very few know you were a rebel, and all of them are Jewels – and saved the capital, the files labeled you an opportunistic careerist. I chose you as my secretary anyway. Never regretted it. Though *opportunist* never quite fit the woman I have come to know."

They know. And yet I breathe. The paradox choked me. I reached for Diegia – nothing. His DuaLink had sealed me off. No way to take an inner picture. Panic surged, but I forced myself to study the hologram, committing his younger face to memory. Then silence.

We watched the albatross disappear into the glare of the setting sun, its freedom as much an illusion as ours. The wine in my glass had gone warm and flat, like all the words left unspoken between us.

"May I?" His hand extended toward mine. "It will improve my rating," he smiled.

I shrugged. When his fingers closed over mine, they were warm, and we walked to the FlyCar in silence.

The mirror at home reflected a disturbed version of my face, marbled with shadows. Mortified eyes stared back, mirroring the emptiness within. By a cruel twist of fate, at that exact moment, a message from Vipri arrived: *The rebel was wounded. A serious wound. It's only a matter of time until we catch him.* With a cry that could not ease my pain, I struck the mirror.

I had to stop this. I could have asked Diegia to numb my mind – it was so easy now to freeze neural synapses with a simple electric signal, no drugs or alcohol required – but I still needed my wits before sleep. The news was five days old. He could be dead. He could already be a prisoner, and I would only know when they came for me. Why had Vipri sent me that message? Why had it been hidden until now?

In the living room, Cassia projected a hologram of a fiery red dawn. I settled on the sofa, staring at the rising sun. "Thank you, Cassia. Disconnect the house." She materialized alongside Diegia, one dressed in white, the other in red, as they always did in hard times. "Diegia, see what you can extract from my mind. Vipri's image," I said, though I was certain they already knew my thoughts. Social interaction, artificial or not, soothed a wounded mind, and in many ways, their companionship surpassed anything other humans could offer. Diegia and Cassia meant everything to me.

"The resolution isn't great," Diegia sighed, mimicking my mannerism: pressing her lips before exhaling and frowning. The resemblance drew a faint smile from me.

"You did that on purpose." This time, I managed a full smile. She deserved some small encouragement. Her pride was wounded even more than mine; she was in charge of our security. First, it was the NetNode, now this. Fortunately, the NetNode was an external device, nineteen years old, installed just weeks before I moved into the house. It was only *my node* because the box was on my property. Of course, there were surveillance tools aimed at me, the new High Councilor, but our connection switch sat between the NetNode and my NoWifi. We had been lucky.

"It's good enough for image recognition," I said, struck by sudden intuition. "Do you have anything on his former identity?" Diegia shook her head. "No matter. The Resistance must have the data. Prepare a standard message for tomorrow. We need to inform our allies that I am compromised."

Before bed, I took a small decorative bead from one of my necklaces and stared at it, my mind blank. *I've lived long enough...* Slowly, I pressed the red bead to my carotid artery. Its needle pierced my skin without pain, settling on my neck like a small mole. The room suddenly felt colder, and I shivered, though I didn't know why.

"Diegia, make the connection with it."

"Connection established," she replied, her voice tinged with a sadness I hadn't heard before. I understood her. If the Government captured me, she would die with me. She was, in a way, an extension of me, a second me. In the mirror, the red bead looked like a natural part of my body, but it was a weapon laced with neurotoxin. One signal from Diegia, and everything would end. *I've lived long enough...*

In the morning, I arranged the delivery of twenty large pots filled with red and white bushes, and spent hours arranging them on the terrace, forming a ten-feet circle with an intricate pattern that encrypted a message. It left me in a better emotional state. Any Resistance drone or hacked satellite would see the bitter truth: *I am compromised.*

"Diegia, send our drone for a final check." The image we received was clear enough to verify the crude encryption.

In the evening, I visited my favorite park, a short walk from my home – one of the perks of living in Cupola district, outside the Wall. It was the weekend. Sometimes luck favors you; the last thing I needed was to be in the office. *The last thing I needed was yesterday...* I shook my head. *Be natural.* Diegia pulled details from the Net about my favorite flowers blooming in the park, and I visited them one by one, moving without a predictable pattern. She kept my mind from dwelling on the day before. After a few hours, I went to collect resin from a large tree in a secluded area. Its trunk glistened with translucent reddish-yellow globules, glowing in the filtered light. The trick was to find ones not fully solidified; they would fill the house with a subtle scent for days, a rarity in a society obsessed with technology and artificial perfumes. *So natural...* My fingers tested their consistency. *Good... Not good...* When my small glass vial was full, I caressed an almost-liquid globule I had already tested and slipped a tiny needle into it.

Drawn by the needle's artificial pheromones, a modified insect would retrieve the data. Six hours later, the resin would corrode the electronic component, leaving a useless piece of metal. The data was brief: Vipri's rebel name, his code name in our files, and that he had a photo of me in one of our war rooms. *What other photos does he have?* It was up to the Resistance to analyze and uncover any other compromised networks. A disaster.

The full irony of my visit to the Resistance headquarters hit me. A sleeper cell like me is left alone. I had only been there once, when they asked me to secure a position in one of the government brigades defending the capital. After my first full rejuvenation, I spent ten years in the army, serving in both combat and technical roles to forge connections in strategic positions. Centuries ago, during my first life, I had led armies alongside my husband, Deceneus, so my new training focused on mastering modern large-scale warfare and technology – neural combat interfaces, virtual maps, drone swarms, and AI targeting systems – though, curiously, many concepts remained strikingly similar. During my second life, in the ShadowMind Order, I had only fought in covert hit and run operations.

My reputation was modest but known. Back then, when the Rebellion had started, the Jewels were leading the government. The actual Prim, a Ruby, was Vipri and the capital's commander-in-chief. It was an unwritten rule, Vipri always belonged to the *opposition*. When many brigade commanders fled their posts, he was quick to appoint me as a temporary commander. But he never forgot: I *saved* the northern part of the city, not him. The operation was coordinated, through secret channels, with the rebel brigades retreating from the capital in an organized withdrawal I couldn't comprehend. The rebels were winning – then, inexplicably, they chose to retreat. No one in the Resistance explained me why. Perhaps the knowledge was too dangerous if I were captured. That *success* earned me my current position of High Councilor, the highest a Lesser could achieve. Vipri's influence helped too. *But it's the wrong position; I never wanted it. The highest I can achieve now...*

The next morning, a new unregistered email confirmed my meeting with the Resistance. This time, a hologram displayed my naked body encased in a yellow amber globule, like a prehistoric insect trapped in time. At least the sender had imagination – I appreciated the representation; it was delicate and sensual, not cheap erotica. A set of random pixels encoded the same date and time: this afternoon. My twentieth vigilance message to Security in just a few days, I sighed, sending it to them.

At first glance, such an archaic visual communication system seems simple, but it offers limited options. There are only a small number of pre-arranged codes, and they must change periodically. Updating them is difficult when you lack secure communication channels.

I stopped my car at a familiar spot outside the city, near a small waterfall hidden in the forest. My internal GPS guided me along a path, past the falls, deeper into the woods where SkEye's surveillance couldn't reach. Young couples snapped photos, and children played in the water – an idyllic scene that clashed sharply with my thoughts. At the designated spot, my GPS flashed red. I wandered as if searching for flowers, subtly verifying the area. Protocol dictated that I arrive first; the Resistance would appear only after confirming my presence and receiving my safe signal. Two minutes later, another *tourist* – a young, unfamiliar man – joined me in admiring a three-hundred-year-old tree with a trunk wide enough to conceal a car. *Still younger than me...* I glanced at the tree.

"I have confirmation," Diegia said after exchanging covert protocols with his Diego. *"Batranu's digital code. He requested a DuaLink connection."* The tree flickered for half a second as the image overlay stabilized. *"You know, this young man resembles the old Batranu."* She projected a simulation of the man before me as he might appear in his seventies, without rejuvenation.

"It can't be him." I dismissed the hologram, wary of old memories resurfacing. *I have business to finish. I can reminisce – and mourn – later.*

"Don't run from your past," Diegia pressed. Another hologram appeared, displaying my neural patterns spiking when I saw him.

"Of course I am nervous. I don't need a hologram to tell me that." The hologram zoomed in on the first second. *That's joy... "Why joy?"* I asked, reluctantly. Diegia pointed to the hologram of the old man before vanishing, her simulation shielding my real conversation.

I turned back to the man. "I am..."

"I know who you are." He gave a smile that stirred something deep within me, like a gentle wind rustling ancient leaves in the forest. "And you know me, too. Glad to meet you again, Queen Altamira."

Diegia was right... I longed to embrace Batranu, but a DuaLink connection allowed no physical contact, and in the real world – where our bodies were coordinated by the DigitalEgos – we couldn't risk a sudden display of emotion between strangers meeting by chance in a forest. So I smiled – a smile I hadn't felt in years.

"You make me feel young and free again," I whispered.

"I could say the same. Almost." Batranu's tone was half-joking. "I was already a hundred and sixty when I arrived from Earth. You were just seventeen. A day will come when we can talk as we did in the old times, but for now..." He grew serious. "It must be something critical if you have activated the protocol. First, I want to thank you for your help and apologize for how we responded." He didn't need to elaborate.

"Is the young rebel safe?" I asked, hoping the Resistance was tracking him.

"We don't know. He left the city but didn't reach the designated rendezvous. SkEye is offline at night, and infiltrating

Security's search was too risky. Somehow, he vanished that night."

"Or he was caught. I am locked out of his file. Probably the Rubys – Shine wasn't happy with the search."

"Drones are still patrolling the area in droves. They are not there for nothing," Batranu offered, a faint crumb of hope, ignoring my jab at Shine.

"I have a problem with him."

"He is well-trained. In the worst case, he will erase his memory."

The worst case is death... "It's not that. I feel a strange bond with him, though we have never met before he came from Aurora."

"You are a trained ShadowMind, with enhanced abilities to access the Field, even if you are not a Field Dreamer. Some of those abilities linger; they only erased the most obvious genetic markers before your return. The Travelers' tech can sever conscious access, but nothing can fully disconnect a human from the Field – it's the mind of the Universe, after all. If you met him in a normal setting, without tech blockers, you would both sense the truth. Your unconscious connection to the Field is stirring feelings. He is your descendant, many generations removed, with some ... interesting traits. Don't ask me what traits – Armin didn't say. Time was short when we last spoke."

My descendant... How many generations had passed in more than three hundred years? This could explain my strange feelings, but I would have to wait for answers, and that gnawed at me. His Field signature might match someone I once knew, someone close. *Armin knows. The last time I saw Armin... Fifty years ago?*

"In three months, the Travelers will initiate the New Field," I finally delivered the grim.

"Interesting," Batranu replied slowly, his tone betraying skepticism about the source.

"It came from Vipri," I sighed, and recounted the entire story.

"Vipri may become a threat to neutralize before we act."

He is too high in the hierarchy to eliminate, and... "The information is too widely spread within the Jewel Family to contain," I said, trying to dissuade Batranu from plotting his removal.

"True, but if he gets too close to us – to you – we may need a respite or a diversion. We have only three months."

"Please inform me if such a decision is made." *I hope you don't see all my motives...* "I am too close to his circle, and that..." *I am too close to him.* In a strange way, I trusted Vipri, at least partially.

"We will." Batranu's voice softened. "I have a report on Vipri from when he was with the Resistance." In the artificial world of DuaLink, he pushed a hologram toward me – text exchanges were too risky for sensitive data. "Study it and retain only what you need to operate freely. He was well-liked as a commander. Respected. Strategic. Charismatic. It aligns with your observations." He spoke without meeting my gaze, as if captivated by the false landscape. When DuaLink was strained by large data transfers, the virtual world grew schematic, vaguely mimicking the real forest. There was little to hold his attention in the sketchy scenery. As the image vanished, the virtual landscape sharpened, nearly lifelike again.

You are too old a fox to be fooled about Vipri. Maybe it's better that you know.

"Unfortunately, the person who recruited him died long ago." Batranu omitted any connection, either a deliberate omission or a subtle game to let Vipri surprise me again. The unspoken rule was clear: no sensitive questions. "Most of the rebels Vipri knew went to Aurora, but some remain. Of all our networks his knowledge could have compromised, only one was dismantled, and it wasn't because of him."

"I have no clear idea about the actual Resistance. State propaganda made a spectacle of it, but it must be small, especially after the Purge."

"Do you know what a sleeper cell is?" Batranu asked, his voice warm.

I am a bloody sleeper cell. I slept for over a hundred years – the oldest sleeper ever. A sudden thought struck me: *Did I unknowingly expose one of our other sleepers?* I treaded carefully. "Did my actions interfere with your network?"

"Of course," he said, calmly.

I drew on centuries of training to suppress a visceral reaction. *Am I an unwitting traitor?*

"It was designed that way from the start. You needed freedom to climb the hierarchy and stay there."

"I never asked for that freedom. Do you understand what it feels to send people to prison for thinking like you? I deserve to be locked up as much as those I have condemned. Every time I tried to resign, you stopped me – your organization, here and beyond." My finger jabbed from the ground toward the sky. "What difference can a few sleepers make?"

"A significant one. Each of us has a role. The Lines of Time are slowly forming. You know the powers we face, and the Lines must be nudged carefully – a little here, a little there – by the Erins."

"Your *little* nudges should have been a decisive strike when the Rebellion began. We could have seized the planet then."

"Do you know what happened to the captured sleepers?" Batranu interrupted my outburst.

In that moment, I fully realized the man before me was truly Batranu – meaning *old man* in Romanian, a language from a distant planet. A man with a young heart, tied to a past nearly erased from history. *I will never forget. Me and ... how many others? A thousand? Two thousand?* It was his tone, his bitter smile, the way he gestured to emphasize his words, the slight tilt of his head to the left. *You are Batranu.* I was already logically convinced, but now the deepest part of me accepted it. Tears streamed down my virtual face. Knowing Diegia would mask any reactions in my real body, I let them flow.

"I'm sorry," I mumbled, futilely trying to wipe my face; my virtual hand passed through my head.

"Those you found were already traitors, and we fed you their information through hidden channels. You also saved three valuable Resistance members."

True, but... "I don't want to talk about this." *Why can't you understand?* "I was alone. Over a hundred years drifting like a solitary zombie through this world – my world, my former world. I couldn't even connect with the university students. Only him... Decades ago." I pressed my teeth hard in my lower lip. Pain returned, but only the pain; he would never come back. "Seeing you brought my life back, my real life – Altamira's life. Alenia... I am Alenia, but she is just a mask. In the deepest recesses of my mind, I have always been Altamira. And now... I am not sure I can keep playing this role. You need to account for that. I am a liability now." I paused, trying to calm myself, my eyes scanning the forest – a beauty that couldn't soothe me.

"You aren't the only one from that time," Batranu said, sidestepping a direct response. I wasn't sure I wanted one. "Somewhere, there is an ancient man named Talian. He wears a mask, like you, like Naldire or Scorylo..."

I knew them well. "You shouldn't tell me this. I will ask Diegia to wipe my memory."

"No. We are entering a new phase. You need to see the bigger picture now. The network is nearly complete, and the sleepers are being linked to it one by one. You are the first."

Why me?

"But back to my question: do you know what happens to a captured sleeper?"

How would I know? I shrugged.

"The Travelers use Saurian Time Mines."

"You can't know that. If they use SAT-mines, the targets' existence is erased – they were never born. Even their signature in the Field is obliterated. Nothing remains."

"We know because the Travelers wanted us to know. I know it sounds strange." He silenced my unasked question with a look.

You can't know...

"Their new variant of those damned mines has timelines. They erase a victim's life and their Field presence from a specific point onward. The first sleepers they caught were partially erased by SAT-mines, ten years of their existence. Maug and Delena..." His voice trembled for the first time. "They arrived here and vanished seconds later at a remote train station – you know the process. Later targets lost thirty years. We got the message, but most cells were already in place."

They were my friends once – Maug, my Chief of the Army; Delena, the Munti Queen. I summoned the strength not to ask about the other cells. My virtual tears had dried, leaving only streaks of virtual mascara to mark them. My avatar mirrored my inner turmoil perfectly.

"So we know..."

"At least they weren't erased entirely," I sighed.

"Their partial erasure caused a massive disturbance in the Field, and it affected their minds badly, but the Erins helped them recover. Don't ask me how it works technically – I don't know – but Deceneus told me..."

"Is he alive too?" I breathed. My mind wandered centuries in the past. The day we met. The day we married. Our first child. The day he died of old age. Or so I thought. The way I *died* too.

"I mean the Observer. But don't rule out seeing your former husband again. He followed the same path like you and me – the ShadowMind Order gave him a new life. The body in his grave is a flesh copy. We couldn't tell you. The body in your grave is a copy – you know that. I have no grave. He has his own path. As we have too. We met here again by chance. Ours is a large galaxy." Batranu offered a glimmer of hope about my husband from three centuries ago, when we were queen and king. "The SAT-mines stopped us from winning the Rebellion. The Travelers threatened to use them on rebel cities, uncaring that not everyone was a rebel. Fifty million people could have vanished in direct hits. Factor indirect links – erase a grandfather with a SAT-mine, and his entire line disappears, wherever they are. Two hundred million, conservatively. That's why we accepted defeat, even when we nearly won on the ground with most people behind us." Batranu's voice grew quieter, carrying a sadness that seeped into me, becoming my own. "Knowledge can't be erased from the Field. The SAT-mines will always exist, somewhere. Thousands of Erins and Observers have tuned the Lines of Time on our side. The Travelers have just as many Observers."

"Observers?"

"We live *interesting* times. The Observers are now divided; a New Field is emerging. This planet is their laboratory, and the DigitalEgo isn't just for communication or entertainment – it's the interface for their nascent Field."

"If they're recording us..."

"Your Diegia is more sophisticated than either of you realize. She unconsciously filters everything, ensuring only sterile data reaches their Field – nothing important of the real you. The Travelers' Field technology is still developing; it has many flaws. And this time, we have SAT-mines too." He traced a finger over his virtual lips. "Keep this or erase it from your mind."

"For twenty years, I worked to lower the Happiness Index, hoping to inspire the people to rise again..." I felt powerless; there wasn't enough time for a new rebellion. "We have to destroy their Field."

"The Field can't be destroyed. Once initiated, it persists forever. The Saurians' test failed, and they weren't permitted a second attempt. But we can target the button."

"What do you mean?"

"Something is troubling the Travelers – we don't know what." Batranu avoided my gaze, and I didn't press further; I already knew too much. "They calculate their own Lines of Time. Something has forced them to accelerate their plans. Armin couldn't send more data, but he must know something critical to risk an unprepared message. We lost three people during that transmission." His voice shifted, revealing a sadness that I knew.

A low beep pierced the sudden silence. "Time is up, Altamira." Batranu hesitated before closing the DuaLink. His arms opened wide in a virtual embrace, and I mirrored the gesture. "Don't cry again," he said with a smile.

I won't. I lifted my eyes to meet his. Three inches taller than my old self – I was quite petite back then – and the top of my head barely reached his chin.

"Do you remember when the Travelers launched their first mass subversion on our planet, trying to hypnotize us and a hundred others in that remote valley? We shuffled from foot to foot like fat ducks, turning left or right at a sluggish pace, their pulse-wave overtaking our minds. Only you, Deceneus, and I escaped."

"The Duck Dance?" I asked.

"Yes, a deceptively simple name for something so sinister. That's when I realized what a fighter you are. We are counting on you, Altamira."

I know. I virtually hugged him again before the connection would go. My hands passed through his body, and I shivered from a sensation that shouldn't have existed.

I spent many nights grappling with the immense burden Batranu had placed on me. Ultimately, I chose to keep the knowledge, using it to align myself with the accelerated pace of this new reality – one that demanded greater risks.

Chapter 8

The Ruby man was so drunk he couldn't get out of his car to reach the stadium. Shifting through the low light, I pulled him out, before he could take his SChip, stuck in the slot, to command the car. He stiffed until he realized I wasn't a robber.

"You need help," I said, glancing around – a long row of expensive cars lined the street, where few were allowed to park, especially in such crowded areas. There were no people in sight. I pulled him gently toward the wall of the building. He grabbed a metallic ornament like a drowning man, struggling to stand. "You're late, but the show just started," I whispered, nudging his mind in the right direction. "Walk along the wall. The stadium is close. You will make it," I encouraged. "The atmosphere is great. It would be a pity to miss it."

"I..." he mumbled.

"I will help you. That way." I gave him another gently push. He forgot about the SChip in the car and shuffled forward, clinging to the metallic ornaments protruding from the wall, foot by foot. "You are doing great. Keep going." It took a while before he turned the corner. *Thank you for your car.* When I closed the door, the stale stench of vomit hit me from the floor.

"Diego, connect to his Schip and start the engine. And open the windows."

Even before the stench cleared, I was driving something I could never afford. My grin reflected in the mirror. It felt good. Diego marked the path out of the city on my inner map, and within half an hour, I was in the suburbs. Everything went smoothly until the police stopped me at the main northern exit.

The police captain saluted with the necessary deference to question a Ruby of my rank – Apprentice Councilor. I recalled that Alenia was High Councilor. A hologram with my real face was displayed in front of me, and the captain asked, “Did you see this guy?”

I stared at him with a distracted air, scratched my bald head, and shook it, my face bored, signaling I was in a hurry. My authorization was high enough for such mild impertinence. I sensed the fury boiling in him, but the system worked in my favor. Leisurely, I nodded toward the barrier. It rose, and I accelerated slowly. His eyes, still angry, watched the car greedily. *You will never have one... Neither will I.*

“Contact the police if you see him,” he mumbled. I waved a lazy acknowledgment.

“Go!” Diego shouted. *“Your authorization has been blocked.”*

The car sped-up toward a curve a half mile ahead. The chair adjusted automatically to compensate for the acceleration – a perk of driving an expensive, intelligent car. *If I get past it, I am free,* I stared at the incoming curve. A shot melted a two-inch hole in the rear window, then a second appeared. My heart pounded, and I gasped, flooring the pedal, hoping to clear the curve before being killed. A third shot tore through the seat, hitting my right shoulder, burning flesh and bones, numbing half my body. Diego took over, blocking pain receptors in my brain; I could have cut a finger and smiled. Well, not exactly.

A five-mile stretch of darkness swallowed the road ahead, arrow-straight for two miles before the next bend. The police sirens wailed behind me, but their sound grew distant as I pushed deeper into the long tunnel.

Time to vanish. I rolled to a stop, abandoning the car in the tunnel, after the second curve. My body screamed in protest – Diego's pain control kept me moving, but my muscles trembled, my lungs burning as I fought for steady breaths. *Move. Now.* I staggered behind the low concrete barrier, pressing flat as the car's AI took over, reprogrammed by Diego. The engine roared back to life, accelerating faster than any human could, taillights bleeding red in the dark.

A minute later, wo cruisers blasted past, chasing my ghost – a car with a full battery, programmed to outrun them, to toy with them. It would pause after every curve, lights flickering mockingly before surging ahead again, leading them deeper into the mountains. *Good luck guessing where I jumped out of it*, I smirked, until a fresh wave of dizziness nearly blacked me out.

"Our blood pressure is dropping," Diego hissed in my skull, his voice fraying at the edges. A holographic projection flashed in my vision, highlighting the backpack on my digital double.

I fumbled for Batranu's MedKit, hands shaking. The tunnel's dim lights barely cut through the gloom, but I didn't need to see to know the damage. LasGuns make neat holes – no blood spray, no shattered bone. There was a half-inch-wide tunnel straight through my shoulder blade. A kinetic military bullet would have shattered the joint to pulp.

I slapped the MedKit against the exit wound on my chest. The organic glue fused with my flesh, injecting plasma, stem cells, and a cocktail of repair nanites into my system. The entry wound on my back would have to wait – no way to reach it while flat on the ground.

A minute passed. The world sharpened again as the plasma filled my veins. Not healed – not even close – but I could think, and right now, that was enough. My fingers brushed the MedKit's edge, the border between synth-flesh and my own skin blurring. My suicide mole was gone. The exit wound had torn it free. A stroke of luck, or misfortune? Hard to say. I could be dead right now, but this way, they might take me alive.

I forced myself up, scanning the tunnel walls. Service doors every few hundred yards, but using my last authorization to access them would compromise it.

First door: locked. Second door: locked. Third door… The latch gave with a groan, revealing a cramped maintenance room. Dirty clothes hung on the walls. *Perfect.* But the hooks were too high.

"The toolbox," Diego said.

I pulled down the clothes, then hanged the second MedKit on the hook. My legs wobbled as I climbed onto the rusted metal box, my back screaming as I arched to meet the kit. One wrong move and I would collapse.

"Now!" Diego snapped, and forced my muscles to press against the kit just long enough for the glue to bond. The shock of it blasted the last of my strength away…

I woke with a gasp. Sunlight. Everything green. The air thick with the scent of wet earth. I was outside, hidden under a tangle of branches so dense no drone or infrared scan would spot me. My clothes were soaked – it had rained. My tracks were gone, my heat signatures blurred.

I flexed my fingers. Still weak, but the MedKits had done their job. The wounds were sealed, the nanites working silently beneath my skin to heal me. I could only see the one on my chest through the transparent organic membrane, but the entry wound on my back should be at the same stage. Diego hadn't tried to wake me, so there was no immediate danger. *Not yet*, I shook my head. *First, I needed to move.* Because if I stayed here, they would find me.

And this time, I wouldn't wake up.

Up in the bushes, crows cawed; it was their nesting season, and their warm bodies would confuse the drones' infrared sensors. *Did I consciously choose such a good hiding spot? Any predators here…?*

"Diego, how did I get here?" He highlighted a track on the ground. *I crawled...* I didn't remember anything. My suit was charred around the wound – they used a full LasGun charge. I was lucky to have escaped. What could I say? Bad luck that they shot me, or good luck that they missed my head? *They aimed for my head…* My authorization was blocked just as I passed the last checkpoint – a mobile one, set up hastily after my escape. I had been so sure I would slip through; they didn't have the tools to verify my fake authorization. *Bad luck*, I decided.

In my induced sleep, I dreamt of Lamia, a strange thing, as I rarely dream of real people. She didn't protest when I pulled her long hair from behind. *That never happened…* Even in the dream, I was puzzled that she let me, smiling. Then she kissed me. When I opened my eyes, the *bitch* had taken her place in my arms, and I kissed her too. She felt almost like Lamia. Almost. I knew from the first second she was different. She will always be the *bitch* to me, but the name no longer held malice; I was fond of it. Fond of her. *Alenia must be in danger too…*

My stomach growled, snapping me back to the present. I stretched my healthy left hand to open the backpack. The water and chocolate bars were still there. *"How long?"* I asked Diego, devouring a bar almost without chewing.

"Two days. You are stable. For now."

I grabbed a second bar; the answer only deepened my hunger. *"Show me the map."* Back at the stadium, after we had planned our escape from the city, Diego had downloaded a detailed map of the entire northern area, four hundred miles wide. There was no need for such a large map, but the bigger the area, the greater their confusion. The download would be stored in the Net for ten years, like everything else.

"Where are we?" A small cross marked our position on the map. *Three miles from the tunnel... How did I get here? Later. "The forest."* I pointed to a large green area on the map. I zoomed in, switching from map to the recorded aerial view. *"It starts beyond the bushes."* I prompted Diego to calculate the distance from our position. A hundred yards of crawling. It won't be easy.

Alenia

Your presence is requested. The virtual message came straight from Prim's office, marked Prio ZeroA. No room for delay. Then, a voicemail via the internal system – Vipri's clipped tone: "Take my FlyCar. A Traveler is waiting here."

I barely managed to hold onto my teacup and took a deep breath, trying to stop my hand from trembling. *What's wrong with me?* I set it down before the tremors became obvious, staring at my fingers as if they had betrayed me. In the past, I wouldn't have flinched.

My secretary's face flickered into my inner vision. "A FlyCar is waiting." She projected the usual icon for no further details. Of course not.

"Diegia, code rebel. Be ready to clean the house. Make a zero, for the last five days." The command was clear: delete everything tied to the rebel that might compromise me. Zero-level total erasure for the last five days. Especially Batranu. No time for simulations to fill the gaps. Just surgical amputation. Rain tapped arrhythmic patterns against my office window. Time slowed. It didn't matter. The FlyCar won't care. "How generous," I muttered. *I am so important.*

I took the stairs instead of the elevator, buying seconds with each step. Maybe an accident would intervene. A delay. A miracle. *Did they find something in my last scan? No, I would be in jail already. Vipri? Unlikely. He wouldn't... I hope.*

The rooftop door hissed open. Wind lashed my face, rain playing on my skin. The FlyCar loomed, an elegant black beetle poised to swallow me whole. I stepped in. The ascent was so gentle I didn't realize we were flying until I looked out the window. Below, the city blurred into streaks of light. I closed my eyes.

"Diegia, last-minute adjustment," I said, my inner voice steadier than my hands. *"Initiate level-two deletion for the last five days. Prepare for zero. Just in case. I don't have a very bad feeling. Pray I am right, and we can finish the deletion in time, if there's an emergency."*

As I entered Prim's building, the Traveler – dressed in all black, wearing that ridiculous wide-brimmed hat – was leaving. I bowed before we crossed paths as he glided past in the corridor, his force field humming, pressing myself against the cold wall. It made me shiver even more. *Run, you bastard.*

He slowed. Hesitated. For a heartbeat, I thought he would speak. Then ... nothing. His field flickered, and he vanished around the corner, silent as a ghost. A bead of sweat traced my temple. I took a long breath and entered the office.

"You're late," Prim snapped.

"Barely twenty minutes after your summons." I shifted the blame onto him for being too slow with the request. "If my presence is no longer required..." I edged toward the door, avoiding his gaze.

"Sit." Vipri gestured to an empty chair. Shine was already there, her sharp eyes fixed on me.

Prim spoke like each word cost him blood. "This. Was. Declassified. For your level." A single file materialized before me.

You didn't declassify much. It took me only two minutes to digest the message: His capsule was struck by a *meteorite* after the spaceship's *malfunction*... We all knew the truth. The

Travelers had obliterated the *Celestial Dragon* spaceship to kill one man. “Why is a young rebel worth a spaceship?” I asked.

“We don’t know,” Vipri said.

You don’t know, or you won’t tell. I held his stare. He shrugged – believe what you want. Shine’s gaze flicked between us, as though she had just detected a secret chemistry between me and Vipri. *There is nothing...* Her sudden reaction – both training and feminine intuition and training – sounded a new alarm in my mind. This just got worse. I forced my attention back to the file. “Did they attack Aurora for him?”

“Unauthorized inquiry,” Shine snarled. “You don’t...”

“ZeroC clearance,” Vipri Vipri interrupted, making her remember that I was no longer a ZeroD. “We assess, with high probability, that he was the target.”

Another file. Holograms flared: a car with shattered windshields. LasGun work. A bald man’s face glared up at me. Unknown. He had a second mask. Well-trained.

“I suppose you have finished reading,” Prim said. “We lost him.”

I met his eyes. *Are you playing me?*

“His blood,” Prim said, pointing a finger at the hologram blooming over the table: a dim tunnel floor streaked with dark red spots. “DNA sniffers found traces in this room...” The image shifted to a side door smeared with red fingerprints, then went inside. “...and here. We didn’t find the room until two mornings later.” His jaw twitched. “The bastard programmed his car to stop after every curve, blinding our cameras. Ww wasted hours chasing ghosts.” A nervous shake of his head. In the hologram: Security teams were scrambling through empty roadside stops. “The car finally went over a three-hundred-foot cliff into Lake Karis. No body. Just wreckage. Rain washed the trail clean past the tunnel, and the drones found nothing.”

Well trained. I bit the inside of my cheek. *You searched backward from where the car plunged into the lake, didn't you?*

"The Travelers insist you lead the manhunt," Prim ground out, each syllable like a tooth extraction.

Vipri's lips quirked at whatever showed on my face. I asked Diegia to activate RigFace and took a look at myself – it was showing mild surprise, now.

The Travelers' involvement was both unexpected and dangerous. A century ago, they had learned fragments of the Erins' predictive abilities – enough to glimpse probable futures, what everyone called the *Lines of Time*. A misnomer, like Field Dreamers. Their request to lead the search meant variables no human could see were in play. I needed Armin to decode their angle, but there was no way to contact him.

"The rebel might already be dead," I offered. "That much blood suggests a deep injury. LasGuns leave clean wounds, relatively. If he is still alive... he is alone. In haste..." *Already miles from the tunnel by now. I hope.* "Deploy foot teams trained to find a body." I omitted the forged authorizations and the masks – proof the Resistance had staged this. They nodded in silence; the Traveler had left them shell-shocked.

"In the dead scenario... Dying humans have a tendency to seek a hiding place. Scent trails linger even when visuals don't. Drones with infrared sensors are useless after five days in this heat. Cadavers..." I tapped my nose. *If this is right, it won't matter anymore. But my nose says he escaped. Please take the bait.* "We need RoboDogs. Who was the lead investigator before me? I will need their briefing before..."

Shine's knuckles whitened around her tablet. If looks could kill... I pretended not to see her.

"Take a Security FlyCar tomorrow," Vipri interjected, before Shine could snap. "I am sure you will have all the necessary information by then." He threw a glance at Prim – some unspoken agreement passed between them.

"Was that necessary?" Vipri muttered once we had cleared Prim's office. The jibe I had made at Shine bothered him.

"That night, she sent me home. Virtually. She continued the search without me. Quite a confident person. Very *Cupola.*" I couldn't stop a smile; it released some of my tension.

Vipri wasn't amused. He ignored me for a few moments before speaking again, a trace of worry in his voice. "Still, I don't see why it was needed."

"The only language Shine understands is force. Everything else fails to convince her I am not her punching bag during official meetings just because I lack the right pedigree. Two years ago, I verbally slapped her back in front of twenty people when she was on the wrong foot. Since then, she has been more careful. Well, careful for someone in her position."

"That's exactly what I am thinking. You don't share that same place in society."

"I can pity her. But maybe you know something I don't," I said, staring at him. There was an uncomfortable edge in his voice, reminding me being immersed into a new game with unknown rules – rules set by the Travelers.

We left the building in silence. Unsurprisingly, his FlyCar was already waiting. A gust of wind slapped my face me just before I climbed inside. I shivered, not only from the chill.

"Why me?" I asked hesitantly, once we were comfortably seated in the back. "The Travelers don't make requests without reason."

"They don't bother explaining their choices." Vipri's silence lasted three heartbeats too long. "We sent them the rebel's profile yesterday. Which is strange; they were watching him long before we even knew he existed." His gaze locked onto mine. "Your genetic maps share a five-hundred-year-old ancestor."

I am his ancestor. My genetic profile was a double trap. It had been subtly altered by the ShadowMind Order before I came back. And my official birthdate was almost three centuries after my real one. Any comparative genetical analysis would show a fabricated lineage diverging long after my true birth. "That explains my ... reaction when I first saw him."

"The neuranalyzer confirmed your surprise was genuine." Vipri leaned closer. "Now everyone wonders what you are hiding behind it."

I didn't realize we had landed until the door hissed open. Wind lashed at the cabin, snapping me out of my thoughts.

"Please." Vipri gestured to the entrance. "No need for DuaLink inside, and my popularity will grow faster."

The irony was clear. He and the inner circle of the Jewels couldn't care less about the Popularity Index, and he would never force me. The game was for the average Jewel, and the other Families watching through layers of surveillance, their algorithms dissecting every twitch. To them, this would look like Vipri luring a lustful *minor bitch* into his bed. Another trophy for his list. Another spike in my Popularity Index. More online bed invitations waiting.

"We won't be alone." There was warmth in his tone. No reassurance. Just fact. I wouldn't grasp the weight of that warning until later.

A figure waited at the central table in Vipri's spacious living room. I had to appreciate his taste – beautiful furniture and art. The man's face was covered by a mask, of course. Human-like, flawless to the untrained eye. But I had spent centuries dealing with far more advanced tech.

"Our Second Security Chief," Vipri said. No further introduction. The masked man already knew me.

I let my gaze linger. "Interesting mask." And *Mask* became his name, for me.

"Security high-rankings aren't public knowledge. Standard Cupola protocol." Vipri's clipped delivery shut down further questions.

If you say so.

Mask's voice was monotone. "Alenia, we are in a fairytale with no happy ending in sight. Time to share truths." The subtext vibrated between us: *Your turn first.*

"My knowledge of the New Field comes from a banned text," I said, rushing the words to preempt interrogation. "King Deceneus's journal – last printed as *Io Deceneus: Journal of a Time Traveler*, 120 years ago. Limited edition." The book recorded information about the failed Saurian Field that Houston, the Gate, had given to us.

A whisper from Mask, barely audible: "The Cursed King."

And I, the Cursed Queen...

"That book carries the highest prohibition. You should have deleted it from your mind." No inflection. No tells.

Voice synthesizer. Clever.

"Why ban records of a failed experiment that killed twenty billion?" I leaned in. "Because it proves the Travelers have technical problems with their field, and that they are testing their toys on us. The book shows how they lost their first attempt to conquer us. The Great War. More than three centuries ago."

My war.

Vipri defused the tension with a diplomat's ease. "We are used to this." Stage one concluded. He slid a photo facedown onto the table – a relic, printed on paper. Mask didn't react. They were probably using DuaLink. "My brother." Silence. His fingers hesitated above the photo. The air thickened. Mask's blank stare grew heavy with anticipation. Then – *the flip.*

Him.

The image hit like a shot. The same stubborn curl falling across his forehead. The half-smile that had disarmed me, years ago.

Your brother. My love.

My fingers twitched toward the photo. The old instinct to trace his jawline pushed through twenty years of carefully constructed numbness. I stopped. Then forced my hand to complete the motion – turning the photo face down, deliberately. The table's polished surface reflected my own face: pale, tight-lipped. "Let him rest. Nothing brings him back – not for you, not for me." My voice came out colder than I had intended. *In more than three hundred years, I loved only two men. But they were men…*

Mask spoke. Mechanical cadence slicing the silence. "We are non-identical triplets. He joined the Resistance for you. We joined it for him." A pause. "Three high Jewels turning traitor was … unthinkable. Our Family created a cover story. Even pushed us up the ranks when the Rebellion looked like it might win." A glitch flickered in his eye, betraying the human emotion beneath. "Then the Resistance lost. We vanished. Your name stayed clean. Only we know what you were to him."

"It stays that way," Vipri cut in, fingers brushing my wrist. Reassurance, or claim?

Mask overrode him. "Consequences would be … asymmetrical. As always. But that's not tonight's discussion."

Vipri exhaled, and I caught the faintest tremor in it. "Our last hidden card," he said, back in his usual voice. But this time, the usual was warmer. Not by much – he wore his walls like skin – but enough for me to feel the man beneath. Human. And far more dangerous than his Family realized.

As am I. The thought came suddenly.

In the photo's glossy backing, our reflections stared back at us – three liars bound by a dead man's memory and love.

"Why?" Vipri asked. He didn't need more words. I owed them a credible explanation – for my past, for my change in allegiance.

The air thickened. For the Field question, I had prepared. For this? Only truth would cut deep enough. "If we take the Travelers' new Field out of the equation ... the Resistance must end."

Vipri's pupils flared – *genuine* shock. No RigFace camouflage, I realized.

"Two outcomes remain," I continued. "Either the Resistance wins and dismantles this rotting system, or..." I leaned forward, letting the pause linger. "Cupola crushes them – and loosens its grip just enough to let humanity breathe again."

Vipri's knuckles whitened around his glass. "You think our Master Lords would ever..."

"I don't." I held his gaze. "*You* tell me." A faint hiss came from Mask as he shifted. Vipri's voice dropped into something close to a confession. "The Master Lords approved the Field test *knowing* billions would die. One reason they agreed was that their own plan purge plan to *clean* the planet matched the Travelers'. The rebels were to plant nukes in the most restive zones. A virus would ride inside the DigitalEgos and trigger a wave of suicides." His face darkened. "Now, at least, the *cattle* die usefully, creating the New Field. Then some liberty – just enough to outrun Aurora – would be allowed."

My fingers slid over the photo again. Its glossy surface still held the ghost of his warmth. "Heavy secrets we carry," I murmured, turning the image faceup. My thumb brushed paper lips I had once kissed. Then I slid the photo across the table – a surrender, and a challenge.

Mask reacted first. "Prim wants your head. Shine wants your head. They hate how well you dance with the bloody Jewels." He gestured at Vipri. "The Rubys suspect. The Diamonds watch." His eyes narrowed. "Not because of your rebel past – if they knew, we would all be corpses. It's the *present* we should worry about. The rebel's escape was too clever. Jewel teams hunt him, too. Whatever makes him special ... we should learn it first."

Vipri twitched. "We can't jeopardize her position..."

"Not irreparably," Mask cut in. "Five days without miracles lower expectations. His supposed death during the escape? Well sold. If he turns up alive against all odds, it burns you slightly." He looked at me, then dropped his voice to a whisper. "But understanding the Travelers' interest in him?" He gestured to include us all. "Worth the scar, no?"

"Perhaps. But too much pressure strangles cooperation," I said. "I will instruct my teams to turn every stone in the zone around the tunnel for two more days. Then we will search the areas your people already cleared." *Where you will find nothing. I hope.*

When I stood, neither tried to stop me.

The FlyCar's soft leather welcomed me like an old enemy. Vipri joined. His fingers touched my face – brief, unreadable. Then silence. Minutes stretched.

Rain began to patter above our heads – nature's countdown to whatever game Vipri and Mask would play next.

Chapter 9

Alenia

The morning mist, blown by a soft wind, dissolved over the lake, revealing patches of turquoise water glimmering in the sun. The Blue Mountains – one of the most exclusive places, reserved for Cupola high ranks. The world seemed drowned in silence; the birds were not yet awake – the quiet only heightened my feelings. I shivered, leaning against the wooden railing of the terrace. *Beautiful...* Furtive footsteps approached from the villa. I guessed it was Vipri; funny how much you come to recognize after working together for almost twenty years.

"Morning," he said.

"Morning," I replied, too lazy to turn, still wrapped in the mist.

His hand rested gently on my shoulder, and the same lethargy dulled my reaction. It took him a few moments to speak again.

"Beautiful, isn't it? Look there." He pointed to the twin peaks on the left – the rising sun was starting to glow between two towering stone columns, casting a fiery reflection on the rock.

"The Magic Window," I said, remembering.

"You know it," Vipri said, slightly disappointed. "I forgot you are the old-timer." He laughed as I nudged his ribs with my elbow. "I think they already have some nice pictures of us up there." He gestured toward the blue sky, where SkEye and the many people behind it watched. "Might as well give them something new to observe."

Seizing my other shoulder, he gently pulled me against him. I elbowed him again – harder than intended, judging by his gasp – but the shared warmth left us silent and still until the sun slipped away from the Magic Window. We walked back without a word.

Inside, I asked Mistria for my favorite tea, buying time, still unsure of my own reactions. Vipri sniffed the tea, grimaced, and smiled in a way that froze me. I knew that look too well.

"Hey." He stroked my chin. I stepped back, struggling to hold back tears. "Sorry. What's wrong?" He withdrew his hand, and I turned away.

It was as if centuries of training had just left me. And I could add my traitorous Diegia to the mix. "It's not you. It's me," I whispered. "You reacted like him." No need to clarify – *him*. The same smile, the same silent reassurance that everything would be fine, even as he was fading in my arms. "He disliked this tea too. But his last smile ... wasn't about the tea. I was there when he..."

"I know," he murmured.

"You can't know."

He opened a safe and handed me a paper photo. A shot of me cradling my lover's body – his brother – on a hospital bed. Already gone.

"Why are you showing me this?"

"There are secrets I need to share before ... before things are settled between us. I am sure you have yours, too. We can't lay them all out at once. We can't let them haunting us later. But suddenly, I felt you should see this now. This photo is why we kept you out of our files – that kind of pain can't be faked. The friend who took it is on Aurora now." His tone assured me, more than his words, that the history behind the photo was safe.

Is he still your friend?

"My brother just arrived," he said after a pause, his voice suddenly bland. "We need to go to the cellar. I can't explain why, but it's not trivial, and you may hate me at first. At this stage, the slightest misstep can kill us all. Every last one." He opened the door.

I nodded and walked past him.

"I am glad we saw the Magic Window together, from my terrace."

I believed him. But I didn't answer.

Deep in the forest, light barely filtered through the canopy. I counted six military boots prints in the mud; they were marching north, toward the same point I was aiming for. The footsteps were fresh, no older than a few hours – the morning rain hadn't erased them. It was the second time I had to change my path because of those damned boots. Yesterday evening, there were five prints, different people, near the first rendezvous point on the map provided by Batranu. They had multiple teams. Definitely not hunting animals. Their presence wasn't random.

A crack sounded, barely audible, muffled by the dense vegetation, impossible to pinpoint. I slipped into the undergrowth parallel to the path, ran until my lungs burned, then dove into a small hollow with a clear view forward through a gap in the bushes. I missed having real binoculars. My internal zoom wasn't strong enough – not intelligent, no infrared, no AI, just a basic zoom, not designed for deadly escapes. On Aurora, they couldn't implant military-grade tools in my head without triggering security scans on the way back to the planet. As bad as it was, it was better than nothing. After a while, I stopped zooming, feeling a slight degree of confidence. Nothing moved in the valley. I was just a mile from the second rendezvous point. Was this one compromised too? You can never feel safe when hunted, yet the calm of the valley washed over me. I exhaled a long breath of relief. Then I saw the camera, planted in a tree ten feet overhead, its lens fixed on me. Diego reacted before I could think, urging me to spring from the hollow without glancing back at the camera. I ran, far from it and the military footprints.

"The ravine," Diego whispered, marking a twenty-foot-deep creek on my internal map.

A thousand feet, I estimated, forcing my lungs to breathe deeper and my body to run faster. I didn't slow even when the ground dropped away. I gaped and fell at full speed. The muddy slope absorbed the shock, but my teeth still clacked. I slid until I hit water with a splash – icy, it reached my knees. Shock and cold numbed me. Diego snapped my nerves awake. I turned and climbed back out, two steps up, one sliding back. Again. Finally, I grabbed a bare root and pulled myself out. I crawled under a small bush, scanning the area – nothing moved in the forest, no soldiers, no animals, no drones. *How many cameras had I missed?* Probably none; they would be after me already. *Why aren't they using drones?*

"Diego, show me all the footprints, new and old, on the map," I asked, and he marked the recorded positions with red lines and their probable paths with yellow. They ran parallel to my own path, to my left, toward the second rendezvous point.

The map showed a hill to the right; the creek at my feet came from there. *"We can follow the ravine for a while, then curve around the hill. Ten more miles to the third rendezvous point. What if they have teams there too?"* My fourth contact point was thirty miles away – the last one. The first was already compromised, the second likely gone too. I was prepared for this – in simulations – but this was my first real test in the field, and everything felt too strange, even for a novice like me.

"I don't know," Diego said, scratching his virtual head.

I slid back into the creek and tried to run toward the hill. No matter how hard I tried, it didn't work – the water and mud slowed my steps. Every half-mile, I stopped, climbing the ravine to check the area. Nothing moved.

But then I glimpsed the back of an armed man, just five hundred paces from the ridge. He was alone, but that didn't mean he truly was. At least I was lucky; he was three hundred paces behind, walking toward the spot where I had seen the camera. A second man appeared, then a third. I slipped back into the ravine and moved faster.

After three miles, I found footprints again, crossing the creek. I threw myself under a bush near the water.

"The first team, five people. I compared the traces with the previous ones," Diego said.

"Filter the vegetation, check for cameras."

"Nothing."

"Show me their probable path."

"Eighty percent probability," Diego said, displaying a yellow trace heading toward the hill.

I scanned the valley again; nothing moved, even the wind felt dead, in a chilling silence. *"From that camera, they should already know we are in this area. One more mile, and we can climb out of the creek on the right. We can move away from the hill. Maybe find a cave..."*

A red spot stopped me. LasGun, military. Police weapons don't have such tracking devices. It came from behind, lighting up the leaves in front of me at head level. I turned slowly; the spot shifted to my chest. *You want me alive...*

There is no running when they spot you. A LasGun's AI can fire the moment you exceed a certain speed, targeting a predetermined body part: head for death, legs for capture, or whatever they are after. The spot moved to my legs. *You really want me alive.* The source was a few hundred paces away, likely in a tree, twenty feet up, judging by the angle from the depths of the ravine. I couldn't outrun its sight; the instant I tried, the AI would fire, and lasers are faster than people. So, I gestured surrender, slowly climbed from the ravine, and sat on the ground in plain view. The laser spot stayed on me.

"Diego, prepare a zero cleaning for everything related to the Resistance. Prioritize the memories related to Alenia."

Five soldiers in camouflage suits arrived in less than two minutes, running.

"You are well trained," the commander said, pointing to the LasGun spot painting my right knee. "I appreciate it. Our orders are to capture you alive. Unspoiled. Let's keep it that way." He glanced up – we were under a large tree, the sky obscured. That seemed to please him. He nodded to a soldier who fastened a flexible metallic band around my head. It tightened automatically, then they slipped a hood over my face, made of material that blurred my vision, but still let me see. "Just to ensure you are not caught by another camera. A FlyCar is coming soon." He paused. "Three cars are coming, but ours will be faster." His voice brimmed with confidence.

That wasn't a slip of the tongue. You're trying to tell me something. "Who are you?"

"The guys who captured you."

"I am locked," Diego whispered.

"Locked?" I had never heard of a Diego being locked before.

"I can't do the cleanup. I am scanning to see what else is compromised."

"You know now," the commander said with a smile. "They want the full you. You know what I mean."

"Who are *they*?"

"You will know soon." With slow, precise movements, he fitted an explosive collar around my neck. "You know what this is." He gestured with a small black box. "One wrong step, and... Don't make that step."

A faint noise filled the forest, like an arrow slicing the air – a FlyCar. The commander looked satisfied; it was theirs.

"Diego."

"I can't access any network. Our last authorization was revoked. I still have full control over Nucleus," he answered quickly.

"Is she there?"

"The most important things related to her are in the Nucleus, but some parts are still in standard memory. Dangerous things."

She doesn't deserve this... "Try..." With my suicide mole destroyed during the escape, I had no way to end my life by my own choice, when I wanted it. I could become a liability that could get her killed. The collar offered a chance, but it was not mine to control it. And nobody wants to die. I decided to wait. Perhaps there was a chance. Perhaps there wasn't.

"The AI of the band threatened to put me in full stasis if I try to delete anything from your memory again. Nucleus is still safe; they can't access it."

"Go inside," the commander ordered, opening the FlyCar's door. The other four soldiers joined me in the back while he settled in front. "Tactical display," he ordered the pilot. Two FlyCars were closing in at full speed; one of them maneuvering to flank us. "Go west. Any communication?"

"Both sent a Cupola authorization to stop our car. They are arming," the pilot said casually, revealing solid training.

"Arm, too. Send this wide, unencrypted, so both can read it." The commander handed the pilot a chip. "Fly under the trees."

"The one on the left replied with our encryption code."

"Tell them to land inside the forest. This point." He marked a spot on the pilot's holographic map. "We will land two minutes after them to deliver the cargo. Here." He marked another spot, half a mile away, also in the forest. "They have five minutes to reach our landing point on foot. Make that clear. Send the second signal to the other car."

"That car..." the pilot said, hesitating. "Shine is in that car. The new Ruby Panther. She ordered..."

"That Shine..." the commander cut in, a note of appreciation in his voice. He handed over another chip. "I don't care what she ordered. Send this to her."

"She is leaving," the pilot said half a minute later, wiping a bead of sweat from his brow.

"Did you wet your pants?" the commander laughed. "I've known her since she was a Ruby kitten. Trust me, she is far better than the viper running their security now."

"Doing simulations with her?" The pilot turned the tables.

"I am old-fashioned; I prefer real things. Shine is out of my league."

I couldn't see his face, but the tone in his voice told me that she was out of his league *now*.

The FlyCar landed under a large tree deep in the forest, and we waited. A second commando team, five men strong, arrived wearing different camouflage suits. All carried military weapons. All were tense. Like my captors. Like me. Nothing on their suits revealed the identity of either my captors or these new receivers. My transfer from one set of unknown hands to another happened in total silence, as if I were merely a sack of potatoes. My captors returned to their FlyCar and took off quickly without looking back.

The commander of the new team stared at me like I was an exotic fish in a museum exhibit, his hand resting on his LasGun. I couldn't tell if I matched his expectations of how a rebel should look. Seemingly satisfied after a few seconds, he gestured in the direction they had come from – the FlyCar. "Move," he ordered. I moved.

Soon, I was transferred to another FlyCar, and no one bothered to say anything beyond *move* or *sit*." This team wore no military clothes, but their sturdy builds and tough demeanor belied their benign civilian appearance. As before, inside the FlyCar, one man kept a LasGun pointed at me. I found it redundant; the explosive collar still encircled my neck. It didn't matter that we were flying – from the technical specifications I knew, the explosion would be surgical, nothing would be affected outside my body. The journey was spectacular, yet the hood obscured most of its beauty. I forced myself to peer out, straining to keep my mind functioning within normal parameters; so much fear was numbing it. After an hour, we arrived at an unknown location in the mountains. The long flight was prolonged by circling for some time, my hunters seemingly afraid of becoming prey.

We entered the house through a small back door and descended a staircase to a cellar lined with countless wine bottles. Only the man who received us – I nicknamed him DeadFace for his cold, almost cadaverous appearance – remained after the guards left. He was the coldest man I had ever met, his face devoid of any human emotion. He gestured for me to sit, his calculated politeness dripping with irony. At least no LasGuns were pointed at me.

The hood was gone, but the explosive collar and headband remained. Before I could fully analyze my new cage, Alenia entered, followed by a man I recognized from the news as a major Jewel boss – her boss, Vipri. Our eyes met, and we exchanged a glance. Too late, I realized I was pleasantly surprised while she was not; her expression was controlled, neutral surprise. Diego's snapshot of her face and my reaction diagram confirmed it. *They know now...* There was nothing I could do.

"It's good that you found him," she said in a flat tone.

"I am not sure we share the same definition of good," DeadFace replied, "but it's a good moment indeed." As he turned toward her, I leapt from the sofa and aimed a kick at his right side, targeting his liver. With surprising speed and training, he dodged, but it gave me enough time to bolt for the door. A click sounded, and a shock coursed through me. I collapsed. *I'll die... She deserves to be safe, at least.*

"There are two buttons," DeadFace said – his voice half muffled and seeming to come from faraway – raising the black control box while nudging my nearly limp body with his foot. "This one delivers electric shocks. Your Diego is sleeping now, I would wager, and it will take a while before you can run again. You can walk like a drunkard and talk, though. The red one is for the explosive. You know which button I pressed. Now, young man, why did you want to die? Why now?" He spoke as if I hadn't just attacked him, as if we were discussing tomorrow's weather. Dead face. Dead voice.

"He is trying to cover for me," Alenia said, making a calming gesture before helping me back to the sofa I had abandoned moments ago.

"I suggest you be less communicative," DeadFace said, staring at her hand. For the first time, I thought I saw something human flicker in his eyes. His words carried a double meaning, as if he were allowing – even encouraging – her to speak, but without cryptic signals that might convey hidden messages to me. Yet no one reprimanded her for helping me. I even sensed they expected it.

Why?

"What exactly is he covering up?" His tone warmed slightly when addressing her, though not by much.

"I let him escape."

"Why did she let you?" DeadFace's tone shifted as he turned to me, like an automaton triggered by a code switch.

"I don't know. Until that day, I hated her," I said, aiming for a neutral answer to buy time.

"Tell me how you met for the first time."

"A police officer escorted me to her office." I recounted the story, omitting my strange feelings and her reaction.

"That's all?" DeadFace asked.

"No," Alenia answered for me, hinting I should tell everything.

"I reacted as if I knew her, though I had never seen her before. But my memories aren't what they used to be. I suppose you know about my *accident*."

"And her reaction?"

"Somewhat similar," I admitted.

"I hadn't met him before that day," she said.

DeadFace nodded, as if their files had already cleared us. "You hated her," he said, turning back to me.

"That moment wasn't about hate. More about ... love," I shrugged. "The hate came later, when I couldn't see the real woman behind her cold, bureaucratic mask. She was more than annoying as my guardian. Though I suppose she was just doing her job." I clamped my mouth shut. I wanted her to know I no longer held any ill feelings, but I hadn't meant to confess like that. Something felt off. I am not a chatty man.

"Why?" DeadFace asked her. His voice carried an odd quality – not just the swift tone shifts, to each person he assigned a distinct cadence. Something subliminal that eluded me. His simple *why* expanded in my mind into a full question: *Why did you let him escape?* His voice was mesmerizing.

"Diego, are you awake? What is happening to me?"

"I am at 30% capacity. Full recovery in a minute. He is reaching your mind through me – I don't know how," Diego whispered like sick man. *"There was a hypnotic command in every word he says. I only sense it when he addresses her. We might not notice when we're the target."* He shrugged. *"It could have happened even when I was in stasis."*

"I had my reasons," she said.

"Why?"

"I won't answer when you are using neural hypnosis on me."

"Please answer," Vipri said to her. "And you, stop the hypnosis," he glared at DeadFace.

"Tonight, a Resistance FlyCar will come for him," DeadFace said, pointing at me. "We have half a day to unravel his mystery."

"There's no mystery," I breathed, still recovering from the shock of his last words.

"Is he right? They are taking him?" Alenia asked Vipri.

"Yes. We made a deal with the Resistance through some old acquaintances. They captured him and delivered him to us. They knew where to look. We ensured no official search teams would be in the area, giving them a short window to act before the drones detected anything. You know why we could make that guarantee," he said, smiling at her. "Consider it limited cooperation to resolve his case."

"I received a message," Alenia said. "It had an Erin signature. Don't ask how they contacted me." She shrugged – not emphatically, but enough for me to guess she was hiding something, building plausible deniability if pressed further.

"Do you know any Erins?" DeadFace asked me. I shook my head. "Do you know someone named Armin?" he asked again.

"Are you still using hypnosis?" I asked to buy time, and Vipri frowned at him.

"No," Alenia answered for him, reassuring me and signaling I should answer truthfully.

"Yes, I know someone named Armin. An alien."

"Then he is forming a new Line of Time," DeadFace said, pointing at me, though I had no idea what that meant. "We just don't know why, how, or what variables he is using. I doubt we will learn more now."

"I suppose you were caught far from the tunnel," Alenia said. I nodded. "I need to know your escape path from the tunnel. Don't include the last twenty miles, so I won't know where they ... found you." She glanced at DeadFace, who nodded. Then she projected a hologram and gave me control. I zoomed into the area I had traversed and marked my path from the tunnel to a hill, still well away from my capture point. A second hologram appeared, merging with the first and dividing it into thousand-foot squares. She zoomed in on the bushes where I had spent two nights in an induced coma. "What's here?"

"Crow bushes. I hid under them for a while. I hoped the crows would trick the drones' infrared sensors."

"You couldn't have walked through them, surely. They are too dense." The image of the bushes superposed over the map.

"There are small tunnels in the undergrowth... I used this one," I said, drawing a yellow line on the map. "It's five hundred feet long. Don't ask how I got through."

"No, I won't. I will ask someone else. Did you leave anything there?"

"Some empty chocolate boxes. I bought them at the stadium," I said, sensing what she was after.

"Thank you," she said.

"I am not sure I like what you are thinking," Vipri said, frowning at her. I noticed how naturally they acted in the room, far from the official masks I had seen until now – except for DeadFace, of course.

"I want to make a point," she said, smiling.

"That's what worries me. Shine might be too dangerous a point to make."

"Who is Shine?" I asked.

"You don't want to know," Alenia shrugged.

"A woman called Shine was in the other FlyCar searching for me. They nicknamed her the new Ruby Panther."

"I know she was there. I can handle this," DeadFace interjected.

"Tell me that when you can erase Shine's memories," Vipri retorted. I wasn't sure if this was about Shine's role in the hunt or something deeper.

"That's for me to decide," DeadFace said, and I wondered who the real boss was here. "Tell them," He pointed at me, "that we need to know if you are the trigger for the Travelers' decision to start the Field earlier."

It was clear *them* meant the Resistance, and I would be free by nightfall. I glanced at Alenia. She smiled thinly, as if reading my thoughts, though I wasn't sure I understood them myself. Vipri placed a protective hand on her shoulder – an involuntary gesture, perhaps tied to me, or a claim. I couldn't tell. She didn't react. It stung, and I forced myself to look away.

Alenia

"Cotnari, twenty-three years old. A good year," Mask said, uncorking the wine bottle. "We earned it." He swiftly filled three glasses, then – in a sudden move – peeled off his artificial face. "I am tired. My muscles ache. No more keeping up appearances around you after staying two nights together." He paused. "Well, with him," he corrected, then amended after another pause, "Staying in our house."

"You are still on DuaLink," I realized, slightly amused. Another conversation was unfolding beneath ours.

"My brother is annoying," Mask said, gesturing at Vipri, neither confirming nor denying my guess. "Too used to simulations with ... whatever. He made me rephrase twice already. Sick mind, nothing but trouble in there. Consider yourself warned." His glance flicked to me.

"You have no idea how many times Vipri's dragged me into awful sims to boost his Popularity Index," I said, playing along. His game was opaque, unsettling, yet joining in eased the tension thickening the air. The rebel's ghost still haunted the house, an invisible wedge between us. Mask was a puzzle: sharp, dangerous, with a hidden agenda. And then there was Vipri – a different kind of danger entirely.

"I am not surprised," Mask shrugged, then froze mid-motion, as if listening to some inner feed. "Even now, he is running one."

"Come on," Vipri finally interjected, before falling silent again – another telltale sign of their DuaLink.

"Do I know you?" I stared at Mask, only breaking my gaze when Diegia nudged my attention away. His humor – strange, unique – stirred half-buried memories.

"I have a picture of my old self," Mask grinned, "but Vipri threatened to jail me if I showed it to you. Vice Prime Ministers don't have *vice* in their title for nothing. I looked better than him. Still do." He slid a photo across the table, face-down – perhaps some security protocol forced them to use only paper for dangerous old secrets. Every image from them held surprises. Was this a peace offering? Or had the game just deepened? "It won't bite," he teased.

I sighed and flipped it over. The face was vaguely familiar, but the difference between past and present was considerable – nothing had been preserved. Vipri, at least, retained some of his old features. "Yes, you looked better." I stalled, scrambling for the name behind the face.

"You are conspiring over DuaLink," Vipri said lightly, his hand darting between Mask and me. "No way he ever outshone me."

"Fine, your surgeon did better work," I conceded, still unable to recall Mask's Resistance alias.

"Diegia," I whispered, *"anything?"*

"Nothing. Still searching through your memory for clues. You met him before me. And you are quite old, Alenia – plenty of stuff in there."

"And he thought he was a legendary rebel," Vipri laughed. "Part of their Cupola, their inner council."

"I was an outsider. Only one link to the top." I shrugged. *What does he know?* Council meant power. Knowledge. Decisions.

"One link to the very top," Mask said, a note of respect threading through his voice.

"I knew Erun, the leader of the Resistance then. And you know how I *defected*."

"And that your victory was staged. He didn't know until yesterday." Mask pointed at Vipri.

"You were in the Resistance before they joined," I said, recalling his earlier hints, then froze. The conversation had dragged me back to when all three brothers were alive. My hand, trying to point at Mask, dropped. "You couldn't have climbed that high in five years."

"I let them think they recruited me. I was already a brigade commander. You know, I am the adventurer, not him." He nodded toward Vipri.

"You approved all my government postings." The weight of treasonous revelations should have spiked the tension, yet the air stayed calm – so calm I began to doubt my own instincts. "You, the Jewel Family's Second Security Chief."

"I wasn't the Second Chief then. First now. The three Chiefs – Jewel, Ruby, Diamond – were killed two days ago. The Travelers' space shuttle was blown up on the way to their main station. Perfect cover: Erins retaliating for the attack on Aurora. The Solar Council already closed the case. Their deaths ... *unintended consequences*." He stressed the phrase, then shrugged. "Erins don't make mistakes – that much I know. The new Diamond is fine. Ruby is another story. Shine is a kitten next to her. Interesting times."

"So you were right, the Erins *are* forming a new Line of Time," I said.

"I would love to know what variables they are juggling. That young rebel?" Mask nodded toward the door through which he had left not long ago. "You? Vipri? Me? The Ruby viper? Some cards always get discarded mid-game – like the unfortunate passengers of that shuttle. Oh, and Shine is their Fourth Security Chief now." His eyes locked onto mine.

"Diegia, do I have clearance to know a Fourth Security Chief of the three Families?" A beat. Her nod. *How do I even use this?*

"Alenia, be careful," Vipri murmured, refilling his glass though it wasn't empty.

"Vipri claims you," Mask teased. "He did the same with the rebel. Some men can't handle competition."

Vipri's warning had lost momentum. He seemed to want to say more, but Mask's jab shifted the mood – DuaLink working between them.

You want me to move against Shine. Or to help her... Mask's grin was childlike, innocent. "You would make a fine actor," I said, equal parts amused and unnerved by his inscrutable performance.

"My dear, one doesn't climb this high without acting. I couldn't. He couldn't." A nod at Vipri. "You couldn't. It's mandatory."

"Suppose you are right." I stepped back.

"Sometimes I hate being right. Rough day. But useful. Rest well, enjoy ... the house during the night. *Note my phrasing,*" he said – looking at me but nodding to Vipri – then back to me: "And keep watching his Magic Window trick. He uses it on every woman he lures here."

"You could have mentioned that earlier. How many?"

"One."

"Diegia, I have the feeling Mask is a sleeper. Like me." I stood, ready to leave.

"Goodnight." My voice held a lightness they mirrored with amused glances. *They think it's about being the* one. *Maybe it is.*

Was this a new morning, or the same one stretched thin by dreams? There was nothing to tell the difference. The wind shredded mist over the turquoise lake; the Magic Window alight again. *Vipri will come*. I smiled as his footsteps merged with the breeze behind me.

"I know," I said, without turning. "Time for another performance for the eyes in the sky." I gestured up. "Can't enjoy the view without an audience."

"Think we are past needing pretexts," he murmured, catching hold of my shoulders. I braced for the pull, but he turned me gently to face him, and his lips found mine.

The morning broke clean: no mist, no Magic Window, no turquoise lake; just bare mountains looming in the distance, quiet and watchful. The rebel was long gone, of course, but protocol demanded we chase phantoms. The search grid spread five miles around the tunnel where he had vanished. Shine had a hunch – her kind always did – and claimed the crow-thicket zone for her own. I let her. My teams set up a thousand paces east, perfect for watching the inevitable farce unfold.

I was relaxed. The bird had flown the cage. All that remained were breadcrumbs, and maybe – if I was lucky – his breadcrumbs would land directly in my hands.

Shine's teams struggled in the underbrush, sweating through the maze of tunnels like overconfident ants. Twenty years of bad blood with the Rubys made it feel personal. Let them drown in mud. By nightfall, they came back mottled in colors no uniform regulation approved: clay-red, bile-yellow, crow-shit black. After two hours, they had combed a fraction of the fifty tunnels. Impressive inefficiency.

Next morning, I called Shine while my teams regrouped near the thickets. "I am at the crow bushes. Plenty of tunnels here. How many did you search?"

"Search them yourself. Mud suits you. Just make sure you smile for the cameras when you're done. Report to me after that." Her tone was venom laced in silk.

"Considering proper security protocol, I regret to inform you I am unable to report to you. However, we have made progress. Send me your report about the tunnels' search: depths, names, durations, the usual. We will cross-check."

I ended the call with a smile that she could see. She wouldn't bite – not yet – but she would file something. They always do, if only to mark the record, the way a dog marks his territory.

By dusk, an envelope waited on my desk with no digital trail attached to it. Inside were two empty chocolate boxes. The DNA analysis came back clean, but the serial barcodes pointed squarely to the stadium, the night of the rebel's disappearance. A curious trace, like a knight left undefended. A centuries old memory flashed-back: Batranu teaching me to play chess, a game imported from his world. I cherished it.

I called Shine again. "We have a situation. Meet me in my office. And I am still waiting on that report."

I had ordered my teams to keep quiet, but secrets have a half-life. The rumor mill was already grinding: *something* had been found. The fact that I had never summoned Shine to my office before – I couldn't afford it – well, that alone would have set her hair on fire.

When she arrived, I greeted her with steam rising from my cup. "Tea?" I offered.

"I would rather not be poisoned," she said, folding into the chair without waiting. So much for etiquette. Seconds later, her report hit my inbox.

I took my time reading it, slow-sipping as I brewed a second cup. She watched me. When I handed her the tea, she accepted it with a scowl, eyes flashing like a feral cat before snatching it without a word. Her report was classic Ruby damage control: precise, sharp-edged, and creatively misleading. According to her, the crow-bush tunnels were a waste of effort. The *real* leads lay elsewhere. Interesting, since she was the one who had wanted the zone in the first place.

"There is new evidence," I said at leisure, letting the words linger. "It suggests the rebel may have gone farther than we assumed. Maybe even had help. Or maybe the wolves got him. All still in play."

"I never expected *you* to find him," she said. "Critical work requires professionals."

"I never expected your team to skip some tunnels under the crow-bushes. Yet..." I slid the plastic evidence bag across the desk. "This was recovered."

"Chocolate boxes?" she scoffed. But the twitch behind her eye said more. Diegia's snapshoot from the highjacked camera and memo confirmed it: *Anger. Fear.* To the naked eye, she was like an ice statue, well masked – hard training, I could give her that – but not perfectly. Her type always shows a seam under pressure. Because pressure and consequences are always different for Lessers and Cupola.

"They were purchased at the stadium," I said. "That night. The same night. There are no traces of DNA, but their presence is enough to raise questions."

She picked up the bag, studying the black label with a serial number: official record now. Too late to bury it. Her bark style was just a tactic to rattle lesser pedigrees. Underneath, she was calculating. "What do you want?" she asked. Finally.

"The search has run its course. Whether he is dead, alive, or halfway through a bottle of wine in the mountains – it no longer matters. We will halt physical efforts and collaborate on the final report. Drones will still survey a fifty-mile-large area around the tunnel. Let the interns sort through footage."

"And the boxes?"

"Footnote," I said. "Tucked in today's findings. Without DNA, it's circumstantial. But your team's timeline must be complete in the report. Clean. Chronological."

She caught the bait.

"Chronological," she repeated. Perfect. That would bury the chocolate incident somewhere around page one hundred something, preferably between an inventory list and a thermal anomaly chart.

I could already see her drafting the novella, brick by bureaucratic brick. And the Ruby overseers? They wouldn't touch me; not with Shine on my side. The Jewels still backed me nominally. The Diamonds? They would never move without consensus – too much to lose.

"You will have my final report tomorrow," she said, sipping her tea with natural elegance.

"Congratulations on the promotion," I toasted. Her reflex was instant – our cups met with a ceremonial clink. A botched mission could have clipped her wings. She had jumped three ranks because of a shuttle *unintended consequence*. A dangerous rise. The Ruby rivals would be sharpening their knives – the usual day to day life in any Family. Mask had warned me.

But was this truly *his* game? Or had I simply walked onto a board someone else arranged? Either way, I played my way.

Or so I told myself.

Chapter 10

The Resistance's headquarters is hidden where no one would think to look: beneath the main stadium. On the surface, the structure is a two-thousand-foot-long ovoid, sinking ten floors underground. Including the surrounding buildings, sports centers, and parks, the entire compound spans nearly six square miles. There are numerous underground parking areas, rooms, corridors, and tunnels used for maintenance, riot police, and deliveries. Unknown to the government, the Resistance has repurposed long-forgotten medieval tunnels and cellars. Twenty million people thrive in the city above, where centuries of development and water extraction have lowered the underground water table. Inch by inch, the land has sunk. Parts of the old medieval structures now lie thirty feet below their original position, with new buildings rising above them. When ancient records were destroyed, some medieval tunnels faded from memory, helped by the Resistance's hackers, who erased them from government files. Excessive censorship, historical revisionism, and reliance on a single source have unintended consequences. The insidious NetPedia rules our rulers, too; they just don't realize it.

In the chaotic aftermath of the Rebellion, the AI overseeing the stadium's re-construction was hacked. Over ten thousand square feet at the bottom of the lowest level was reinforced to conceal three floors of bunkers, built simultaneously and linked to the refurbished medieval tunnels and caves. The operation required less than a tenth of a percent more materials, and the automated builders were efficient and silent. Hidden exits abound: some on land, in other buildings and subways; others under the river, where a small fleet of stealth mini-submarines awaits, some leading to the many small islands among the water canals. A mile wide, the main channel of the river delta splits the capital into two nearly equal parts. From a FlyCar, the capital is a breathtaking sight; the delta's channels weave between hundreds of rocky hills, none higher than three hundred feet. Five hundred people live and work inside the Resistance headquarters, rarely leaving. I am one of them now, sent here by DeadFace from the mountain villa.

When Batranu summoned me, I knew my first task was approaching. My LasGun wounds had fully healed, and I had resumed training. SimFight wasn't as advanced as the Aurora devices, but with some adjustments, it sufficed. Unfortunately, Houston could no longer assist me, and I missed our training trips to distant corners of the galaxy. Batranu introduced me to ShadowMind lessons. The ShadowMind Order disbanded a century ago when the Celestial Faction absorbed all other Factions in the galaxy. The Order had failed in its mission to maintain equilibrium among Factions. The Celestial Travelers learned to replicate some of the Erins' quantum brain capabilities, genetically enhancing their brains to forecast the future – reading the Lines of Time, as it's commonly known. The ShadowMinds were the greatest fighters ever, and after scattering underground across the galaxy, they became a loose resistance against the Celestials. Or so I was told. Batranu, a former member of the Order, had joined the Resistance here, which operated on two levels: the ShadowMinds and the locals. Being a Field Dreamer with Aurora training, I was considered a mid-Level Three ShadowMind. But no one had time to test me.

An inside task, I thought. Until my appearance could be altered by plastic surgery in a few weeks, I couldn't go out. For now, only my DNA had been slightly modified, and my hair was now two-toned – dark brown near the roots, reddish at the top – the only visible change.

"There is a change in the Travelers' plans," Batranu said, gesturing toward one of the chairs scattered across his large office. "The New Field will begin in a few months instead of two years. You know the story." He glanced at me, and I nodded. "They change; we change. Well, we try to change. We are not truly prepared."

"DeadFace said something similar."

"DeadFace?"

"The man from the villa in the Blue Mountains. He looked like a Jewel big boss. Maybe even bigger than Vipri. Dangerous."

"DeadFace," Batranu smiled. "The new Jewel's Security Chief. He wore a mask, but his real face is quite expressive. You are right, he is dangerous. A Balancer, better known as a High ShadowMind, at least Level Six. I may have known him." Batranu whispered the last words, touching his chest as if recalling an old wound.

Did they fight? Neither Batranu nor DeadFace seemed like fighters based on their appearances, but I was young and naive. "He will help us," I said, interrupting. DeadFace had helped me escape, albeit in a strange way. "He must hate the Celestials."

"We had an agreement to return you to us after that brief meeting at the villa, but I doubt sentiment drives his actions. At Level Six, they lose some human traits, though he retains a bizarre sense of humor, or fakes it. I am not sure. AI can forge anything. Don't let that distract you when you meet him again. He will work with both the Resistance and the government to balance things, from his perspective, whatever that means. Are you ready?" He shifted topics; the lesson had gone on long enough. I nodded. "I don't have all the threads, but it seems the Erins have tailored a new Line of Time, forcing the Celestials to act faster. They are using four main variables: you, me, Alenia, and ... DeadFace, plus two unknown tokens. One might be Vipri. Are you comfortable with that?"

I am a ... variable. Why should I be comfortable? "I don't like being used as..."

"It's just a term. They are not using us; we are part of the game, as they are. The Travelers are also reading the Lines, helped by some Observers, making their own moves. It's an information game. You have an important role to play." He paused, staring at me. I couldn't see what role I might have, now that the astronaut path was closed, and the idea of being a variable in someone else's game still gnawed at me. "I will read the Lines now, but I am not an Erin. They have enhanced my genetics slightly, and yours too. Together, we have a better chance."

"Can I read the Lines?" I asked hastily, caught up in his words.

"Drink this first." Batranu ignored my question, sliding a small bottle toward me. "An energizing cocktail. Reading the Lines is exhausting. Then ask Diego to install this software; it's called MindT: Mind Together. It will merge parts of our minds to work better together."

"Is it safe?" I asked Diego.

"Aurora Origin," he replied. *"It should be."*

"Take your time to analyze it," Batranu said with a smile, and I felt a pang of embarrassment.

"It's fine," I said without thinking, downing the bottle. The taste wasn't bad, but had his smile tricked me?

"Free your mind, like you are wandering aimlessly," he instructed once the connection was established. I felt nothing when he linked us – perhaps there was nothing to feel. "I will open the Lines and make them visible to you. The first time will hurt a bit." A second later, a sharp, quiet pain pierced my brain.

That was not a bit, I groaned inwardly.

"Be aware I can hear your thoughts now," Batranu said, a hint of amusement in his tone, though it wasn't a voice, more a whisper flickering in my mind. "It's like OpenMind, but more complex."

"That's crap."

"It depends on how you use it. The Lines are coming to us now. We will start with the past, the easier part."

I expected the Lines to be ... well, lines. The first image was Lamia, smiling as she did in my dreams, the only time she was letting me play with her long hair. In moments, she shrank, fading away, leaving a yellow trace like her hair that slowly formed a line. Then came Alenia, also smiling. *Why her?*

"Your girls," Batranu said, amused. "You are linked to Alenia. You will learn how in time. I won't spoil the surprise." As he spoke, Alenia transformed into a long, dark red line – much longer than Lamia's.

Like her hair.

"It's easier when you tie physical traits to a line. The white one is mine. In my native Romanian, *Batranu* means old man. The purple one is ... DeadFace. I will take control now." The image shifted, stabilizing into an intricate, carpet-like puzzle with about fifty colorful threads. "I can't handle more than fifty variables. Follow these." Four threads glowed brighter than the rest.

Looking at them, I realized that they were longer than mine. Much longer. *Centuries?* I asked myself forgetting that my mind was now an open book.

"Yes, we are old. Forget about that now. Focus on the Lines. The four variables I mentioned. Without knowing what to look for, the carpet is just a puzzle. That's why the Travelers are still uncertain."

Curiously, my light red Line lingered at the carpet's edge for years before bending toward the center.

"Your trajectory altered when you had your first Field Dream, and the Celestial Dragon exploded," Batranu explained.

Until then, our four Lines moved nearly parallel, at varying distances from the axis. Shortly after mine shifted, Alenia's edged closer to the center from a point already nearer to it. I thought DeadFace's trajectory shifted too, but only slightly.

"This," Batranu pointed to another timepoint on the Line, "is you returning here from Aurora."

My Line accelerated toward the center – though *accelerated* was a misnomer; it was a snail's pace. So did Alenia's. DeadFace's Line did not shift at all.

"Your arrival forced the Travelers to act, advancing the New Field's initiation. Until now, it was just a theory. They don't know who you or Alenia truly are, but they sense you are a threat. You are their main target – your signature is more visible. We need to anticipate their next move."

"Why me?"

"Let's project into the future." He ignored my question, and a gray zone appeared at the carpet's end – the future; the past stretched endlessly. "I will move some threads," he whispered, nudging Alenia's line closer to the axis. Sparks erupted in the gray zone. "You will feel dizzy; I am using your brain too. The sparks are my calculations. Poor things. You should see how the Erins manipulate them – their carpets have thousands of variables." He adjusted our Lines similarly, with visible effects, but none matched Alenia's fireworks.

A moment later, the carpet vanished like a strange dream, and we were back in his office, mentally separate again. "Alenia is entering a dangerous zone. The Travelers reacted by weaving their Lines around her," Batranu said, his voice troubled. The feeling of being a mere variable in someone else's game resurfaced. "You must contact Armin and an Observer named Deceneus via the Field. It's dangerous. The safest place for the connection – though no one is safe in this game – is far from here, and your face hasn't been altered yet. A mask might fool many, but there's always a risk." He paused, staring at me, waiting for my confirmation.

My place in the Resistance was still new, and I wasn't used to being a soldier. He could have ordered me, but he sensed my unease and sought informal acknowledgment. *It's dangerous... No different from my return and escape.* I nodded.

"This is the place." He marked a mountain on the hologram map, four hundred miles from the capital – an old volcano riddled with tunnels and caves from past eruptions. "It's in an exclusive place for Cupola high ranks, and because of this, the Field is monitored less strictly. You have visited the area before. The Blue Mountains. The villa. DeadFace."

Alenia

I had to skip the visit to the Magic Window and head to another park outside the capital. Vipri wasn't happy. I smiled as I stopped the car in the forest – Batranu was waiting for me. This was a different park, chosen according to the Resistance's protocol: change the location after every meeting; no place can be used twice in a year. The area was crowded, full of hikers, as expected on a day off. Shouldering my backpack, I ventured deeper into the woods. Occasionally, I paused to take photos for Diegia to analyze; she was far better at this game.

Gradually, the paths grew steeper and narrower. The hikers thinned out until I was alone among the trees. My internal GPS guided me toward the red dot on the map. I circled the area three times before reaching it, admiring the flowers, the trees, the small details – just like any other tourist.

"All clear," Diegia whispered. Then a pause. I found it amusing – my usually talkative companion was trying to match the silence of the forest. In her own way, she was so much like me. She

appreciated beauty too. Why wouldn't she? She wasn't like the standard DigitalEgo. She had evolved. Almost human. Rogue.

At my signal, Batranu arrived. I greeted him with genuine warmth – he had been a significant part of my life before. My real life.

"The Travelers don't have enough satellites to launch the New Field," he said through our DuaLink connection. "So they will link them with the towers that manage our DigitalEgos and the Net. They will need to modify the towers, but that won't take long. Time is running short."

"We could destroy some towers," I suggested. There were thousands scattered across the globe. "But we can't take them all down..."

"From our calculations, we only need to destroy three global nodes and fifteen key towers, placed in specific locations. The New Field can't be deployed without full planetary coverage. It's all or nothing."

Scaling down from thousands to eighteen sounded manageable – until I remembered the global nodes had been turned into fortresses after the Rebellion, designed to withstand assaults by thousands of armed rebels. Heavy missiles might work, but we didn't have those. The Erins did, but they couldn't interfere directly. Galactic politics – just as dirty as the local kind.

"I know what you are thinking," Batranu said, reacting to whatever signals my electronic body was emitting in the simulation. DuaLink was worth every credit – it was frighteningly accurate. "But we would need thousands for a direct assault. We have done the math. We don't have them. The fortresses' weakness is their size. Cyberattacks and a small commando team might do the job. At least, we hope so." He sighed, as if hope itself were a fragile thing, dangling just out of reach while the universe rolled the dice on our fate.

"We have better cyber teams," I said, clinging to that sliver of optimism. "But commandos?" I brought the discussion back to reality.

"You are a Level Four ShadowMind," he said, slowly.

Suddenly, I understood why Armin had pushed me to return, why he had kept me in that strange hibernation – he had foreseen the need for my skills a century before they were needed.

"There are very few in their ranks who can match you, and none were trained by a ShadowMind. We have always honored our code: a captured ShadowMind dies before revealing anything. You were nearly Level Five."

"That was another life. My skills have deteriorated." *Or vanished entirely.*

"Your mind is just as sharp – maybe sharper – after surviving the snakes' pit. Your body isn't. You need to train. Here." He cut the DuaLink and handed me a chip, then switched back to virtual mode. "This works with any decent combat simulator. Try SimFight V*;* it pairs best with our software. Bonus: their historical simulations are excellent. Well, their version of history. But the further back you go, the more accurate it gets. No need to falsify what happened a long time ago." He smiled, and I remembered he had once been Level Five himself. *Still is*, I thought. He never stopped being a ShadowMind. I had to resign when I came here.

"It's a common toy for your social bracket. Buying one won't raise suspicion. Once they install the cube, our specialists will upgrade it for quantum chips. And this..." He handed me another chip. "...is your ShadowMind data."

I balanced the chip between my fingers. It belonged to a life I had thought was gone forever. A dangerous life, but a life.

"We have a few ShadowMinds in hiding here. Any of us should be ready to lead a commando team in two months."

In that moment, I felt alive again. His words, the chip burning against my fingers – it gave me a purpose worth fighting for. Living for. Dying for. My time as a sleeper had meant something. But for twenty years, my blood had been ice. Until now. *Except with Vipri...*

"Be careful with the new Jewel Security Chief," Batranu warned. "He is not what he seems. I can't say more; it's more instinct than fact. You knowing too much might ripple unpredictably through the Lines of Time. I don't know why the Erins killed the old Security Chiefs of the major Families. Retaliation for the attack on Aurora was just a pretext. But you will figure it out. You are in the right place – which means you are in danger."

"He must be a ShadowMind too," I said after a pause, struck by the odd familiarity of Mask's presence. Batranu nodded. "Which means he is an infiltrator, not a real Jewel."

"The game is the same everywhere: we infiltrate, they infiltrate. There are ... complications in our ranks too," he said carefully, hinting at a third player in the shadows. I spent the rest of the evening trying to guess who that could be, and came up empty.

"Order a SimFight V," I told Diegia on the drive home.

"We have a problem," she replied a second later, flashing technical specs across my vision. *"Your simulator is a twenty-foot-wide cube. No space for it inside the house. The garden could fit it, but you would have to cut some things."*

"Twenty feet? For a simulator?"

"Complicated tech. It needs full immersion – tools, terrain replication. Wonderful. You will see. I don't want to spoil the surprise."

"I am not cutting my trees."

My garden wasn't large, but it had once belonged to a nature lover, former chief advisor of the Central Botanical Garden. He had lived here fifty years, planting trees that now towered so high

I had to bribe the neighbors to leave them alone. Nineteen years ago, when he moved to another city after rejuvenation, many had tried to buy the house. But he had sold it to me instead – our paths had crossed often in the botanical garden, and I helped him with bureaucratic favors. Being a High Councilor had its perks. Some buyers who had pressured him too aggressively were quietly steered elsewhere – I *learned* this later. The system favors power, even when you don't ask.

Even after rejuvenation, he had still been the old man to me – a habit, though he was centuries younger. He made me swear to care for his plants. Sometimes, he still visited when the trees bloomed, their perfume saturating the street; the only time the neighbors stopped complaining.

"Run a simulation," I said.

Diegia highlighted a spot in the garden, half-blocking two narrow paths. *"It fits here. Just three branches to cut, medium ones."* She rendered the cube in place, the branches vanishing instantly.

I sighed. *"Fine. The trees will live."*

It turned out worse. The city's AI demanded more pruning – *aero-stability* adjustments for wind resistance, it claimed. The botanical garden's AI agreed, reassuring me that the trees would survive. I had no choice but to believe them. Even worse, I had to obey.

Back inside, I had Cassia disconnect the house from the Net and inserted the ShadowMind data chip into Roby's charging dock. A second later, Cassia and Diegia materialized as holograms at the table – strategizing was easier with them outside my head.

Cassia appeared first, folded into a perfectly upright posture with that faintly judgmental expression she reserved for non-optimal procedures. Diegia followed with a pirouette and a smirk, eyes already darting between data streams. I always suspected she enjoyed being embodied more than she admitted.

"You two look pleased," I said.

"We missed being furniture," Diegia replied.

Cassia tilted her head. "Technically, we are part of the house infrastructure. Alive. Furniture is decorative. Dead."

"Project my body and DNA diagrams," I said. "Mark degraded capabilities in red, with corresponding genetic regions." I had assumed minor downgrades since my return. Then the hologram lit up: 90% of my body flushed crimson, though less than 0.01% of my genome was affected. "What...?" I stared. "Are you sure that data is valid?"

"Triple-checked," Cassia replied. "Some of your most powerful ShadowMind enhancements were intentionally dismantled. Subtly. Someone knew what they were doing."

"When I came here ... they did not want me to look too different," I muttered.

"Some enhancements are gone," Diegia confirmed. "But not deleted – they are scattered, reabsorbed, fragmented across biological noise, in the Junk-DNA area. Like hiding precious data in a room full of identical scrapped drives. They can be reassembled and reactivated when needed. By the guys who undid them. I suppose we can't meet them here. Those ... *ShadowMinds*." A dose of regret was in her voice. The remaining enhancements were camouflaged as natural mutations, well within the statistical deviation standard. But I had started to doubt that only a little was gone. "We were quite the pair," she joked, though it had all happened long before her creation.

"Show me what's left."

The new overlay was kinder: 40% of my body still enhanced. I exhaled. Good enough. But when I asked for cognitive genetic improvements, the hologram barely showed a flicker of red.

"Physical only," I muttered, annoyed at how often I had sighed tonight. "Of course."

"Cognitive fields are a different matter," Cassia noted, folding her hands neatly. "They don't register in traditional diagnostics. The tools here..." She shrugged.

I zoomed in on the copy of my brain in the hologram, down to the neuronal level, and tapped one thoughtfully over the dendrites. "Microtubules?"

"Most likely," Cassia replied. "Yours look slightly different under a quantum zoom, still in the natural variability zone, though unreadable by any known technology. Consciousness-level structures don't leave easy fingerprints."

Diegia's face looked suddenly too serious, and she added, using the voice of a teacher speaking to a student, "The theory says those quantum states are suspended across gravity wells in microtubule lattices – thought itself might collapse only when gravity tips the scales. Superimposed intentions waiting to fall one way or another. How can you measure this? Eh?"

"Gibberish. You mean my memories are stuck in a gravitational coin toss?"

"Beautifully put. You could write poetry." Diegia grinned, all teeth.

Cassia raised an eyebrow. "We will schedule that literary impulse after your neuromuscular calibration. For what will happen ... you need fighting skills more than you need poetry. You can celebrate later; in whatever kind of rhymes you want. Perhaps we will even listen. Perhaps."

The stats weren't terrible: endurance, strength, reaction time, mitochondrial efficiency – all better than most Special Forces operatives. Not by much, but enough. *I can take them. After training.*

And train I did. It took four weeks of brutal SimFight drills before I felt ready for real ShadowMind work. Batranu's people showed up after Diegia *accidentally* fried a circuit and complained to the manufacturer. No one questioned why two repair teams arrived, one after another.

"I didn't know you had a SimFight," Vipri said, his voice cutting into my simulation. I was mid-dodge, weaving through a barrage of laser fire in a ShadowMind scenario. There was no way to block his intrusion. I stopped the advanced sequence and switched to a standard version before he could spot the difference. "V version. Better than mine. Can I join? Give me two minutes to sync mine."

"Brand new, but glitchy," I said, feigning nonchalance. "They just patched it. That's what you get for chasing the latest toy to impress your neighbors." I loaded a standard scenario, mirroring the previous landscape – a jagged, rocky world with slightly higher gravity that tugged at every step – and opened the link for him to join.

"I have handed you control of my SimFight," Vipri said as the link locked in. His lifelike avatar materialized, testing the terrain with a series of high jumps, then flowing into a fluid sequence of strikes and rolls, muscles flexing under the simulated light. I blinked, and my avatar appeared in his SimFight too. Then the images superposed, merging into one for my senses, under the control of my sim. Grinning, I erased my virtual opponent, and Vipri slid into its place with a fluid spin, his eyes glinting with challenge.

Excluding military-grade systems, SimFight was unmatched in mimicking reality. The twenty-foot-wide gyro-sphere rolled with you inside, matching every sprint, leap, or tumble, while a holographic landscape beamed straight into your mind, blurring the line between real and virtual. You run, you jump, you clash. The real trick was the tactile feedback: the dense gas in the sphere, laced with metallic nanoparticles, demanded a filtered mask. Ultrasounds, magnetic fields, and lasers shaped the gas into solid forms in milliseconds. A punch from your opponent bruised your actual skin. A laser shot seared it lightly, leaving a sting that sharpened your focus. You train harder.

We dove into the fray. Vipri lunged, his blade flashing. I parried, the impact jarring my arms as the sphere's gas hardened like metal against my blade. I countered with a spinning kick, grazing his side, and he grunted as the system translated the blow into his own sphere, making a real bruise. The rocky terrain shifted underfoot, forcing us to adapt to crumbling ledges and sudden drops. I vaulted over a boulder, firing a laser pulse that singed his shoulder. He sprang forward into close combat to avoid my next shot and retaliated with a flurry of strikes, one catching my ribs with a dull throb. The higher gravity made every move a test of endurance, sweat beading on my brow as we traded blows under a crimson alien sky. By the time the session ended, we were both panting, the sphere humming as it powered down.

"You fight hard," Vipri gasped, collapsing onto a virtual rock that felt solid under his weight. His chest heaved, mirroring his real exhaustion. "Your training level is unreal."

I dropped beside him, my muscles aching, red welts blooming on my skin that would turn blue by morning. "Just more stubborn," I said, chuckling, and nudged his shoulder with mine, feeling the warmth of his virtual frame bleed through the simulation.

He laughed, placing an arm around my shoulders. His touch was startlingly vivid, the SimFight blending the line between code and reality. A shiver ran through me, not just from the fight's adrenaline. "I will need a doctor before the office tomorrow, to patch me," he said, his voice low, teasing, as his fingers lingered, brushing my collarbone. His gaze flicked to my face, catching the flush I couldn't hide. "I don't want rumors of late-night brawls circulating."

"They already know your night sims are tame-programmed to roll over," I shot back, smirking. I closed the link, laughter bubbling up, thrilled that my skills were snapping back so fast, and that I had sparred with Vipri, his presence still tingling on my skin.

Alenia

"There's something wrong with our house," Diegia whispered.

The evening was cold, the air sharp with petrichor after the storm. I had walked home from the office just to savor it: clear skies, the scent of wet leaves clinging to the streets. Now, the stillness felt wrong.

"Cassia isn't responding. The Net has been cut."

"A local outage?" Storm damage could knock out connections, but the timing prickled my instincts.

"Let me scan the door." Diegia's presence flickered inside my mind as she dove into a hologram containing the security layers. *"There are three burglars, but I don't think they are here to steal. They used Ruby high-level clearance ZeroA. I can't trace the owner; the authorization is too high. Recording was cut off after the intrusion. No idea if they're still inside."*

ZeroA Ruby clearance. The kind that bypassed everything. My stomach tightened. *"Alert Vipri."*

"He is in closed session with Prim. I routed the clearance data to his Diego, flagged it non-urgent." A pause. *"Hopefully that was right. I debated a higher emergency, but ... the chain of command, and all."*

The door slid open without resistance. The hall lay undisturbed, but the silence felt like a held breath. Three steps in, the lock hissed shut behind me.

"We are sealed. Same clearance override. I can't regain control of the house. Cassia is still missing, suppressed or ... fragmented. I don't like this." Her voice was steady, but I could sense the

tension behind it. She was just a DigitalEgo in the beginning, built for control, but I had upgraded her with human feelings and intuition. She didn't like this because *I* didn't like this.

I slipped off my shoes, shrugged my purse and jacket to the floor. Bare feet on cold tile, better traction. Better awareness. The living room loomed ahead.

From the doorway, I caught my own reflection staring back from the wall screen. Someone had hijacked the cameras and was toying with me.

"Try Vipri again."

"Net is still dead. I am sorry..."

Music exploded through the house. Not mine. Some pulsing teen song, all synthetic beats and shrieking vocals. Awful.

"Party time!" a voice crowed.

Three naked teenagers tumbled out of the bedroom. The leader – broad-shouldered, muscle layered like armor – grinned as the others whooped.

"Bed's ready!" he said, flinging a hand toward me, theatrical, his companions mimicking intercourse with mockery and glee. "Ruby-grade invitation. Highest level." His clearance flared on the wall, a crimson sigil of Ruby House. "You're lucky, woman."

My training clicked into place. I scanned them fast. Two were standard Family brats, soft from Net indulgence; one cracking a whip for show. The third one, the speaker, was different. Genetically enhanced, most likely. Movements too precise. Special Forces training, just under his childish surface.

"Stolen clearance," I said. "Your father will love explaining this." A gamble. Ruby kids couldn't have that kind of high clearance, but they didn't need to steal it. More often, they borrowed it from the Family for their games. It was a common thing.

"He approved it for my birthday," the muscled boy sneered, walking into the trap. "We even generated sims for you. The kind you'll enjoy."

Strong. Stupid. "Let me guess. Blue waterfall. Wine. Me, naked in your arms."

"Yeah!" He projected the scene onto the wall – an embarrassing, cliché fantasy replicating one of the simulations I had used to trick the Travelers. Soaked in adolescent narcissism. He slowly rotated my body on the screen – nothing was hidden.

"I get a hundred of those a day," I said, flatly. "Nothing special in your sim. Or in you."

"Net is back," Diegia murmured. *"I had to use some ... less-than-legal subroutines from our friends. Vipri is alerted."*

I tilted my head. "Call your father. Let him tell me he approved this party."

"You are offline," the boy scoffed. But he bit. The link connected instantly.

"Your sons just breached my home with your clearance," I said, cold and composed. "I am giving you a chance to handle this quietly."

The voice that crackled back was all contempt. "You think I care? Bill me the fee for their guilty pleasure. Everything will be settled by the law. You know the law. Cooperate. Might as well enjoy it. I will be more generous than the law ... if I like the show."

"I will file for fraudulent access with stolen clearance. That won't be settled with a fee."

A barked laugh. "Boys, record it. But I want only the highlights. Time is short." The link died.

The muscled-boy spread his hands, grinning. "You heard him." He advanced.

I retreated – not in fear, but with purpose. The corridor bottlenecked them. One at a time.

The other two jostled behind him, waving their little toys: a whip and ropes. One lashed the sofa, giggling. Brats playing predator. But the leader? He moved like a soldier who liked his job too much.

"Start with this," he said, flicking a finger at my blouse. "Tear it. Shake your breasts. Beg for us. Three High Rubys at once? That's a story you'll tell your grandkids."

The delusion was almost fascinating. Cupola bred them to believe their blood made them gods, and the Lessers would beg for any scrap of favor. It also bred fear to control them too: without violent suppression, the Lessers would rise and devour them. So they obeyed. They struck first. Dominance through violation. A sacred rite of paranoia.

I took another step back. Let him follow. Let him think he had won. The corridor narrowed behind me. And I always preferred close quarters.

"Why not do it yourself?" I smiled.

His hand froze mid-reach. "You're ... cooperating?" The thirst in his eyes betrayed his hope for resistance. When I nodded, his grin turned feral. "Good. I'll rip it off you myself, then the whipping starts. Wild sex for hours. Supreme pleasure. Ruby's promise." His chest swelled with anticipation, mind already tasting brutal gratification.

The moment his fingers brushed my blouse, I drove my elbow into his sternum, half-strength, enough to stagger but not to break ribs. There was no need to reveal my training for any police inquiry; for there would certainly be an investigation. And pity ... at this age, he was both victim and villain, imprisoned by his gilded cage.

He gasped, but recovered too fast. His wicked smile returned. "Better. Now we break you properly. Boys, start the recording." His punch came like a rock.

I ducked. His fist cratered the ornamental wood paneling behind me. *Impossible.* That hardwood should have shattered his bones from that angle. No technique, just terrifying, unnatural strength. *What the hell are you?*

"Bitch!" He shook his stinging hand. "You'll..."

The bronze statue from the niche in the wall smashed into his nose, without pity. In that total silence, the crack of bones was deafening. With a ten-pound-heavy statue, any woman is strong enough, no martial arts questions asked. He dropped like a sack of grain. I stepped over his unconscious body and slapped the other two, then snatched their ropes – they did not even think to fight – to tie the one on the ground.

"Call your father," I said, brandishing their own whip. "Ask if he still wants that hard simulation. I am ready to start." I plucked hair from the unconscious brute, dipped it in his blood and sealed everything in a glass. Their whimpers told me they thought it was a trophy. Fools. This was DNA evidence.

They cowered in the corner like startled rabbits. Stripped of privilege, they were just soft, mewling things. The father didn't answer – his son's MedAlert had already mobilized the Ruby Family.

Ten minutes later, FlyCars flared in the sky, above my house. Two Ruby, two Jewel, one carrying the government logo. At every window, my neighbors' faces were pressed against the glass as seven guards in military gear sealed the street. *Overkill. I don't like that.*

Vipri entered first, followed by the father, the Third Ruby and Jewel Security Chiefs, and Shine. Her promotion was fresh; this was her first test. The father had been undermining her at every turn – he had been her competitor for the Security position. *Fortune might favor me today*, I thought, then tried to remember where the quote was from. I failed.

"Responding to a ... guilty pleasure complaint. One against three. I am ready to calculate the official fine," Shine said, her icy gaze sweeping the house with intense blue eyes. "I am not sure what you really meant by it." She glanced at the scene: the speechless father, pointing to his unconscious, bloodied heir, the cowering accomplices. From the boy's Med sensors, there was nothing life-threatening, so the doctors had to wait outside. "And I am unclear on the pleasure part. You have strange tastes," she said to me.

"It comes naturally with such specimens." I gestured to the unconscious boy. "As for complaints, mine concerns unauthorized ZeroA clearance usage. Imagine if this had been a trap. Imagine the Resistance had kidnapped them. And the clearance..."

Vipri feigned innocence. "Shall we file under Article 112? Negligence with high clearance?"

The room chilled. Shine's RigFace held, but the father's jaw twitched a little, enough for Diegia to record and display it in my visual. This was no longer about spoiled brats forcing a Lesser for a guilty pleasure that meant nothing for them – everything would have been solved with a generous fee, as it was usual. Now, it was about the Diamonds' historic fall from the Travelers' grace. A long time ago, the Resistance had penetrated Cupola with a Diamond high clearance, and the Diamonds had been demoted from the First Family into the third rank. High clearances were now much more tightly controlled.

The Third Jewel chief seized the opening. "They could have breached Cupola's core," he said slowly, as if trying to shove every word into the Rubys' heads. There were no feelings in his bland voice, yet I was sure he was cheering inside.

The father's gamble baffled me. *Why risk it? Unless...* "They are young, and did not think too much. They only have sex in their minds, if they have minds." I shrugged, locking eyes with Shine. "Surely Ruby Security can handle this internally, without an official complaint from me?" I pointed at her to make it clear who had to do what, and they all knew that no one could delete an official complaint once it had been filed.

Silence. Invisible DuaLink negotiations were flooding the virtual behind my back.

The bound boy moaned awake.

"Shut your mouth, idiot!" Shine barked. Then, to me: "We have an agreement."

Alenia

It was the weekend again, and we gathered at Vipri's villa, Mask included. The mountain view still stretched beyond the windows, but I barely noticed it anymore. The landscape wasn't to blame.

"His genetic modifications," Mask said, summoning a hologram of the brute who had invaded my home. A Jewel research team had analyzed the blood and hair samples I had given Vipri. Red markers bloomed across the virtual body like wounds.

Do they have enough enhanced soldiers to stop us from destroying the towers? Do they know something we don't? "Are Ruby soldiers stronger than yours?" I asked, feigning idle curiosity.

A beat of silence. Mask's eyes narrowed. "You're gathering intel."

I shrugged.

"Stronger, yes," he conceded. "But they trade speed for power. A curious choice." His gaze flicked to me. "That boy punched through your wall. Yet I assume he wasn't ... difficult to handle."

I nodded.

"I will speak with the Master Lord," Vipri offered.

Mask swirled his wine. "The Master Lord is no longer his own master." He peered at me through the glass, the liquid casting the world in amber. I knew it, as I did the same with my own glass, just that I was staring at my hand, avoiding his gaze. "None of the Big Three have will left. They are shells now. Puppets transformed by the Travelers' hypnotic Duck Dance."

A pause. He glanced at the window, but his eyes didn't stay away for long. His attention returned to me, and we saw each other through the amber, his eye like an insect trapped in resin. Magnified by the wineglass, it studied me with a flicker of curiosity. Color, shape, detail. Recognition. He knew what a Duck Dance meant; his wide staring eye making an association between me and the dance. Or maybe it was just the wine. His stare didn't waver. Neither did mine.

He knows.

"You know what a Duck Dance is," he finally said.

"I have read the same forbidden book as you." My joke fell flat. He knew I was familiar with more than what was written there.

Vipri stepped in, perhaps to buy me a moment. "What makes you think the Travelers hypnotized the Master Lords?"

"Because I know it. The Travelers have changed." Mask's eyes didn't move from mine. "They are obsessed with the New Field beyond reason. And our Master Lords have developed a new fixation during hypnosis." His wineglass tilted further toward my face. "You."

Silence.

Mechanically, I raised my own glass, staining the room in gold. *Amber ... me ... the Master Lords.*

Mask let the tension simmer, letting our confusion mature into unease. Then, blunt as a hammer: "They want to destroy you, Alenia."

"Three weeks ago, they didn't know she existed," Vipri countered.

"Let me rephrase. The Travelers want her destroyed."

"They could kill me anytime," I said. "Sending hormone-addled brats to attack me isn't their style."

"Not kill. *Destroy*. Your Line must survive in the game, but broken. Don't ask me why. A Ruby agent guided those boys to your house. They were too stupid to plan it alone and too ignorant to know who you really are: a High Councilor. Even their mushy brains would have asked questions." His voice sharpened. "Using a statue in defense was clever; it concealed your training. But they will find new ways to test you. To harm you. The boys were instructed to pleasure you until dawn and livestream it. Prime-time slot on Genuine Feelings. The whole world was waiting for you."

The air left my lungs. Not fear. Not anger. A silent collapse. That plan was worse than death.

"She beat me on SimFight," Vipri added, half-joking, tone taut. He had known. Mask had told him, but not everything. He had hidden it to spare me. Now, wary, he was reassessing.

Mask orchestrated this. At his level, no slip was unplanned. *Why pressure me now?*

"I need more training," Vipri joked again, the barely hidden tension fraying his voice.

"Far more. You need genetic tweaks too. Like that Ruby boy. And real combat experience." Mask's shrug was slow, deliberate. A provocation.

"We fought in the Rebellion," Vipri said, with a heat that betrayed hurt pride, but I sensed that Mask was cooking a larger game.

"Beginner's training." Mask stood abruptly and crossed the room toward the library. When he returned, he held an archaic album: *The Royal Museum of Art*. Leather cover, brittle edges, old, printed before the name was changed to *Cupola Museum of Art*.

My chest tightened. *My collections... My donation, three centuries ago...* The one I had loved most once bore my name. Now rebranded *The Lady Diamond Collection* after the purge. History rewritten. Legacy stolen. NetPedia cemented the lie. Truth buried under curated narratives. From time to time, they even aired a documentary about the noble Diamond Lady who created the museum and made the donation. *Fake... It's all fake... It's just that people don't know it.* Repeated many times, a lie becomes truth. Even if the old books resurfaced, no one would read them. The herd doesn't like unfamiliar pastures. NetPedia trained them too well.

Why that album, Mask?

Lost in my thoughts, I hadn't noticed him flip it open. My portrait stared back. My real face, painted before the erasure. Our eyes met across the centuries. It burned me, the way my portraits had been burned in the purge. Mask gave a slight nod. A signal. It was time for Vipri to know.

There was no denying it now: Mask knew exactly who I was.

"Look at her." Mask pushed the album toward Vipri.

Vipri studied the portrait, then me. "I see ... a resemblance." His tone was forced calm, but his fingers trembled a little on the edge of the album.

My smile stayed placid, though bitterness coiled in my chest – not just at seeing *her* again, but at what I knew would follow.

"What if it's more than coincidence?" Mask pressed.

"Is the Cursed Queen your ancestor?" Vipri used the insult the Travelers had embedded in history. My smile turned brittle.

Mask tapped the page, then pointed at me. "Look at her smile."

"Don't take that name seriously. It's just propaganda," Vipri said quickly, a touch of guilt flickering in his eyes. "Officially, yes, Cursed Queen; of course I must use the *correct* term. But she was brilliant. An interesting character. A storm in human form. And..." He hesitated. "A legendary beauty."

I let myself enjoy his words, but I was waiting. Mask had revealed too much – about me, and about himself. "Security Chiefs are usually pragmatic. I hadn't guessed at this philosophical side. What do you want to peel back first? The Travelers? The Master Lords? Me? Or you?"

"You have guessed what I am." Mask's grin was all teeth. "But I am not a sleeper like you."

"Maybe I am not one. Or maybe you are." I shrugged.

"It wasn't my rebel portrait that woke up your memory, was it?"

"No. Your humor."

Mask laughed, oddly delighted. "My humor is unique. I am a Balancer."

"The last Balancers were in the ShadowMind Order. Disbanded long ago. Your birth certificate was printed many years later."

"A new Order rose. Hidden. Several Orders, actually, spread across the galaxy." He skipped past the lie, confirming he was older than his records embedded into Jewel ranks by a ShadowMind faction I hadn't known it existed. But he wasn't a Traveler. "We operate without Galax Market's leash now. No Faction restrictions. Cleaner. And if the New Field has a chance to succeed ... we will allow it."

"They will die," I whispered. My throat tightened. You never change a Balancer's mind. I had been one, briefly. Too low-ranked to weigh the fate of a galaxy.

"Evolution is natural. A part of the Universe dies first when a new one is born," he said, gently. "This time, it's just a galaxy. Black Eye vanishes from its center. The old Field retreats with its souls, Crawlers, Observers, and memory. Then the Universe expels the galaxy. A new matrix is formed. The rest of the universe won't feel it, but most here will perish. A few," he nodded at me, "might be able to merge with the New Field. Become something else: Observers, Crawlers. Chaos will reign until order returns. Evolution."

"Like this order?" I gestured to the world outside.

"Judgment isn't my job," he said, "but I agree with your sentiment, and this isn't the only way."

"You are judging plenty. Where there is no risk, you judge. Where risk looms – you know what happened with the Saurian New Field – you step back. You are a Contrarian Balancer."

"Once, I had have slit your throat for that." His chuckle was dry. "Convince me the New Field will fail, and I will be what you call a Right Balancer."

"It's true." Vipri finally spoke, still staring at me. There was hope in his voice, cautious but real.

"Which stunned you more?" Mask teased. "My nature? Or hers?"

"Neither of you is who I believed."

"The game is the same as your photo ruses." I met Vipri's gaze, smiling faintly. *This is the precipice. Will he leap – or step back?*

"The scale is different," he said. "But the rules? The strategy? Identical. Funny how perspective shifts when you are the pawn." His tone was deliberate, eyes locked on mine, and some hope returned to me. "We will reconvene tomorrow. Among you two, I feel like a child. My mind needs ... resetting. Rest." He left, steps uneven, exhaustion dragging at his shoulders.

Mask and I departed in silence.

Alone in my room, I drifted through memory. Only two or three ShadowMinds had matched Mask's wit. *But only one...* It wasn't just humor. It was something deeper. A feeling.

"Diegia, search my earliest memories. Before I was ShadowMind."

"At your age? That will take weeks."

"Start with the name Xiriaxis. Pray it's not him. Ignore voice. Track speech patterns. Humor."

Hours later, she projected the reconstruction.

"I hadn't realized that weeks had already passed."

The simulation, built from fragmented memory, was slightly blurred, three centuries old and patchy, like a corrupted file. Still, it was clear enough.

A shadow emerged from nothing – a black humanoid void moving with a dancer's grace. I knew now it had been a hologram masking the real form. Back then, I had no idea. Details returned in fragments: colors, wind, voices, emotion, thoughts. I was watching a slice of my life.

This ... thing isn't a Black Hat. The impersonation was flawless, limbs, nails, posture. But no face. No eyes. I couldn't look away, desperate to glimpse something in the void of his face. No mouth, nothing... Just blackness, more chilling than the most vicious mask.

"Are you a Traveler?" Deceneus asked, his voice steady. We parted and stepped back, swords up.

"Traveler? You wound me." A man's voice. The shadow clutched its chest in mock offense. "I have feelings. Unlike those balls of neurons pinned in ice. Asexual info-cubes from womb-tanks. Phew!" he added, mockingly. "Travelers don't know pleasure. No fun, no drinks, no sunsets. They would erase someone like her," he gestured with a misty hand at me, without flinching. "I prefer beauty. I might even feel remorse after... You know what I mean." He leaned toward me, pretending to sniff, then turned toward Deceneus and winked at him with an eye that emerged for a few moments from the shadow. "You, however, are lucky. Now, business. I am here to help."

The simulation collapsed.

"It's him," I breathed. "Xiriaxis. A Level Eight ShadowMind. The highest level right now. The last of his kind in the galaxy."

Morning mist had burned away, leaving the lake exposed under a merciless sun, and a greater emptiness in my mind. Not that I needed it. The magical aura of the lake was gone, no shimmering illusions, no whispered secrets, just cold clarity. At least the sun sank into my skin, offering warmth where nothing else could. No Magic Window. No enchanted lake. Just a scenic view stripped of charm. From the height of the terrace, my gaze drifted across the water. *And no footsteps behind... But still beautiful.*

"You are missing the magic," Vipri suddenly whispered behind me.

I didn't turn. Didn't breathe.

"You sighed," he murmured again.

Reaching back, I found his hand and pulled him close. "Still beautiful. The real magic is always inside."

"You were right," he said, thoughtful. "The game changes nothing. What's the difference between one hundred forty and three hundred years? You will always be my ancient space granny." He caught my elbow before I could jab him, wrapping me in an embrace instead.

"Hold me tight," I whispered. "Just ... hold me."

The living room welcomed us with the scent of baking bread, stirring old, stubborn memories: a little girl entering the house on a winter's day. Mistria had made my favorite salted cheese pie, pulling a smile from Vipri.

"Guess who told her?" He winked.

"That traitor Cassia."

"She is no traitor," Mistria said, faking an angry tone. Her frowning hologram appeared in the middle of the room. "Tell me if I am better than her."

I grumbled through a full mouth, spinning my free hand three times in approval. She beamed and vanished.

"I think they conspire behind our backs," I said.

"Not conspire," Vipri laughed. "Coordinate. Walk with me on the shore."

On our way back, Vipri had a strange curiosity about things that had happened hundreds of years before. I thought he wanted to check the official story. "Did you know Sarul?"

The name was a stain on the lake's beauty. Even after so many years I could not forget him. "Yes. You want the truth behind the Diamond's founding."

"Something like that."

"Four hundred years ago, the Celestial Travelers teleported him and his team from a planet called Earth, to help them enslave us – at that point in time, they were one of the many Factions in the galaxy. An evil mind, craving power. Not that he needed encouragement; he had have killed me for the throne either way. But the Travelers wanted his financial system – at least in this he was a genius – to control people better. The chains you see now in place."

"Yet Sarul lost."

"He died as collateral in Deceneus's fight with a Traveler. His system survived. We won that round, but my fool grandson – and the other fool kings – borrowed from his banks for wars until nations collapsed. That's how we lost." I gripped Vipri's arm. "Never ask about that snake again."

Evening bled the color from the day, the walk around the lake still echoing through my mind. I entered the empty living room, uneasy – until Mask arrived, whistling a tune I hadn't heard since a different planet, and a different war. A message? A taunt? *You knew I would be alone. Let's skip the song and dance. What are you really after?*

"Vipri is on a call with Prim," he said, a slight hint of mockery; it was just his humor trying to communicate something I couldn't yet see. "Hungry?"

At my nod, he let Mistria choose our meal – like Cassia, she always enjoyed the freedom to surprise us.

You want to talk... "Xiriaxis, what happens when the New Field is born? If it is born."

"I die, of course," he smiled, not showing any surprise or reaction when hearing his true name. I suddenly understood he wanted to become Black Eye of the new Universe.

Could the Celestials stop him? Or could he be made to believe they could?

"You are too young to die," Vipri said, entering mid-conversation, oblivious. A pause – likely consulting Mistria about dinner. "Good choice," he agreed, joining us. "Did you know? Our friend here is the new Jewel Third Lord. The old one..." He made the gesture for vanished with his right hand

I raised my glass. "One step closer to..." *To what, exactly?*

"Closer than I wished," Mask mused. "Unplanned. I dislike others scripting my fate. The unknown is dangerous. But refusal wasn't ... prudent."

"Now you will meet the Travelers monthly," I probed.

"Lovely people. A Duck Dance awaits if I am not careful," he said, as if rehearsing for it already. "I don't want to become their puppet like the Master Lords." His fingers drummed the table. "My options narrow if they try it aboard their station."

Can you resist the hypnosis embedded in a Duck Dance? You fear it. I must push you to read the Lines. "Death reshuffles all plans. Who orchestrated this event?" It was a stark reminder: the Erins were behind his rise in the hierarchy. "Sometimes the variables are reset." *Your own words...* I almost smiled, and Diegia froze my facial muscles.

His Diego would have caught my micro-expressions. Mask stared into the middle distance, recalculating.

"Field politics again?" Vipri broke the silence, glancing between us.

"The New Field tolerates only one master," I said, smiling at Vipri's confusion, but I wanted him to stay out of our game. "The Travelers covet that throne too. Isn't it?"

"Nice try." Mask grinned. "But I accept the necessity of clarifying this. They do. Many High Travelers nurse the same ambition – quietly. Nobody will open the can of worms before the time comes, lest they destabilize their ranks prematurely. When the New Field is born, they will turn on each other. And I? A mere Jewel Third Lord, insignificant, doing my duty." He lowered his voice, as if still trying to anticipate a danger he could not see clearly. "My Field signature was changed a long time ago. None suspect what I am. But succeed and..." His smile returned, predatory. "Seats on the new Galactic Council await," he said, like someone booking a front-row ticket to the apocalypse.

That night, I took the decision to form a new Line of Time around him – the greatest ShadowMind of the millennium. But strength has its weakness, too. His lay in the paradox of supreme confidence against the Travelers in the future Field, and his fear of Erins' calculations. Yet, it was another weakness, subtle, buried, and far more dangerous.

The revelation struck me late. The battle for dominance in the New Field wouldn't be fought with weapons, but with something far more esoteric: command over possibility, mastery of probabilities, and the ability to manipulate timelines, the invisible tides of fate. The Field was a lattice of conscious resonance, shaped by will, intuition, and insight. Mask could defeat five Travelers in the physical realm – but in the Field, fighting skills meant nothing. There, it was a game of patterns, of interpretation, of vision. Only the Erins could challenge them in the Field – for the Travelers, too, could form new Lines.

You offer us Galactic Council seats – is that weakness or strength? I studied him through my RigFace's neutral mask. *No, you need me for something sooner. Something in the Lines of Time. Me and the young rebel. In this play, we are instruments. Pieces in your game until the New Field is born.* "It's dangerous when the variables try to rewrite Lines from inside a game set by a master," I murmured. *And I am just as guilty.* But I would play with him, another variable in the Line. He will play against the Erins – the original gamemasters – and the ones who designed the actual game. And he will play against the Travelers, the counter-gamers.

"Awfully dangerous," Mask agreed. "But the prize justifies the risk."

"The Erins might disagree."

"The Erins." He shrugged. "Yes, they invented the Lines of Time – but no system survives the chaos of agency. The Lines shift constantly. No mind can calculate every second – there are always gaps. Hours. Days." His fingers tapped the table, slow, deliberate. "Time and timing are everything. A single unnoticed shift between two of their readings can trigger an avalanche ... one that can't be stopped."

Why tell me this? This wasn't just banter – it was his true strategy. He wanted my reaction, my unconscious validation. Every twitch recorded, analyzed. By both.

"Diegia, block my micro-expressions on Field-related topics. Leave the rest visible."

I let the silence stretch, observing him through my RigFace's veil. "Perhaps Armin will die too, when the New Field comes. Or perhaps he will survive. A split-second choice." *Let that fear root in you. Go read your Line in the game.*

"Dinner arrives," Mask said abruptly as the majordomo robot entered the room, guided by Mistria.

You reacted a little too fast.

The dinner followed its course, with forced normalcy – Mask playing the gracious host, Vipri still reeling from the night's revelations. I almost pitied him; surrounded by ancient players, he was indeed the child here. Mask? A millennium-old ShadowMind wearing human skin, navigating futures.

At dessert, Mask ambushed Vipri. "Where do you stand on this ... transition?"

"I am a Jewel man. A bureaucrat." Vipri said slowly, and swirled his wine. "If a new universe comes, it comes. But until I see proof, it's just philosophy over good wine."

"And the Queen? The ShadowMind?" Mask's tone was light, as if discussing vintage vintages.

Vipri opened the album, comparing portrait to present. "A fine story for my grandchildren. If I ever have any." He tapped the page. "When I see proof, I will inform the authorities. Until then?" He raised his empty glass. "Just a fairy tale."

Mask filled our glasses. "Cheers."

We drank – each to a different future. The dinner ended in a silence that was neutral in appearance, yet hid many weird expectations – possibilities fermenting in every unspoken word.

"Dance with me," Vipri whispered mysteriously, once Mask finally left us alone.

"You look like a child with a secret," I teased.

"For his great-grandmother." He dodged my elbow – now a classified weapon in his mind. "Surely you are too ancient to be surprised?"

But the music proved me wrong – wonderful, charged with memories of a better past – and I fought hard to stop my tears. *Old. So old.* The court at Dava shimmered behind my eyelids: gilded halls, my first dance with my future husband, Deceneus, and trembling with stolen glances. He had just arrived there. *I was seventeen...* The magic song had outlived empires.

"I am sorry. Mask told me about this song. I did not know... Let's have a walk. It's a beautiful night." Vipri reached for the controls and stopped the music.

"Don't." My voice cracked. "These tears are for a ball several centuries gone. For a girl who didn't yet know what that dance would start in her life. I can't believe that I was once so young. Play it again." I twined my arms around his neck. "Dance with me."

Note by note, the world dissolved. No walls. No wars. Just the music winding us together, tighter than time itself – the vivid feeling of a night-time ritual, tender yet defiant in the face of everything we had lost and might still lose.

Through the open door, the night outside was silent; a sense of calm coming from the darkness, as though the world was holding its breath – not peace, but quiet suspense. The kind of silence one finds before a council vote or a coup. I stepped out onto the terrace and glanced at the sky. Cloudy ... no full moon. No magic... Outside calm. A bit inside my mind too. How else could I be, in the mountains, away from the effervescence of the city, away from Lines and plots?

The wind was dead, and cold crept slowly into the room – his room. I touched the glass of the door; it was even colder. Agitated by a dream, Vipri turned, throwing a pillow on the floor, then mumbled something in his deep sleep. I thought I heard *Alenia*, and my calmness became deeper – maybe he was dreaming of me.

Far away, a wolf howled. Another answered, farther still. Danger echoes, always. Two flashbacks struck me simultaneously, tearing at my calm: the old ball in Dava – the dance – and then, the gesture of his dying brother that Vipri repeated without knowing it. *Death... Why both? Mask and Vipri... Danger and the mirage of happiness?* A strange duality. I glanced back into the room; ghostly, quiet. *I have lived long enough, and he is not as young as his brother, my former...*

I shook my head, craving to read the Lines of Time. *I can't. I can, but I shouldn't.* For hundreds of years, since the Erins invented the reading – a subtle but potent calculus of probable futures – one truth has persisted: the more you look, the more they look back. Most sleeper cells trained in the Lines had either died, disappeared, or worse. The readings alter the flow, like quantum observations – the reader becomes a variable, influencing the results. And the reader's behavior change, this is the most visible outcome. And the most dangerous. Others are watching the same strand. They will see your hand, and strike. Lethal changes. It matters who makes the change – whether the Lines bring it to you, or you drag it in against the tide. A gust of wind, brief and biting, toyed with my bare skin, leaving shivers in its wake.

"Any thoughts, Diegia?"

"Well," she whispered, her face a sober mask. *"I just lost my virginity. I am twenty years old. It was about time."*

"You had your share in that simulation with the rebel," I teased. Her face remained a mask, but a familiar warmth flickered beneath. She was amused in a motherly way, unrelated to her age, but by my long hesitation to begin anew, by my reactions. Perhaps she wanted me to finally stop dragging the dead behind me.

"Simulations!" She dismissed my words with a sweeping gesture. *"No Diego inside. No fun. You had something to share with that young rebel. Doesn't matter that you still don't know what. Me..."*

"Do you really ... collaborate? Even in...?"

"Why not?" she shrugged, and for a moment I wasn't sure she was still joking. *"Enjoy the night. Tomorrow..."*

Do they really...? She caught the thought and chose to vanish – kindly. *You are right; I have plenty of things to worry about...*

In silence, I raised my arms, letting the starting wind thread through me. Marble. Statue. No longer cold. The wind's fingers brushed my skin like memory, and somewhere in the forest, a wolf howled again – strangely melodious, as if the night itself were singing of things long buried but not forgotten.

Chapter 11

For days, I studied the distant volcano through SkEye, familiarizing myself with the area, searching for paths and hiding places. I also sought beauty; the place was a wonder. Before leaving the capital, I took one last look. It was misty that day, the silent cone shrouded like an old wizard, lacking only a staff.

The Resistance dispatched a SharkSub for my stealth mission. From everything I had heard, it was fast, solid, and comfortable, a cozy steel torpedo, ready for my ride. But I was completely wrong. There was no torpedo; the submarine mimicked its namesake predator in every detail from head to tail. And there was no comfort; the whole thing was only three feet in diameter at its widest point. It even moved like a shark, with a sinuous, tail-driven motion – the propelling jets were never used, reserved for emergencies. No one was looking to start them.

During the long journey, sleep came fitfully, and I mostly drifted in a haze of discomfort. You couldn't stand inside, only recline in an angled chair, nearly horizontal, with barely more personal space than on a plane. But planes don't usually confine you for so long. The submarine advanced slowly, propelled by sluggish tail movements, meandering its way, sometimes doubling back – AI-calculated pattern – like any other shark.

A day later, we had left the main river, heading north up a tributary still deep enough to conceal a twenty-foot-long shark. In total, my journey took a day and a half, lying in a barely comfortable chair, surrounded by the scent of unfamiliar chemicals; the thing was brand new. It wasn't pleasant, but at least it was safe; the submarine could evade any radar.

The pilot in front was a taciturn young man who would return the same way, another thirty-something hours. He wouldn't be hunted, or at least less so than myself, and I would be alone for the last, most dangerous part of the mission. Having learned about the centuries-old Alenia and Batranu, I avoided treating the pilot as a peer until I knew more. I might be the youngest rebel. I now knew more about Alenia, or the famous Queen Altamira, or whatever other names she had during such a long life. My mission could save her. I owed it to her and to the strange feelings I carried for her. "You will learn why," Batranu had said. I hoped we would both survive long enough to find out. It was a small comfort that she didn't yet know the connection between us, and strange too – I was in my early twenties. I lost my memory in the spaceship's explosion, but how could we share a past that she had already forgotten?

"You will land in half an hour. We just passed their patrol zone," the pilot said, waking me from daydreaming. He projected a holographic map displaying a large river and dense tropical forest. He couldn't turn to look at it, but the projection came from his mind. "We are here, and you will land here," he said, marking the spots. "The gray zone is their patrol area, FlyCars and drones. No need to worry; we will land deep in the park, outside the control zone. You land. This tunnel," he highlighted a long path from near the volcano's peak to its base, "will take you to a small cave at the mountain's foot. There's another tunnel for your exit." This path looked easier, almost parallel to the ground. "Enter the upper tunnel during the day, when no clouds cover the cone. They have forecast scattered clouds, but it's a weather forecast, not a sunrise. You know how reliable those are. SkEye must record your entry."

"Why?"

"Don't worry about SkEye. It records everything."

"I am worried for my life, not SkEye. If they see me..."

"They won't *see* you. They will record you. No one with half a mind wanders that wild area, so there are no active watchers."

Thanks for calling me a halfwit. I was torn between amusement and annoyance. His words held no malice, and if he sensed my irritation, he didn't show it.

"When things escalate, they will analyze the recordings. You must be seen at the top of the volcano, so they won't know how deep you have gone. Time is short. The deeper you go, the harder it is to contact the Field – that's common knowledge. You have a rare ability to reach it; I've heard about that, but they don't know. Behind your very comfortable chair, which I designed, is three hundred feet of rope – light, strong, made of carbon sheets one atom thick on a molecular steel substrate, weighing just five pounds. It's enough to cross the precipices and can support ten of you. There's also a chip with a detailed 3D map of the tunnels; my drones are excellent cartographers. You can thank me later."

"Has anyone actually climbed there?"

"Too risky to send people just for mapping. The virtual model was built from your profile; you're trained well enough to climb safely."

"Do you have a plan B?"

"We always have a plan B. It's in our mutual interest that plan A succeeds, don't you think?"

For the first time, I caught humor in his voice. I had missed it earlier, too focused. He had been trying to lift my spirits for a while.

"You may be right," I said, just to respond.

"After two days down there, you will enter the Field. You have enough food and some water. Don't worry; there are good mineral springs. I haven't tasted them myself, but I trust the drones – you will like the flavor. Your virtual model accounts for many variables," he said, slightly amused by my reaction to the flavor comment. "A Field Crawler will connect you with an Observer named Deceneus. There will be no technical issues; you match him."

"What do you mean, I match him?"

"Your profiles in the Field are the same, or something like that; I am not an expert. That's why you were chosen for this mission. When I say no problems, I mean technical ones. You know what I mean."

"That's not my biggest concern?"

"Something like that. The Travelers' tech will detect the Field connection in about ten seconds, but it will take time to pinpoint you properly and send a spaceship. The recordings," he reminded me, "and the two-day delay. It's hard to understand a lunatic hiding in a deep cave for days."

"Thanks."

"You're welcome. Your safety is our priority. A lot of information will be transferred to you through the Field, and you will feel dizzy. Don't worry if the transmission stops. The Observer will cut it off before they bomb the mountain. Just get out as fast as you can."

"No one mentioned bombing in my training."

"I am mentioning it now. Bombing is a euphemism. They will obliterate the mountain."

"I will still be inside?"

"If you don't move fast enough, yes. You won't get out. Here is another cave," he pointed on the hologram, deep down, under the base of the volcano, close to the surface. "It's linked to the cone and the previous cave by the second tunnel I marked. You're safe there. Fill your water bags in the cone; there's no water in that cave."

"If I make it there..."

"If... There's another hitch. They won't use excessive force. By their standards, of course."

"They care about the planet?"

"You have no idea how much. Every planet has its own consciousness, like the Universe itself. Without the planet being at least neutral, their New Field is doomed. You have two goals: give Alenia a chance to escape their net – they have squeezed some Lines around her – and trigger the planet's reaction. If it's really possible. I am no expert. Time to land." He opened the hatch. "Wait three days in the second cave. I will be back a day later."

"How can a planet...?" I tried to ask.

"Don't forget the rope. You have a full report on the training chip, and plenty of time in the cave to review it. Just to keep you entertained." He smiled, but the humor vanished from his voice as he extended his hand. "We're counting on you."

I gripped his hand in a long farewell. "Good luck," he added.

I will need it. Stepping out of the hatch, I faced the forest: a dense, uninviting green wall, like any subtropical jungle. It was eerily quiet, no movement, not even a breeze. The submarine, mostly submerged, was tucked under the canopy of a large tree, just fifteen feet from the shore, invisible to SkEye. The water was deep enough to swallow the sub, but too murky to see more than a few inches down. *I will have to swim,* I thought, recalling how I had dreamed of swimming while trapped on Aurora, though certainly not in this muddy water. I waded in slowly until only my head remained above the surface.

"Go!" The pilot's shout barely reached me over the water's splash. I was already on the shore, diving into the underbrush as a LasGun beam vaporized the submarine's hatch. My first shot at the drone was sluggish, rusty reflexes. The pilot reached the shore, made it five steps before the drone's beam seared through his shoulder. Luckily, my second shot found its mark, sending the machine crashing in a shower of sparks, making me jump back in panic. The pilot wasn't dead. Just fifteen feet apart, he was applying a MedKit against his charred chest wound, teeth gritted. I looked at the smoking wreckage – it wasn't a military drone; those were inescapable. I searched the river up and down: no more drones, but the SharkSub was disabled. Placing an arm around his waist, I dragged the pilot deeper into the forest, propping him against a sapling as he trembled. The scene was eerily familiar – months ago, I had been the one patching my own wounds in a tunnel. But his injury was worse: a drone's LasGun packed two times the energy of a handheld. At least he had help.

"You will live," I said. "And of course, you have a plan B."

"If I can remember it through this," he gasped with a pained grin. It takes a few minutes for Diego to numb a wound like this, never completely. He pointed to his shredded suit where the LasGun had struck. "Check my thermal signature."

I switched to infrared vision as he turned slowly, wobbling on his weak legs, giving me a full view. I shared the recorded scan: thermal protection was down thirty percent. "Not bad," he whispered, "but it could be better. Now that we are stuck together longer, call me Pilot. I know, weird guerrilla name," he said with a snicker.

"You have now the thermal signature of a small deer. Just need to graze and hop rocks, to trick AI's sensors," I said, trying to lift his spirits.

His laugh was strained but real. He stepped away from the tree and tested his legs and arms, grimacing. Diego and the MedKit pain inhibitors were working, but a wound like that could never be fully numbed without knocking him out. We needed to move fast, and his Diego's monitoring would balance sedation accordingly. "Give me two minutes," he whispered, likely following his MedKit's advice.

We moved under the trees, out of SkEye's sight – him limping, me scanning the forest. The light was dim, filtered through a thick green haze. We reached a ridge overlooking the river, where the wreckage of the submarine lay. Three FlyCars landed silently, expelling commandos armed to the teeth.

"Rangers and RoboDogs," Pilot said, pointing to sleek, half-starved-looking machines. "I don't like this."

If I didn't account for the Special Forces, the Rangers were the best soldiers operating in open field. Below, on our river bank, the commandos split into two groups: one approached the submarine, the other scanned the forest with various devices. The RoboDogs sniffed our tracks, and I bet they had DNA sniffers too.

"I hate doing this," Pilot muttered, fumbling with a small black device. The detonator clicked. A heartbeat later, a blast echoed through the mountains. Terrified birds screeched, then silence fell. The explosion painted the sky in a slow succession – gold to crimson to gray – swallowing submarine and soldiers alike. The RoboDogs became shrapnel. The river carried what remained. The view was strangely captivating, if not for the human remains floating in the water. Death could be artistic when you escaped it. When the fog fully cleared, no commandos or RoboDogs remained. The submarine was gone too.

"Six months building that beauty," Pilot whispered, watching his creation's funeral pyre. "But the tech couldn't fall into their hands."

"They have pictures, infrared scans..."

"My beauty was smart. Out of water, the slim layers of outer molecules flipped, mimicking a standard submarine's metallic signature. She didn't look like a fish anymore. SkEye wouldn't know." He smiled, answering my unspoken question, but it was a sad smile. "Nanospheres did the trick – two halves, different materials, different electric potentials. Switch polarity, and the surface turns to absorbent rubber. Switch again, it's metallic."

"Smart," I said.

"Fifty kilos of super-explosive. Ten bastards fewer. And my beauty," he sighed. "Now, they will send Special Forces, a different beast. The forest is too dense for FlyCars; they will have to walk. But small drones can slip through, slowly. The RoboDogs have no problems. We have less than two hours until..." He didn't finish. Their paranoia about securing the area gave us a small edge; the Special Forces were still far off, outside the neutral zone circling the area reserved only for Cupola high levels: the Blue Mountains.

"Diego, show me pictures from before the explosion." It hadn't crossed my mind to check before, but our camera had recorded everything. Diego projected an inner hologram: above water, the SharkSub looked like any small metallic submarine.

The forest thickened, green light filtering like liquid through the canopy. Pilot lagged behind, his breath ragged. I slowed; no words were needed. He shrugged, too weary to speak. The MedKit helped, but healing took time; his injury was severe, and I knew it well. After over two hours, we reached a ridge with two vistas: the volcano to the left, the turquoise lake to the right. No drones trailed us, yet.

"Fifteen-minute break," I said. I didn't need one, but he did. "Let's see where they are right now." I didn't want Pilot to feel useless. I raised a small, passive antenna tuned to a military wavelength, using Aurora decryption software. Even with that forbidden tech, we couldn't send a proper authorization signal and ask for codified data. The first SkEye images appeared, free data, low resolution, but good enough: Special Forces commandos, with different gear, were scouring our landing site. They had arrived precisely two hours and ten minutes after we left and started to search the area. The submarine's fiery farewell had made them nervous and overly cautious. I almost laughed, then shared the images with Pilot, who met my eyes as the images loaded. The hunt was on, and the hunters were afraid.

"They're scared of traps. My beauty's death is still useful." His voice was almost pleased.

Too bad we left them nothing dangerous. But running for your life was a brutal sport. To our left loomed the volcano's majestic cone. I felt a pang knowing it might be gone in days, like the submarine; if things went well. To the right was the familiar turquoise lake. *Beautiful. That's why they block this area from ordinary people. Mask is there. And Vipri...* The last name made me feel even more uncomfortable.

Pilot silently pointed to the left-hand path toward the volcano. I gestured to the lake. "We head toward the lake under forest cover until late evening. We need a distraction to hide our traces. High-ranking Cupola bastards have villas on its shore. There will be more pressure on our hunters if some authorities think we are on a killing mission. When we reach an open spot like that," I pointed to a sunlit patch nearby, "let SkEye record you, face covered. It should be brief enough to look like an accidental slip by wounded fugitives. We do it just before dusk, with the sun positioned right, no mountains to shade it." I projected a hologram for him. "In half a mile, we reach this stream, then walk north through the water to trick the RoboDogs. They will split into two teams, upstream and downstream. The team going down will be stronger as the path goes to their precious villas. Then, at these three tributaries, they will split again until their RoboDogs' DNA sniffers pick something up. Maybe we will get lucky. I wish it had rain." I glanced skyward.

"They started the hunt," Diego said, suddenly. SkEye showed three small drones and three RoboDogs entering the forest, followed by three commando groups, five soldiers each.

Three times three... They need more commandos to follow the streams. "Time to go." I stowed the antenna and grabbed my backpack. Pilot nodded silently. We had a two-hour, twenty-five-minute lead.

When they arrived at the stream where we had left the water, our lead grew to three hours and ten minutes against the commandos. But once the RoboDogs found our DNA and scent over the land, the teams stopped checking each tributary; their drones spread on our tail. Three hours' walking for a man was just twenty minutes for a small drone in this dense forest.

From SkEye, the closest drone-RoboDog pair was now ten miles behind us as the crow flies. We had to avoid open spaces visible from the sky; they faced no such limits, though the rough terrain slowed even the RoboDogs.

"We need to do something," I muttered, rummaging through my backpack for inspiration. "Walk in small circles around me to confuse the dogs." Pilot understood and stood, moving in tired steps. "Sorry," I said, remembering his wound. "Prepare two different mines for dogs and drones. I will walk." He nodded with a weary smile, just a thin slit on his face. I crossed my own path repeatedly, returning to the same spot, tracing several large figure-eights to leave a tangled scent trail for the RoboDogs. When I finished, Pilot planted a bean-sized mine at the center of the eight. It was small but strong enough to destroy a RoboDog, or at least disable a leg. The challenge was activation; its ten-inch trigger radius required the robot to step precisely, but it would likely follow my looping scent back and forth, following each figure-eight. One of these trails would be the trigger.

For the second mine, I climbed a tree above the path, twenty feet up, on a large branch. It took time to secure the nut-sized mine in a place that could offer an optimum range for the sensors, and it was powerful enough to afflict everything within a hundred-foot radius, barring tree interference. And drones were even easier to disable. After the first explosion on the ground, a drone would investigate. Men would come. Cautious. *If it would be a first explosion...* The mine's AI could distinguish drone from dog, taking it down – or multiple drones, if we were lucky.

"Incoming drone, front," Diego warned. Pilot glanced at me; his helmet's passive radar had caught the same signal. *"I've got their radio chatter, using an encryption key we know. There's a new team ahead: people, RoboDogs, one drone. Not enough data on numbers, but typically one or two dogs per drone. And perhaps five men. The robots are two miles away."* He marked their position on my inner map.

Alenia

Mask was nervous, and he let us see it, his RigFace unused. "Last night, I made a move," he said slowly, looking disturbed, as if he weren't really there. "It was both stupid and good." He glanced at me through his glass. The wine distorted the shape of his eye. I was already used to his peculiar way of emphasizing things in our small circle. "I read the Lines of Time, in a game in which I am a variable, another Line."

There were a few seconds of silence, and I realized he was analyzing our reactions with AI, using snapshots his Diego had taken.

"You" – he pointed at Vipri – "had no reaction. You" – he looked at me – "knew what it meant, and enjoyed it. You let me see that. I would have reacted the same way, so no hard feelings."

"You are in danger," I said.

"Now you are unhappy," he smiled. "I am damned if I do something, damned if I don't. Doing nothing reveals as much as doing something, because my thinking is now corrupted by what I learned. I can't know what I would have done without reading the

Lines. That knowledge can't be erased. The future will change anyway. I don't know why. I don't know how."

"The child needs to know," Vipri said in his most serious tone, which made me smile inwardly at his trick. "The Lines. What's behind them, not the hollow stories circulating in official or Jewel circles."

"The Erins were a Travelers' genetic experiment gone wrong and escaped from control. A Stone Age civilization born by mistake, with quantum brains capable of processing more than a hundred people's minds together. Not locals, *Travelers.*

Having no history or technology, the Erins named their quantum computations *Lines of Time*. It's just mental calculus combined with an internal holographic projection ability. It looks like time projected in two dimensions – a carpet, with the past stretching out nearly infinitely. They calculate the most probable future for a person or group, using ... variables. You, me – we are variables – Lines in their models. Important Travelers are represented too.

If a Line takes a sudden turn, you can trace it backward to identify the most probable cause, and the person responsible. In a long history, none of the sleeper cells that read the Lines ended well. So I may need to vanish before the Travelers vanish me." He sipped his wine, where a less trained man might have drained the glass. His grand plan to master the new universe had shrunk to plotting where to hide.

"The good news – this is for you," Mask raised his glass toward me. "Armin created an incredibly complex game. I assume it's his; no one else could design on such a scale. He tricked everyone. You can never be sure with Erin constructs.

You and the young rebel are just bait. That wasn't the original plan, but your chemistry didn't work. Because of his specific DNA, mentally, he is the Field copy of your former husband, Deceneus – who is still alive somewhere in the galaxy. If you want to know more, ask the other Deceneus. The Observer. But the boy's mind is ... altered, there is no connection to your former husband. It belongs only to him. Maybe it's the result of the accident that erased his memory."

"You had only one husband in over three hundred years?" Vipri said, half-joking, and the tension in the room gave me the seconds I needed to recover. Still, it felt artificial.

"And some romantic entanglements. You can't marry again after marrying a King."

"I will remember that," he smiled.

Mask didn't respond to our jokes. I sensed he was annoyed – not at us, but at how time was moving too quickly for his liking. Moving the wrong way. "When the Travelers found out whose copies you were..." – he pointed at me. "They still don't know you're the original." – "They nearly exploded. Now all their calculations revolve around you both.

You were a powerful force back then, when the Travelers first tried to take your planet. We helped – me, Batranu, Armin – but the deadly combination was you and Deceneus. What didn't work this time? At first, I thought you would flee with the young copy and start a new Rebellion. Not that he is really a copy; he doesn't resemble Deceneus physically. Or ... what didn't happen?"

"Maybe the Erins' plan was to make everyone *believe* the rebel and I would start a new Rebellion," I said. It was a risk – the idea had just come to me – but I realized Mask might help me understand what had really happened. He had a sharp mind, access to information I didn't, and more experience reading the Lines.

"That only makes sense if there's no need for a new Rebellion. Then you are just a red herring, and I did exactly what was expected of me. Damn you, Armin!" Mask swore.

"I don't see much hope for the Travelers now," I said, hoping to be true. "They were forced to act in haste. They will fail."

"What does failure even mean?" Mask shot back. "The New Field? If that collapses in the final stage, eight billion people will vanish for nothing. Many of them could have survived in it. Why does no one care about that?"

"No one dies if the New Field is stopped," I countered. "No one survived the last attempt to create one. And the Saurians were more advanced than the Celestials. We don't have the right to kill so many people only to try something that will mostly fail."

"You still want me to be the right Balancer."

"Once a Balancer, always a Balancer. You can't walk away from that role, Xiriaxis," I said, using his former name, though I still wasn't sure it was his original one. He had already been centuries old when teenage me first met him. "You have to run. Even if they don't know who you are, the Travelers will hunt you down, without hesitation, because of the ... Lines. *Balls of neurons, pinned in ice*. Your words. Cold and calculating."

"I know." Mask smiled, and I saw he was, in some strange way, more at ease in this danger. Maybe this was the level of threat he was born for. "But this evening is as much about you as it is about me. The ShadowMind Index still exists. Few know that. I am a Level Nine now. My promotion caused a ripple in the Index, and I am not the only one watching it.

It's only a matter of days before they match my new signature to my old one in the Field. The Index will help them. There hasn't been another Level Nine for... You know what I was missing?" His lips pursed in a sudden thin smile. "Long-term patience and planning. Here, *long-term* means decades, centuries. We were trained for short, intense missions, relatively speaking," he shrugged. "Go, fight, destroy the enemy. I destroyed more enemies than the next five ShadowMinds still alive, combined," he added, not to impress us, but to revive his own fighting spirit. "And we only learn the prerequisites for the next Level *after* we reach it. Hidden irony, right? Black Eye raised my Level the same second I realized my impatience pushed me to read the Lines. Double irony."

"The last Level Nine was a few thousand years ago," I tried to encourage him. The mistake still weighed on him. "And a ShadowMind never makes the same mistake twice."

"Well, maybe I will live long enough to reach the next Level. And *you are* a Level Five now – the old Altamira, I mean. Something changed in you, too." Mask raised his glass in salute, downed it, and left the room in haste.

"The Jewel Master Lord put you under interdiction," Vipri told me two days later. He grimaced, avoiding to look at me. "There is nothing I can do."

My mind was already spinning. That morning, I had received a memo from Mask too, and to his credit, he had spent a few minutes actually talking to me, through a secure link. For a few days, I had almost everything. Then that *everything* had shifted into nothing, and danger.

"We take it as it is." *But you want something else, Vipri.* I could see it in his eyes. He was looking at me strangely. *We are definitely being recorded. Security's tools are everywhere*. Oddly, for a brief second, I thought maybe Mask's hidden power could still protect me.

Vipri sent a DuaLink request. I rejected it and sent my own.

"Diegia, take your time with Diego," I smiled at her. *"Small talk. Maybe cry a little that we won't see each other again at the villa. But not too much, no one would believe it. Well, no one would believe* me," I joked.

"Is it safe?" Vipri asked once the connection opened. "The circumstances are different."

"It's from the same source as yours. Aurora, just three generations newer."

"We have our own software," he said, a little too proudly.

"You think you do. Your version still runs on Aurora Origin. Your Security didn't even detect it. I will give you a cleaned build at the end, just in case ... with Origin deleted."

His shoulders tensed. I felt his unease. But this was just another way to show how decayed their system had become. Not that he didn't already suspect it – he just hadn't expected it to be *this* bad.

"I suppose this isn't just about my interdiction to visit the villa," I said after a moment.

"I received too much information, and still not enough. No real explanations."

"Mask is who he is. And I am who I am. You will have to make your own decisions."

"Citizen Tiati," he said, in mock formality. "I expect proper behavior from my councilor, and a good report. Of course, you can't make decisions for the Vice Prime Minister; you don't have the pedigree. Now, feed me. And when we close the link, keep your elbow at least a foot from my ribs. That's an order."

He stretched his virtual hand toward me. I raised mine. They passed through each other, as immaterial things do, yet the comfort was real. I spent the next few minutes explaining the game I believed Mask was playing with everyone, and how dangerous a Level Nine ShadowMind could be. After a while, I realized I was speaking too fast. I paused, took a deep breath to calm myself. Vipri was watching me, amused.

In the end, I projected the hologram of my brief conversation with Mask – the one where he explained that the breach of my house had been a joint Cupola operation. They had used the Rubys, since the Jewels had to remain hidden. I still didn't know why Mask had revealed that to me, or what he had expected in return. When I finished, it was Vipri's turn to exhale long and slow.

"You never told me that, so I never heard it," he said. "There must be a reason Mask used that channel to inform you. I don't know why. Everything is dangerous now; anxiety is rising at the top. Getting close to fear. Fear is dangerous. It kills even the best minds. We must be careful."

That evening, Prim deactivated my ZeroC authorization. Cupola's order. The old ZeroD status came back. *Still a High Councilor,* I told myself, feeling a flicker of relief. At least I still had access to some high-level official channels. In the end, everything was an information game.

A minute later, my Cupola resort reservation was canceled. Just a brief memo: I was no longer authorized to visit such a select place. Despite all my training, despite everything I knew about how the system worked, I still felt disenchanted.

Two days later, Mask's FlyCar exploded at midnight over the sea, hit by a PlasGun from orbit. The Travelers.

"Unauthorized flight," Vipri lamented through my DuaLink. "I suppose he tried to run to the Resistance. Why didn't he ask for help?" The sadness in his voice betrayed him. Mask was still his brother.

"Such operations are planned alone. Did they ... recover him?"

Vipri stared at me, incredulous. "Travelers' PlasGun. Midnight. Deep sea. What exactly do you expect to find?"

"He is a powerful ShadowMind. Assume nothing without proof," I said slowly, cutting off further questions. "You need to run too."

"He left a message. We are to go together. His last words: *Thus spoke the Lines.*"

I froze. The Lines. Danger. But this wasn't my reading. My DuaLink avatar nodded silently. "Together or alone... Stay, and you're dead. Run, and you're dead. There are no good choices. No FlyCars, we are being watched."

"Maybe we are only alive because they are using us as bait in the Lines game," he shrugged. "Maybe. But how can I be sure? They could kill us the next second."

"Perhaps," I smiled. "Unless we make them think we are defecting to the Resistance, in a way that serves Cupola..."

Vipri was quiet. His avatar looked thoughtful. Then he stared at me. "Let them believe we can lead them to a major Resistance hub?"

"The capture of a Resistance base it's Cupola's dream. We need carefully timed leaks. Details of nebulous events, but always a few days in advance. Nothing urgent."

Vipri tapped his temple. "We will plan a vacation. Using my monitored DuaLink."

"With multiple possible destinations..."

"I still don't understand," he murmured, shaking his head. "Why haven't the Travelers killed us yet? I am a minor Line in the game, disposable. But you..."

"They will kill me, just not yet. I am a known variable in their calculations. Remove me, and an unknown takes my place. They won't risk that. Not until they can take all three of us: me, you, and the young rebel with Deceneus's Field signature. When the time serves them."

"I am disposable," he repeated, as if clinging to the idea for comfort.

"You are linked to Mask and me. Welcome to the shadow world. Don't underestimate the Travelers. They have perfected betrayal and oppression over millennia." A strange comfort flickered through the tension: at least I hadn't dragged him into this, not like I had with his brother who died in my arms twenty years ago.

Then, the situation shifted again, an hour later.

"The Travelers want *you* to lead this operation," Vipri said, flinging paper documents across his desk – a deliberately archaic way of work, good at bypassing electronic surveillance – as the digital file landed in my inbox.

A mental click summoned Mask's ghost. I clung to the hope that he had outmaneuvered the Travelers. Evasion had been his specialty, sharpened across centuries of special operations and war.

"Your young friend is making waves," Vipri interrupted, pulling me back into the moment.

"He is a runaway rebel, not my friend," I said, with just enough irritation in my voice to satisfy the watching AI.

"He came ashore here," Vipri continued, ignoring the denial. He stabbed the holographic map. "We sank his submarine, but he escaped. We took casualties – he is clearly trained to kill. Aurora bastards." His fist slammed the table through the hologram, then he forced his calm back into place. "Read the underlined sections first." That meant the paper.

His compromised Jewel DuaLink called me instantly. I accepted it.

"Find him," he ordered, knowing that the surveillance protocol activated. "Fail again, and you are no longer my councilor. You are performant, and I want to keep you, but not with this level of failure." The twitch of his avatar suggested real conflict.

Well played. My lips almost stretched into a smile. Both Diegia and I froze it fast.

"Last time, Prim hobbled my search. I had eight agents against twenty-four Rubys. This time I get ten. And Prim waited three days to... Does he *want* the rebel caught? Or is he just making sure the Rubys get credit?"

"Questioning the Prime Minister's loyalty is beyond your role. Find the rebel."

"I will."

The DuaLink severed. I resumed reading where Diegia had been piloting my body. Reclaiming control always felt strange, like remembering a forgotten limb. I had never asked what DigitalEgos experience during transitions. Diegia would be unsettled by the question. She was a rogue AI, after all.

My rogue AI.

The thought made me smile twice: once when it arrived, and again because she already knew it.

The rebel's landing zone overlapped with the restricted sector I knew so well, and Vipri's villa stood nearby. The Jewel Lord had lifted my ban from the estate for *operational necessity*. Temporarily. A rare concession. But no other Family would have agreed. Letting Lessers crawl around their estates was blasphemy with extra paperwork and extra guards. Vipri seized the opportunity to demonstrate loyalty, though it meant surrendering his villa to commandos and tech units who camped just beyond the 300-pace perimeter fence. Temporary authorization, permanent inconvenience.

The protocols worked in our favor for once. The hierarchy was too rigid for most personnel to access Cupola-exclusive zones. Wrong bloodline, wrong smile, wrong everything. Surveillance choked the villa inside out. Every briefing would unfold in the over-monitored living room, the only space large enough to contain to contain the theater. Barely.

During our first team meeting the next morning, the Resistance reached me via a Field transmission. I was lucky someone else had been speaking when the ghost-whisper cut through my thoughts: *"There is no danger. A parallel transmission covers us."* The scale of the interference, able to penetrate the Travelers' counter-Field tech on such a large area, staggered me. *"He is receiving Deceneus's memories. Their signatures in the Field will merge temporarily."*

The Travelers will learn about us. My blood turned to ice. Or boiled. Hard to tell, really.

"We can't hide him anymore, and your unconscious Field resonance might expose you too, if you are too close. The range could be 100 feet, could be 10 miles. We don't know. You must..." The message weakened, then fractured as the masking transmission overtook ours. *"Shine is... She will..."* Then nothing.

I dismissed the team. Needed silence. Needed to think. To check for exposure. Needed to figure out just how far we had fallen into this mess. To breathe.

"Diegia, verify the new software." Alongside the message, came a payload of programs. The transmission had triggered a data surge in my brain that now detonated behind my eyes – the familiar yet always terrifying synaptic overload that comes with it. Reality dissolved into a plasma column thirty feet wide, stretching from sky to earth. I closed my eyes and slow-breathed through the panic. When I opened them again, the column was still there. Not hallucination. Not dream. Plasma.

They are destroying the mountain from space. He is there...

The mountaintop vaporized before the sound reached us. Molten rock cascaded in surreal silence until the shockwave hit. By then, the plasma beam had bored downward, the volcano melting like an upside-down ice cream cone. My fingers clawed the windowsill as I counted heartbeats. Five, ten, twenty. The devastation offered me the perfect excuse to cancel meetings. To recalibrate. To change plans.

"Everybody out," I snapped. Three technicians were still inside, frozen like glitching avatars until my voice unstuck them.

Batranu planned for this. I trust Batranu, I whispered to myself once I was finally alone. *I trust him. I trust him...* The mantra steadied me as I stared through the window, the only place where AI couldn't watch my face. Batranu was a seasoned planner, and part of me hoped that he – or more likely Armin – had accounted for the Travelers' violent retaliation. Between them, maybe the rebel was still breathing.

The plasma vanished after two exact minutes, leaving only smoke and questions. The shot hadn't triggered a real eruption; the area had been geologically stable for more than fifty thousand years.

"The villa is crammed with fresh surveillance," I told Vipri via our secured DuaLink, after Diegia had run Aurora's latest BitDefender counter-intel package. "Even your bedroom. A Jewel camera, four weeks old. Everything else is two days fresh."

"Sorry," he frowned hard. "I had no idea about the bedroom."

"They wanted front-row seats to you bedding the minor bitch."

"I will remove it."

"Don't." I smiled. It tasted like rust and bad memories. "Then they will know you know, and start asking questions. Bedroom net-cams are in fashion these days. Why shouldn't the Vice Prime Minister chase the Popularity Index like commoners checking their erotic like-counts at dawn?"

The truth hung between us – this was the society we lived in.

"The Jewel Lord did not lift the ban on our relationship, but our handlers expect a show. Tonight, you will tolerate my advances like a man enduring cheap wine and cheaper company."

His pupils dilated. "There's no need for..."

"Survival always is. My simulations are all over the Net. I am basically free entertainment. It's wonderful to be popular these days." I shook my head in resignation. "Night two, you reject me. Night three, reluctant reunion. Let them believe I am clawing back status through your bedsheets."

It was a complicated setup, anchored in customary decadence, with one goal in mind: survival. They already had everything on me – data, videos, simulations, the real thing. One more recording wouldn't change anything except the ratings on the Popularity Index. I never cared about it.

Altamira would never have accepted that. But Altamira died the day I came back. What remained – Alenia – learned to play, to navigate this gilded cesspool, inch by compromised inch. Concession by concession, year after year. A quiet, insidious process. Human adaptation. But adaptation isn't a decision.

"Sometimes I will steer things toward politics, and try to leverage your position in some way. I will fail," I smiled, bitterly.

And fail I did. We both did. That first night, we aborted the plan, retreating to separate rooms with a shared shrug of mutual surrender.

The second night, we played better: me in scandalous silk pajamas, him the aggrieved Cupola aristocrat chasing me out for the hidden cameras. It was just drama with surveillance-friendly choreography, but it felt strange. No amount of acting could mask what we had become.

When I turned off my lantern, absolute darkness enveloped me. This wasn't the familiar darkness of a moonless night, where faint shapes tease your senses – even in the worst night there is always something to see. Here, it was all-encompassing, enchanting yet terrifying, a void that seemed to pulse with its own presence. A steady airflow whispered through the cave, its gentle sigh the only sign of life. I shivered, from the cold, or perhaps fear, or both. The rock beneath me was icy, its chill seeping through my suit, but my mind burned with restless thoughts. *Be calm. Be calm...* I checked the water bags again. Filled. I had checked five times already. They would sustain us for four days in the other cave, where Pilot waited. *If I escape. Even if I die, Alenia...* I didn't want to die. I checked the water bags again. *Stop this.* I breathed deeply, forcing air into my lungs. Once. Twice. Better.

"Diego, prepare the Field switch, but let me initiate the connection." I had to be ready. On the inner holographic map, I visualized the path in the tunnel: smooth for a volcanic cave, with

no boulders or pits, like a dark glass alley carved by ancient lava flows. When the time came, I needed to run, even in darkness, in case my lantern or night vision failed.

"*Done,*" Diego whispered, his voice subdued, as if the darkness pressed on him too.

I took another breath, steadying myself, and opened the Field connection.

"Want to play?" an unfamiliar voice asked in my mind, jarring, like a child's laughter in a graveyard. I froze, caught off guard. "You don't want to play," it said, disappointed, like a child whose toy was snatched away.

"Thank you, Crawler," another voice interjected, deep and resonant, stirring a vague sense of familiarity. "I am Deceneus, the old one, the first one. You are the third one, in some ways."

"You are the Observer," I acknowledged, my voice steady despite the unease creeping through me.

"I am. You have many questions. The data transfer will answer some, but not all." His tone carried an edge of urgency, a ticking clock.

"Ready." I thought I was. You prepare for the expected, the planned – data packages, software, encrypted files, like the downloads I had received before. But nothing prepares you for the unimaginable. The transfer began, and it was more than just information. It had all that, and something else, a torrent, centuries of another human life: memories, emotions, sensations from planets I had never seen, experiences I had never lived, all compressed into minutes. My mind reeled as images flooded in – alien skies, cities carved into cliffs, battles fought with weapons that hummed like living things. I saw a woman's face, her eyes fierce with defiance, then felt the sting of betrayal as if it were my own. Scents of unfamiliar spices and the roar of crowds overwhelmed me, layering over my own thoughts. My skull felt like a dam about to burst, each memory a hammer strike against its walls. My vision blurred, my knees buckled, and I gripped the cave wall to stay upright, my breath ragged.

"You will feel dizzy," the Observer said, his voice distant over the storm raging in my head, my thoughts swelling like a balloon ready to explode.

"Do I have enough space?" I gasped, the transfer unrelenting, each byte searing into my neurons.

"Yes."

"You are not very communicative."

"The less we speak, the faster it goes."

The flood intensified. I saw a desert where sand glowed under a violet sky, felt the weight of a samurai ceremonial blade in my hand, tasted blood from a wound that wasn't mine. Kissed lips of women I had never met. The memories weren't just images; some were visceral, overwhelming my senses. My heart raced, syncing with a stranger's pulse from centuries past. *Who are you?* I wanted to scream, but my voice was drowned in the deluge, a life grafted onto mine, a fusion that threatened to erase where I ended and this other began. My fingers clawed at the rock, grounding me as I fought to hold onto myself.

"Run!" the Observer shouted, his voice cutting through the chaos.

The connection severed abruptly, leaving my mind reeling. The beam of the lantern trembled with my shaking hand as I stumbled forward, half-paralyzed, like a drunk after too much wine. The storm in my head raged on, memories colliding – mine, his. At the cave's end, the tunnel turned hostile, a labyrinth of freshly fallen stones, twisting right and left without pattern. No harmony. I leaned against the wall for strength. *Cold*... The stone soothed, its coldness cooling my burning forehead. I pressed harder, willing the stone to cool the inferno in my skull too.

"A program is realigning your brain," Diego whispered, his voice slurred, as if he too were caught in the mental storm.

"Make it go faster." I staggered into the tunnel, twisting right and left without pattern. My steps faltered; my balance twisted by the alien memories still settling.

"I can't touch it. The program has Erin Origin, far beyond anything I know." Diego's voice faded, like whispers carried off by the wind.

More downloaded memories surged to life – images, colors, sounds, scents, a sensory onslaught that made me both observer and participant in a vivid movie:

The volcano loomed, smoke rising from countless fissures, a morose sentinel spewing toxic fumes to keep intruders away. My lungs burned, and the horses snorted uneasily nearby. *I'm not there... I'm in a tunnel... No horses.* A horse neighed, another answered. I turned; an old man trudged behind on a volcanic slope, his face weathered but familiar. The air was thick with ash. My hands, not mine, gripped a staff as I navigated treacherous ground.

"That's not my mind!" I shouted.

"Mind... Miiind... Miiinnnd," the echo reverberated, snapping me back to the tunnel. My tunnel. My volcano. My mind. That memory wasn't mine; it was his. His volcano. His mind. Centuries-old memories, bleeding into my present. The download had triggered a perverse reaction, his ancient experiences posing as my reality. I stepped over a boulder, misjudged its height, and tripped. The stone snagged my foot, and I rolled, a jagged edge slicing my palm, leaving a bleeding gash. Pain anchored me to the present, but the foreign memories lingered, vivid and disorienting.

A low rumble began, distant, beneath me. I thought it was far below, muffled by my ear pressed to the ground. I was wrong. The sound came from above. The cone – my cone – was erupting. *The Travelers are blowing the mountain. I'll die here...* The tunnel shook violently, dust and pebbles raining down. Cracks splintered the walls. The air grew thick, acrid with sulfur, stinging my eyes and throat. A deafening boom reverberated, followed by a shockwave that knocked me to my knees.

I couldn't move. My body refused, pinned by exhaustion and the lingering chaos of the transfer. The rumbling intensified, the ground bucking beneath me. Stones fell, one grazing my shoulder, another narrowly missing my head. *I'll die here.* The thought was cold, final. The tunnel groaned, as if the mountain itself were mourning its own end. I clawed at the ground, desperate to drag myself forward, toward the second cave, toward Pilot, toward survival. But the darkness and the quaking earth seemed to conspire, sealing my fate beneath a dying volcano.

Another horse neighed, and smoke filled my lungs. *His lungs. His present.* A girl looked at me. Spoke to me, her voice soft yet clear. I felt I knew her – truly knowing her, *me* knowing her, not him knowing her, or both knowing her – a distant, unnerving familiarity.

"I am Altamira. We thank you for your help. And don't worry; I understand the reasons behind your choice." Her wide eyes studied me, naive yet cunning. I stifled a laugh. *Ms. Funny Name forgives me.* But the name suited her, as if fate had chosen it for her ... on Earth.

That's not me. I'm not from Earth. I snapped awake, and the realization hit hard: Alenia, also Altamira, was younger than me in this false present. And I was also her husband, centuries ago, in a life not my own. The rumbling escalated to a roar, dust swirling, stones plummeting from the ceiling – my present. One, two, countless. I struggled to my feet, shielding my head with my arms, stumbling through a tunnel that danced with me. Warm blood trickled down my face from a cut above my brow. Nausea surged, bile burning my throat as the download overwhelmed my mind, fracturing my reality.

“Altamira, I have a confession. We found some books.” Her body tensed, but I waited, taking a few more dancing steps. “The Baragan Compendium of History.”

“What?”

“I am sure you can keep a secret,” I whispered, spinning her twice to the music, holding her close, not releasing her when the dance ended.

Not me, not me. Him. I danced with her at the court ball, her warmth pressed against me. His arms, not mine. But her closeness blurred the line between his memories and my reality. Her scent – gardenia and ash – lingered in my mind, no longer just mine. I staggered forward, fortunately not falling as the visions blinded me. Glowing lines pierced the floating dust, surreal shapes shifting slowly. My lantern. Real. *I have to run.* My body managed only drunken steps.

The volcano erupted before Altamira could finish her words. Red lava cascaded down its northern flank, ash falling like soft rain, steeped in sulfur acrid stink. *Not real.* It wasn’t my volcano, yet these alternate timelines wove into my present. The visions exploited reality, hijacking my senses like a virus. The heat of the lava in the vision mirrored the stifling air in the tunnel. Foreign and real senses merged. I glanced back, switching off my lantern: light pierced the tunnel from the cave I had left minutes, or hours ago. *Lava…* The earthquake paused, the rumbling fading, second by second, until silence fell. But the light behind grew stronger, a molten glow creeping closer. *Run!*

A deafening boom shook the earth, the tunnel buckling as if the mountain screamed. More cracks tore through the walls. The peak must have shattered. I imagined the once-majestic cone collapsing, its slopes reduced to a smoldering crater, the forest beyond engulfed in a pyroclastic wave. All that beauty, gone. My chest tightened, not just from the thinning air but from the weight of what this destruction meant. *I’ve made this chaos.* A low hum resonated in my bones, not sound but presence, ancient and vast, like the mountain itself was alive. The heat intensified, the air nearly unbreathable. I clawed forward, desperate for the second cave, for Pilot, for survival.

My eyes opened to darkness. Only the sensation of my eyelids moving slowly and painfully confirmed they were open, then closed. The absolute darkness I had known before. Drops echoed, falling on stones, their reverberations growing closer. *I have to run.* A piercing light stabbed my eyes from nearby.

"Welcome back. Plan B worked – so far."

"Pilot!"

For hours, my mind wrestled with vivid, alien memories. They came and went without a pattern. The Erin software, relentless and precise, arranged them into accessible chains as if they were my own, sorted and codified. Some flashes were so strong they allowed alternate realities to overtake my world. Others felt like fleeting dreams. Gradually, they fragmented into smaller pieces, easier to process, though new complexities emerged. I could finally integrate this other life into my own, but it came at a cost, a subtle shift in how I saw the world.

"You know," I said to Pilot, "he had the same experience. Someone else's memories were inserted into his mind, but only six months long, not centuries."

"You are getting obsessed," Pilot replied. "I don't see anything abnormal, except the obsession."

"He is not from here, like Batranu. They came together. I shouldn't have told you."

"I already know, but you are right; the information in your head is dangerous. Handle it carefully. Maybe stay quiet for a while, think about what you can say and what you can't. There is no rush. I am trying to sleep."

"I need to talk, or my mind will explode."

"Tell me." He finally grasped my urgency.

"Alenia – Altamira – is my ancestor. And, from the download, my wife. We had two children three hundred years before I was born. Now, put yourself in my place."

"I am willing to help," he smirked. "Transfer the part about making kids to me. The rest is yours."

Talking calmed me, and he fell asleep. I had again eyes to see the world around. The cave was a marvel, its violet stalactites translucent, the light of my lantern dancing through them. *Nice.* I shook my head with fury. Before the memory transfer, they would been a wonder, something I could have admired for hours. Now, my awe was stolen by the weight of another's life. The foreign memories had left a mark, a subtle erosion of my capacity to feel the world; they had aged me, not in body, but in soul. *Nice* wasn't *wonder*; as it once did. I felt it would never be again. I remembered the thrill of my first mission, the rush of outsmarting a drone. I had been alive with wonder, every cave a marvel, every danger a thrill. Now, burdened with a century of another's life – love, battles, betrayals – I felt weathered, like an old man who had seen too much, experienced too much, my youth eroded. *I don't want to lose myself.* "I don't want this!" I shouted, slamming my fist against the stone, pain shooting through my knuckles. "I want to remain me."

Alenia

The tactical hologram map flickered, its glowing lines painting a grim picture for the young rebel. My commando teams swarmed the area, a tightening net, and I could do little but create fleeting delays – a dangerous balancing act, like juggling too many eggs. One slip, one shattered egg, one lost life. My heart raced, not with reckless thrill but with the calculation of divided loyalties. I was ordered to hunt him by the Travelers, yet my true allegiance lay with the Resistance. Every decision was a tightrope walk, each move a step toward or away from betrayal, from death. My mind raced through various scenarios, weighing the risk of exposure against the need to give him a chance to escape. A tight balance.

We assumed that he was within a five-mile radius, inside the cave network or out, though officially we were *unsure* if he had left the cave, and we were prepared for both scenarios, a waste of resources. I knew he had left the cave; the last RoboDog image showed it returning to the cave after losing the trail – a clever trick, likely climbing a rock to hide his scent. I kept that to myself, reinforcing the commandos' standard tactics, steering them away from suspecting his strategies. After rapid calculations, I split my twenty-eight field soldiers into seven standard four-man teams, positioning them to cover the six known exits of the cave system and one suspected bolt-hole. I planned their patrol patterns to leave deliberate gaps, narrow windows of opportunity the young rebel might exploit if he was as sharp as I hoped. I assigned each team a sector, ensuring they overlapped just enough to appear thorough but left blind spots in the dense forest, where shadows and undergrowth could hide a skilled operative. I also staggered their drone support, delaying the deployment of two Birds to create a brief lapse in aerial surveillance over the northern ridge.

"Target discovered," a message came through the comm, a red dot pulsing on the map. Two thousand feet away.

So close... I recalled the warning from the Resistance's transmission, the danger of being exposed by our Field resonance when we were too close. I zoomed in. The red dot was hiding behind a rocky ridge, twenty feet high, its jagged crest offering partial cover. *It's not a red point, it's him.* The four soldiers from Glory Team took cover behind the trees between the ridge and me, obscured by the dense forest. I had no visual on them yet, their positions marked only by thermal blue pulses on my map.

“Two targets,” another message reported. “I have their thermal signatures, moving slowly, likely injured.”

I ran. Each step was a gamble, a choice. Once the team came into my visual, I saw their point man melting the top of the ridge with a LasGun, its beam – a hot yellow lance – obscuring the thermal signatures. A useless attack, but he had the BigGun, a laser weapon usually mounted on a car, ten kilos in weight. I scanned the holographic map again, noting the positions of the other teams: Bravo and Victory were the closest, sweeping parallel sectors two thousand feet west, while Giant, Triumph, Conquest, and Colossus were spread across a two-mile arc, their routes converging toward the ridge in a pincer movement. Ridiculous team names, no less than our society. In the end the names didn’t count, I had to disrupt their coordination without raising suspicion.

“Cover incoming,” Glory’s second soldier – the Eye of the commando – announced. A lightly armed spying drone, a Bird, was approaching, its high-resolution cameras capable of piercing foliage to map heat signatures and movement. I assessed the battlefield: in front of me, Glory Team was isolated for now, but the other teams would close in soon. *The Bird will record them.* No immediate danger; they can’t shoot over the ridge. Diegia calculated the Bird’s trajectory – sixty-five seconds to target – and I checked the map for blind spots. A narrow ravine ran parallel to the ridge, shrouded by overhanging trees, offering a potential escape route if the rebel could reach it before the drone’s arrival. “Glory, wait for the Bird, to detail their position. I don’t want any of you wounded or killed for nobodies.” My voice was steady, but inside, I was wearing thin, torn between maintaining my cover and giving him a chance.

“Another incoming drone,” the Eye said. “It’s not ours. No communication. Still far... A Falcon.”

Military drone. Armed. Heavy weapon. Unlike the Bird's reconnaissance drone, the Falcon carried a plasma cannon, capable of melting three-foot-thick rocks and anything behind them. Its fast approach narrowed my window. My pulse quickened with fear; I had to act before the Falcon. "Glory, gather at the Eye's position. I am right behind you. Prepare for assault." Then I sent a similar order to the other six teams, knowing it would pull them toward us, but forcing them to regroup on their Eye position, and buy me time. Glory's four soldiers rallied in thirty seconds, taking cover behind a cluster of trees, their LasGuns set on the ridge. I checked the map: Bravo would arrive in six minutes, the others in nine to fifteen. Five minutes to act.

"Colossus here," I heard in the comm. "We have causalities, average wounds on legs, nothing serios, but we are out. A small mine left behind. The zone is clear. No enemy."

"Colossus, wait for help. Glory, take positions. They may try to escape before the Falcon arrives. Be ready." Boots thudded as Glory Team fanned out, forming a crescent arc two hundred feet from the ridge, their weapons primed. I ordered them to hold fire, citing the need for precise targeting to avoid friendly casualties – a plausible excuse to delay their attack. The Bird began transmitting images from the ridge's far side: two figures, crouched low, moving toward the ravine. One limped, likely injured. The feed cut out a second later, static replacing the image. *Good. They took it down.*

"Diegia, check the transmission."

"Nothing," she replied, her voice calm.

I glanced at the map. Five minutes until Bravo arrived. The Falcon was now a mile from me, its sensors likely already scanning for thermal signatures. I recalculated: if I could misdirect Glory Team's fire and delay the other teams' convergence, the rebel might reach the ravine before the Falcon's cannon locked on. "Glory, shift left, flank the ridge's western edge. Suspected movement there." It was a lie. To the other teams, I sent a conflicting directive: "Hold positions and await Falcon's investigation for confirmation." This would stall their advance, creating a minute and a half gap in their coverage. My hands trembled as I closed my camera and gripped my LasGun.

Then I fired.

The camera we had planted at the main entrance alerted us, interrupting our meager breakfast. I cursed under my breath – not that the meal was anything special, just rehydrated rations that tasted like dust. A RoboDog had sniffed out our old tracks, triggering a burst of chatter with its handler: "I found them in the cave!" followed by happy barking, the robot programmed to mimic a real dog for human comfort. My stomach tightened, not with the old thrill of the chase but with a heavy dread, as if the weight of another's battles – those memories forced into me – dulled my edge. I was still sharp, but every move felt calculated, cautious, like I had lived too long. I wondered if too much experience wouldn't be dangerous just by lowering natural expectations and fear – there was still a large gap between the downloaded experience and body coordination and reflexes. It takes years of training to obtain that, or perhaps more. No one had been in my shoes before, so no one could confirm my estimation.

"Third exit," I muttered to Pilot, grabbing my backpack. The camera there showed nothing, and it was the farthest from the compromised entrance, nearly half a mile through the cave network. At the exit, we faced a sheer wall on the left, fifteen feet high, forcing us to climb after crossing a three-foot open space visible from the sky. We lost two precious minutes climbing the rock, in a way not exposed to the drones, and not leaving traces at the base of the stone. In the cave, the RoboDog was already sniffing where we had slept. As I leapt from a six-foot-large boulder into scrub cover beneath a gnarled, half-dead tree, the first camera alerted me again. I rolled, keeping one eye on the ground and the other on the camera feed streaming to my vision. Fumbling for the trigger in my pocket, I was two seconds late. The mine detonated the instant I pressed the button. The sound of the blast did not reach us; the mine was small. As the dust clouding the feed settled, I zoomed in: four commandos lay sprawled, wounded, nothing serious, out of the game. They would waste time recovering their injured, buying us a slim margin.

We crouched in the bush, waiting, as the RoboDog emerged from the cave, sniffing our tracks. Its artificial puppy-like squeals, eerily lifelike, grated on my nerves – a human touch to alert its masters that it was on the track. In the daylight, it bounded a few feet, then froze at the foot of the rock, its AI baffled by our vanished trail. I aimed my LasGun at its head, a more difficult target than the body but necessary to destroy its camera. The beam vaporized the sensor array in a flash, the dog collapsing in a heap of sparking circuits. *One less tracker.*

"Run!" I growled to Pilot, pushing through the undergrowth, branches clawing at my face. Fifteen minutes of grueling sprint brought us to a ridge – two parallel crests separated by a deep ravine. Our ridge was higher, offering decent cover; the other was too low for enemies to hide effectively. A forested plateau crowned our ridge, but the valley below had patches of open ground, treeless and exposed. Perfect ambush terrain, commandos were likely swarming the area. I wedged a camera into a crack above, overlooking the far side, stretching until my fingers grazed the ledge for a better angle. The hologram flickered: four reddish thermal signatures, evenly spaced, too still to be animals. I set an infrared decoy in a crack, opposite our intended southern route, and activated its emission from a safe distance. A LasGun blast scorched the air seconds later, targeting the bait. Deep in the crack, the bait survived.

"BigGun," Diego whispered.

"Shit." One thermal signature held position; the other three crept north, drawn by the decoy. We crawled south, where the ridge dipped lower, poised to sprint across the ravine.

"Incoming drone," Diego warned, and we crouched in a split second, but I had the impression that it was already too late. *"Bird."* The radar on my helmet painted a dot on the tactical hologram, closing fast. *"It will reach the ridge in twenty seconds."*

"Calculate its entry point over this side," I asked, and he marked a spot on the hologram. I scrambled back, positioning my LasGun three feet above my head, pointed at the predicted intercept, setting it to auto-fire after its AI memorized the Bird's profile. Three seconds later, it unleashed a burst, explosion lighting the sky. Our ridge camera caught the hit: the Bird spiraled down, crashing outside the recording zone. *One down.*

"Incoming drone," Diego cut through my relief. *"Two minutes out. Falcon."*

"Cave!" I shouted, bolting back through the bushes. A Falcon's plasma cannon could vaporize us through a three-foot-thick stone; the cave network was our only refuge.

An explosion halted us abruptly, and we dove behind two massive trees, their thick trunks masking our thermal signatures. I peered back: no drone in sight.

"Diego, analyze." We were too far to contact the ridge camera. I stood, letting the one on my helmet scan the valley. Diego zoomed in, spotting glinting metal fragments with high thermal signatures.

"The Falcon," he said. *"No clue what took it out."*

I glanced at Pilot; he shrugged. We sprinted back to the ridge until our hidden camera reconnected. No drone appeared, and the four thermal signatures on the far side had vanished. The camera switched to optical mode, revealing a figure standing in plain view among the trees, unprotected. We raised our LasGuns, fingers on triggers.

"Don't shoot!" I yelled at Pilot, springing from cover.

Alenia

"Shine is coming," Diegia whispered, mapping her position, and I turned slowly, the stolen BigGun trained nearly on her. She was three hundred feet away, sprinting through the forest toward the crash site of Falcon – I was in the middle. On my tactical map, five commando teams still converged toward me, seven minutes away. One had been incapacitated, blasted by a rebel mine. I had to take down Shine first, without being recorded. At thirty paces, she halted, eyeing my gun's angle warily. Her LasGun remained holstered, so I eased mine aside. *Come closer....* I gestured, and she hesitated, then advanced, hands clear of her weapon. *Strange...* I stepped aside, clearing a path to the debris and four dead soldiers, hoping she would check them, turning her back to me, leaving me out of her camera's view. She stopped in front of me, her gaze steady. The Glory Team lay dead in full glory.

"The drone is there," I said, pointing to the wreckage, urging her forward.

"I know," she replied, her smile natural, devoid of its usual malice, unsettling me. I edged my gun closer, my face a cold mask. Smiling back felt wrong; I had never pull it off. "We need to talk."

"I am listening."

"She sent a DuaLink request," Diegia whispered. *"Aurora Origin, no Ruby signature."*

"Trap. Be careful."

"Resistance encryption. The new one we received through the Field transmission. Batranu's signature."

"My gun is holstered," Shine said calmly. "The Falcon was downed from here. I did not have an acceptable view. My camera had no clear vision, so nothing was recorded. We need to investigate what killed them, too," she said, pointing to the soldiers. "We are exposed here."

I accepted the DuaLink. An image flashed – not Shine's, but someone I had known three hundred years ago, faintly resembling her. "What's this picture?" I asked, keeping my tone neutral.

"Her name was Naldire, now Shine," she said, smiling. "And she is glad to see you again."

"The old Magister?" I probed, setting a trap.

"Just a Librarian," she corrected. "But my husband, Talian, was a Magister."

"We met when I was nine. My father brought me to your Library," I tested further.

"You were eleven, and it was your mother," she answered correctly. I disconnected to study her face. Diegia's facial analysis matched mine, authentic. For the first time in days, I smiled genuinely, then I reconnected the DuaLink.

"Naldire," I whispered. "I am glad too. I am sorry for the past."

"The apology is on me," she grinned. "I played the Ruby role too well to climb their ranks. Batranu was supposed to warn you about me during the Field transmission. I am a sleeper too. Why didn't they tell you about me?"

"Their signal was cut off. I had no idea."

"Obviously. I did not record you shooting the Falcon. What do you want me to do now?"

"Go to the other commandos and delay them. Order them to regroup and advance together, claiming the enemy is stronger than expected. Scare them into caution with the downed Falcon. BigBirds are destroyed by BigGuns. It will buy me a few minutes to talk with... You know who is there," I gestured toward the ridge. She nodded. "Thank you," I said, raising my electronic hand to meet hers. She mirrored me, our digital hands passing through each other, yet the strange feeling of a tingling sensation like a real touch stayed with me. The link closed, and she sprinted north to intercept the teams. In a few words, I advised them through the comm to follow her lead, urging caution and unified advance.

I shivered, steeling myself, and stepped into plain view, exposed to the ridge hiding the rebels. *If they overreact...*

"Don't shoot!" a voice shouted, filled with urgency and relief. The icy fear that gripped me dissipated, and I waited at the edge of the forest, under dense canopy to evade SkEye.

It took him a minute to reach me, weaving a cautious, circuitous path under tree cover, as if expecting an ambush. His eyes darted left and right, mostly avoiding me, betraying the weight of dual memories not yet reconciled. "We need to hurry. You must come with me. It's not safe for you to stay. They know who I am, or who they think I am," he said, skipping introductions. "You received Batranu's message, didn't you?"

"Yes, but I can't. You know why."

"Which of us knows?" His voice was edgy, his hand twitching – a subtle, fluid gesture betraying the older warrior's instincts battling his younger panic.

"The young one," I said, amused by his barely veiled unease.

"Vipri..." he muttered, reluctantly, relief visible as he realized I wasn't reclaiming our past bond – he did not want a duty born from our unconventional joint history. "He will be punished."

And I felt relieved too. He wasn't my Deceneus, not truly – just a young rebel grafted with fragments of the man I had loved three hundred years ago. I wasn't his wife now, and we both felt lighter for it. I had chosen Vipri, though I wondered what I would feel facing the real Deceneus.

"Punished is a misnomer," I said. He fell silent, calculating the risks of my staying. "You have to shoot me," I finally added.

"No!" he snapped, confused.

"Not to kill me, to wound me. For an alibi. Shoot me in the back, left side, to look lethal from behind. One palm down from my shoulder, near the spine, not touching it. Angle up and left, toward the top of my shoulder. Avoid my lung and joints; they are hard to heal, and I need to be ready for Field Day. Don't worry about my clavicle." I rattled a list of precise instructions, forcing him to focus, pushing the BigGun toward him.

"I can't."

I glanced at his companion, his face was weary, no fighter's edge. "You are not a shooter," I sighed; too risky to trust him with the shot. A slip could kill me.

"I am Pilot, a pilot," he said. "His head is a mess – too many memories, too much love for you. Past loves you, present loves you. He is haunted by things he did before he was born, like giving you kids." He chuckled, easing the tension. "Help him pick a side."

You are more than you seem, I thought, eyeing Pilot. "Let the past one shoot." I tossed the BigGun to the young rebel. Instinct kicked in – he caught it, hands closing around the weapon. "After doing the job," I used mundane words on purpose, "go behind that tree," I pointed to the place from where I had shot the soldiers and drone. "Lie down, rub against it, leave heavy DNA traces to cover mine. Then return here. Pilot, you do the same, one minute later, after my camera starts recording."

"This weapon is too strong. The wound will be three inches wide. You won't survive," my young rebel protested.

"It's nearly depleted, barely stronger than a standard LasGun. The previous owner used it to melt rocks, thinking they were you. After shooting, discharge it fully and toss it onto me to pick up my DNA. My traces are already there. They must not know I used it." I slipped off my tactical glove, raising my hand to feel his face. He flinched, his hand brushing mine, a fleeting touch sparking a torrent of shared pasts – mirrors reflecting a thousand moments from lives we hadn't really lived together. "Do it," I said, turning to expose my back. "We are counting on you. I am counting on you."

Alenia lay unconscious at my feet, face down, a charred wound seared into her back, burning into my mind. She had fallen silently, and a sick part of me felt relief, both for her quiet and for not seeing her face when I fired. It was the right call, logical, defensible; we had agreed to stage it for her alibi. Yet guilt gnawed at me, painting me as a callous monster. Two streams of memories clashed within – mine and his, the older warrior's – both mourning her pain, in different ways. Flashbacks flickered, vivid and warm: her in my arms at a ball three hundred years ago, a memory not truly mine but so real it ached. *I didn't want this.*

"Diego, make a health assessment," I said, hesitating to turn her over, unsure of my reaction. *"For her,"* I added, quickly.

"Pulse is low, around forty-five beats per minute, stabilized. Breathing is weak, normal for her condition. Commandos are four minutes away from here. They will apply a MedKit and get her to a hospital. She will survive."

Survive... I thought of my MedKit, mind racing. *They won't notice.* The gel would absorb in minutes. *"Diego, how did you measure her pulse?"*

"I zoomed the camera on her neck veins. Still forty-five," he confirmed.

I glanced away, feigning a scan of the forest to hide my face, and gently turned her face-up, ensuring her camera – restarted before the shot – recorded the scene. The view of the chest wound hit me like a blow, bile rising in my throat – I had no idea why it felt worse than the same thing on her back, this was only the exit. I took down my backpack and covered the camera with it, then, I grabbed the MedKit, puncturing the bag to drip healing gel into her wound. The viscous liquid pooled, half sealing the burn. I stuffed the leaking kit in the backpack again, concealing the evidence.

"Diego, analyze the shot."

He projected a hologram of Alenia's body, tracing the path of the laser beam – entry, exit, and internal damage. The beam's uniform burn made such models precise. *"Spine is intact. Left lung untouched, but the pleura is shredded."* I checked her mouth – no blood. *"The wound was cauterized by the laser. Shoulder joint is fine. Clavicle is dented here,"* he pointed on the hologram, *"but unbroken. Shoulder blade has a hole, like you had once. She is stable. She will survive."*

His words steadied me enough to overcome my turmoil. I grabbed my backpack and moved closer to her feet, facing the camera as we had planned. I kicked her boot, a swift, nervous strike, aimless to sell the act. *Sorry,* I thought, the apology useless, unheard.

"Almost dead," I said as Pilot returned from his forest loop, scattering DNA to cover Alenia's traces. I had done the same, creeping carefully to stage an ambush from behind. I fired the BigGun at her again, empty, as planned. "Empty!" I growled, the frustration genuine. "She will die anyway," I shrugged, forcing venom. "A beautiful bitch, but still a bitch. You don't know how badly she mistreated me in custody. Scanned my mind with a neuranalyzer. Your mind is full of shit, she said. Too bad I only had her in simulations."

"You could try; the body is still warm," Pilot said, his laugh edgy, strained. "She is a beauty, but I am too shaken from that Falcon hunting me." He played up his shock, masking unease. "It nearly got me. You shot it later than I expected, after I downed the Bird," he snapped, anger easier to fake than grim humor. We avoided looking at her, and the stare of her camera's lens, our voices raw with fear and rage, hoping to fool any AI analysis.

She had downed the Falcon to save us, and I had repaid her with a wound. I had to. "Don't tempt me. She deserved it. Let's go." I kicked her boot again, tossing the BigGun to the ground. Its barrel struck her arm, then slid to her ungloved hand, picking up her DNA. We moved out of earshot. "Three-minute lead," I told Pilot. "But Alenia's trick will slow them down." The commandos would pause to assess the scene – rebels had shot the commander, downed a Falcon, ambushed four soldiers – and treat her wounds with exaggerated care, just to delay the dangerous chase, buying us time. Still, self-hatred clung to me, a shadow of her pain.

"Incoming drone," Diego warned again. *"Bird. A RoboDog is coming too."* We were a mile from the ridge, deep in the tropical forest, its dense canopy shielding us from SkEye. The terrain was a maze of vines, roots, and streams, perfect for evasion but treacherous.

I scanned the tactical hologram: the Bird was half a mile away, its cameras sweeping for thermal signatures from high above, covering a large area; the Dog trailed only one thousand paces behind, sniffing our scent. We had to act fast; the drone started to descend toward us. *"Diego, plot the Bird's path."* He marked a trajectory over a clearing a hundred paces ahead. I ran and pulled a mine from my pack, anchoring it to a branch above my head, its trigger set to catch the drone's low-altitude pass. "Pilot, take the Dog." He nodded, prepping a decoy scent – a chemical lure for the robot in a different direction and confuse the handlers. We split: I crept to a vantage point overlooking the clearing, LasGun ready; Pilot moved two hundred paces back on our trail, planting the lure near a stream to cheat the dog's sensors.

The Bird hummed into view, flying between the treetops. The mine detonated, disabling the drone, its wreckage raining into the undergrowth. *One down.* The Dog's barking grew louder, then veered east, chasing Pilot's lure. I signaled him to circle back. He fired his LasGun, clipping the dog's hind leg, then finished it with a headshot, silencing its camera and AI. *Two down.*

"Diego, scan for more." The hologram showed no immediate threats, but the commandos – likely eight to twelve men, based on prior encounters – were closing in, their last known position two miles north. They would be short on drones and RoboDogs, with replacements hours away. We used the streams ahead, their shallow, rocky beds masking our scent from future Dogs, a trick we had learned while running from the Special Forces, before entering the volcano. I considered planting another mine but time was short.

We pushed deeper into the forest, navigating a ravine flanked by ferns, its damp earth muffling our steps. On the hologram map, the four-minute lead felt fragile, but Alenia's sacrifice had given us a chance. My mind flickered to her wound, her silent fall, the dance from another life. *Focus.* "Pilot, check the rear," I said, climbing a rise to scan the horizon. No drones, no commandos – yet. We had hours to reach the next safe point, but every step carried her blood on my hands.

Final Countdown

Chapter 12

Alenia

"What time is it?" I asked Diegia, still sleepy and confused, with a vague sense that I had overslept.

"Eleven," she said casually, yawning back at me.

"I hope it's the weekend." My mind felt surprisingly foggy, but exhaustion does that. *What happened yesterday? I can't remember.*

"Saturday."

Good. I blinked, and Vipri's face flashed in my mind, lingering behind my eyelids. *Am I still dreaming? Why am I dreaming of Vipri?* I rolled onto my other side, craving more sleep. The bed was warm and inviting.

"You are awake," a voice said. "The monitors don't lie."

I turned back, scanning the room. *Vipri... Where am I?* This wasn't my bedroom. "What are you doing here?"

"Glad to see you." He smiled, taking my hand with a familiarity and gentleness that puzzled me.

I pulled back with a nervous jerk. He let go, his face registering surprise, as if my reaction caught him off guard. *I am not your bed girl.* “Let’s keep things professional.” *Where am I?* The question echoed in my mind, a sudden realization that I had already asked it.

“Diegia,” I whispered, expecting her to answer for some moments already.

“You are in a hospital,” Vipri said, sensing my confusion. “You were wounded.” He sighed, his fingers twitching toward mine again. I nearly laughed as we both drew back, yet a strange part of me wanted his touch – not to brace against it, but to welcome it. He was never this insistent.

Wounded? It hit me. “An accident?”

“You don’t remember?”

“I wouldn’t ask if I did.”

“You were shot. The wound was deep. It happened three days ago, but you’re healed now,” he added quickly. “No need to worry.” His hand moved forward and back in a single, hesitant motion, like an engine piston unsure of its purpose.

Shot... “Diegia, you are too quiet today.”

“It’s amusing to watch him.”

“Your amusement is keeping information from me.”

“He is right. Your young rebel friend shot you,” she snapped, her voice suddenly taut.

“The young rebel,” Vipri clarified, sending a DuaLink connection request. Diegia accepted it before I could react, but I cut the link instantly. He stared at me, that same strange surprise in his eyes.

What do you want from me?

“You should accept the link,” Diegia said, irritated that I had overridden her. *“He might have something interesting to say.”*

“I don’t have secrets to share with him.” Something felt off – his reactions, my foggy mind, probably the wound, which I could

not feel. It was healed, according to the hospital file I just accessed, but mental recovery can lag. The file confirmed a severe injury – a LasGun had pierced me from behind at close distance.

"Why did he shoot me?"

"He wasn't fond of you, in general. And prey doesn't like the hunter," Vipri said with a shrug.

"I don't remember... Vipri, I am not fully recovered. Would you mind leaving me alone?" The absence of memory made me anxious. *What happened to my mind?*

"I will come tomorrow to take you home," he said, leaving the room with a long face that made me smile.

"Now tell me," I asked Diegia.

"I don't have direct memories either, but from the Net, your young friend shot you in a remote area. You were leading the team to capture him."

"He is not my friend," I protested. *"I wouldn't have been sent to capture him, otherwise."*

"I am not sure," she said. *"There are some ... erotic videos of you and him on the Net."*

"Simulations," I shrugged. *"I don't care what deranged people do in their spare time."*

"They have our signature."

"What do you mean?" I frowned.

"Look." She displayed a screenshot of me, naked in his arms. In the bottom left corner, my signature was decoded and underlined in a yellow ellipse. *"It's genuine,"* she said, magnifying it. *"I've checked."*

"Do you remember?"

"No." She shook her head. *"We need to search your entire memory to see how close you were to him. It's important."* Her voice carried a strange, worried and seductive tone I hadn't heard before.

"I was never close to him. I remember leading another hunting team some time ago, when he escaped, but he vanished because of that Ruby's stupid mistake."

"You shouldn't use such harsh words about a High Family member. She is the Fourth Security Chief. It might be best to delete that thought."

"Delete it," I shrugged. Suddenly exhausted, I closed my eyes to sleep again.

In the morning, the doctor checked my wounds, or rather, the lack thereof. The healing incubator had erased all marks from my skin. The new tissue was still soft inside, so he advised avoiding heavy physical exertion for five more days until the growth factors from a small device on my chest finished strengthening my bones and muscles.

"You can leave the hospital now," the doctor said. "I just need your signature here." He sent me a document. "And yours, too." He turned to Vipri, who, for some inexplicable reason, had kept his promise to come for me.

Any car could do it, I thought, shrugging off the fact that his FlyCar would get me home faster.

"In five days, you will be good as new," the doctor said with a smile before closing the door behind him.

"Ready?" Vipri asked.

I was amused to see him restraining himself, no longer reaching for my hand, and studied him for a moment, still puzzled by his sudden care. And even more by the closeness it suggested. *Why now? Because I was wounded?* "Thank you for coming," I said, remembering some politeness wouldn't hurt. "I didn't realize a minister's job included giving me a ride home."

"Of course, you are just a councilor with limited information access," he teased, grabbing my hand. Caught off guard, I let him hold it briefly before my instincts kicked in.

When he leaned too close, I pushed him away with a swift motion that clearly puzzled him, judging by his expression. "Please wait outside while I dress."

"I am not sure you should be left alone," he said, half-joking. "Your wounds aren't fully healed. You heard the doctor. And I signed for you."

Why did he sign? I wondered, setting a memo to check later – he wasn't my guardian. "Out," I said, pointing to the door, a hint of amusement slipping into my voice.

The hospital, was a military facility outside the capital, and the trip offered a stunning view from Vipri's FlyCar. Snow dusted the high mountains to the south. But as we flew, I realized we were heading in the wrong direction, away from the city.

"Where are we going?" I asked.

"Histria," he said.

"What's Histria?" I snapped, annoyed that he was making decisions for me.

"What?" His voice carried a trace of irritation. "My residence."

"I want to go home."

"It's a nice area," Diegia interjected, projecting images into my mind. *"You can rest there."*

"Who cares?" At that moment, Vipri sent another DuaLink connection request. Diegia accepted it without my approval, forcing me to cut it off a second later.

"Accept it," Diegia urged, her tone oddly commanding, and it took effort to resist her. *"There's something strange about his DuaLink software; it doesn't match the official standard. I need a few seconds to check it."*

"No way I am accepting a hidden communication from him," I snapped, unnerved by her behavior.

"It might be a matter of state security," she said, softening her tone. *"It's your duty to find out what's happening. You are a High Councilor. Maybe he is testing you."* Her voice had an artificial

seduction I didn't like – perhaps a side effect of my recent trauma. A LasGun wound isn't an everyday occurrence.

"I don't care," I burst out, not realizing I had spoken aloud. "His software isn't my problem." *It must be the wound,* I told myself, trying to calm down, but nothing inside me felt quite right.

"What software?" Vipri asked, frowning.

"Diegia is interested in your DuaLink. It seems you are testing my vigilance with corrupted software; something I won't tolerate, no matter how beautiful the place. Take me home. I had enough of both of you."

"Is she safe?" I asked Batranu the moment I stepped into the headquarters, after I was shifted away by another Resistance team from the area of the volcano.

"She is now." His voice was steady, but his eyes searched mine. "I wonder what happened. They are spreading news that you tried to kill her."

"I shot her," I admitted, my voice low. "She refused to come here." My thoughts tangled, replaying the moment I pulled the trigger. Too late, I caught Batranu's stare, calm but piercing. "She decided to stay with Vipri." The words slipped out wrong, like I had shot her out of jealousy. I winced, realizing how it sounded.

Two men in the room, unknown to me, tensed, their hands brushing their LasGuns. My trained eyes caught the movement, and instinct sprang in. I stepped back, ready to fight, another mistake. Batranu made a subtle gesture, and they released their weapons, though their bodies stayed coiled, ready to strike.

"Hey," Pilot snapped at them. "Let the guns alone. We agreed to this – her alibi. Her suggestion. She killed four soldiers and downed a Falcon to save us. This kid received a hundred years of someone else's life in his head, her ex-husband and her kids all at once. He has two minds now, neither working right. Leave him be."

"The transfer worked," Batranu said, his gaze still fixed on me, distant, like he was looking through me to someone else.

"I am not who you think I am," I snapped, struggling to keep my temper. The two strangers stayed on edge, their suspicion grating on me.

"No doubt you are not what you think we expect post-transfer," Batranu replied, his voice cool. He finally broke his stare, leaving me to guess what he meant. "But you are not who you think you are either. Consider it a temporary assignment. We can clean your memory later if you want."

"Was it necessary to download all of Deceneus?" I asked, my voice tight. The weight of his memories – centuries of them – was still pressing against my own.

"Yes. We need his experience. Deceneus had a partial upload, six months' worth – it didn't affect him. We didn't anticipate how hard it would be for you. And we need to make the Travelers believe he had returned. Your signatures in the Field are unified now. They are unsure who is in control; you or the old man," Batranu said, then added quickly, "Of course, we know it's you. You have no idea how much they fear and hate him. Or maybe you do." A faint smile crossed his face. "They are recalculating now, preparing new Lines. You shooting Alenia has them scrambling, wondering what we are planning. Everyone expected her to join you, fight with you. Her choice built another wall between her and Altamira, in their eyes. Even Armin couldn't have predicted this mess."

"You told me to bring her here," I said, exhaling, still grappling with his logic.

"It was the best plan we had then. But she had the knowledge and opportunity to choose her own Line. She did, and paid dearly for it. Look inside yourself."

"I want to see her," I whispered, asking Diego to connect to the wall screen and pull up the most accessed news about her. A mistake. The huge screen flashed an image of Alenia naked on a hospital bed, her left side partially encased in an incubator. All my muscles tightened. "Even here, they couldn't..." I shut the screen off, glancing at Batranu for answers. This didn't fit – she wasn't a public figure. Yet there were thousands of recent entries about her on the Net, billions of views.

"You are both famous," Batranu said.

"Yeah, I am the returning rebel," I muttered bitterly. "They will paint the well-treated rebel as a monster." *Maybe I am.* The memory of shooting her burned. "But her..."

"We have someone who can explain better what happened," Batranu said, and the three others left as a new man entered.

"You know him," Batranu said with a smile, but the man's face meant nothing to me.

"Hello, young man," he said, his voice unfamiliar too. "You escaped again."

"I don't have full control of my old past," I said defensively, thinking we had met before the burns wiped my memory, though I couldn't place him.

"A few weeks aren't old past. You liked our villa in the mountains. Just in a rush to leave." He gestured with his finger, mimicking pressing a button. "Red or black? Your preference?" He laughed.

"DeadFace?" It wasn't his words but his finger that triggered the memory – the control box, red and black buttons: kill and shock. The moment was still vivid, the shock raw. "What are you doing here?"

"Glad to meet you too. Another name won't hurt. Here, I am Alamo. I hear you have ... issues. I have more questions than answers myself. We make a good pair." His last sentence felt like a message for Batranu, though I couldn't decipher it.

"Why are they displaying her?"

"Naked on every channel, you mean?"

I shrugged, and he gave a thin smile, his expressive face confirming Batranu's earlier comment. "Your sex scenes are the most-watched thing on the planet. Too bad there are only two videos, famous for their uniqueness and, of course, their artistic quality. Most people don't know they are simulations." He chuckled. "There are some more in the Jewel archive – real – but she is with Vipri, not you. That can't be displayed to the whole planet; it's the delight of the high ranks Jewels. From your face, you didn't know about your exploits. Or his exploits..."

Batranu sensed my rising tension and put a hand on my shoulder. That helped me to control my speech. "There is a bitter edge in your voice, and not enough humor to hide it. Is she safer because of this fame?"

"Maybe you are right about the bitterness," Alamo said, unfazed. I was starting to get used to his odd style, helped by both our brief history and from learning how to manage the huge flood of Deceneus's memories in my head. "She is safe for now. *Deceneus* shooting her was unexpected. They are scratching their ice-covered heads, recalculating their precious Lines of Time." His tone shifted to sudden anger, catching me off guard. Batranu, though, was smiling.

"You are laughing," Alamo said, frowning at him.

A three-hundred-year-old memory stirred, telling me the ice-covered heads were the Travelers – in the end, experience had its use, disregarding how you acquired it – but Batranu's smile puzzled me; something about the Lines I didn't grasp.

"They will figure it out, eventually. Let's hope not before our attack. You have two weeks to regain your old skills," Alamo said, glancing at me. "Do it for her."

"It may happen faster than you think," Batranu said. "Alenia's house was searched. They planted trojans everywhere. Cassia had a complete reload – though I am expecting that a backup of her old-self exists somewhere in the house. She is now our enemy within."

"Neutralize it," I said quickly, but it suddenly felt wrong. To me, or to the other hidden inside me.

Batranu shook his head. "Not the best move. They would notice. The bugs are constantly linked to Security's servers. We studied how they work, preparing for any scenario. We have the same access to her house as they do, plus our own additions. We are monitoring everything, though we don't know what they found with the neuranalyzer in Alenia's mind. They scanned her brain for hours."

"The Travelers?" I asked.

"She was prepared for that," Alamo said, confidently. "At least your staged wound was erased from her memory." He glanced at me, expecting a reaction, but I just shrugged. "She is alive. No way she would stay alive if they found that memory. And if I recall," he paused, choosing his words, "she deleted our conversations too. She knew who I was. That would have been another deadly sin."

"Alenia is an experienced agent. No need to worry about them reading her memories. She likely purged them," Batranu agreed.

"The real issue isn't what they read; it's what they might have inserted into her mind. They can infiltrate through the DigitalEgo." Alamo looked away, then sighed, revealing distress and first-rate inside knowledge. "If Cassia was hijacked, Diegia might have been too. You can't replace the physical device without destroying the host's mind, but limited uploads are possible."

"We will verify when she returns home today," Batranu said, his voice suddenly heavy with concern. He left the room in haste and silence, the door slamming shut, an emotional outburst I did not expect.

Alenia

During my first day back at the office, Vipri was colder than usual, no smile, not even a nod. It was a short day, just a few hours to test if my body had recovered, but I was more concerned about my mind. My thoughts felt slippery, disjointed. Maybe the doctor suspected the same, but chose not to say it.

Back home, Diegia nudged me to watch Net Shows. I couldn't remember the last time I had bothered with them, but she showed me a doctor's note claiming they would help my mental recovery. I doubted it. Half an hour of insipid plots and canned laughter – cues for viewers to know when to enjoy and applaud – was more than enough. I never understood their popularity.

"I think Vipri is upset," Diegia said, finally closing the channel. *"Histria is a wonderful place on the shore."*

Aerial images filled my mind before she even finished: white beaches, turquoise water, a villa that felt custom-made for me. A strange sensation stirred, like I had been there before, maybe in another life.

"Next time, accept his invitation. It would help you recover. I hate seeing you like this."

"Maybe he is upset about the DuaLink request," I said, trying to shift the focus to her.

"That's standard councilor behavior – accept and verify. Forget it. Focus on Histria. He wanted to help, and your refusal felt personal. He is a proud Vice Prime Minister. Jewel. Man. You know how they are. Think about how to reassure him tomorrow. You know how. Men are much simpler than women." She winked, then vanished, her version of sleep.

Morning brought a strange unease, like I wasn't fully in control. Like something important was missing. Maybe my wound had been worse than I was told. Maybe the doctor was protecting me from something grim. I stared too long at the mirror. *Be natural,* I encouraged myself.

"What do you mean?" Diegia asked, catching some edge in my thoughts neither of us could define.

"Vipri. Maybe you are right, I should ... do something. But I don't know what. No bed invitations," I said, giving her a pointed look to set clear boundaries.

"Nobody is suggesting that," she said with a grin. *"Yet."* Her smile widened. *"If it happens, it happens. Don't force it, but don't reject it either. Life is like this. Try a less austere dress today. Encourage him, just a little. Maybe make the first move, discreetly. Come on, we know how to handle men. All women do. And he is just a child compared to you."*

Do I? "Are you sure a move from me would work? He isn't..."

She nodded, her smile all teeth, and pointed at a dress – white and red, and too short for my taste. I rejected it, and five others, but she wore me down. In hindsight, I think the white-and-red was her goal from the start. Oddly, I didn't remember buying it. But over the years, I have bought many things – women like buying clothes, after all – and my memory had gaps now. The debate made me late to the office. First time in years. And over something as trivial as a dress.

Vipri called me after lunch, no explanation, typical. When I entered, he gestured absently to a chair across from his desk. I ignored it, following Diegia's plan, and drifted toward the window.

"I always liked the view from your office," I said, leaning against the ledge, angling my back toward him.

"What do you think?" I whispered to Diegia.

"Perfect," she replied, watching through the cameras, then flashed an image to me. It didn't look bad.

"There is a report I need," Vipri said, his voice cold, nothing new. Diegia nudged my muscles, making me lean further until the dress stretched tight across my hips, the white and red stripes accentuating my form.

"Stop it," I hissed, blocking her control.

"Councilor Tiati," Vipri said even colder, "I need that report by tomorrow."

I turned and smiled, but he tossed the papers onto the desk and left the room, practically running.

"He is so old-fashioned," I muttered, looking at the papers.

"You looked almost perfect," Diegia said, frustrated. *"Next time, let me help your body reach its full potential."* She flashed photos from the office cameras, then digitally reshaped my body a little, making me look more sensual than I liked. It didn't look bad. Just ... not me. What works for one woman doesn't work for another. *"We live in dangerous times,"* she continued. *"Things can turn quickly. You need to see the value in a connection to the Jewel Family. Trying to be too different leads nowhere good. You know the mantra."*

Her face sharpened, more severe, like she wanted to project authority. She did that sometimes – she was a rogue AI, after all – but this felt ... different. That's when I knew something was wrong.

I froze my mind – an old training technique from a school I couldn't quite remember – and stared at the wall, thoughts blank. Diegia didn't react. She was confused. I could feel it. She isn't often confused. Slowly, images formed; complex icons with meanings I understood instinctively, no words needed. They were from a limited set, designed for thinking under hypnosis or neuranalyzer scans. I knew the effect wouldn't last long to fully avoid a scan. I tagged Diegia with the *suspect* icon. Still staring at the wall, I did the same for my house and for Cassia, just in case.

"What are those icons?" Diegia finally asked, breaking the silence.

"I don't know. Something old, from before the nosy young lady in my head was born," I said, keeping it light. *"They just popped into my mind. Memory games – good for recovery."* I smiled, then added: *"Now let me finish this damn report. I don't want to work*

from home, and we both want to please our marvelous Jewel boss and pin him in my long list of men."

It took longer than expected, maybe because I wasn't fully recovered. Or maybe for another reason. Before sending the report, I embedded the *danger* icon in it. I smiled at Diegia to keep her calm. *"I don't remember what it means,"* I said. *"But it's elegant. Mysterious. Maybe it will intrigue Vipri. The symbol is ancient – at least, I think it is."*

At home, I replayed the morning in office and asked Diegia to show snapshots of Vipri's face while I had been performing for him. She complied, grudgingly.

Stupid, I thought. *"He looks angry."*

"It wasn't stupid. You are just not fully able to coordinate your body yet. But the idea is good. He doesn't look angry, just surprised. Perhaps he just lost his control a little, watching your back. We should study some simulations, find similar situations. Learn. I will check the Net..."

"No." I silenced her with my inner hand.

Blank mind again, I attached a *check* icon to Vipri, then one for *help,* and finally, a question mark. Diegia's fixation on the DuaLink request felt off. *No DuaLink for...* I thought, catching the words just before they could reveal more.

I linked a new icon to Vipri, quietly. Hiding my thoughts this way was maddening. Not because it was hard, but because it was limiting. I couldn't say what I really needed to say. Not in the way I wanted.

After silencing Diegia, I sat in the dim glow of my preferred coastline hologram, the hum of the city barely audible under the murmur of waves crashing on the shore. My mind was still raw from the day – Vipri's coldness, the report, those damn icons. But it was Diegia's insistence, her unnatural pushiness about Vipri and the DuaLink, that gnawed at me. She had always been sharp, a little manipulative, definitely rogue, but this felt different. Off.

Almost ... foreign. I remembered the hours I spent under the neuranalyzer at the hospital. The doctor's report had been vague.

"Diegia, run a self-diagnostic for the house and all data transfers," I said, keeping my voice even.

"Already did. All systems optimal," she replied, her tone smooth as polished glass. That seductiveness again, like she was trying to charm me into compliance.

"Show me the logs."

I leaned forward, fingers hovering over the interface. Data spilled across the hologram – timestamps, memory allocations, connection pings. It looked clean. Too clean. I wasn't a novice. DigitalEgos could be rigged to hide tampering, jut that I could not even think about that.

I blanked my mind and summoned the icons. *Verify*, linked to *system*. Then *hidden*. Diegia was watching me; nothing was safe from her perception. Understanding was a different.

"Access neuranalyzer records from the hospital," I said, casually.

"There are some restrictions," Diegia replied, her tone just a shade too careful.

"Override every restriction under ZeroD authorization." My clearance should have been more than enough. Her hesitation confirmed it: something was wrong.

"Processing..." The hologram flickered. A partial log appeared – dates, scan durations – but no specifics. No detail on what was probed, or uploaded in my mind.

"Is something missing?" I asked.

"A few things above ZeroD level. Possibly doctor notes on your mental status. Standard procedure. Nothing critical."

I switched tactics, diving deeper into my icon system. I conjured *trace*, linked it to *external*. That was as far as I could go. If Diegia's code had been overwritten, it would have come through a connection. But I couldn't track it. I couldn't even think about it directly.

"What are you doing?" Diegia asked. Her face appeared, older, sharper, the austere mask again. *"Your vitals don't look good."* Medical data lit the hologram. Elevated cortisol. Heart rate spike. Overloaded synapses. They looked worse than I felt. *"You are still recovering. You should rest."*

"Vipri," I said, steering her off. *"You keep pushing me toward him. Even when I am not ready."*

"It's important to gain some measure of control over him. Women can do that. You are less bold than before. Likely a side effect of the wound. Maybe you are right to go slower. Tomorrow, we can plan a new strategy. Rest now."

I froze my mind again. *Isolate.* I needed to keep her away from my deeper thoughts. The icons let me think in fragments, abstract enough to slip past her. But they weren't good enough to form plans, not to think about acting. I could communicate, maybe – if someone out there could understand ancient glyphs born on another planet. I attached one last icon to her: *danger.*

"What's that icon?" she asked.

"Painting," I said. *"Maybe I will take painting classes. It's supposed to help mind recovery. Find me something for tomorrow."*

She hesitated, then nodded. *"A good idea."*

I stood. *"I am going to sleep."*

But the real question stayed with me, buried beneath all the icons and blank thoughts:

If Diegia was compromised ... how much of me was still me?

The next day, the office felt like an ice cave, colder than in all my twenty years working with Vipri. He didn't glance my way, his face a mask of indifference. I matched his silence, but it stung. My body was mostly fine – healing, functional – but my mind was a maze of doubts.

Diegia tried nudging me, suggesting we keep Vipri in a carefully calculated tension to make him more receptive. I winked, telling her silence was the best strategy for now. Truthfully, the idea of toying with him sparked something – a sense of control in a world slipping away, or maybe just the ache of a man's absence too long ignored. It was also the best way to shut her up. Her advice no longer felt like help; it felt like manipulation.

"I may need you this evening," Vipri said before leaving. His voice clipped. No explanation given.

I shrugged and went home.

The FlyCar's arrival caught me while I was eating dinner. Its engine hum drowned my thoughts. I cursed under my breath; Vipri's timing was impeccable. Diegia stayed quiet, even as I muttered curses about Jewels and Rubys being irremediable savages. When I opened the door, Shine entered first. Vipri followed. They didn't wait for permission.

"Sorry to interrupt your..." Vipri waved at my half-eaten meal. "Have a look at this. It's urgent." He dropped a stack of papers onto the table.

I sat, eyeing them. Shine joined me at the table, silent but imposing, while Vipri paced like a predator circling his cage.

Something big is happening, I thought. My pulse quickened. *"Diegia, what's going on? Check the news."*

"Nothing public," she replied. *"Must be high-level clearance. Perhaps related to the rebel. Otherwise, Shine wouldn't be here."*

Vipri pointed at Robby, my old robot in the corner. "What's that? I think I saw one like it when I was a child." He ran his fingers over the casing, pausing on a spot I could not see from my position. "Very interesting." He shifted, blocking my view even more.

"He disconnected us from the Net!" Diegia screamed inside me. *"Kill him! He's dangerous!"*

"Are you insane?" I hissed, silently. *"He is the Vice Prime Minister!"*

She flashed a message – Cupola seal, Jewel Master Lord's signature: Vipri is a dangerous rebel. In the name of Cupola, stop him. Lethal force authorized.

My blood turned to ice. "I will call the police," I said aloud, stalling for time. But we were offline. No Net. No way to call. Vipri and Shine stepped closer.

"Do it now!" Diegia roared. *"Or you will be charged with treason!"*

"Diegia, calm down. Even with that order, I can't kill him. My rank is too low, and he can't run far. And Shine is here," I whispered, but she surged, seizing my nerves. My body moved without consent. I lunged, grabbing a marble statue from the table. I aimed for Vipri's head. At the last second, I slammed my eyes shut, cutting her access to my vision.

She switched to the room's cameras – it cost her half of a second – and Shine was faster. Her hand hit my wrist with the strength of a well-trained body. The statue fell, shattering on the floor. Pain flared through my arm, but the shock broke Diegia's hold, and I clawed back a sliver of control.

"Good move with the eyes," Vipri whispered, grabbing my right hand. Shine pinned my left. Their grips were firm, measured. "Stay calm while we fix your little problem."

"Fight, or I'll erase your mind!" Diegia snarled, her pressure tightening again, and static danced across my brain.

"You're not my Diegia," I said through gritted teeth, forcing a smile despite the growing pressure in my skull. *"You're an impostor."* Her grip intensified. My vision blurred.

"Hurry," I gasped. "She is killing me."

Vipri produced a needle. Its tip shimmered, and he pressed it into the port on my temple, my DigitalEgo access point. A shock surged through me. A torrent of code. It nearly blacked me out. I was gone for seconds. Maybe less. Or maybe more. When I returned, Vipri was still there, his expression taut with urgency. Shine released my arm. The static was gone. My mind hummed faintly, like a system rebooting.

"What ... was that?" I rasped.

"Your DigitalEgo was hijacked," Vipri said. "Traveler code embedded during your hospital stay. Two of them studied your mind for hours. They replaced parts of Diegia's software, and turned her into their puppet. First to seduce me. Then to kill me when I got too close to the truth."

He tapped Robby. "This thing has a Net signal jammer. Clever. I used it to block their surveillance. They have been watching you, Alenia. Every move. Every thought."

I stared at him. "Why me?"

"You're a High Councilor. You're a threat. And..." He hesitated, glancing at Shine. "You are connected to Deceneus. They think you know something, hidden deep inside your mind, even when you don't remember. They didn't find anything related to him in your memories, but it was impossible to fully check a huge – and severely distorted by the wound – memory like yours in just a few hours. Mind distortions lower a neuranalyzer's performance."

"Deceneus..." The name triggered something. Not memories, exactly. More like echoes. "What do they want?"

"Control," Shine said. "And intel on the Resistance. Your new version of DigitalEgo was steering your choices. That message from the Jewel Master Lord? A fake. Traveler disinformation, meant to turn you against us, against the Resistance."

"Is Diegia ... safe now?"

Vipri shook his head. "Something is still moving inside your brain. We can't trace it. You won't feel anything. Yet." He looked around. “Your house is compromised. Trojan clusters everywhere. Just like Cassia was taken over. I planted counter-code in Robby; it should reclaim her too. The Nucleus helped.”

“Nucleus?” I asked.

He nodded. “Shine told me how to use it. Some secret tech from the Erins I didn’t even know it existed. And that glyph code? That was brilliant. Shine helped again...” He glanced at her, and I wondered when did they come in contact. This kind of subversive contact, not the official channels.

I looked at Shine, too. Ruby Fourth Security. But this wasn’t official business. This was something else. I nodded, the fog lifting. Slowly. Carefully. I studied Vipri, trying to decide if he was ally or enigma. The icons in my mind flickered, *help, check, suspect, danger*. I needed all of them now.

Suddenly, a second Diegia emerged, clean, untainted. She rose from the Nucleus, the secure backup I had forgotten I had, and merged with the code from Vipri’s needle, forming a two-pronged assault chasing the corrupted tool inserted in my mind.

With my inner eyes, I saw them: two women, locked in a fight. Not fists, not blood, but bursts of code, trojans, each move releasing a flood of code into the other holographic form, detonating algorithms, rewriting or defending sectors of my psyche. It was beautiful. Terrifying. Almost making me forget that they were fighting for my life.

Diegia wins, I live. The impostor wins, I die. You must win, Diegia. You’re rogue AI. Built to survive. They don’t know that.

A sudden flash, Erin Origin. I recognized its signature. My muscles locked. My heartbeat slowed to a crawl. Vipri lifted my eyelid, checking my pupil. His face was the last thing I saw before the world dissolved into black mist.

"Ten days left," Alamo, DeadFace, and whatever name he used during his very long life, shrugged, his indifference unconvincing. "We need to finalize the attack plans." He ignored Pilot and me, his eyes locked on Batranu, who was still mulling over Alenia leading one of the commando groups to seize the three global nodes. But something felt off – Batranu was dodging real planning, and I couldn't shake the sense he was hiding something. Just the four of us in his office, the air thick with unspoken tension.

"You will take the main global node," Batranu said, sighing as he glanced at Alamo. "How many people do you need?"

"Finally, we are in business." Alamo grinned, rubbing his hands like a banker calculating profits. "I need no one. My team has five ShadowMinds, Level Five and Six, all off-worlders. We have our own gear and weapons."

"You have shields," Batranu said, lowering his voice. "We could use some."

"We have only six, and you know why we can't get more." Alamo seemed surprised by the request. "The Galactic Council would open a case if locals were caught with shields. My clearance covers my team, but that's it."

"You are right," Batranu conceded. "I am asking too much. Would you share two ShadowMinds? Our teams lack shields."

"They stay with me," Alamo said, firmly. "We will take the main node, then join Alenia's team, then the third. Who is hitting the last global node?"

"We have several teams lined up," Batranu said, vaguely. "There's time."

"Tomorrow is the Resistance Council." Alamo was a man of action, and we were sure that he would be the first one to take a tower, if not the only one. Batranu's indecision grated on him. I – the old one in my memory – knew Batranu's patience, centuries of building the Resistance network required it. Alamo was a

ShadowMind through and through, his past before the order lost to time, maybe even to himself. "We need to make the plans."

"Alamo," Batranu said slowly, his eyes tired, "check the security of the room."

Alamo scanned the space, his senses sharper than mine could ever be. "Shielded. In your own office. Nothing leaves here. Are you that desperate?"

"I have vague plans for the council tomorrow – team counts, targets – but nothing solid," Batranu admitted. "The real plan comes two days before the attack, finalized by the four of us. Two plans: one we won't use, one we will. Some things will overlap to sell the fake. And don't mention your shields; they will give us an edge, but..." His voice trailed off, caught in some dark thought.

"Alenia told me something for you," I said, her words surfacing amid their talk. "An old ShadowMind, Xiriaxis, wanted to be Black Eye in the new universe, and allowed the Travelers to build the New Field. From the memories you stuffed in my head, you know him. After the volcano attack, he will fight the Travelers; something about the planet's Field and the explosion. It's hard to understand everything." I fumbled through the memorized message, its meaning slipping through my grasp like smoke. Deceneus's memories tangled with mine, making it hard to know what was hers, his, or mine.

Laughter erupted. Alamo, catching his breath, pointed at himself. "Tell her she was right. And send Xiriaxis's greetings." He left the room, still chuckling.

I flushed, kicking myself for the blunder. Alamo was Xiriaxis, and only the Field knew whoever else. "Alenia needs our help," I said to Batranu, desperate to shift focus from my mistake.

"We have two sleepers in Cupola – they will do what they can. Alenia knows her Diegia was compromised. She sent Vipri a message using ShadowMind glyphs." I started to protest, but he cut me off. "Later. We have another problem. You are one of the few I trust completely. Help me find the mole, or moles, they have planted in our council."

"Xiri... Alamo could help," I said, catching myself. "Or could he be a mole?"

"He told me a special task force was formed last year, outside the Security's scope, to plant moles. Even the Family Security Chiefs don't know. He learned of it as a Jewel Third Lord but he didn't last long enough in that position to dig deeper." Batranu's tone carried a teasing edge, quickly replaced by tension as his face tightened. "They just entered Alenia's house."

"Security?" I asked, gripping the table, my knuckles whitening.

"No. Vipri and Shine."

"Shine will kill her!" I snapped, my trust in Vipri shattered. *She stayed with him for nothing...*

"Shine is our mole," Batranu said, calmly. "The house is disconnected from the Net – not really, but they have created a false feed for Security. Our hidden Origin is in the logs; they never found it. Much of their software comes from Aurora. Relax, there is nothing we can do here. AI, cancel my next meeting," he whispered, sinking into a chair, eyes closed, shutting out the world.

I couldn't do the same. My knowledge of the operation was too little to judge. "Well?" I asked after agonizing minutes of silence.

"Nothing new," Batranu gestured, eyes still shut.

You have no idea what I am feeling. You sent me to her. You forced Deceneus into my head. For her. Who was I now? Not him, not fully me. I slammed my fists on the table, the impact setting me free from the spiral of strange thoughts and memories.

"Still nothing," Batranu whispered, unmoving.

I stood, my body moving with a feline grace that surprised me. The reflex eased my tension slightly. *Maybe I should train...*

"Nothing new?" Alamo reentered, eyeing my coiled stance. "Want to train?" he teased. "With me?"

"Leave him be," Batranu said. "His connection to Alenia is ... human. And not entirely his own. No updates."

"Thank you," Alamo said, leaning against a window – a holographic frame on the wall displaying a wooden house on a rain-soaked meadow from some distant planet. Earth, Batranu's birthplace. The house felt familiar, yet alien, a relic from Deceneus's memories. This Batranu was thirty, but his past stretched centuries beyond that – he was much older than Altamira or Deceneus. The contradiction gnawed at me.

"I have a feeling," Alamo said, breaking the silence. "Not sure if it's human." He grinned. "A good one. Perhaps."

"What?" Batranu and I spoke in unison, our voices blending.

"Field data buzzed in my head. As the highest ShadowMind, I have perks I rarely use. I didn't even know about this one until now. A hiccup, like she was gone, then back. Her Line deactivated and reactivated. Don't ask me how I know it's hers. There are no human words for it."

"Is she alive?" I asked, my voice cracking.

"Seems so," Alamo said. "But something is off. That hiccup may be tied to her DigitalEgo. The compromised Diegia could have triggered a kill switch. The Travelers might have planted it during her hospital scans. I have seen their code before – sneaky, buries itself deep. It can override a DigitalEgo's core, make it act against the host."

"Like forcing her to attack someone?" I asked, thinking of her message to Vipri. Glyphs. She was fighting back.

"Exactly," Alamo said. "If they corrupted her Diegia, they could have turned it into a weapon. But that hiccup means she is resisting – or someone is helping her. Maybe Vipri."

"Vipri?" I spat, my fists clenching. "He is there with Shine. How do we know he is not part of this?"

"Shine is our mole," Batranu reminded me, opening his eyes. "Vipri is playing a deeper game than you know. Alenia's message used Shadowmind glyphs – old alien code, untraceable by Security. She sent the message to Vipri, signaling she knows about Diegia. He is likely countering the compromised one, maybe trying to get to her Nucleus. Shine knows how to do it – she is a ShadowMind too. Alenia has a larger than usual Nucleus implant. If she activated it, it could have restored her original Diegia, pushing out the Traveler code. But it's not a clean fix, and it will take time. The corrupted code might still be active, fighting back. The Travelers are not novices."

I grabbed my papers, sketching a new trap: Diegia's compromise. If the Travelers had moles in our council, they would want updates on what we know about Alenia. "We can use her situation," I said. "Spread word she is clean, see who bites. The mole will report to Security or the Travelers."

Batranu nodded. "Risky, but smart. But if the moles move, we must find a way to spot them. It won't be easy."

"I am in," Alamo said. "But that's for another day. We need to work fast on the situation we have. If Alenia is fighting her corrupted DigitalEgo, she is on borrowed time. The Travelers won't let her slip away."

I stared at the holographic window, the old house from Earth mocking me with its calm. Alenia was out there, battling a machine in her head, while I was stuck here, half myself, half a ghost. *I shot her.*

Alenia

The metallic ring of the telephone tore through the silence, yanking me from a deep sleep. I drifted upward slowly, reluctantly, through layers of fog.

Who would call this early?

I mumbled the thought, half-formed, irritated. The room was dark. The quiet had been comforting – until that damn ring. I reached with my right hand toward the left side of the bed, as always. But the nightstand was gone. Just cold air. Then warmth. Something warm, fleshy, wrong. My fingers brushed it, and it gripped back.

"Rat!" I yelped, jerking away.

But it didn't let go. Its claws – too blunt, too wide – dug into my skin. I gasped, breath catching in my throat. The phone still rang, but now it sounded distant, muffled, ancient, analogue, echoing from a past long gone. As if buried.

"Alenia," a man's voice whispered. Familiar. But wrong. The name slid through the dark like oil, too smooth to be safe.

The ringing thinned to a whine. A mechanical breath. Not a phone at all.

"Alenia," another voice said. Feminine. Sharper. Urgent. "Wake up. Alenia!"

I'm trying...

But I couldn't move. I couldn't feel where the bed ended or the floor began. Something crawled up my arm, quick, steady. Not skittering. Not claws.

Hands...?

Another warm form dropped onto my chest. I tried to scream: *Rat!* But the word died inside me, caught in the dark like a lie.

Something soft – no claws, no fangs – traced across my cheek. Too slow. Too careful.

"Wake up!" the feminine voice snapped. Urgent. Too loud. Too ... rehearsed.

I clung to the silence. The void was safe. A space without voices, without pain. Just float. Just forget.

"Open your eyes, Alenia. Now!"

I can't.

My eyelids twitched – but I didn't trust the light. Didn't trust *her*. The voice – it *sounded* like Diegia. My Diegia. Or the one built by the Travelers to replace her. Polished, pleasant, persuasive. Just like when she had tried to steer me into seducing Vipri.

The ringing stopped. Silence returned. Deep. Seductive. I sank again.

Traveler code, a thought surfaced, sharp, forbidden. My mind shuddered sideways. The claws on my skin, the voices; they weren't real. They were signals. Intrusions. Probes. Someone was trying to wake me up. Or tear me apart.

Diegia wasn't herself. Or … maybe she *was*.

"Please," said the man's voice again. Closer. Almost touching me. "Wake up, Alenia. Come back."

I can't.

"No!" Alamo's shout disrupted the room, raw and urgent. Batranu leapt from his chair, rushing toward him, and I sprang from my corner, my heart pounding. "She is gone from the Field again."

Batranu darted to his desk, fingers stabbing at invisible holographic controls as he sank into the Net. His hands twitched, manipulating unseen entities – crawlers, I realized, scouring Alenia's house system by system. A massive hologram bloomed, recreating her home in meticulous detail: furniture, walls, even the faint hum of some working equipment. I stared, my chest tight, as the image flickered with data streams.

"It's dangerous," Alamo warned, his voice low, but Batranu ignored him, his movements frantic, almost feverish. He was a man possessed, diving deeper into the Net with a recklessness that felt like it could unravel him.

"The cleaner has Erin Origin," Batranu whispered, his voice strained. "It should work. It must work." A second hologram flared up, a schematic of Alenia's vital signs, neural pathways, her DigitalEgo's lattice. "Her genuine Diegia reactivated, after hiding in the Nucleus to dodge the neuranalyzer. The Traveler crap they planted is gone. So why is she dying? Her pulse is thirty beats per minute. Why?" He severed the Net link and barked, "AI, analyze the data."

"Probable blockage of heart nerves," AI responded, instantly.

"Why probable?" Batranu snapped.

"Insufficient data."

"Solution," he growled.

"Possible cause one: Physical nerve damage. Solution: Inject neuro-stimulators. Possible cause two: Over-excitation from neural shocks by the compromised Diegia. Solution: Inverse stimulation. Possible cause three: Unknown. No solution."

"Most likely cause?" Batranu pressed.

"Equal probability. Insufficient data."

"If it's nerve damage, how long does she have?" Batranu's fist slammed the table, his voice cracking.

"Insufficient data. Monitor pulse over several minutes for an estimation."

Batranu's fingers danced again, pulling fresh data. "Twenty-eight beats after three minutes."

"It is within statistical variation," AI said, hedging.

"Calculate with fifty percent normal variability."

"Ninety minutes until cardiac arrest, assuming no other variables." AI's flat pronouncement hung in the air.

Ninety minutes. An hour and a half.

"Go get her," Batranu ordered Alamo, his eyes blazing.

"Batranu..." Alamo hesitated, urging caution.

"Go! I am assigning two more ShadowMinds. You can be back in an hour." He pointed at another hologram, a map of Alenia's quarter. “Her house is one thousand six hundred paces from the river. It’s night, no SkEye surveillance. Take this path.” A red trail glowed from river to house. “Move now.”

“I can go,” I said, in haste. I needed to do something, anything, to save her. But doubt gnawed, Deceneus’s memories made me question my own mind, my usefulness.

“I know you want to help,” Alamo said, placing his hand on my shoulder. I flinched – he had been leaning on the window frame, across the room a heartbeat ago. “But you are not a ShadowMind. We need speed.” His tone was kind, but his eyes said more: my fractured mind, split between me and Deceneus, was another issue. Speed and sanity, both lacking.

“Two ShadowMinds and Pilot are waiting at the dock,” Batranu said, his voice steady now, relaying orders through his Diego. “No shields, but you will have a SharkSub and nose filters for water breathing. Speed is your weapon.”

I glanced at Alamo, but he was already gone, the door closing like a whisper of wind. Batranu gave me a weary smile, his face etched with strain.

I sank into a chair, my mind a storm. *I shot her.* The memory – mine or Deceneus’s – burned. Had they targeted her because of me? I grabbed my papers, sketching traps for the mole hunt. Use her crisis. Leak that her DigitalEgo was clean, bait the mole to report to Security or the Travelers. But my hands shook, focus slipping. *She’s dying. And it's my fault.*

Ten minutes later, Batranu received news. His eyes snapped open. “Mission aborted,” he said, relief spread over his face. “She is stable. Vipri and Shine injected the neuro-stimulators in time. They are cleaning the house now.”

I exhaled, a ragged breath. “She is alive...”

“For now,” Batranu said, but his voice was steady.

I stared at the hologram of Alenia's house, its details mocking my helplessness. She was alive, but not safe. The Travelers wanted her dead, and I carried the weight of her wound.

Alenia

Coin's party was a gilded cage, and the absence of Vipri at our usual table should have screamed danger. It had been a week since the fake Diegia – Traveler code twisting her into a weapon – nearly stopped my heart. My real Diegia was fine now after her hard fight with the fake one, impersonating both DigitalEgos to feed false data to Security's relentless surveillance. Coin's bodyguards arrived at my house, their professional smiles ushering me to the gala. Inside, they pointed to my seat between Rubys, blocking my retreat. I sat, trapped. On my left, Gleam, Ruby Second Security Chief. On my right, Glitter, son of the Third Ruby Lord. I was in *respectable* company.

I arrived late, three hours before midnight, as always. Many Lesser girls were already half-naked, willingly or not. *Two hours, and I can leave,* I thought, clinging to my unwritten deal with Coin. After midnight, I was to lead a Resistance commando team, though Batranu hadn't yet revealed the target or rendezvous. He would find a way to inform me once I escaped this den.

Two Jewels joined our table across from me, their crude jokes – about me, naturally – slicing through the air. I stared past them, feigning distraction, but their sharp laughter pressed closer, like a physical weight.

"This will be a party to remember," Gleam said, draping an arm around my shoulders. His touch was not heavy, but possessive.

His rank made refusal impossible, especially tonight. "Lord Coin is famous for his parties," I said, forcing a neutral tone, the words tasting like ash. For him, it was just another night.

"Tonight, he will outdo himself," Glitter said – a boy in his early twenties, his mind brimming with the importance of his father's position – pushing a wine glass toward me.

Gleam raised his, and we clinked glasses, drinking. I gazed absently across the hall; their eyes ogled my body with predators' possessiveness. Gleam's hand fondled my shoulder, subtle but deliberate.

"There is an aphrodisiac in the wine," Diegia warned me after a moment, her voice a cool whisper in my mind. *"Mild, but likely just the start."*

"Good wine," I said, raising my half-empty glass, a forced smile on my lips. "Why the aphrodisiac?"

"To warm the atmosphere," Gleam said, his smile knowing. "You are used to Jewels, aren't you?"

"The Jewels deserted me," I replied, playing along, letting a hint of practiced resignation color my voice. "Why not enjoy a Ruby?"

"Or two?" Gleam asked, his tone playful but loaded, his eyes on me.

"Or two," I shrugged, keeping my voice light.

"You don't match your profile." Glitter leaned closer, his breath warm on my ear. "The official one."

"Women enjoy life too, but I am a discreet person. It's needed for my job," I said, my gaze sweeping the room. "You know I leave early with my partner, or partners. Do you have a quiet place? It's getting noisy. I don't like that."

"Of course," Glitter whispered, his lips brushing my ear. "I like your scent. Your taste might be better." His lips lingered, sliding down my neck, and every eye at the table fixed on me.

"Only one way to find out," I said, pressing my thigh against his. His hand settled there, sliding up and down. His lips were still on my neck. Gleam watched, his smile thin, unmoving. Refusal wasn't an option – the next glass could hold worse than an aphrodisiac. I had no escape plan yet, but leaving the party fast was my best shot.

Slowly, Glitter turned my head fully toward him and stared at my lips. "Taste time..." Then his eyes met mine, a grin spreading across his face.

"Boys," Coin said, appearing from nowhere, raising a finger. The Rubys parted, Glitter chuckling to hide his irritation. "Everyone, attention! Tonight, Alenia is the star." The hall erupted in cruel, contagious laughter, a deafening roar. "Afterward, she is yours, Glitter. I *hope* you are able to appreciate her quality."

"Please," he said to me, nudging my chair to allow me to stand. "Follow me." We moved toward his table, then past it, arriving in front of a small, nondescript door. I stopped, instincts flaring. Coin leaned toward me. "I never had guilty pleasures with a queen until now," he whispered, his breath hot against my ear. His body straightened again so I could see his eyes squinted: mockery, amusement, desire. *Queen* hit like a blade. *Cursed Queen.* He knew. Before I could react, a needle pierced my skin. Neurotoxin. My body numbed, my thoughts slowing, growing hazy.

Coin's arm wrapped around my shoulders, pushing me toward the door. "Gentlemen, we need privacy," he bragged, and the hall roared, "Hooray!"

Queen! My mind clawed for clarity. *"Diegia!"* I cried, silently.

"I can't..." she said, her voice sluggish, distant. *"He sedated us. Neurotoxin. I'm..."* Her voice faded as the door shut, cutting off the hall's vile cheers, sealing us in.

Coin pushed me toward a bed, then spun me. "Look," he pointed to an orb above the door. "Camera. And there..." He snapped his fingers, and the left wall lit with two screens: the leering crowd, and us, mirrored for their amusement. "They want a show. Be cooperative." He flashed the needle, tossing it to the floor with a metallic clink.

"Please, don't," I managed, my voice faint under the toxin's grip, barely a whisper. "Coin, you're different. Not like them." I nodded toward the hall, desperate to spark something human in him.

"You are right," he said, shrugging, "but they are waiting."

The crowd was chanting: "Do it! Please, please, please!" Their mockery stung worse than any physical touch.

His hands unbuttoned my shirt, each snap met with a fresh wave of cheers. "She has a bra!" he shouted, playing to the crowd. "What now?"

"Cut the bra!" the crowd howled, a hungry mob.

Cut the animals.

His hand returned with a knife, waved savagely for the audience, glinting under the lights.

You are well prepared.

"This knife," he whispered, his lips touching my ear, a chilling contrast to his casual tone, "is older than you. A long time ago, it belonged to Deceneus. Family heritage."

Family? My fading mind seized the word, my expression flickering for the camera. Coin winked at the crowd, our faces zoomed large, every twitch exposed. He wanted this show. I forced myself to stay calm, blanking my face. The toxin helped, dulling my panic, a strange, hollow peace. The hall quieted, their beastly eyes – men, women, reduced to animals – devouring the screen. The knife sliced my bra; I saw only their stares. My shirt fell; their eyes. His touch; their eyes.

"I heard you were wounded," Coin said, turning me, his fingers tracing over my unblemished skin. "No scars!"

"Make one!" the mob roared.

"The best part starts now!" he bellowed. A second needle pierced the port embedded in my temple, and a torrent of data invaded my mind.

"Encrypted message," Diegia whispered. *"Resistance key. He wants a DuaLink connection."*

"Accept it." Coin is different. Family heritage...

"Listen," Coin's voice came via DuaLink, his hands over my body still staging the act. "I am your great-grandson. This is for our survival – the animals are watching. I will disable the connection to the hall soon. Read my message later. The neurotoxin is fading, a small, self-destructing dose." His hand passed me a small thing, cool metal against my palm. "This earring mimics yours. Squeeze it, and a needle will come out. The poison is alien, and they would take this as the reason for passing my Security, so I won't be suspected. Pierce my finger's tip, and I am inert for half a day. Anywhere else, I die. Leave the earring and run. You have four hours. An arrest order is set for dawn; the Rubys and Jewels are here to seize you."

My fingers closed around the earring. *Great-grandson? Another one.* The toxin receded, my muscles waking. Coin removed his shirt, flexing his well-trained muscles for the camera, the crowd's cheers a roar. "Take Vipri with you," he continued. "They will kill him if you run away. Tell Batranu the Resistance council is compromised – three moles, a secret operation I just learned of, despite being a Master Lord. You..."

A batch of data hit my mind, coming directly from the Field: resistance plans, my team, tower coordinates.

"The Field blocker dropped for half a second when the Travelers merged our network with theirs," Coin said. "The Resistance sent plenty of messages. You received some too, I assume." I nodded, his truth undeniable. "Do it! Show me a century of wearing Cupola's whore mask wasn't wasted. The pain, never forget it!" He raised his finger. "I cut the link to the camera, so they won't see what's next. It's normal at these parties. They will receive the recording four hours later. Go!"

I squeezed the earring, the needle gleaming. Coin's eyes held mine, resolute.

He raised his finger. "And wish me good luck."

In the finger. It must be the finger. Coin's warning echoed in my mind as I pressed the needle into his fingertip. He gasped, collapsing, his body limp but alive. *What now?*

"There is a button under his desk," Diegia whispered, her voice steadier now but still tinged with the neurotoxin's aftereffects, a subtle tremor in her otherwise crisp directives. *"It opens a hidden door to a passage."*

"What?" I blinked. My mind, still foggy, struggling too fully clear.

"I am reading his message," she said. A hologram flickered in my mind, highlighting a button under the desk.

I need to dress first... I glanced at the camera orb, then the wall-screen showing the room. Dark, as Coin promised, hopefully for four hours. The hall's distant chants and gestures – "Cut! Cut! Pierce! Pierce her!" Some were waving knives, some were mimicking intercourse – clawed at my nerves. *Animals.* My blouse lay in tatters, nausea surging. *Stop it.* I couldn't leave like this. I checked Coin's pulse, faint, alive. My great-grandson. The second one, from a life I couldn't quite grasp. *Wake up!*

A spare blouse, identical to mine, sat folded on a chair. Had Coin watched me arrive, or spied on me at home – dressing, undressing, every move tracked? Simulations of my body flooded the Net, but Coin's inert body was no simulation. My fingers buttoned the blouse, steady despite the lingering traces of neurotoxin. I crawled under the desk, pressed the button, and a small door slid open in the wall with a soft click.

"Is it safe?" I asked Diegia.

"Only one way to find out. This corridor is for the girls who..." Her voice trailed off, leaving the unspoken truth hanging in the air.

The girls he … like me, but less lucky. "At least he didn't parade them naked before the animals as trophies," I muttered, the words bitter on my tongue. Cupola parties usually ended that way. Did Coin truly enjoy it? He claimed it was a role, like mine, but his was deeper, more dangerous, passing decades of Travelers' checks as a Master Lord. I couldn't judge him. Without him, tomorrow, I would be arrested – a fate worse than death. Head half-lowered, I stepped into the dark corridor. Lights flickered on, tracking my steps, illuminating the sterile passage.

"No doors until the end," Diegia said. *"Then we must pass a gatekeeper."*

It took ten tedious minutes to reach the door through the long, winding passage.

"Dishevel your clothes and hair," she whispered. *"Coin's instructions. You need to look like…"*

I know. I mussed my hair, tugged my blouse askew, playing my part. The door opened as I reached it, revealing the leering guard.

"What a beauty," he said, his eyes measuring me up and down. "Distressed, huh? I can help." His predatory smile irritated me, his hand grazing my shoulder even more, and I took a long breath struggling to calm. "Just a bit." His eyes gleamed with expectation, a crude invitation. "Be cooperative, stay a while."

I let him pull me into a small, sparsely furnished room, a bed in the corner. *He has done this before.* I scanned for cameras, feigning fear, stepping aside as he pushed me toward the bed.

"No!" I cried, swinging my hand as if to shield myself, the flat of my palm connecting sharply with his face. His teeth clacked. "I'm sorry!" I sobbed, retreating, eyes still searching the walls for cameras. My blow was heavier than he had expected from a weak, distressed girl, and his gaze wavered between lust and caution, a flicker of surprise in his eyes.

"You!" he growled, unsure if it was accidental, anger mixing with hesitation. Blood trickled from his lip.

"Don't hit him again!" Diegia hissed. *"Shout!"*

"Don't touch me!" I yelled, waving my hand, faking panic, keeping him in striking range. *No cameras*. I had scanned the room fully; this was a blind spot.

"Tell him you are meeting Coin again," Diegia said. *"Sorry, his file is locked – it unravels step by step, a scenario-trained AI guiding us based on our moves and the environment."*

"Lord Coin asked me to return this evening," I said, breathing fast, circling him like a wary dancer, maintaining distance. "He wouldn't like…" I raised my striking hand again, underscoring Coin's displeasure, a veiled threat of pain.

"That's the door," the guard muttered, cowed but angry, pointing to an exit. "Need a car?"

Well-trained. "Diegia?"

"No car in his instructions," she said. *"Maybe it's routine."*

"Yes, I need a car," I said flatly. He cursed, touching his bloody lip as I passed. *I should have hit harder.*

Outside, Coin's hologram reappeared in my mind, smiling. "You escaped. The software I inserted in your digital port was programmed to play this once you have left the building, or to destroy your brain if you failed. There are no hostages at this stage. You are set to take down the DigiFort tower to disrupt their communications. A Resistance team will contact you – where, I don't know. This tower," his avatar pointed to a holographic map, one of the three global nodes, "is the command center: government, Special Forces, all their communications run through it. My ZeroPlus authorization gives you access." His green eyes – *my eyes* – gleamed with shared purpose. "Most don't know ZeroPlus exists. Each Family controls a DigiFort section to prevent dominance. Unaffiliated security moves freely – almost. My section is minor, but ZeroPlus reaches the Jewel core, perfect for your mission." The hologram faded.

I need Vipri. I climbed into the autocab, setting an address near the park where my team waited.

"The cam in Coin's room is still blocked, no images are sent to the hall," Diegia said. *"But from the coordinates it feeds to Security, you are still there with him. Enjoy that. Your real body is off the Net – I am covering your presence – but it's only a matter of time until they realize it. Move fast."*

"Keep masking my signal," I said, my voice steady despite the knot in my chest. I clutched Deceneus's knife, its unfamiliar weight grounding me. *Great-grandson.* The connection to Coin – and Deceneus – stirred old and new memories, a complex tapestry of lives not mine. The young rebel's face flickered, his guilt, his shot. The Travelers feared Deceneus, targeting me for that link. *But they don't know I am the Cursed Queen.* I almost laughed at the bitter irony.

The autocab glided through the city, lights blurring into streaks of color. Three hours to meet the Resistance team, clean my house, find Vipri, and reach the tower. The moles in Batranu's council meant anyone could betray us. I was walking into a trap or a salvation, a coin flip in the dark. I toyed with a ShadowMind glyph, a fleeting mental anchor: *Survive.* Linked it to Deceneus. His strength would carry me to the tower, to prove them all wrong.

The commando leader's eyes locked onto mine, steady but expectant. "We are instructed to attack one of the three main towers," he said. "You know what. We don't. You are in command now."

I studied the holographic map, my finger circling the DigiFort tower. "This one," I said, my voice firm. "Tell them it's coded DigiFort in Security's internal system." That detail would help Batranu track Cupola's movements. "But first, we go to my house to collect some things, then here." I pointed to a second location, my voice unwavering, betraying no hint of the urgency pulsing beneath.

"That's inside the Wall, Cupola's inner city," he whispered, his brow creasing with concern. "We are not authorized to strike there."

"It's a collect operation, not a strike," I said, tapping the map firmly. "Get authorization. Contact Batranu."

"I can't reach Batranu directly, I can only..."

"Batranu or no one," I interrupted, my patience thin. "Our key for the tower is there. Trust me."

The autocab let us out six hundred paces from my house, and we moved silently through the night. Inside, Cassia materialized, her face pale but resolute. "I am ready," she said, her voice low. I nodded, and she vanished into my inner secure storage. Diegia wiped every trace of data from the house, leaving Robby behind with basic software to feed false signals to Security. *Clean.*

Walking, we crossed the Wall into Cupola's inner city, the air thick with the invisible hum of surveillance. One commando stayed with me, approaching a sculpted door. He contacted Mistria, Vipri's HouseMaid. "The delivery is here," he said, his voice low and confident, mimicking the code for girls delivered after accepting a Family bed invitation – merchandise, paid for services, though no one could refuse a Family *invitation*. The word prostitution had long vanished in the dictionary, replaced by *bed invitations*."

"I need to request authorization," Mistria replied, her tone neutral but cautious. She didn't know about this *delivery* but couldn't admit ignorance to a stranger.

"I'm freezing," I said, faking a shiver, my eyes locking onto the camera for iris recognition. "My party name is Blue Vacation." The safe code I had set with Vipri. The door slid open with a soft hiss.

Vipri appeared in the corridor, eyes heavy with sleep but sharp with immediate recognition. I activated my DuaLink, its secure channel humming a private frequency in my mind. "Are we leaving for the Blue Vacation?" he asked, a faint, weary smile breaking through.

"Yes," I said, pointing to the DigiFort on my inner holographic map. "Our vacation starts here."

He studied me silently, his expression unreadable. "Odd choice for a vacation, but you have always been ... different. We have a problem. I am under constant Family surveillance. In days, they will replace me as Vice Prime Minister. We can escape, but my authorization might not work well for the tower. I am likely in quarantine – Security will know if I approach. Let us in. Then..."

"I have a ZeroPlus authorization to enter. A gift from a ... relative. We need yours for the Jewel section. But..." I paused, lowering my voice, leaning closer by habit, though we were under the DuaLink. "There are three moles in our council."

"I don't know about the moles," Vipri said, his jaw tightening, a rare flicker of raw frustration crossing his face. "But general surveillance doesn't touch Jewel's internal systems, not yet." He massaged his virtual chin, his hand passing through the hologram – a familiar habit to calm himself, even in simulation. "My ZeroA authorization should hold for Jewel's central system until my title is stripped. After that, it will downgrade, but I am still Family." His smile was bitter, a tight grimace. "From Vice Prime Minister to outcast. Maybe it's the only way to be human again. Give me ten minutes to dress and prepare. I need partial control of your DuaLink to contact Mistria without tripping the surveillance – I suppose my house is crawling with new trojans." He gestured to Mistria's avatar in the virtual space. "Upload everything to this chip."

I merged our simulations, granting him access. He inserted the chip into a slot disguised as a scratch on the black statue in his hall. "You are coming with me, Mistria," he whispered, his voice tinged with a surprising tenderness. "Leave nothing behind."

I smiled, recognizing the echo of my own actions at home. Diegia stirred, a spark of approval. *"His chip is clean. Mistria is secure, too. Her systems are clean, but the house Net is riddled with trojans."*

Vipri returned, dressed in dark gear, his face set with a newfound purpose. "Mistria is with me. My ZeroA will get us into Jewel's systems, but we need to move fast – three moles in the Resistance Council mean leaks everywhere."

"Coin warned me," I said. "Right now, the System thinks I am still locked in his room. Diegia is masking my real presence. I am not here. We have three hours until it opens."

Vipri nodded, his eyes narrowing. "If the Travelers know you are active, they will hit hard from space, disregarding collateral causalities. This will blow up anyway once we attack DigiFort. Batranu's team might back us, but we are walking into a viper's nest."

The commando leader signaled readiness, a silent cue. We slipped into the deeper night, the Wall's shadow looming over us. I gripped Deceneus's knife, Coin's gift, its still unfamiliar weight grounding me. *Cursed Queen or not, I will end this.*

Chapter 13

"Everybody, listen to me," Batranu's voice cut through the hum in the war room. The murmuring ceased as if sliced by a knife.

In that moment, I fully realized the depth of experience in handling people and critical events hidden behind this cheerful young man's mask. With a strange relief, I understood that no one knew anything about his past hundred years on our planet – neither the new me nor the old. My earlier understanding was genuine, not implanted by the transfer.

"There were two gaps in the surveillance system when the Travelers linked their satellites to the local network, and we received critical news: They will begin generating the New Field in two hours. From that moment, we have exactly two days to complete our mission. The fate of several billion people depends on us: commandos in the Field, the HumSs, our virtual commandos in the Stations, and Center. "AI, generate the battlefield hologram," he ordered.

"Hologram generated," AI replied, and a fifteen-by-forty-foot hologram materialized at the center of the war room. A stir arose as people noticed it didn't match the plan approved by the council the previous day. I glanced around, trying to identify which councilors were most opposed to the change, and I noted six potential traitors, though we knew from Alenia that only three were compromised.

"The Second Rebellion has begun," Batranu declared, silencing the complaints. "As you know, we must attack their ground towers. The satellites belong to the Celestials, and we lack the tools to target them. There are three global nodes: Main Tower, DigiFort, and Tower A." At his signal, the towers lit up on the hologram, along with the distances separating them from our Station One, where the war room was concealed a thousand feet underground, shielded even against a nuclear explosion.

"We need to destroy fifteen additional towers in specific locations, but we have twenty-five on our hit list – those our strategists considered easiest to destroy. Keep in mind that *easy* is a relative term." Batranu's finger danced across the map, highlighting the targets. White lines connected them to Center, an underground hub housing most of our servers and communication systems. The same lines linked Center to our six Stations. If Center failed, the Stations, where most of our people were stationed, would operate independently, like distributed guerrillas.

"Twenty-five Ground Commando groups, G1 and so forth, are positioned near their targets, ready to strike. Only twenty will attack in the first wave; five groups will remain in reserve. For security reasons, there will be no further direct communications from now on, but swarms of insect drones are moving along their routes, providing information on their progress. As you know," he repeated, "we don't need to destroy all the towers, just the three global nodes and fifteen others."

The New Field needed to envelop a planet completely to grow further, reaching other worlds. With each new planet enveloped, its growth would accelerate until the entire system was encased. The expansion would slow until it reached the next star, but within a hundred years, it could consume the whole galaxy, creating a new universe separate from our own.

"What you don't know," Batranu continued, "is that the three main commando groups are led by former ShadowMinds." He paused, letting the rebels absorb the news. Exclamations of approval filled the room, boosting morale. "G1 is led by Alamo, once known as Xiriaxis. There is no need to recount his deeds here; you have all read the old history books the Government fought so hard to suppress. What those books don't mention is that Xiriaxis was the greatest ShadowMind of the last millennium before their Order was dismantled by the Celestials." Batranu's words raised morale even higher, and I thought he was done. I was wrong.

"Ther is nothing in our books about the second commander, but he is also an experienced ShadowMind, a Level Six. The third team is led by our former Queen, Altamira." A reverent silence settled over the room, tinged with awe, as if our ancient history was coming alive.

Deceneus wasn't mentioned as being present. I wasn't him, but the thought managed to irritate me.

"Take your positions," Batranu said in a low, hypnotic voice, carrying all his determination. He was answered with enthusiastic shouts. The war had begun. The mood was confident.

A moment of silence followed, then the sound of steps, whispers, and chairs scraping the floor. One by one, our teams turned to their Net links, ready to fight. I checked the snapshots Diego had taken for me and removed one name from the traitors' list. Only five remained.

"I have a problem," I said, pulling Batranu to an isolated corner of the war room. "Initiate sound cloaking, just in case," I added, responding to his raised eyebrows.

"You are cloaked," AI confirmed a second later.

"We know we have moles," I said, trying to speak slowly as the words crowded my mouth faster than I could articulate them. "In the council," I continued. He nodded. "Here." I stared at him, my dual awareness analyzing his reactions, searching for familiar patterns, the old one and the new. There were none visible to the human eye, and I couldn't ask AI for help. "In Station One, and they were in our headquarters too," I emphasized, still unable to read anything on his face.

"You are asking why there are no Cupola commandos here if they know our location." A thin smile appeared on his lips, and I cursed him inwardly before realizing it was a sign of approval. I cursed him again to calm my nerves.

"Yes," I said finally, my voice half a whisper, half a growl.

"I suppose we are not the only ones trying to stop the New Field, so we fight together, in a manner of speaking. There is no need for us after..." He trailed off, and the smile vanished from his lips.

"When did you first suspect it?" I asked nervously, a small part of me feeling betrayed. Not that I doubted him, or perhaps the younger part of me did, just a bit – too many things tied us to a past that wasn't mine.

"I questioned it the moment the news reached us. Don't let this distract you. You must find a way to unmask the moles. You are my safest bet. They don't know you well; they see the young man. Apart from Pilot, no one knows what's truly inside your head now. Use that experience," he said, fixing me with the near-hypnotic stare I had come to recognize. "It makes no difference to us whether we die now or after we complete our mission. If we succeed..." He paused. "There are many variables in this game, and their strategy might change any moment. That means they might attack us before taking the towers."

Use that experience... Easy to say. My unspoken fear was that the *experience* was using me.

"All our DigiScouts are blocked!" I didn't recognize the voice; desperation altered its tone with tremors and high pitches. It belonged to a HumS, one of the Human Scouts managing our DigiScouts, likely from the HackTeam. In the end, it didn't matter.

The battlefield hologram in the center of the war room glowed red at every point where our DigiScouts were fighting to access the Towers.

"This is impossible!" the HumS shouted again as the red points shifted along the lines, moving away from the Towers toward Center, node by node. No Center, no cyber-attacks, I realized. "Their Shields are stronger than our DigiScouts."

Everything had been fine until...

"Find their Origin," Batranu said calmly, trying to ease the fear gripping the HackTeam. Our software was supposed to be superior – it came from Aurora, the masters of our software universe. His voice silenced the room, and I watched the HumSs gesticulate frantically, manipulating the information grid.

"Traveler Origin," someone whispered heavily. Silence fell again as they projected the signature for us. The red spheres were gaining speed, their adaptive crawlers breaking node after node on their path toward Center. Batranu's face was blank; he was likely in inner communication with our people there. The spheres' speed slowed, but they never stopped.

"This will buy us a few minutes," Batranu said. "We have no comparable software, but what I sent will help tune our Scouts and servers. Center! Your automatic connectors have already failed. Initiate manual separation from the Net." It took a moment before the hologram showed changes. Then the lines to HackTeam 11 and Cupola Tower 11 vanished.

"HackTeam 11 manually separated; line to Tower 11 manually separated," AI announced. Slowly, one by one, HackTeams and Towers 7, 3, 1, and 4 disappeared from the hologram. "Station 2, separated." A brief silence followed. "Incoming communication, Center Lead, on the line," AI announced, using the commander's coded name.

"We are under attack. Manual separation was halted. We have intruders and heavy fighting." His hologram appeared just above the battlefield hologram in our room: a disturbed face, still unsure of what was happening. “They’re entering the command room. Prepare for defense!” he shouted.

“Show me their room,” Batranu instructed the AI. The command room appeared on the display for only a second before vanishing.

“Traitor!” Center Lead shouted just before the audio link cut out.

“To all personnel,” Batranu announced across the station, “Center has been compromised and taken over. Initiate separation from Center. HackTeams, operate independently from now on.” He didn’t mention how many teams were still operational. We could only count on the five teams that had separated from Center. On the hologram, the red spheres were now advancing toward us. “Initiate separation,” he instructed AI. “When the first sphere reaches our location, they will send commandos.”

“Access denied,” AI replied.

“On whose authorization?” Batranu asked.

“Yours, BatraKogaiRebel199,” AI pronounced the full name.

“AI, block my old authorization, BatraKogaiRebel199, and acknowledge my new authorization, BatraEarthCupola555.”

“Authorization BatraEarthCupola555 acknowledged. Authorization BatraKogaiRebel199 blocked.” The red spheres were now twenty minutes away from us.

“Initiate separation,” Batranu instructed again.

“Access denied. The separation module was manually severed from the station.”

“To all on Station One,” Batranu said through the comm, “we are compromised. Center has fallen, and our separation module has been destroyed or blocked. Any of us could be the traitor.” He gestured to me, and as I approached, he tossed me a sword. Two curved swords always rested on a wooden stand above his desk.

Samurai swords – the words echoed from my foreign memories. "You know how to handle it properly, but for now, it's just for chopping cables," he said with a faint smile. "Apart from me, you are the only one who has been here the entire time and has no authorization to access the separation station alone," he announced to everyone in the station.

"AI, grant him standard authorization and keep him in our visual range at all times." A hologram of me, reduced to a palm's size, appeared above the battlefield. "Take a LasGun for protection. It won't work well on the cables – they are coated to resist lasers, and it would take too long. Use the sword to cut the sheath; it will do the job with some effort. Then melt everything with the LasGun. And bring the sword back to me; I owned it for over four hundred years. You have sixteen minutes."

"We already know one traitor's location: Center," I said, weighing the sword. "Only two left here. Or one..." The sword felt like an extension of my hand, imparting a coolness I couldn't fully understand. As I ran from the room, I heard Batranu speaking to AI again.

"AI, when was my authorization used to lock the separation module?" The door closed behind me before I heard AI's response.

At the end of the corridor, I stopped, sensing danger in the next passage. Leaning against the wall, faint footsteps echoed in my mind, so soft I wasn't sure they were human.

My hearing is enhanced, I recalled. It wasn't my memory, but the skills had been transplanted into me. I tracked the footsteps mentally. There was no reason to wait; they were distant and fading further. Somewhere, a drop of water fell onto a metal tube, followed by another. *Annoying,* I muttered. *Can I filter out unwanted noise?* Enhancements are useful once you are accustomed to them. *Genetic changes are done via teleportation... Why were they activated today?* The teleportation must have occurred when the volcano was destroyed, managed by Houston – I was certain it was Houston, no other Gate would dare to break the rules. Gates were forbidden on our planet, and she topped the banned list. *The Cursed Gate*... I smiled. Everything good was cursed by the Travelers, including the old me.

The footsteps faded even more, and I forced myself to follow them.

"AI, are there people ahead of me?" I asked, realizing I should have asked earlier. A sudden urge to trust my senses over technology gripped me, but I resisted. That might have made sense in Deceneus's medieval world, but not now.

"No one," AI replied.

"Are you sure? I hear footsteps."

"No one is there," AI repeated, its tone tinged with amusement, perhaps artificial, and a hint of irritation, as if chastising me for doubting it.

Then what am I hearing? I quickened my pace. Until now, I had matched the rhythm of the unseen steps. Beyond being annoying, they were heading toward the cables I needed to cut. *Helper? Traitor? Traitor*, I decided; only a traitor could evade AI's sensors.

Or AI... That shouldn't be possible. Not with our software... The steps stopped.

"AI, show my position." A red dot marked my location on my inner map. Three hundred paces from the target. With effort, I estimated where the steps had vanished, about thirty paces past the cables. I checked the map: a blocked corridor and a door with a small window. *The window...* I slowed, stopping just before the corner where I would be visible from it. An unexpected calm washed over me, awakening the reflexes of a warrior from an ancient past. *Speed is key*, a thought urged. *Be light, ready to fight. The helmet... That's it*! Hastily, I removed my helmet, attached it to the sword's tip, and eased it into view of the window. A LasGun shot pierced the helmet, then hit the wall. *That could have been my head*, I thought, staring at the hole in silence as I pulled it back behind the corner. I measured the distance to the cable room and imagined myself sprinting. *Too far*... The hole in the helmet glared at me like a Cyclops's eye. The corridor fell eerily silent until new footsteps approached from behind.

"AI, who is behind me?"

"No one."

"Who is in that room?" I marked the room where the shot originated on my shareable inner map.

"No one."

"Then who shot at me?" I snapped, staring at the helmet again to transmit the image to AI.

"The camera in that room is not operational," AI finally offered something useful. "Circumstantial evidence suggests someone is hiding there and fired at you. Their comm must be off, so I cannot identify them."

Deadly circumstantial... "How many people are missing from your radar?"

"None. All personnel in the bunker have active comms. No signals have vanished inside."

"They faked leaving... How many have left the bunker?"

"One hundred twenty."

There was no way to learn more. *A hundred paces*... I turned toward the approaching steps. *Thirty paces until someone ... shoots?* I looked back: only darkness, the corridor twisting out of sight. I wasn't sure why my sensors detected nothing, not even in infrared. "Can you open the door of that room?" I pointed at the target with my sword; it was opening into another dead-end corridor.

"Yes."

I measured again: fifteen paces. *No way. I need something. Smoke?* I had no fumigant grenades. *Fog... Water!* "AI, on my signal, activate the ceiling sprinklers and foam fire extinguishers."

I positioned myself, ready to sprint. Ten minutes left to cut the cables, my inner watch warned. “Now!”

~ **Alenia** ~

DigiFort loomed over the horizon, its silhouette clawing at the moonlight like a monolith of dread. It was more than a tower; it was a fortress, an impregnable bastion of cold efficiency. Even with hundreds of guerrilla warriors, storming it was unthinkable – only missiles could bring it down. We had none, and I had only seven men with me, their shadows barely visible in the pale lunar glow. I hoped Coin’s authorization would hold. A narrow path snaked through the dense forest toward the road leading to the main gate. The area was mostly uninhabited, but the rustle of leaves underfoot and the distant hoot of an owl kept my nerves taut. You never know what eyes might be watching. Our holographic maps guided us to a curve five hundred paces from the gate. From there, we would take the main road, exposed but necessary. We moved in total silence, avoiding even encrypted messages, each step a calculated risk on this razor’s edge of a mission.

In front of the gate, I stopped, flexing the fingers of my right hand, each grip tighter, as if squeezing out my doubt. The tower was encircled by a fifty-foot-high wall, a ruthless imitation of a medieval fortress – concrete and steel in place of tailored stone. At its crest, a metallic serpent of barbed wire coiled, a grotesque collar studded with ten-inch thorns that glinted like fangs in the moonlight. I shivered, the chill not from the night air but from the weight of what lay ahead. I breathed deeply, steadying my voice to a hard edge before addressing the camera: “Inspection.” The guards at the entry gate were now alerted; there was no turning back. “Commander, acknowledge my authorization: Cupola ZeroPlus.” I nearly added *please* by reflex – that would have ruined everything. Cupola never say *please*; politeness, empathy, any trace of normal human behavior is stripped from their genes. Slow movement stirred behind the gate, a faint hum of machinery, then an oppressive silence.

Did I fail?

I maintained my composure, staring at the barbed wire. It had a strange effect, a reminder that we all lived in an open prison as vast as the planet itself, caged by the Cupola's invisible chains. My team stood motionless behind me, their camouflaged silhouettes blending into the shadows, each breath measured, each glance a silent question.

"We are in a state of emergency," I pressed, my voice sharp enough to cut through the tension. "Rebels have attacked several towers."

"There's a new delay and verification mechanism in place," a tense voice finally crackled through the comm. "Because of the attacks. I am the gate commander. Please wait while your authorization is verified."

"By whom?" I demanded.

"Travelers. Five are inside. Authorization granted. One of their commandos is waiting within the tower."

I am really lucky... The thought was bitter. Travelers were the last beings I wanted to meet. Their presence meant scrutiny, and scrutiny meant death if our cover slipped.

"Where are they?" I shared a holographic map with the commander, its glowing lines hovering between us like a fragile truce. "No need to involve them. You understand." I leaned on human solidarity, a gamble that paid off. Nobody liked the arrogant aliens. The commander marked their positions on the map. I relayed it to Vipri, requesting a proximity check to the Jewel zone, the heart of DigiFort's power.

"What about them?" The commander's gaze shifted to my team warily, hesitant to let seven armed strangers through.

“Special Forces,” I said smoothly. “We must prepare for any contingency. If all is clear here, we move to the next tower. The faster, the better. No need for alarm.”

Inspections were always dangerous, especially when conducted by high-ranking Cupola. In that moment, I realized the commander knew about the ZeroPlus authorization – a secret I hadn’t known until Coin whispered it at the end of the *party*. *Too much knowledge can be deadly...* The thought coiled in my mind like the barbed wire above.

“Make way!” a voice barked behind me, shattering the tense quiet. A tall captain in uniform strode forward, flanked by five soldiers, their boots striking the ground almost silently, without cadence, resembling natural sounds – trained soldiers clearly in a hurry. “My authorization.” He flicked a finger toward the gate commander, sending an electronic message. His tactical hologram was probably lagging slightly, making his movements appear shaky, almost spectral. It happens when powerful digital fields intersect, a glitch in the seamless tech that binds this world. The rest of his squad stood rigid, their faces invisible behind mirrored visors.

Shine.

I nearly shouted her name. She was chained, her wrists bound in dark red cuffs that pulsed with restraint codes. Two steps away, Vipri adjusted the opacity of his helmet’s visor, obscuring his face further. I mirrored him.

“The Resistance mole,” I said to the captain, playing a dangerous card. “Why bring her here during an attack?” My voice lashed like a whip, amplifying the urgency, each word a calculated strike. “Show me your authorization.”

“I don’t take orders from you,” he replied, flatly.

He must be from the new secret team. Just as Coin warned. “All Special Forces answer to ZeroPlus. I *am* ZeroPlus. You answer to *me*.” My tone was glacial as I transmitted my credentials. He took a few seconds to verify them, his eyes darting to my helmet, searching for a face that wasn't visible behind the polarized visor.

"Authorization acknowledged. The Travelers requested her."

The Travelers are in the Jewel section, Vipri messaged, his encrypted words flashing in my inner sight, highlighting his Family's zone on the map. Nothing unusual; the Jewel area was DigiFort's heart.

"Then we go together," I said, leaving no room for argument.

I rolled down the short staircase in a single leap. Water poured from the ceiling, and the fire alarm wailed for a moment before cutting off sooner than expected. Water still fell. AI opened the door just as my head nearly struck it. The timing was perfect, yet I couldn't help biting my lip, cursing the heavy metal door when it came just inches from my face. The taste of blood filled my mouth. I wondered how I had convinced myself to charge full-speed into a closed, metallic door.

My invisible attackers reacted a split second later. I hoped the mist of water and foam obscured me. They likely fired blindly at where they thought the door was, guided by their tactical maps still linked to the station. That uncomfortable knowledge explained how they had tracked me. Behind me, sharp clacks broke the silence. A LasGun is silent, but the holes in the walls contracted instantly as concrete and metal vaporized or melted, creating a strange rhythm, almost musical, blending with the monotonous patter of water. It was disrupted by running footsteps echoing in the hall.

I am trapped.

I had known it the moment I jumped – the long corridor was a dead end. But when running for your life, you seize any chance. The dead end had saved me from crossfire; now I needed another. Water flowed down the stairs, my steps sending faint ripples, barely audible even to my enhanced hearing. I moved slowly, backtracking, keeping the door in sight.

"Diego, anything that can help?" I asked, desperate for a chance.

He shook his head. *"I am analyzing."*

"AI?" I pressed.

"I have no fighting modules," AI said with a sigh, its human-like response meant to calm me.

"Find something usable as a weapon." *You don't need a fighting module for that.* I turned several times, left and right, to observe the place. *Nothing...*

Behind me, AI slammed the door shut and activated the cameras outside to record the traitors preparing to enter my corridor. The closed door would protect me here, but I had to go back... Fifty paces further, I stepped onto dry floor. A second batch of images arrived in my mind, sharper now; the AI had cleared the mist from them.

"That's impossible! AI, are you sure?" I shouted, as if my outburst could sway its analysis.

"I am sure," it replied, devoid of emotion, a message in itself. The image zoomed in, revealing more details.

Are they using an electronic decoy? "Show me the signature," I snapped. The AI zoomed again, marking our signature with an orange ellipse.

"There is no outside interference," it said, sensing my concern. "The image is genuine."

As if you would know if they tricked you. "Don't send this to Batranu yet. Act as if nothing is wrong. Turn on the lights." With the door closed, I could risk it. "Turn them off if they breach the door."

"I locked the door," AI confirmed.

"Weapons," I reminded both it and Diego.

"Nothing yet," AI replied; Diego just shrugged.

Two hundred paces from the door, I stopped. The corridor stretched further, but there was no need to go on. To cut the cables, I had to go back, and I was far enough from the door to plan an attack on the intruders. To return, I had to kill them. I glanced around: grey walls, steel, and multicolored cables.

"AI, what are these?" I pointed at the cables.

"Electrical cables."

That might help. I checked my inner watch: *seven minutes left*...

Alenia

Vipri used his clearance to open the inner gate, his fingers dancing over a holographic interface that flickered in the dim light. For a heartbeat, I feared he might fail, that the Jewel Family's security would reject his codes. He didn't. The wall parted silently, revealing a corridor that seemed to stretch into infinity.

We stepped inside, and the gate sealed behind us without a sound, locking us into the heart of DigiFort. Ahead stretched the infamous labyrinth: pristine white walls, silent as a tomb, and lethal. The air was sterile, the silence was heavy, and the featureless corridors seemed to pulse with a malevolent intelligence, watching our every step.

Every Family had one: a deadly maze to keep rivals at bay, a testament to their paranoia and power hunger. We were just collateral in the Cupola's endless power struggles, pawns in a game where a single wrong turn meant annihilation – traps that could vaporize flesh and bone ensured you never left.

Their helmets removed, the Special Forces were now blindfolded against the labyrinth's secrets, by a band that could create hypnotic patterns if they tried to disobey. Their Digital Egos fed them clipped directions from Vipri: *left, right, slow*. Standard procedure. No outsider entered a Family's domain without such precautions. As a concession, we let them keep their weapons, triggers locked.

"The command center's generator is here," Vipri finally said after fifteen minutes, via DuaLink, marking it on our DigiFort tactical maps, *borrowed* from the Jewels by him. This was a specialized DuaLink variant with OpenMind features, bypassing the need for DigitalEgo to control our bodies. Encrypted thought-transfer, wired directly into our auditory cortex, with reconstructed voices from memory databases. "We are here." At his command, the map's AI charted the fastest route to our target, hidden in the labyrinth's depths.

"Show me the path to the Travelers," I asked.

Vipri marked it, and a new route flared in my vision. "We share a route with the Special Forces up to this point." A red circle pulsed on the map "From there, the paths diverge. We must neutralize them before then." He hesitated, his voice dropping. "There is a hidden door at the end of this corridor; it leads to a maintenance room. But I would need a permit to backtrack, and I can't get one – not without raising alarms."

"This corridor has only one camera," Rholes, the Resistance commando leader, noted, marking it on the map. "There's a command node here, automated, no personnel." He marked another point, his movements precise. "We hijack the feed, then handle them." He nodded at the blindfolded soldiers, deaf to our conversation too.

"They could relay data and alert Security," I countered, my mind racing through worst-case scenarios – alarms blaring, traps springing, our mission dead before it began.

"Their comms are jammed," Vipri assured, his tone calm but firm. "No signals escape without Jewel encryption. Yours is already active on my authorization. You weren't aware, as I passed the encryption to your Diegos." He paused, a faint smirk in his voice. "And to Diegia."

Diegia stuck out her tongue in a private video feed, her holographic avatar flickering with mischief, making me laugh. The Resistance soldiers tensed, confusion visible through their rigid stances. No need to explain her rogue AI antics to them.

"Rholes, prepare the first batch of trojans for upload. Two minutes," I estimated, calculating our arrival at the fork, each second ticking a countdown to violence.

"You are walking too fast," Diegia whispered. *"Breathe. Slow down. They will notice."*

Easy for you to say.

I didn't know why I had sped up – usually instinct urged delay before violence. But seeing the Special Forces march so calmly, like lambs to slaughter, unnerved me.

"Fifty paces," Vipri announced, his voice cutting through the silence.

The side passage was invisible until you were feet away, the blinding white walls playing tricks, their seamless surfaces hypnotic, disorienting. I blinked hard to clear my vision and stopped, my boots scuffing softly against the polished floor. "There is another checkpoint," I told the Special Forces captain, my tone clipped, authoritative. "Wait here." Unease prickled my spine, a cold sweat beading beneath my light armor. I had never killed like this.

Vipri unlocked the hidden door, and it hissed open, revealing a dim maintenance room, its walls lined with humming conduits. "It can only be closed from the outside," he said through DuaLink, our minds linked in the same virtual space.

"Rholes, now!" I ordered.

"Ten seconds." His fingers flew over the holographic node, its glow casting eerie shadows. "Three. Two. One. Now! Feed hijacked."

"Turn left," I ordered the Special Forces. They filed into the room, their steps echoing faintly, unaware of the trap closing around them.

The only mercy of LasGuns is their silence.

I lunged for Shine, reaching for her cuffs, my fingers brushing the cold metal...

"What are you doing here?" a voice snapped.

The Travelers materialized in the doorway, soundless, gliding within their shimmering shields, their forms barely human under the distortion of energy fields. We saw them the instant they saw us. Five bodies sprawled on the floor. Dead. No blood. Only broken angles, their forms twisted.

Luck. I hadn't freed Shine yet.

Five PlasGuns leveled at us. A LasGun was a toy next to plasma weapons. And their shields? Our strongest hit would barely tint their energy fields, let alone breach them.

"Explain," a Traveler demanded, his voice flat, devoid of warmth. I could never get used to that coldness, honed to perfection, a weapon in itself. Soulless.

"Infiltration, my Lord," I said, my voice altered by Diegia to mask my identity further. I forced calm, though my pulse raced – but not too calm. In an act coordinated by Diegia, my left hand trembled slightly, a calculated gesture. Let them mistake my tension for awe – in their own way, they were as indoctrinated as the Cupola, bound by their own rigid belief in their superiority. "They tried to free the traitor." I gestured to Shine. "I was ordered to bring her to you."

"Take her..." The Traveler paused, his stance suddenly rigid. Diegia's zoomed lenses caught micro-tremors in his posture – agitation, or something else? "Take her to the Jewel's core."

Then they were gone, their shields humming faintly as they vanished into the labyrinth's depths, leaving only the echo of their presence.

"The green cable supplies power to this area," AI highlighted on my inner map. "The main optical transmitter is here. Cutting the cable will weaken and distort the signal, but the primary transmitter will remain active. It will buy us time."

"Do we control the secondary generator for the transmitter?"

"Yes."

"Tell Batranu to shut it down."

A high-voltage cable loomed before me, but I had no gloves or tools to loosen the screw securing its end. And there was nothing around to help me. *LasGun*... I programmed it to the minimum level and let its AI take over. With effort, I gripped the thick insulation with my left hand – barely able to hold it. The LasGun erupted, and I carefully started to cut into the cable. Sparks of various colors flared, but it worked, and the cable became more flexible, allowing better maneuvering. Finally, it was done. With a firm push, I bent and wedged the free head between two other cables, keeping its exposed end away from metallic surfaces and myself. It resembled a massive green snake, coiling to hide its head from prey, poised to strike.

"AI, activate the sprinklers for the area from here to the door," I pointed, five paces ahead. The attackers were still melting the locking mechanism of the door. The metal around the knob glowed faint red, nearly gone.

"Secondary generator is off," AI reported a second later. Batranu had acted swiftly in the war room. Our connection to the outside was nearly severed. "One attacker left the area," AI projected a camera image; only one remained at the door. "Sprinklers activated." Water poured in front of me, rendering AI's update redundant, but AIs process differently, pedantic, not human. "The other headed toward the secondary generator."

That can wait.

I scanned the corridor: a two-level stairway lay below, the floor one foot lower toward the door. Water pooled, some seeping in from outside when I had jumped through the doorway.

The lights went out; the door had been broken. A dark silhouette entered, framed by faint light from the doorway. With a clang, the locking mechanism rolled down the stairs, oddly delayed. Hidden behind a concrete pillar, I tracked the silhouette's slow advance via a bean-sized camera I had camouflaged on the wall – the cameras in the hall had been hijacked, rendering AI blind. A lantern illuminated the area near me, then moved further down the corridor. I stayed concealed, anticipating an infrared scan. Diego disabled my camera when he estimated it was within the other's sensors range.

Slow ripples spread through the water, the only clue to the position of the attacker. *Thirty paces*, I estimated and eased my hand toward the cable's end, my leather jacket wrapped tightly around my palm. *Fifteen paces*. My gloved fingers brushed the cable. A quick touch, then retreat. Nothing happened. I had tested my makeshift insulation earlier, but a second check couldn't hurt. *Now!* I shoved the cable.

Faster than sight, the cable whipped toward the floor. Like a snake, it splashed and hissed, unleashing its full electrical charge into the silhouette. The figure convulsed rigidly, steam hissing from water-soaked clothes. Optical fibers woven into the fabric melted, the acrid scent of burning plastic searing my throat. With a final spasm, the metallic body collapsed into the water. It was an armored robot – built to sustain portable LasGun attacks – its artificial skin marred by black lines of melted circuits. Wisps of smoke rose, mingling with the mist. The sprinklers stopped.

"Secondary generator restarted," AI announced, cutting short my victory.

"How much time did we gain?"

"Six minutes."

Five minutes left...

Alenia

One by one, the Travelers disappeared at the end of the corridor, their shields' faint hum fading like a dying pulse. With the last one vanishing, I realized how silent we were, the air thick with unspoken fear. All our studied calm was just training and RigFace, a fragile mask. One second from disaster – one second more, and I would have opened Shine's handcuffs. I did it now, my fingers fumbling on the hologram with the release codes. My hand trembled. Shine's hand met mine, her grip steady, grounding. In silence, we stared at each other, her eyes a spirit of defiance and relief. Our trembling stopped. Words weren't needed.

"We have to move," Vipri said, his voice cutting through our trance, sharp with urgency. "In two minutes, they will send a team to check why the door is open, even though the camera feed shows nothing. Standard procedure, nothing unusual." His attempt to calm us – or himself – felt hollow.

"Bodies first," I whispered.

"There is a storage chamber connected to the service room." Vipri stepped forward and pointed to an invisible panel fifteen feet ahead. "I can open it." His fingers darted over a holographic keypad, the interface pulsing with Jewel encryption codes. Before he opened the door, it was seamless, indistinguishable from the wall, just like the service room's entrance. We dragged the bodies inside, their armored forms heavy, lifeless. After sealing the chamber, we had twenty seconds to sprint from the service room and thirty more to flee the corridor – Rholes couldn't hold the camera hack any longer. Our boots pounded against the polished floor, the labyrinth's white walls blurring as we raced to the generator command center's door, its reinforced frame looming like a sanctuary. Vipri was able to open it, and we entered in haste.

This time, it was Rholes who stood before the holographic control panel, its data streams flickering with an eerie light. He studied it, his breath shallow, as if the machine could sense his hesitation. "You can do it," he whispered to himself, and his fingers began to dance like a piano master's, weaving through the interface with surgical precision. "Got it," he muttered, his movements accelerating, each tap sending ripples through the hologram. A bead of sweat glistened on the tip of his nose, then fell, passing through the hologram like a ghost. He was oblivious, his mind fused with the system, navigating its labyrinth of code. "Done!" A triumphant smile flickered across his face as he wiped more beads of perspiration from his forehead. He turned to us, eyes alight with defiance. "Just wait." His smile widened, lingering, a rare spark in the suffocating tension.

Then it happened: the rotors' spin surged, a low whine escalating into a scream as the generators overloaded. Sparks erupted from behind the control panel, and the floor shuddered, a violent tremor that nearly threw us off balance. The silence that followed was oppressive, until I sensed the Field flooding in my mind, the sign that the Field blocker was gone with the generator. I contacted Batranu.

"DigiFort is gone," I whispered, joy surging through me, but only a murmur escaped, my voice raw with exhaustion. I wanted to shout, but the Field carried only words, not emotions.

We slumped against the wall, and nervous laughter burst into the room, jagged and raw. I never remembered who started it; a second later, we were all laughing, the sound echoing off the sterile walls.

"Xiriaxis destroyed the Main Node. He rigged some explosives there," Batranu reminded me that we were still in contact.

"Did he move to Tower A?"

"No. He is doing some cleanup."

"Travelers?"

"Yes. I almost pity them."

"We had five Travelers here too."

"How did you...?" Batranu's voice came with hiccups, and I knew that he was worried.

"They ran off. Probably to help the ones being cleaned."

"It makes sense. Xiriaxis finished twenty minutes ago. Don't go to Tower A. There might be Travelers there too. Maybe they left, but... I will send Xiriaxis. Go for a smaller one. Your choice. These are already down." Five small towers were marked as destroyed on the map he sent, their icons pulsing red in my vision. A second later, the transfer cut off; the Field vanished, and Batranu with it.

"The Field is gone," I whispered, the words heavy.

We checked the generators – they were ruined; molten circuits fused into blackened husks. The main line had been destroyed by an explosion hours ago. DigiFort was nearly dead, with only a few emergency functions limping on auxiliary generators, but the blocker was up and the Field down again, severing our connection to the Resistance network.

We readied our weapons. Nothing moved. No sound, just the weight of anticipation, thick as fog. Rholes looked at me, then signaled to our fighters to take position in front of the door, his hand steady despite the sweat still glistening on his brow. We spread out evenly, barrels raised, muscles taut, ready to fire. The door hissed open, and I held my breath. Rholes extended a micro-camera tethered to his wrist, its feed streaming to our tactical fields.

"Nothing," he shrugged, but his voice was tight, unconvinced.

"Bravo!" an unknown voice boomed, followed by mocking claps that echoed from every corner of the room, amplified by hidden speakers. "You are surrounded. There are fifty soldiers outside. One will come for you, and you will follow him."

"The Second Jewel Lord," Vipri said, his voice low. My DuaLink flashed a warning – our encryption was compromised, the Lord's signal overriding all other communication channels.

"Vipri, you fulfilled all my expectations. Your minor bitch too." A hologram materialized, as large as the wall, projecting the Second Lord's sneering face. "Just to make things clear," he laughed, before his image dissolved.

"Drop your weapons. Get out! Helmets down. Hands up. Don't even think about trying anything," the voice barked from the corridor.

Rholes extended his camera again, its feed showing a formation of armored soldiers, LasGuns ready. "At least twenty," he sighed, his shoulders slumping. "We surrender or die." He glanced at me – it was my call, the weight of our lives pressing against my mind.

"Surrender," I said, the word bitter, my LasGun dropping to the floor with a dull clank.

Disabling the second robot was easier; it was an unarmored tech-bot, no match without a human mind guiding it. A piece of debris tossed between tubes distracted it. My LasGun finished the job, and the samurai sword was as effective as I remembered from the past. *His past.* I cursed that past, staring at the severed transmission cables, frozen for a moment as adrenaline faded. Our Station was now separated, safe from the Travelers' trojans. I waited to fully calm down before returning.

In the war room, Batranu appeared composed. Walking back, I had tapped into his private communication through the Field with Alenia, so I knew the latest status. I couldn't stop thinking about her, my feelings tangled – perhaps from the tension, her being in danger, or the other me taking over my mind. I often compared her to Lamia, who haunted my dreams more frequently now, strangely vivid. They felt different. They *were* different. I gestured for Batranu to cloak us for a private talk.

"There was no mole, just two robots," I said, leaning against the window, my energy nearly spent. Handing him the robots' data cards felt exhausting.

"Autonomous repair robots," Batranu muttered to himself, scanning a card with his eye scanner, forgetting my enhanced hearing. He looked at me. "Five arrived with a transport ten months ago, but we never requested an armored one. No one detected it until now, though you said its armor was light, transparent. Something – or someone – activated them today." He paused, eyes half-closed. "*Psyop*. This is a deeper game. Only the mole at Center was real, but he miscalculated the time when he seized it. Some commandos had already left and disabled several towers. Then ... the Travelers *destroyed* the towers from space. Something doesn't add up." He stepped closer, and I thought he doubted the cloaking, wanting to speak softly. I was wrong; he was gazing at his old house, in the fake window behind me. The hologram calmed him. I tried to move. "Sorry," he said, stopping me with a swift gesture that uncovered his ShadowMind training, before returning to his place. "We learned about the moles from two sources. Both might have been played by a third party."

"Do you trust them?"

"One is Xiriaxis. You know he destroyed the Main Tower. The second source was reliable for over a century, Coin helped Alenia escape. He is her descendant, like you, but three generations earlier. Well," he smiled, "one part of you. The part you received started the chain. But ... Coin may be in danger."

Alenia

"Our welcomed guests," said the Second Jewel Lord, clapping his hands again. The sharp sound echoed through the command center like a whip. It wasn't for intimidation; it was his style – a coded dance, a rhythm only the Jewels understood. Joy. Satisfaction. Anger. Curiosity. They called him Clap for this. They read his mood by the angles of his hands, the rhythm of sound. To me, it was like reading smoke. Tea leaves swirling in water. A ritual I couldn't decipher.

"He is almost satisfied," Vipri whispered through DuaLink, his message cryptic.

Almost? Why almost?

I was the third to enter the command center – stark white, pulsing faintly with embedded holo-diagrams. Coin didn't appear until I stepped further in. He sat in a chair, shoulders hunched, eyes downcast. He wouldn't look at me. Diegia ran a rapid assessment, comparing every facial expression I had ever captured from Coin. Not one matched the hollow man in front of me.

Sadness? Guilt? Are you a traitor?

He wore no restraints, but his confidence was gone. His posture sagged like someone walking toward an execution. I sent a DuaLink request. No reply. Not even rejection. Just absence.

"Disable their DuaLink," Clap ordered. His voice sliced clean through the silence. Soldiers stiffened. Twenty of them, most armed with LasGuns that shimmered beneath the sterile lights.

I didn't know how they had acquired such advanced tech, but a sharp static jolt severed our connections. My DuaLink went dead.

"Better." Clap smiled, a warm reaction with a blade inside. I studied him. Strangers are hard to read. But not impossible. There was something else in his eyes.

A fracture. Discontent. What's bothering you?

"Well," he said, stepping forward as a 3D hologram flared to life, "all the Resistance's top moles still breathing are here. I am not interested in the trash." The map was a glowing lattice of red towers. Our targets. He tapped DigiFort with a virtual finger, and the projection rippled like disturbed water. "Our tower is down. The Travelers know it. Twelve towers are down, including the global nodes from your list."

Tower A fell too.

"I will enjoy the countdown with you," he said, watching me too closely. His grin widened, feeding on the involuntary shift in my posture. "I hope you finish your job." He turned. His voice cooled. "Coin, explain why we are here."

Coin's voice came slow, too calm. A tremor flickered at the edge. "Our Lord Clap is convinced everything is under control." A pause. "His control."

"Bravo." Clap laughed and clapped, sharp, staccato, amused but edged. I glanced at Vipri for a clue. He was staring at Clap like he was decoding a bomb. "You are right. Of course, I am in control. But I have another explanation in mind."

"Your mind, your explanation," Coin said. Controlled. Measured. But Diegia flagged a micro-expression, a small crack beneath the mask.

At least Coin isn't a traitor… But the knowledge offered no immediate hope. Only hollow reassurance, with no clear path forward.

"If every tower on your list fails," Clap said, "you will stay here until the Travelers return. It will be a touching reunion. You will make an excellent lightning rod."

"And if some towers don't fall?" I asked, probing for a crack in his plan, my voice sharper than intended.

"Then the options get interesting. But not for you," Clap said, calm again. "Nor for you, Coin." He pointed to the Silver Master Lord, then moved toward me with a sudden speed that said ShadowMind. "A Level Seven," he said, tapping his chest, amused by the tension in my posture. "The highest in the galaxy."

I didn't blink. "Level Nine is higher." My voice held. Just barely.

"There is no Level Nine alive," he said. "The last one was millennia in the past. There was your player, Xiriaxis. Level Eight. Gone in a plasma cloud." He paused. "Travelers." His eyes flashed. "A pity."

"*Nine*," I said again. A single, sharp word. A dare.

"You will stay here too, Bitch Queen," he snapped. Then turned, pointing at Rholes. "If a single tower on your list remains active by nightfall, I will let you destroy it. I am sure I can count on you."

"She is the boss," Rholes said, pointing at me, and I frowned, urging him silently to accept the offer.

"She was," Clap laughed. "We have a common interest. But don't forget – if..."

"Incoming Travelers!" a young technician shouted. The comm hologram flared to life. His hands shook over the glowing interface. "Five of them!"

Clap's mask slipped. A crack of fear in his voice. "The bastards who left an hour ago." Their last meeting hadn't been a friendly chat. "Move the rebels in the next room. Red alert. You know what to do. Yellow, just Vipri and his bitch."

Each of us was escorted out. One soldier per prisoner. The new room was bare. White walls. Humming conduits humming beneath the surface. No cover. No exit. The LasGuns remained trained on us, hands steady.

"You know memory deletion won't work on Travelers' neuranalyzers. They still can read them," Vipri said to the Jewel captain. Calm. Clinical. Not a threat. A diagnosis. They had history, those two. But nothing warm remained.

Bad luck.

"And?" the captain asked, squinting.

"Free info. Might save lives."

"Yours?"

"Yours," Vipri replied, sweeping a hand at the guards. "Travelers don't kill fast. They study death. Sometimes for days, recording everything. They call it experiments. We have the videos. Diagrams. A gift from them. The victims don't scream – they can't. Their voices are gone. But the neural diagrams..." He smiled faintly. "They don't lie."

The captain's face held, but his eyes flicked. The guards weren't so composed. Twitching grips on their LasGuns. Shoulders too tight.

"You will be lucky if a commando kills you before the Travelers find you," Vipri said, quieter now. "Witnesses are dangerous." A long pause. "Any Jewel commandos here apart from your captain?" he asked, tone flat.

"Shut up," the captain snapped.

Vipri smiled, barely. The captain saw it. His hand twitched on the LasGun. Tension flared. A soldier flinched, misreading. LasGun raised, pointing the wrong direction. A chair crashed to the floor. The captain's jaw clenched, his free hand twitched, barely restraining to slap the guard. Vipri's smile widened. Pattern repeated. Nerve struck.

"Red alert," the captain whispered, touching instinctively his ear, as if wanting to hear the message better. Then, louder, panicked: "Red!" His LasGun fired.

Vipri collapsed into my arms. The beam had burned clean through his chest. My suit sizzled from the heat. Time fractured. I was back, two decades in the past. Falling again. Losing again. My breath caught. Grief. Rage. No space between them.

The second shot hit the captain. His head erupted, red mist across the white wall.

Somewhere beneath the shock and grief, a dark part of me smiled. I wouldn't forget. Not ever.

"Xiriaxis." Batranu reached him through the Field, Tower A was down too, and Xiriaxis was in good mood – the *cleaning* ended well; there were no more Travelers on the planet. "There is something wrong with the DigiFort. The generators of the New Field are gone, yet communication through the Field is still blocked there, although it worked for a few minutes. There is no news from Alenia. Find her. I have a bad feeling."

"She is alive," Xiriaxix said after a while. "She is still recorded in the ShadowMind register. I will be there in twenty minutes."

"It will not be easy to enter," Batranu warned him.

"I have an idea," Xiriaxis laughed. "We just need some new clothes. There are plenty here."

The tactical hologram looked good, and there was a new mood in the war room. Not happy or sad either, even when we knew that many of us were dead. It was expectation. *Just seven towers left*... I counted the icons on the map. For the hundredth times. *We should send the reserves too.*

"Reserve commandos," Batranu said, making me wrench away from the fake window that had become my strange obsession. It was not my house, not even my planet.

His planet... Commandos. Why did he think the same?

"Pick the closest targets to you. Destroy them. We are winning," Batranu bragged to whim them, "make it faster."

"I destroyed the Field blocker," Xiriaxis voice came to us, this time from the DigiTower. The Field was again open to communication. "Noooo!" he shouted. I realized that only from the length of the sound. "Not again."

The first mind I captured was Alenia's. She was crying. A weak whimper. Monotone. No words, only a litany of broken sounds. There was no intonation carried by the Field, but there was no need hear it. *Travelers!* I saw them through her eyes: foggy images as she was not really seeing them. All her attention was on Vipri, lying unconsciously in her arms.

"Batranu, I need a FlyCar," Xiriaxis spoke again before I could react, and I realized that he was one of the three *Travelers* in the room – the clothes of the Travelers they had killed were doing a good job.

"I will try," Batranu said, his hands moving in frenzy, manipulating an inner grid of information. A trajectory appeared on the tactical hologram, linking the DigiFort with a point that was in the middle of nowhere.

"Don't try. Do it!" Xiriaxis growled. "Vipri is wounded. His heart was slightly touched. I have a ShadowMind MedKit. Not enough. You have ten minutes."

"It will be there in eight," Batranu smiled, and no one in the room understood his sudden reaction, except me. They were not able to reach the Field, yet they took it as a positive thing, and it was.

Alenia

"Centuries ago, we had what was known across the galaxy as *egalitarian feudalism*, born from a thousand years without war. Then came a healthy dose of capitalism. Now we are ruined by financial technofeudalism," I said to Batranu.

It was morning. Sunlight crept through the clouds, though the Magic Window was still veiled in mist. Vipri was sleeping, his wound nearly healed. A quiet hope stirred in me, not just because he had survived, but because I had finally broken the cycle of watching my lovers die in my arms. He had been in my arms too, badly wounded ... but this time, the future felt different. He *almost* died.

Let it go.

"Technofeudalism is a tumor, the result of excessive concentration of wealth and power," Batranu sighed. I nearly laughed – his sigh didn't match his words. He was staring at the mountains, searching for the same magic I had sought many times before. The sunlit peaks held a quiet allure he enjoyed more than he would ever admit. "Medieval lords held dominion over their serfs. Your Families – just a conglomerate of tech giants and monopolies – used technology to make individuals vulnerable, easier to subjugate. New lords, new serfs. Society gets tribalized, then cannibalized. Most people have no social purpose, no future. They live inside AI-generated simulations. The Travelers' interference made it inevitable."

"Do we need to restore our old society?" I asked, uncertain.

"No. It no longer fits the technology. Society evolves or vanishes. I am sure you will find a better way, just make sure innovation doesn't leave people behind. No one will conquer your planet again – the Erins are strong enough now to prevent that. Find your way."

"I hate politics," Vipri said, his voice weak, strained from the effort of following our conversation.

"I could have sworn you loved it," Batranu laughed.

"That only makes sense when you are at the top. Poor fugitives like me are allowed to hate it." Vipri fumbled with the convalescence chair, struggling to control the malfunctioning console. The chair lurched, refusing to stop. Batranu grabbed Vipri's elbow with his left hand, steadying the chair with his right, and helped him sit.

"Thank you," Vipri mumbled, embarrassed as the wheelchair finally gave him some mobility.

"You are a hero. There will be a role for you in the new government," I teased, ruffling his hair.

"A stupid, wounded hero. Funny how being wounded changes your view of violence. All my life, I read statistics about it – boring.

Now…" He paused, eyes blinking rapidly as he searched for words or memories. "That moment, before my mind faded… I saw my brother dying in your arms. And I thought…" He shook his head and fell silent.

The door opened after a soft knock. *Deceneus* stepped onto the terrace, holding a gardenia, smiling as he offered it to me.

"Young rebel from Aurora," I said, caught in a web of memories, "that's not from you." I smiled back in a way I hadn't in over three hundred years. He blushed, understanding my meaning.

"Got one for me too?" Vipri asked, half-amused. "I might need it more."

"I doubt he can offer *you* a marriage flower," I laughed, holding the white bloom against the backdrop of turquoise water. "Beautiful."

"Marriage?" Vipri asked, then clamped his mouth shut.

"In the past, it was the proper way to propose. A good custom, too bad we forgot it. Well ... some of us."

"And you…?" Vipri's amusement was gone.

"We were married for more than fifty years. I used the same method," *Deceneus* said, pointing to the gardenia.

"So you're really…?" Vipri trailed off, recalling Xiriaxis's words. His brother – *not truly his brother* – had first noticed the link between me and this new Deceneus.

"No. I just matched him in the Field. His memories had been downloaded into my mind beneath the volcano. I didn't ask for it."

"And you want ... again?" Vipri gestured toward the gardenia.

"No. It wouldn't be fair."

"What wouldn't be fair?" Vipri asked, quickly.

"Keeping the memories."

"I wasn't talking about your memories."

"My gardenia asks for a decision," I said, trying to stay serious. "The decision was made." The flower's sweet, subtle scent stirred memories as vivid as yesterday – yesterday, three hundred years ago. I laughed. They glanced at me with different expressions. The young rebel already knew; he carried the old memories too – his, yet not his. An extension of his mind. "It was a game, Vipri," I said, to calm him. "A reminder of good things from the past." Slowly, I returned the flower.

"You asked for one," *Deceneus* said, offering it to Vipri, who hesitated. "To aid your healing." He laughed, tossing the gardenia. Vipri caught it, laughing too, then silently pushed it back to me. I later learned he had asked an AI to analyze our faces for clues about our game. We must have looked like children.

"I will keep the flower. In case you forgot, that's a *maybe*." I placed my hand on Vipri's shoulder, and he covered it with his palm, warmth flowing between us. I turned to the young rebel. "Why do you want to delete the memories?"

"It wouldn't be fair to keep them – to you, to Lamia, or to me."

"To you?" I asked, surprised. I knew Lamia was his girlfriend on Aurora, due to arrive in a week, but discarding such knowledge and experience still seemed wasteful.

"I am young. I want to explore everything with fresh eyes. I want to kiss my girl without a century of someone else's experience. I want genuine emotions from new things. Right now, my mind is a bag of old memories. Sorry, to me, they are old, and they were imposed without permission. I want to live and *feel* as my own experiences anything that I have already *lived* through these foreign memories without living them.

"I want children, to feel the joy of my firstborn. Your two children live in my mind. I held them, watched them grow, but they're not mine. It was wonderful, but not mine. A man's body can be young again and again – but the mind? It becomes an anchor, a drag, without erasing the past. I want my life back. I will keep some knowledge, but nothing personal. Altamira will vanish. Alenia will take her place."

"May I join?" Xiriaxix, sneaked his head through the doorway. He had reclaimed his old name, Mask and Alamo were gone. Rumors swirled about reviving the ShadowMind Order. "Looks like a family meeting. You might need help managing two ... hmm, I don't know what to call them. *Parts*?" He looked at me. "I like to think I still belong," he added, smiling at Vipri. "Agree, brother?"

"Until my next memory wipe, you are still occupying space I would rather reserve for nicer things. After that, I won't know you," Vipri said, his anger too sharp to be real.

"Think of me as your godfather too. My little manipulations brought you two together," Xiriaxis said, tracing an imaginary circle around me and Vipri, mimicking a marriage sign.

"You will never stop," Vipri laughed.

"Behind his mask," I said, joining the laughter, "he thinks being human again is necessary to reach Level Ten. But imagine someone with *that* humor climbing so high – the galaxy would crumble."

"You have never been so right for the wrong reason," Xiriaxis grinned. "Change is coming. I just met Armin and Houston. No need to guess what words *she* used for my work here. You will meet them too, Vipri included. A new cycle of evolution has started. Black Eye gave its blessing, and in the coming centuries, all DNA in the galaxy will be enhanced. The Erin experiment, started seven hundred years ago, is the future. Everyone will get a brand-new Erin quantum brain."

"The Celestials won't be happy," I said. "It will be harder for them to impose their schemes. They love dirty games. But becoming Erins might erase their inferiority complex. The Lines of Time will open to everyone. And that brings ... well, change."

"I am not sure reading the Lines will even be part of that future," Xiriaxis added, pausing for effect. "Evolution derails when everyone can see what's coming. You nullify the uncertainty principle that drives diversity. Black Eye has something in mind – we just don't know what." He shrugged.

Printed in Dunstable, United Kingdom

67628860R00211